CW00496268

# Now I Am A Soldier

## Tulloch at War
### Book 1

## Malcolm Archibald

*FOR CATHY*

*"War is nothing more than the continuation of politics by other means."*
*On War*: Karl von Clausewitz.

*"From about 1300 hours onward, they were only able to gain ground slowly and with continual fighting against an enemy who defended himself stubbornly."*
War diary of the German XLI Corps, speaking of the 6th and 8th Panzer Divisions, facing British Territorial infantry, Belgium, May 1940.

# Prelude

It was Private Brown who started the singing. Private Brown, who ran the gauntlet of Waziri fire in the Shahur Tangi defile on the Frontier and told bawdy jokes at the colonel's expense. Now, when Tulloch looked across to him, he saw that Brown was dying. He lay behind the remnants of the farmhouse wall, a desperately wounded man within a shattered building.

> *"Oh, we're no awa' tae bide awa,'*
> *And we're no awa' tae leave you."*

Brown sang softly through broken, swollen lips, spitting out blood with every word. One by one, the other members of Four Platoon of B Company joined in, some growling the words defiantly, others using the old familiar song to hide the fear that none would admit they possessed.

> *"We're no awa tae bide awa.*
> *We'll aye come back tae see you."*

"*Here they come again,*" Tulloch said, checking his men. There were not many of them left, forty-five out of the original ninety-eight, with eight wounded. He felt his pride stirring as he looked over the survivors. They settled behind the ruined buildings, holding their Lee-Enfields in dirty, calloused hands as they faced their front. Tulloch counted his remaining cartridges and snapped shut his revolver.

"*Aim low, lads, and don't waste bullets.*" He wondered how many British officers had said that to a beleaguered company over the centuries.

The dead lay before and among them, German in field grey and sinister black and Lothian Rifles in the new British khaki battledress. Beyond the dead, a line of sad trees concealed the massing enemy. The singing died away. A lone voice shouted, "*Gin ye Daur!*" - If you dare, a defiant challenge to the overwhelmingly strong enemy force that waited on the far side of the trees.

"*Any fags, chum?*" Private Aitken rolled over and asked Private Baxter, who absently passed over a Woodbine. Aitken lit up, shielding the match in his hand from long habit, and drew on the cigarette.

"*I'd rather be on the terracing at Tynecastle,*" Aitken said, releasing a long spume of smoke.

Baxter grunted. "*You're welcome, you Gorgie bastard. I'd rather be with Betty Grable.*"

The shelling began again, German 37-millimetre artillery with its ferocious bark and vicious explosions. As often before, the German artillerymen were efficient, dropping their shells squarely on the British positions. The Lothian Rifles scrabbled into whatever cover they could, hugging fragments of wall and trying to burrow into the French earth. Or was it the Belgian earth? Tulloch was unsure if they had crossed the frontier or not, nor did he care as the shells landed like hail on an Edinburgh November, and the ground shook, trembled, and erupted under him.

Private Kelly died then. A red-headed, cheerful man from

Bonnyrigg, one minute he was there, and then the shell landed, and he was gone, leaving no trace except a single leg and a muddy boot.

Private Lightfoot looked at the bloodied remains of Kelly, swore softly and looked away, covering his head with his hands.

"*Hold on, boys!*" Tulloch shouted hoarsely, then ducked as another salvo crashed down. Earth and stones clattered onto his steel helmet, with one sharp pebble opening a small cut on his cheekbone.

> "*Oh, we're no awa' tae bide awa',*
> *We're no awa' tae leave you,*
> *We're no awa', tae bide awa',*
> *We'll aye come back and see you.*"

Brown bawled out the words, aware he was dying and desperate not to show fear. "*Come on, you Nazi bastards! Come out and fight! Are you feared of the Lothian Rifles?*" Raising his rifle, he fired at the distant trees, a gnat challenging an elephant, forty-odd ragged men facing the most powerful army in Europe.

The shelling ceased. Smoke slowly drifted away, leaving one more dead Rifleman and Private Baxter screaming with the right side of his chest blown away and half his lungs exposed. The cigarette dropped from his mouth to lie on the ground, slowly smoking.

"*Stretcher-bearers!*" Tulloch yelled, but Baxter mercifully died before they reached him. Baxter was an Edinburgh man from the Old Town, an ex-brewery worker who had joined the army when his employer dismissed him for drinking. Tulloch found him a model soldier, strictly sober, conscientious, and now dead.

Tulloch controlled his trembling and walked the length of the company's defences as the dust settled. He heard the distant bark of a sniper's rifle, ducked instinctively and saw the bullet strike a chip from the wall two inches from his hip.

*If that had been a Pashtun, I'd be dead by now.* He realised the men were watching him and straightened his back, trying to look nonchalant.

*"We'll aye come back tae see you!"* Brown roared, firing, working the bolt of his Lee-Enfield and firing again. Tulloch let him continue, aware the action was futile. He wondered at the power of music as some of his men still sang despite the carnage. Another song entered Tulloch's head; he remembered his platoon marching through the unforgiving mountains of Waziristan on India's Northwest Frontier. He shook his head, remembering himself as a callow one-pip second lieutenant fresh from Sandhurst.

As an unhealthy hush fell over the Rifles' defences, Tulloch relived another song that whispered down the years.

*"I love a lassie, a bonnie Black Madrasi."*

Down the years? It was only four years ago, although it seemed a lifetime since he thought he knew it all, an officer keen to teach the other ranks how to soldier. He grinned ruefully, remembering how the officers in the mess and soldiers in the barracks exchanged glances, grunted, and waited for reality to bite.

*"She's as black as the coals in deepest hell."*

Tulloch had learned the hard way, step by bitter-experienced step.

*"Sir!"* Private Hogg, squat, flat-faced, and imperturbable, nodded to the sky. *"Aircraft, sir, and I doubt they'll be ours."*

Tulloch saw the tiny black dots rapidly approaching and knew that German aircraft would soon be pounding the Lothian's positions, softening them before another assault.

*"I love a lassie,*
*A bonnie black Madrasi."*

Tulloch shook the song from his mind.

*"Down, lads!"*

The Lothians were already tearing at the ground, trying to burrow even deeper holes for protection, pulling their steel helmets closer to their heads as the mind-tearing scream of the aircraft battered at their sanity and nerves. The Lothians had experienced Stuka attacks before and knew what to expect.

The aircraft arrived far too soon, descending into near-vertical dives one after the other immediately above the British positions. Each plane released a single bomb, with the Lothians covering their heads with their hands. One man screamed involuntarily while Brown and Sergeant Drysdale raised their rifles and fired at the attackers. Drysdale's face was twisted with concentration, aiming each shot as he worked the bolt.

The explosions shook the defences, pulverising walls, tearing craters in the ground and, miraculously, causing no more casualties except headaches from the concussion. Tulloch coughed as the combination of smoke and dust caught his throat. He saw Sergeant Drysdale recharge his magazine and stand up, shake off the dust and stalk around the defences.

*"They're coming, sir!"* Hogg sighted along the barrel of his rifle. *"Here they come!"*

Machine gun fire ripped from the trees, and then the Germans advanced in a series of short rushes, professional and deadly. They had already defeated Poland, Luxemburg, the Netherlands, and Belgium and had no doubts that this handful of British soldiers would either surrender or flee.

*"Pick your targets,"* Tulloch ordered. *"Fire when you can."* Most of his men were veterans of the Northwest Frontier; they did not need his advice. He raised his chin as Kinloch started playing his pipes, the Lowland Pipes unique to the Lothian Rifles. The sound encouraged the men, and Hogg snarled *"Gin ye daur,"* the regimental motto as he narrowed his eyes and fixed an advancing soldier in his backsight.

Brown fired first, hitting a tall German sergeant and spinning him in a half circle. The Germans moved faster as Hogg and the other survivors aimed and fired, working the bolts of their Lee-Enfields with the precision of the professional soldiers most were. The Spandau fired again, far faster than the Bren that Innes aimed at the advancing Germans.

More of the attackers fell, some dead, others writhing and moaning on the ground.

*"Fix bayonets,"* Tulloch ordered and heard the metallic snick as the men fitted the long eighteen-inch sword bayonets to their rifles. For a moment, the weak sun glittered on the blades, making a bleak beauty out of the wickedly dangerous weapons, and then Tulloch looked forward. Bayonets were puny weapons when compared to the Panzers of the enemy.

A German officer shouted an order, and the attackers moved again, rushing towards the slender khaki line.

Tulloch checked his revolver was loose in its holster and lifted his rifle with another song ringing inside his head.

*"Vivas Schola Edinensis,*
*Schola Regia venerabilis,"*

The old well-remembered Latin phrases lifted inside Tulloch's head, transporting him back to a time when his world was full of hope.

*"This is no time to think of my old school song,"* Tulloch told himself as the Germans advanced, yet the power of music transported him back to when his military career began and, before that, to his school days.

# Chapter One

"There are three wants which can never be satisfied: that of the rich, who want something more; that of the sick, who want something different; and that of the traveller, who says, 'Anywhere but here.'" *Considerations by the Way*: Emerson.

The Door had dominated Tulloch's thoughts throughout his sixth and final year at Edinburgh's Royal High School. Massive and imposing, it sat beneath a marble pediment, solid wood and closed, a barrier between youthful academia and the adventure of adulthood. In common with most of his peers, Tulloch viewed the Door every time he sat in morning assembly, wishing it was time to step through and escape the thralldom of compulsory education.

Now that day had finally arrived. Douglas Tulloch sat in the great hall of the classical building on his last-ever assembly, singing the old school song as he contemplated the huge door and desperate to progress with his life.

The rector stood in front of the assembled school, with his senior masters sitting behind him, their black cloaks adding to

1

the air of dignity the Royal High School attempted to portray. Tulloch sang the words that six years of repetition had drilled into his brain.

> *"Vivas, Schola Edinensis,*
> *Schola Regia venerabilis!*
> *Sicut arx in colle sita,*
> *Sicut sol e nubibus densis,*
> *Splendes, splendeas in aeternum,*
> *Alma Mater atque amabilis."*

Tulloch watched his fellows, youths he had known for the past six years, and wondered if he would ever see them again. Oh, he knew they would make promises of eternal friendship and exchange addresses, but life would intervene and spoil the sincerest of intentions. Tulloch looked sideways at their eager, fresh faces and wished them well even as he shivered at their prospects. He could not imagine himself with a sedentary life in an office or furthering his education at university.

The deputy rector only opened the Door one day a year when the men of the sixth form finally departed from the Royal High to enter the post-scholastic world. About a fifth would continue their studies in academia, progressing to Edinburgh or some other university; the majority would go into business or enter a profession, and others would find work in the Colonies. Tulloch watched the rector walk forward with his black gown rippling in his wake and his highly polished shoes gleaming in the light. When the rector gave an order, the deputy rector solemnly produced a large key and ceremonially unlocked the Door. Although he had witnessed this occasion once a year for five years, Tulloch still felt a ripple of excitement.

The sixth-year students watched the heavy door open to their future, and sunlight flooded into the great hall. The pupils continued to sing as the refrain rippled around the hall.

*"Vivas Schola Regia,*
*Vivas Schola Regia,*
*Vivas, vivas, Schola Regia!*
*Schola Regia!"*

One by one, the sixth-year men, all eighteen years old, edged forward under the envious eyes of their assembled juniors, shook the hands of their teachers, and walked through the open door. Tulloch was in the middle of his class; he was an average student, not particularly distinguished academically, good at history and had played rugby for the second eleven and was a member of the school boxing team.

"Rummel them up!" Mr Rutherford, the PE teacher, was a Borderer born and bred and taught rugby as he had learned it in Galashiels. "Don't let them settle!"

Tulloch could see his bright eyes watching as he waited in the queue to leave. His mouth formed silent words. *Rummel them up!*

"I heard you are going into the army, Tulloch," William King Gillies, the rector, shook his hand while holding his gaze with penetrating eyes.

"Yes, sir," Tulloch replied.

"That's a fine career, Tulloch, and I am sure you will do well."

"Thank you, sir," Tulloch said.

"Is there any particular regiment you wish to join, Tulloch?" King Gillies asked.

"The Argyll and Sutherland Highlanders, sir," Tulloch replied. "The regiment that made up the Thin Red Line."

"I see. Work hard at Sandhurst, Tulloch; it's a fine institution," King Gillies said. Tall and imposing, he gripped Tulloch's hand for a second longer than necessary.

"I will, sir," Tulloch assured him.

"Don't forget to keep in touch and let us know how you get on," King Gillies repeated the words he had said to the hundreds of anonymous boys he had ushered through the Door in his time as rector.

"I won't, sir," Tulloch said and stepped on as the rector moved to the next boy in line. He had noted some relief in the rector's tone, as though he was as glad to see Tulloch's back as Tulloch was to bid farewell to his scholastic career.

The Edinburgh air greeted Tulloch with its habitual surprise, mixing the brightness of late June with a bite of still-remembered winter. The green slopes of Calton Hill rose above them, and the dark mass of the Old Town below, with the stern slopes of Arthur's Seat breaking the horizon. Tulloch took a deep breath of freedom and looked around at his schoolmates.

"I wonder if we'll ever meet again," he said as the sixth formers emerged one by one and stood, some wondering what to do, and others talking excitedly.

"Oh, we're bound to bump into each other somewhere," Beaumont said. "The world's not all that big a place." He laughed, with his round, freckled face creasing in good humour. "Where are you off to now?"

"Home," Tulloch said. "To change out of these togs into something fresher. I've worn school uniform for so long it's nearly part of me."

Beaumont laughed again. "I'll miss the old place," he said, glancing around the dark building that had dominated his life for the past six years.

"I doubt I will," Tulloch replied. "I'll be too busy." He held out his hand. "Good luck, old man."

"Well, good luck," Beaumont shook Tulloch's hand. Two or three rugby players wished Tulloch well, and Robertson, his rival in the boxing ring, grinned as they parted. The others were too busy with their own affairs.

Tulloch glanced back as he left the building. He remembered the long, tedious hours inside the classrooms, with Latin his least favourite subject as the master stalked the aisles between the desks, twirling his black cloak between his fingers and searching for transgressions.

"Your translation is wrong, Tulloch! Write that out forty times!"

"Yes, sir."

Or the equally common. "Come to the front of the class, Tulloch; hold out your hand!"

Tulloch swore he had worn out at least one school belt with the palm of his hand in his long-drawn-out feud with the Latin teacher, but it was all history now, and he held no grudges. The past was gone, and the future beckoned.

He remembered the better times when he panted on a muddy rugby field, expending his youthful energy. He had never made the rugby firsts, being more an enthusiastic than a skilful player, but he had been a useful addition to the seconds. Playing the old rivals of George Heriot's school had been his peak when he scored three tries in one victorious match. More than one PT teacher had warned him about his over-aggressive attitude on the pitch, but he had played to win and never backed down from a tackle or in the scrum.

Tulloch realised he was alone as his classmates drifted to their post-school destinations. His school days were over; the days of chalk, stifling boredom, and excited chatter would never return; and life beckoned. Conscious of his new status as a man, he straightened his back, had a final glance at his *alma mater*, and walked away.

Saying goodbye to old friends had been difficult, but leaving his boyhood home was positively painful.

Tulloch's final term had ended in June, while his junior term at Sandhurst did not begin until January. During the intervening months, his father employed him in a junior capacity in his legal office, and he headed for the hills most weekends. Although Tulloch was slightly guilty about not spending time at home, he felt his parents' eyes on him as they also relived his childhood.

"Are you sure you want to join the army?" His mother said, hiding her anxiety behind a small smile. "It's not too late to change your mind."

"I'm sure," Tulloch replied, stifling the guilty doubts that his mother could always place in him.

"There's always a place for you in your father's practice," Mother reminded.

"I know," Tulloch replied. His father expected him to follow into the legal profession, but Tulloch could not envisage himself spending his working life in that stifling office, struggling with legal terminology as he bought and sold houses or dealt with court cases. Tulloch's grandfather had been a forester in an estate outside Edinburgh, but his grandmother had a larger vision for her four sons. By iron will and a leather belt, she had forced all four into university, ensuring they made something of themselves. Tulloch's father had graduated from Edinburgh University and worked his way up in the legal profession until he had a solid position in a Queen Street firm. They had moved from a terraced flat in respectable Comely Bank to a house in Nelson Street in the middle-class New Town, and every evening, Tulloch's mother walked through Queen Street Gardens to meet her husband.

The house was filled with fine furniture, Walter Scott's novels, legal books, and militaria from the First World War, or the Kaiser's War, as Tulloch's mother insisted on calling those four years of slaughter. Mrs Tulloch enjoyed pictures, painting, and buying, so they decorated every wall with a mixture of self-painted watercolours and purchased Victorian and Edwardian oils and an occasional print.

One picture had caught Tulloch's attention. It hung on the wall in the hall, and Tulloch spent hours of his childhood staring at it. According to Mrs Tulloch, Robert Gibb had painted *The Thin Red Line* in their house. The picture captured the instance when the 93rd Highlanders had stood against Russian cavalry at the Battle of Balaclava during the Crimean War. Tulloch's mother had intended to inspire an artistic streak in Tulloch, but instead, he had become interested in the subject matter rather than the style.

"I want to be a soldier like Colin Campbell," Tulloch decided as he indicated the officer commanding the Highlanders.

"You're going to follow your father into law," his mother told him severely.

"I'm going to be a soldier," young Tulloch decided, lifting his head.

"Oh, no, you're not," his mother said.

The arguments continued for years, with Tulloch's mother reinforcing her point of view with logic or brute force and Tulloch stubbornly refusing to alter his mind. Apart from such discussions, Tulloch's boyhood was happy as he explored Edinburgh, graduating from the serene privacy of Queen Street Gardens to Arthur's Seat. As the years passed, he rambled in the Pentland Hills and the Ettrick Forest, growing more adventurous with every expedition. He tested himself with trials of endurance, walking faster and further every trip, finding rock faces to scramble up and sleeping in the open with the stars as a canopy.

"Why are you doing all this outdoors activity?" Beaumont asked curiously.

"I want to be fit for the army," Tulloch said.

"Why?" Beaumont asked, genuinely curious.

Tulloch did not mention the picture in his hall. "I can't see myself doing anything else," he said honestly.

Beaumont shook his head. "You are strange," he said. "Well, when you're sitting in a muddy trench in some Godforsaken corner of the world, think of me sitting on my comfortable leather chair in my warm office."

Tulloch laughed. "I will," he said.

In his last year of school, Tulloch applied to sit the competitive entrance examination for Sandhurst. He was an adequate pupil at the Royal High and surprised himself by finishing in the top half of the year for Sandhurst.

"I'm starting Sandhurst in January next year," Tulloch

informed his parents. He saw the anger on his father's face as his mother closed her eyes.

"I'm sure you'll do well, Douglas."

"Thank you, Mother," Tulloch said as his father walked away.

On his last day before leaving for Sandhurst, Tulloch paced the familiar house in Nelson Street, wondering when he would be back. Now that the time had come, he felt a mixture of excitement and sadness. He stopped in the kitchen and looked down to the tiny triangular back garden with its high stone walls and the stone birdbath and smiled at the memories.

"Remember to feed the birds," he said.

"I will," his mother said. She touched his shoulder, opened her mouth to speak and walked away.

Tulloch's upstairs bedroom was full of memories, with his childhood books, the pair of rugby boots under the bed, and the stain on the carpet where he had spilt ink many years ago. He glanced out the window at the houses opposite with their black-painted railings above dark basements and watched a car rumble down the steep cobbled street.

"Goodbye, old room," Tulloch said as his history crowded around. He was aware that his mother was hovering on the landing outside and wondered how she could have been so stern all his life and now looked sad at his departure.

"Put away childish things," he told himself resolutely and began to pack.

# Chapter Two

"To be prepared for war is one of the most effectual means of preserving peace." - George Washington, January 8th, 1790.

"Gentleman Cadet Douglas Tulloch!" The Regimental Sergeant Major – the RSM - was four inches taller than Tulloch and twice as wide. He addressed the cadets who mustered before him on the steps of the Old Building at Sandhurst. "You are in No. 4 Company."

Two storeys high and with a massive columned gateway, the Old College or Old Building had trained British officers since 1812, the year of Wellington's victory at Salamanca. The Union flag hung damply from the flagpole above, and the row of six brass cannon from the Battle of Waterloo stood in immaculate attention facing the immensity of the Square and the grey waters of the Lake.

There were only four companies of cadets at Sandhurst: One, Three, Four, and Five. Four and Five lived in the Old Building, and One and Three in the red brick New Building, half a mile distant and dimly seen through the drizzling rain.

Tulloch looked at his fellow cadets from the corner of his

eyes. They stood at attention, most looking desperately keen and efficient. One dark-haired cadet caught his eye and winked before directing all his attention at the RSM, who read out the names alphabetically, snarling which company each cadet would grace.

Despite all Tulloch's research on Sandhurst, the Royal Military College was much larger than he had anticipated. He stared at the pine trees and rhododendron bushes, sad now in the bleak January weather, beside the Lower Lake and the smooth gravel of the Square. Soaring columns marked the main entrance to the college, while a momentary break in the cloud and rain allowed the weak winter sun to gleam from the brass cannons.

"Double!" RSM roared. "Number Four Company to the East wing of the Old Building!"

Tulloch doubled, and the dark-haired cadet doubled at his side.

"We'd best get used to this," the dark-haired cadet said. "I'm Carlton. Hugh Carlton."

"Douglas Tulloch." They shook hands while running along the corridor with a dozen other junior cadets behind them.

"It looks like we're neighbours," Carlton said as they moved into adjoining rooms.

"It looks like it," Tulloch agreed as he entered his room.

The army had allocated each junior cadet a bed-sitting room and allowed them time to unpack and settle in before training began in earnest the following day. Tulloch glanced around his room, decided it was larger and more comfortable than he had expected and put away his meagre possessions.

"Learn all you can, do your best, and remember your goal," Tulloch told himself and decided to explore his new surroundings. He saw other cadets in the stone corridors, young men like himself, some confident, others assuming confidence. Some were junior cadets like himself, while others carried themselves with the arrogant swagger of men who had already passed their first term at Sandhurst and were well on their way to becoming officers in the British Army.

Tulloch collapsed into bed that first night, convinced he would never sleep with so many new images dancing through his mind. He heard the rap of footsteps in the corridor outside his room and closed his eyes.

"Wake up! Wake up! Show a leg! The sun's burning your bloody eyeballs!"

Tulloch started as he heard the shouting in the corridor, realised where he was and jumped out of bed to attend his first parade as a gentleman cadet. He dressed hurriedly, opened the door, and saw Carlton looking equally bemused outside his room.

"Where do we go?"

"Company steps!" Somebody advised as they hurried past.

"Company steps," Tulloch said, and they followed the crowd, making last-minute adjustments to their clothes as they ran.

Number 4 Company stood on the steps facing the vast parade ground, with the RSM and company sergeant already present. Tulloch was in the middle, with Carlton at his side and a jovial Ulsterman named Masson near the front.

Regimental Sergeant Major Noble, late of the Royal Welch Fusiliers and Welsh Guards, was six foot two of military efficiency packed into the most immaculate uniform that Tulloch had ever seen. The array of medal ribbons spoke of a career that spanned half the Empire and all four years of the First World War.

"Get fell in!" RSM Noble shouted with a blast of sound that scared a parliament of rooks a hundred yards away into immediate flight.

The cadets clattered down the steps with their nailed boots striking sparks from the stone and stood at what they hoped was attention. Tulloch caught Masson's eye, realised the Ulsterman was trying not to laugh, and looked away in case it was infectious.

The RSM shook his head in disgust.

"Horrible! I've seen infants at school better. Get fell out again!" Noble did not move as he surveyed the cadets scrambling back up the steps, with Tulloch wondering what he had let himself in for. He slammed to attention, saw Masson's shoulders shaking with suppressed mirth and tried to concentrate.

No sooner had the cadets formed up on the steps than the RSM bellowed again. "Wait for it! Now move! Get fell in!"

Tulloch ran back down the stairs, looking to his right and left to see how his fellow cadets behaved. He was relieved to see they looked as nervous as he felt, except Masson, who seemed to be enjoying himself, and Carlton, who was as composed as if he were strolling through a park.

The cadets lined up, panting, as RSM surveyed them through eyes like gimlets. When he spoke, even Masson stopped smiling to listen, and Colour Sergeant Blackwood, a few paces to the rear, scanned the cadets with his broad face intent.

"You junior cadets will address all NCO instructors as 'staff.' I am RSM Noble. You will address me as 'sir.' I also call you 'sir.' The difference is that you mean it, and I don't."

Masson began to laugh, swallowed as he realised nobody else found the RSM amusing, and turned his humour into a strangled cough. Noble slowly walked to him, pushed his forehead against Masson's and remained static in the most intimidating silence that Tulloch had ever experienced.

"Mr. Masson, sir," Noble said after a long two minutes. "I thought I heard you laughing. I know I must be mistaken, Mr. Masson because you are an officer cadet, and officer cadets don't laugh when a member of staff talks to them. Do they?"

"No, sir," Masson said.

The RSM stepped back. "The rest of number Four Company will thank you for a full morning's drill, Mr. Masson."

Tulloch felt the atmosphere change as some cadets swivelled their eyes towards Masson. He faced his front, closed his mouth, and concentrated.

For the remainder of that morning, the RSM had the cadets on the square, marching and parading until their feet ached, and their minds buzzed with his repeated commands. Noble was relentless, pushing them to their limits while expecting nothing less than perfection.

"That man there! Idle! Take his name, Colour Sergeant!"

"Got him, sir!" Blackwood said, scribbling a name in a small notebook.

Tulloch learned that "idle" could mean anything from being a fraction of a second late to obey a command to not having all the tunic buttons polished to the correct sheen. Masson had his name taken for being idle three times that morning, and Tulloch wondered what the penalty would be even as he sweated and stamped in the January rain.

The first day was an introduction to weeks of what Tulloch called unremitting hell. When they were not on the parade ground, the cadets were on the firing range or in classroom lectures, learning to ride a horse, physical training, or polishing their kit. The staff demanded that every item of clothing and equipment be perfect, with boots, belts, and chinstraps so bright they dazzled.

"You don't want to fall out with the RSM," one grizzled old soldier whispered from the corner of the room as Tulloch polished his boots. "Next to the Commandant, he's the most important man in Sandhurst."

Tulloch looked around in surprise. A handful of old soldiers haunted the barracks, acting as batmen and general advisors to the budding officers. Most had done their twenty-two years or more and watched the cadets through wise, cynical eyes. The speaker was around sixty but could have been older, with a face that told of a lifetime of experience and tattoos from wrist to neck.

"You're Corporal Dunn, aren't you?"

"That's right. You're not from a military background, are you, sir?" the soldier said.

"No," Tulloch replied. "I'm the first in the family to join the army. How did you know?"

"The way you carry yourself, sir," Dunn wore the twin stripes of a corporal. "Look, sir, you'll never get a decent surface on your buttons like that," he took the tunic from Tulloch. "Do it this way, see? And don't forget the back as well as the front."

Tulloch watched and learned. "Thank you, Corporal."

"You're due a surprise kit inspection on Friday," Dunn said, buffing up the buttons with the ease of long practice.

"Are we?" Tulloch asked.

"The adjutant is coming round," Dunn said. "I'd have everything perfect for him. He'll look for faults in somebody to set an example of his efficiency. Don't let it be you."

"Thank you," Tulloch said. He wondered if he should reward the old soldier and realised he had nothing to offer.

Dunn read his mind. "No," he said, shaking his head. "You don't give me a tip. I'm here to advise and help. You should polish underneath your dress boots as well, sir. You won't wear them before Friday, so a nice surface will last and look better."

"Thank you, Corporal Dunn," Tulloch said.

He heard the noise at about midnight and lay in bed for a few moments, trying to work out what was happening. First came the hammer of dozens of feet and then the raucous shouts of raised voices, accompanied by a rhythmical thump Tulloch could not place.

"What's happening out there?" Tulloch opened his door and peered along the corridor.

"I don't know," Carlton stood in a plush dressing gown and bare feet. "There's a commotion at the far end of the corridor."

"We'd best go along and have a look," Tulloch said.

A crowd of cadets clustered around one of the rooms, most watching, but some engaged in hauling out the contents and pouring water over the bed.

"What's all this?" Tulloch asked, pushing through the crowd.

"Masson," a short, narrow-faced youth replied. "He got us all extra drill."

"Are you wrecking his room?" Tulloch asked, unsure whether to be amused or irritated. "We're officer cadets, not schoolboys."

"It's a Sandhurst tradition," a tall, erect youth of nineteen told him.

"He didn't do anything," Tulloch saw Masson in the corner of his room with two of his fellow cadets holding him secure. Masson was struggling, red with anger at the vandalism.

"He got the RSM angry." A tall, arrogant youth, Simpson stood at the back of the crowd with a smaller cadet named Preston at his side.

"The RSM looked for an excuse to give us extra drill," Tulloch said. "He found Masson; it could have been any of us." He saw Preston whisper to Simpson.

"Keep out of this, Tulloch, or we'll do your room next," Simpson said.

"If anything happens to my room, I'll be looking for you, Simpson," Tulloch said, "and you, Preston." He recognised that Preston was stirring up trouble and using the tall and muscular Simpson as his weapon.

Tulloch realised that the atmosphere had changed, with most of the cadets shuffling away and the two holding Masson releasing their grip.

"We've taught him a lesson," Simpson said, glaring at Tulloch. "That will act as a warning." Turning, he stalked away, with Preston pausing for a final smirk at Tulloch before he followed. The room cleared, and Masson took a deep breath.

"Thank you, Tulloch," he said.

"You've made an enemy of Simpson," Carlton said as he began to pick up Masson's scattered possessions.

"And of Preston," Tulloch agreed.

The more senior cadets looked down on the juniors, much as prefects at school had viewed the more junior pupils. Tulloch kept out of their way, watched how they acted and dressed and imitated their demeanour. Apart from the brief encounter with Simpson, the first few days at Sandhurst passed in a blur of constant movement, with Tulloch's fellow cadets only names and faces until he got to know them as individuals with personalities, habits, patterns of speech, and idiosyncrasies. He grew to like Carlton, a cheery, spontaneous youth from Northumberland, and Masson, the laughing Ulsterman everybody called Paddy. At the other end of the scale were the devious Preston and tall Simpson, destined for the Guards and happy to let everybody know it.

"I hear you're joining the boxing society," Simpson said as they hurried along the corridor to the first parade of the day.

"That's right," Tulloch said.

"I'll see you there, then," Simpson gave his broad, counterfeit grin. "On the knuckle end of my gloves."

"I'll look forward to it," Tulloch told him, leaning backward to meet Simpson's amused stare.

In common with the other cadets, Tulloch wore brown canvas drill, a loose canvas jacket and trousers in unflattering brown, designed to slip over a uniform to keep it clean. In his second week, he endured the ordeal of being measured for his uniform. He stood still while the military tailor from Camberley poked and prodded him, stretched his tape around every extremity and made non-committal noises.

"We'll soon have you looking like a proper officer," the tailor said as he wrote neat notes in a small black book.

"A proper officer?" Simpson, Tulloch's neighbour, repeated. "He wants to go into the Argylls."

"A fine regiment," the tailor said without looking up.

"They'll never accept him. They want Highlanders, not civilians from Edinburgh," Simpson said, grinning.

"Which regiment do you hope to join, sir?" The tailor asked Simpson.

"The Scots Guards," Simpson replied.

"Ah," Tulloch responded. "Didn't they run away at the Alma?"

Simpson's face darkened with anger. "We did not!" he denied. "We were on the Army List a hundred years before your mob was even thought of. Namur, 1695, Dettingen, Salamanca, Waterloo, Inkerman, Ypres, Somme, Arras, Sambre," he listed some of the Scots Guards battle honours.

"Oh," Tulloch said and shook his head. "All that, and they still ran away at the Alma."

The tailor worked on, hiding his smile. He had heard the like a hundred times before as he measured cadets and listened to their inter-regimental rivalry.

"That's you, sir," the tailor dismissed Tulloch with a few words. "I'll let you know when your uniform is ready."

"Thank you, sir," Tulloch said.

"Sir?" Simpson repeated and smiled. "If you ever become a proper officer, Tulloch, you'll learn when to say sir."

"Are you next, Mr. Simpson?" the tailor asked, promptly pressing a long pin into his leg. "Oh, I do beg your pardon," he said as Simpson started. "Fortunately, officers of the Guards ignore such minor discomforts."

"I'll see you in the ring, Tulloch," Simpson promised.

"Whenever you like," Tulloch told the taller and heavier man.

After the tailor came the bootmaker, a morose gentleman with slender hands who measured Tulloch's feet and nodded.

"We'll have your boots for you soon, Mr. Tulloch."

"Thank you." Tulloch had never worn hand-made boots before, but as a potential officer in the British Army, he had to look the part.

"Ensure you polish them well, sir, to make them supple, and the RSM likes a surface on his cadets' boots."

"Thank you, sir," Tulloch replied.

Tulloch soon adjusted himself to the size of Sandhurst. The cadets learned that marching was only one method of progress and used bicycles to travel to the often widely separated parades. The bicycles were especially marked for each company, with each cadet possessing his own, numbered on the rear mudguard.

Sandhurst had a specific drill for mounting and riding bicycles, with the cadets standing with their bicycles in columns of half sections as a sergeant instructor shouted, "Prepare to mount!" and then "Mount!"

Although Tulloch was used to bicycling around Edinburgh, the Pentland Hills, and the Borders, cycling in a disciplined formation was a new skill. He worked hard to fit in with the rest while remaining in the middle of the class, neither shining nor letting himself down. However, with so many potential officers together, many cadets strove to prove their suitability for leadership.

"My father is a lieutenant-colonel," Simpson drawled. "I aim to outrank him before I am thirty."

"Thirty?" Carlton said with a laugh. "The best of British luck to you. Unless we have a war, we'll all still be lieutenants until we're in our forties."

"This Mussolini fellow might oblige with a war," Masson said.

"Or Hitler; he's doing a good job in Germany," Carlton said. "He'll want to expand his boundaries soon and cause all sorts of bother."

"Back to the trenches, eh?" Preston said.

"Even Japan is getting a bit uppity," Masson observed. "They've been fighting in China for years now."

"The Japanese?" Simpson laughed. "They're hardly a threat."

Tulloch listened. He knew many of these cadets came from military backgrounds and expected they had discussed such matters at home. His father had rarely touched on international affairs.

"How about you, Tulloch?" Preston asked. "What rank was your father?"

"He wasn't in the army," Tulloch admitted. *As you well know, Preston.*

"Not at all?"

"Not at all." Tulloch became aware of the interest in the room.

"What a clever man," Preston said smoothly. "Avoiding all the slaughter." He looked away with a smile, having made his point and hinted that Tulloch's father, and by association Tulloch, was a coward.

When the conversation moved on, Tulloch wondered if his popularity had waned. It was a thought that remained with him as the cadets marched back to the parade ground.

"Idle!" RSM would scream at anything less than perfection. "Idle!" he yelled at even a speck of dust on a uniform. Idle meant extra duties or being confined to barracks. Idle meant working twice as hard with even less time off. Idle became a byword to the cadets, who used it to describe everything they disapproved of or disliked.

"I'm off to the pub as soon as I get the chance," Masson said as he polished his boots with such energy that he threatened to wear out the leather.

"You're idling," Carlton told him, smiling. "I'll come too. How about you, Tulloch?"

"Ask me nearer the time," Tulloch said. His parents were both tee-total, so he had no encouragement to drink, and the prospect of spending what little money he had in a public house was not appealing. He felt people's eyes on him and realised he had slipped further down in popularity.

Everything in Sandhurst was at the double as the staff hammered their cadre of brash young civilians into something resembling junior officers. They learned to work as a team on the Square and as individuals in their various classes.

"Eighteen months of this!" Carlton gasped as he rushed to change between two classes. "I won't survive."

"Yes, you will," Tulloch encouraged. "We're here for three terms, remember, and the first term is always the worst."

"I might not survive that long," Carlton said.

"You will," Tulloch replied.

"You might not, Tulloch." Preston had been listening. "You've avoided Simpson in the ring so far, but he'll find you." He smiled. "I'm looking forward to that."

"I bet you are," Tulloch said, pushing him away. He had no fear of fighting Simpson in or out of the boxing ring, but he did not want the distraction yet. He would bide his time and let the bigger man wait.

# Chapter Three

*"Learning is not child's play; we cannot learn without pain."*
**Aristotle: *Politics***

"Most of you will have handled a firearm before," Sergeant Reynolds, the musketry instructor, spoke with a Welsh accent as he looked over the cadets. "Some of you will have been in the Officer's Training Corps at your school, and others may have fired rifles or shot-guns on your daddy's estate." He waited for the expected murmur of mingled humour and agreement to pass. "Some of you may even have handled the SMLE, the Short Magazine Lee-Enfield rifle."

About half the cadets nodded in agreement. Tulloch hefted his rifle. It was heavier than he had expected but felt well-balanced. He looked along the length of the range, with the targets a distant blur in the February mist, and hoped Reynolds did not keep talking for long.

"There are many variations of the Short Lee-Enfield," Reynolds continued. "The rifle you have is forty-four and a half inches long, with a barrel length of twenty-five inches and weighs eight pounds and ten ounces when empty."

21

The mist altered to a drizzling rain that blew into the cadets' faces. Tulloch lifted his chin, thankful the weeks he spent rambling and camping on the Pentland and Border hills had inured him to all sorts of weather.

"The extreme range is two thousand eight hundred yards," Reynolds said, "but you'll be lucky to hit anything at more than a mile. It's deadly accurate at three hundred yards, with a magazine of ten rounds of .303 and another up the spout." He demonstrated how to load.

"A good infantryman can fire fifteen aimed rounds a minute," Reynolds said, "with twenty-five rounds rapid fire. You gentlemen hope to be officers and, therefore, should be as good as the best. I will not tolerate anything less, and the worst of you will be a first-class shot, or I'll ensure you fail the course."

Tulloch felt a ripple of apprehension along the cadets' ranks. The highest level at the ranges was a marksman, with a first-class shot next. He felt the rain making his grip on the rifle slippery and hoped he did not disgrace himself.

Reynolds marched the cadets to the rifle range and gave instructions on how to aim, with the backsight lined up with the foresight. He walked along the line of cadets, correcting where required.

"Aim," Reynolds ordered. "Fire!" He stood back to watch the results.

Tulloch pulled the rifle into his shoulder as ordered, lined up the target and fired. He was surprised at the ferocity of the kick and swore when he saw the result.

"Outer," Reynolds told him. "Have you ever fired a rifle before, Mr. Tulloch?"

"No, staff," Sturrock replied.

"Take first pressure, then second pressure. Don't snatch at the trigger and accept the recoil," Reynolds said quietly. "The SMLE is a beautiful weapon if you look after her; treat her like a wife. She never jams and will accept rough treatment, but don't give her any." His words caressed the weapon. "Keep her clean, bright, and slightly oiled; use the pull-through and oil bottle in the butt trap, boil her out after prolonged firing, and she'll serve you well."

Reynolds realised he was smiling and adopted a ferocious scowl. "And don't waste bullets! Each bullet costs threepence! One bullet, one Hun! Now try again, Mr. Tulloch!"

Tulloch nodded and hugged the Lee-Enfield closer to his shoulder. He allowed his body to flow into the weapon, as if they were both part of the same entity and aimed, took a deep breath and released it slowly as he took first pressure on the trigger.

"Squeeze the trigger, sir; squeeze it; that's the way," Reynolds said.

Tulloch rode the kick and looked up, knowing his shot had been better.

"An inner, Mr. Tulloch," Reynolds said. "Now you've got it! That's another of the king's enemies dispatched." He walked away to give encouragement and advice to the next cadet.

"Kneeling, sir, kneeling! Left elbow resting behind the kneecap, eyes level with the backsight!"

"I am sure Sergeant Reynolds sleeps with his rifle," Masson said later that day. "I can see him cuddling it like a wife, breathing sweet nothings into its breech mechanism as he fondles the muzzle."

Tulloch laughed. "Maybe so," he said. "He certainly knows what he's doing."

Added to the drill, musketry, sports, and physical training, Sandhurst added classes in military law, history, military adminis-tration, tactics, geography, and engineering. Tulloch studied harder than he ever had at school, absorbing knowledge for a career he often wondered was a mistake. The topography classes in map making and field sketching saw him bicycling further afield, exploring the local countryside, and returning to his old love of walking.

"You're a bit of a loner," Major Outerston, the Company Commander, observed as Tulloch returned from one of his map-making expeditions. "That might not be the best thing for a regimental officer."

"Yes, sir," Tulloch agreed. He already knew his weakness.

"I'd advise you to join one of the clubs and improve your team-playing skills," the major said. "I know you're in the boxing club, but that's a solitary sport. You played rugger, didn't you?"

"Yes. Sir," Tulloch stood at attention in front of his desk. "I was in the seconds at school."

"Good; the company team could always do with new blood. How's your shooting?" Outerston was an erect man with a fair, neatly clipped military moustache and the ribbons of the MC and DSO on his chest. His manner was deceptively mild beneath sharp grey eyes.

"Fair, sir," Tulloch said, knowing that the major would have every cadet's score at his fingertips.

"It's on the plus side of fair. Join the rifle club and get better."

"Yes, sir," Tulloch said.

"That's all. Dismissed."

Tulloch saluted and left, unsure if Major Outerston had encouraged or rebuked him.

The company rugby team welcomed him with the usual mixture of frivolity and foolishness. The initiation saw Tulloch running naked around the Lower Lake with the other club members flicking him with wet towels, but he accepted the horseplay with grim good humour. He found himself playing in inter-company matches within a week, surprised at the serious-ness with which some of his fellow cadets took the games.

"We're playing Lovely Five Company," Cadet Jarrold, the team captain, told him. "They've swept all before them so far, and we aim to stop them. Nobody has ever beaten Lovely Five; we'll ruin their record this time."

Tulloch nodded. Now he was part of the rugby club and

determined to make his name. He knew that Outerston would watch, noting everything, and focussed on the game ahead.

"You're not heavy enough to be a forward," Jarrold said. "But you seem aggressive, so rough them up."

Tulloch nodded. He knew his strengths and weaknesses. He could run and tackle, but his kicking could have been better. He stood on the pitch, stamping his feet as the opposition filed out, sizing each man. They were a tight-knit team under a formidable captain who planned to enter the Royal Norfolk Regiment, known as the Holy Boys or the Fighting Ninth.

Tulloch viewed the opposition captain. *You're mine,* he said, stamping his feet. Tulloch's rugby philosophy was simple. Go in hard and fast. "Rummel them up!" his old rugby master had preached, and Tulloch never had cause to disagree.

As soon as the whistle sounded, Tulloch played his usual game of pure aggression. He never flinched in a tackle, ran with the ball, and hit hard. He had little idea of tactics or subtlety but headed for the opposition's line and encouraged his teammates to do the same.

A small crowd had gathered to watch the game, including Outerston, Simpson, and a young woman that Tulloch had never seen before. He ignored them all, mildly irritated that they might spoil his concentration if he allowed them.

Number Five Company was well-drilled and played as a team, passing like a machine as they swept forward. Tulloch made it his duty to upset the passing by tackling a man the instant he got the ball and running hard, handing off every attempt to tackle until a hefty forward flattened him, and he passed the ball.

"You're not letting them play their game, Tulloch," Jarrold said as Tulloch staggered up and checked no bones were broken. "Keep it up."

When the game ended in a draw, Tulloch left the pitch to see Outerston watching.

"You're still a loner, Tulloch, and a bit of a maverick," Outerston said. "Learn to be a team player." Yet as the major walked away, Tulloch thought he saw a hint of warmth in his eyes. The young woman was also watching, with Simpson standing at her side and whispering in her ear. When she looked at Tulloch and laughed, he walked quickly away, with the studs of his boots sinking into the soft mud.

"She's a smasher," Carlton observed. "Trust Simpson to land a peach."

Tulloch grunted. "Yes, trust Simpson."

————

THE CADETS ATE TOGETHER AT LONG TABLES AND VISITED THE Fancy Goods Store, known as Jesus, for extras. They grew to know each other's habits and backgrounds, who to avoid and who to befriend. Although Tulloch made no close friends, he found himself in the company of Carlton and Masson more than anybody else and avoided Simpson and Preston, despite the former's popularity.

The entire company was present at the inaugural military history class, with Tulloch in the middle of the central row.

Major Morrison of the Army Education Corps smiled at his students. "Well, gentlemen, I'm teaching military history, a subject you should all study to learn from the mistakes of the past. You, Jarrold, who would you say is the best general in history?"

Jarrold looked blank and stuttered, "Napoleon Bonaparte, sir."

"Even though he made a mess of his 1812 Russian campaign and lost to Wellington at Waterloo," Morrison said. "And you, Preston?"

"Marlborough, sir."

"A man who accepted thirty per cent casualties without a qualm." The major toured the class, asking each cadet the same question. "And you, Tulloch?"

"Either Colin Campbell, Lord Clyde, or Henry Havelock, sir," Tulloch said.

"You're not sure, then?" Morrison asked.

"No, sir."

"Why pick them?" Major stepped closer, with his eyes sharp.

"Havelock won three battles in a few days, each one against great odds, while Colin Campbell was the only British general to emerge from both the Crimean War and Indian Mutiny with an enhanced reputation, sir."

The major nodded. "Don't you think they had the advantage of fighting against inferior troops?"

"No, sir," Tulloch said. "I don't think Indian sepoys are inferior to Europeans as fighting men, and the Russians are doughty fighters."

Morrison smiled. "Which of the two was the better commander?"

"I don't know yet, sir," Tulloch said. "I hope you can teach me." He felt a surge of satisfaction at the ripple of faint applause from the cadets.

"I hope so too, Tulloch," Morrison said, nodding.

Tulloch enjoyed the military history classes as an escape from the stress of Sandhurst. Ignoring the barbed remarks from Preston, who suggested he was studying too hard, he spent much of his leisure time reading military history books and shone in class.

"One German general divided officers into four classes," Morrison said. "The clever, the stupid, the industrious, and the lazy." He looked over the cadets, watching who were taking notes. "He believed that every officer possessed at least two of those qualities. Write down which two you think you possess; no false modesty now, lads."

Tulloch considered for a moment and wrote, "industrious and clever," adding a question mark to the latter word.

"All right," Morrison said. "Our German friend believed the

clever and lazy were suited for the highest command. Who thinks that applies to them?"

Masson and Carlton were among the cadets who raised their hands.

"I'll agree to the lazy part," Morrison said and waited for the laughter to die away. "Who wrote clever and industrious?"

Tulloch, Simpson, and Preston were among the cadets who raised their hands.

"You may be bound for a high staff appointment, according to our general," Morrison told them. "Stupid and industrious?"

When nobody agreed to that label, Major Morrison smiled. "I'm glad to see that," he said. "Stupid and industrious officers tend to send men into impossible situations, get them killed and lose battles." He paused for a moment. "The lesson is to think before you give an order. You are responsible for men's lives, and the higher in rank you advance, the more British soldiers you can lose."

The cadets were silent as they digested Major Morrison's words.

At the end of the first or junior term in July, Outerston summoned Tulloch to his office.

"Well, Tulloch, how has the first term gone?"

Unsure how to reply, Tulloch said. "All right, sir, thank you."

Outerston nodded. "I see you joined the company's rugby team."

"Yes, sir."

Outerston smiled faintly. "I saw you play, Tulloch. And you joined the company rifle team."

"Yes, sir."

Outerston touched his moustache. "You're certainly not a star cadet, Tulloch, but you obey orders and work hard. I'm going to take a chance on you and promote you to lance corporal for your intermediate term. Congratulations."

"Thank you, sir."

"I hope it makes you less of a lone wolf, Tulloch. Dismissed."

Tulloch left the company commander's office in a daze. He had not only survived his first term at Sandhurst but had also been promoted to a lance corporal, the most unforgiving and unwanted rank in the army.

*I don't care how low the rank is,* Tulloch told himself. *It's still promotion, the first long step towards being a field marshal.*

# Chapter Four

*"Force and fraud are in war, the two cardinal virtues."*
**Hobbes: *Leviathan***

"A woman?" Tulloch repeated Carlton's words. "I've never considered a woman."

"Never?" Carlton asked, drawing on his elegant Turkish cigarette. He had seen a fellow cadet with Turkish cigarettes and thought they were more suited to an officer than the more usual British equivalent.

"How can I afford a woman?" Tulloch asked. "We earn nothing here, and my father is hardly a wealthy man." He did not add that his father grudged every penny, hoping to starve him away from Sandhurst and back to the legal office in Edinburgh.

Carlton smiled. "It depends on the woman," he explained. "Some are expensive, while you can have others for next to nothing. It all depends on what sort of woman you want and what purpose you want her for."

"I don't want any woman," Tulloch said after a few moments' consideration. He thought of the expense and the possible effects of using a prostitute. He had no desire to lose his position at Sandhurst because he caught some venereal disease.

"As you wish," Carlton exhaled aromatic smoke. "I'm in love, you know. I'm going to get married."

Tulloch smiled as the image of the girl who watched the rugby entered his head. "Subalterns may not marry," he quoted the old maxim. "Captains may marry, majors should marry, colonels must marry."

"Amelia's bringing a friend," Carlton said urgently. "I need somebody to come with me; you're the only man free." He raised his eyebrows, hopefully. "Could you come, Tulloch? I've got some spare cash if that worries you."

Tulloch sighed, knowing he had to try and fit in. "I'll come along," he said. "But I warn you that I'm not great with women."

Having no sister and attending a boys-only school had not prepared Tulloch to deal with women. He had heard his colleagues boast of their sexual prowess and often wondered how much was true.

"You don't have to be great, Tulloch," Carlton told him. "Just smile and nod as they chatter, praise their looks and hold their chair when they sit down."

Tulloch forced a smile. "I'm sure I'll manage."

Carlton had booked a table for four at the King's Head in Crowthorne, a few miles north of Sandhurst, and Tulloch wore his best civvies, hoping they were not out of place. He was more nervous about meeting a girl than anything he had experienced at the military college. Still, he persuaded himself it was all part of his education to become an officer.

"You look terrified," Carlton said.

"I am," Tulloch admitted, laughing to give the impression he was joking.

The King's Head was little more than a country inn, not the plush hotel Tulloch feared, and the two women arrived ten minutes late as he waited outside in Carlton's borrowed car.

"This is Amelia," Carlton introduced a blonde woman with a ready smile. Unsure what to do, he shook her hand. "And this is Amelia's sister, Elizabeth."

Tulloch took a deep breath and faced the woman he intended to entertain for the evening.

"I know you," Elizabeth tossed back her dark hair under the fashionable hat. "I saw you playing rugby."

Tulloch smiled. "You were the only girl watching," he said.

"Woman, please," Elizabeth told him, smiling. "I am twenty-one years old now."

"Woman," Tulloch corrected himself with a slight bow. "I do apologise."

Elizabeth had a pleasant smile, which crinkled her eyes and showed small white teeth.

Tulloch was thankful that Elizabeth seemed content to talk about everything from women's fashions to the state of affairs in Europe. All he had to do was nod, agree and field the occasional question about himself or Sandhurst.

"Do you like Sandhurst?" Elizabeth asked.

Tulloch considered the question before replying. "Like might not be the best word," he said. "I find it interesting, and I am learning a lot."

"Oh, good," Elizabeth said and began a long anecdote about her school days.

Tulloch looked sideways at Carlton, who was laughing happily with Amelia. He glanced surreptitiously at his watch, decided he should smile as Elizabeth paused for breath and wondered why he was not as excited as he should be in female company.

Elizabeth and Amelia expected wine with their meal, and Carlton ordered in an assumed French accent that set both women laughing.

"What regiment will you join?" Elizabeth asked at last, and Tulloch relaxed a little as he spoke of the Argyll and Sutherland Highlanders. Elizabeth listened for a few moments and then talked of her father, who was something in the City, and how she loved London life.

"Do you like London?"

"I've never been there," Tulloch confessed.

"Never?" Elizabeth looked astonished. Leaning across the table, she touched his arm. "Oh, Douglas, you must see London. There is so much in the Capital!" She began to extoll the virtues and attractions until Carlton noticed the time and said they had to return to Sandhurst. He paid the bill with a flourish as Tulloch tried not to look embarrassed.

"Don't I even get a good night kiss?" Elizabeth asked as Carlton deposited the women at their eight-bedroomed country home on the outskirts of Crowthorne.

Tulloch nodded, hiding his momentary confusion. "Yes, of course," he said and looked sideways at Carlton, who was busily engaged with Amelia.

Elizabeth pressed her mouth against him, pulling him closer. Tulloch found the sensation more pleasant than he had expected and responded willingly, allowing his hands to stray until she pushed him away.

"That's enough, Douglas. Don't eat me!"

"Come on, Tulloch," Carlton said, and they raced back to Sandhurst at top speed, with Tulloch musing about what had happened. He had found the evening more frustrating than exciting and wondered if he was ever destined to find a woman. Tulloch shrugged; that could wait. He had to pass Sandhurst first.

---

"TULLOCH!" SIMPSON PUSHED TULLOCH'S SHOULDER FROM behind. "I want a word with you!"

"What do you want?" They were outside the building with the sun setting, reflecting from the Lake and on the brass cannon. A few cadets marched past, with one or two turning to see what was happening.

"You're a bastard!" Simpson snarled.

Tulloch saw Preston standing a few yards away, smiling. "What are you on about, Simpson?"

Simpson pushed Tulloch's chest, sending him two steps backwards. "You kissed my girl!"

"Your girl?"

"Elizabeth Brownlow," Simpson said and pushed again, harder.

Tulloch pushed back. "I didn't know she was your girl," he said.

"Liar!"

Tulloch drew back his fist and swung a punch that would have broken Simpson's nose if the taller man had not ducked. Even so, the blow caught Simpson on the forehead and knocked him back.

"Enough!" RSM Noble strode between them. "What's all this about?"

"A woman," Preston said. "Tulloch went out with Simpson's girl."

Noble grunted. "You have a choice, gentlemen," he said. "Either I take you to the Company Commander, who will take a bleak view of cadets brawling, or you settle this in the ring."

"In the ring," Simpson said immediately. "Tulloch's been avoiding me in the ring since Junior Term."

"I'll see you in the ring," Tulloch said, leaning back to meet Simpson's gaze as Preston smirked in the background.

"He's inches taller than you and two stones heavier," Carlton said when he heard the news.

"I know," Tulloch agreed.

"You haven't got a chance, man," Masson said cheerfully. "Lead with your chin, tale an early knockout and stay down. Avoid punishment."

Tulloch shook his head. "Simpson's been needling me since my first day. I'm going to have a crack at him."

Masson began to intone Chopin's *Funeral March*.

"He'll kill you," Carlton agreed with Masson.

"Maybe," Tulloch said and lifted a military history book.

————

QUITE A CROWD GATHERED IN THE GYMNASIUM TO WATCH what they knew to be a grudge match.

Carlton had agreed to act as Tulloch's second and gave a stream of advice.

"Have you ever boxed?" Tulloch asked.

"Never," Carlton admitted.

"Then attend to the sponge and the water and let me attend to Simpson," Tulloch told him. He saw Private Dunn at the back of the crowd, a good six inches shorter than most cadets but looking teak-tough.

One of the staff sergeants acted as referee, eyed the height and weight disparity between the two men, and shook his head.

"No low blows and no hitting after the bell," the referee ordered.

Simpson glared at Tulloch. "I've been looking forward to this, Tulloch."

Tulloch walked to his corner without a word. Stripped for the ring, Simpson looked even more impressive, with a deep chest and broad shoulders.

When the bell rang, Tulloch came out quickly and led with a series of jabs, catching Simpson above the eye with his first, only to have the taller man block the rest with a raised right arm. He ducked a powerful right cross, landed a right of his own and winced as Simpson scored with a left to his temple.

Both men backed away after the initial encounter, circled each other for thirty seconds, and then Tulloch advanced again, jabbing with his left as he looked for an opening with his right. Simpson had expected the attack, blocked the jabs and caught Tulloch with a left hook to the ribs.

"Fifteen rounds, Tulloch," Simpson said as the timekeeper

rang the bell for the end of the round. "I'll make you suffer before I knock you out."

"Told you so," Carlton said, sponging Tulloch's injuries. "It's a mismatch. I'll throw in the towel any time you like."

"No," Tulloch said. "That was only the first round."

As the bell rang again, Tulloch advanced to the attack, and Simpson met him with two smashing blows to the ribs and one to the solar plexus. He grunted, straightened up and threw a straight right that bounced off Simpson's upper arm.

"I'll break your ribs, one by one," Simpson sneered. "Twelve rounds of pounding. I'll make you a cripple, Tulloch."

By the end of the fourth round, Tulloch believed Simpson was correct. His best punches did not affect the bigger man, while Simpson's blows set his ribs on fire.

"Mr Tulloch," Private Dunn stood at his corner at the end of the fifth round. "You've got all the aggression in the world, but you'll need more than aggression to defeat Mr Simpson. He's got height, weight and reach advantage over you, and, if you don't mind me saying, sir, he's a better boxer."

"He is," Tulloch agreed through split lips.

"Well, sir, you need guile if somebody is stronger than you. Nobody can doubt your bravery, now prove you're more intelligent as well."

"Guile?"

"Out-think him, sir," Dunn said. "Do what he doesn't expect."

Tulloch nodded, dripping watery blood from a cut above his eye. "Thank you, Dunn." He staggered to his feet and saw Simpson bouncing in the middle of the ring, tapping his gloves together.

"Come for more, Tulloch? You can always throw in the towel and prove you're a coward or face me and end up a cripple, too badly injured to attend the graduation parade."

Tulloch slumped, favouring his left leg, and limped around the ring. He breathed heavily, gasping when he threw a weak punch that Simpson fended off easily. Simpson laughed and jabbed into Tulloch's ribs. Tulloch doubled over, gasping again.

"Are you fit to continue, Mr Tulloch?" The referee asked.

"Yes, staff," Tulloch said, rose, crouched again and rose a second time, with his face twisted in pain. He saw Simpson relax, grinning at the crowd.

"I don't believe so, Mr Tulloch," the referee turned to Carlton when Tulloch rose, feinted a jab and landed a tremendous uppercut to Simpson's chin. It was a single blow, but it carried all Tulloch's weight. He knew it was a good punch even before his fist made contact and saw Simpson's head crack back as the glove landed.

Tulloch stepped back with his guard up and his feet square on the canvas. Ignoring the grinding pain in his ribs, he waited for Simpson to retaliate, but his opponent lay face up with his legs apart and arms spread out. The referee pushed Tulloch back as he counted.

"Back to your corner, Mr Tulloch," the referee said, holding his arm aloft. "You've won."

The crowd were silent, except for Carlton, who was jubilant, and Masson, who watched with a broad smile and helped Tulloch unlace his gloves.

"I thought you would win," Masson said.

"That's the way, sir," Dunn said. "A combination of aggression, courage and guile."

Tulloch winced and tenderly massaged his ribs as the referee approached him. "I'll have the medico tend to you, Mr Tulloch." He eyed Tulloch with new respect. "You took quite a beating, sir, and kept going."

"I feel like I've been hit by a steamroller," Tulloch said, sinking onto his stool.

"You kept coming, Mr Tulloch, and learned some guile," Dunn handed Tulloch a mug of water. "You led Mr Simpson into a trap."

"Yes," Tulloch said. He knew he would never forget today's

lesson. Aggression and courage alone were insufficient; a successful officer also needed cunning and the art of deception.

———

A COMBINATION OF SHEER HARD WORK AND STUDY KEPT Tulloch in the top half of his class, and towards the end of the senior term Major Outerston called him into his office. Wondering what military crime he had committed, Tulloch marched in and stood to attention.

"I have decided you're going to graduate, Tulloch," Outerston growled, fixing him with a ferocious look. "Fill in this form and bring it back to me tomorrow." He handed over a pre-printed War Office form.

"Thank you, sir," Tulloch said and saluted. Returning to his room, he placed the form on his table and read it with growing satisfaction. The first line told Tulloch everything.

*Name in order of preference three regiments into which you desire to be commissioned.*

Tulloch did not have to think hard. He had spent much of the last eighteen months and much of his youth dreaming of the regiment he hoped to join. He wrote Number One: Argyll and Sutherland Highlanders at the top of the page and stepped back, smiling. With his high marks and attainments, he knew the Argylls would accept him, and he did not need to put down any other formation. However, the form asked for three regiments, so that is what he would give them. He quickly scribbled the Royal Scots as his second choice and the Lothian Rifles as his third.

He knew the history of all three regiments, but the Argylls had been his favoured unit since childhood when he had examined every detail of the Thin Red Line painting that hung in his hall. The Royal Scots was the British Army's oldest and most prestigious line regiment, and belonged to Edinburgh. They were Pontius Pilate's Bodyguard, the old First of Foot, with battle honours that stretched back to Tangiers in the seventeenth century and roots that were even deeper in the past. The Lothian Rifles were the youngest of the three, having been raised for the French Revolutionary War as recently as 1793. Tulloch knew less about them, for his heart was with the Argylls.

Tulloch handed back the form and awaited the outcome with confidence. Simpson had avoided him since the boxing match, and his cracked ribs had slowly healed.

"You fought well, Tulloch," Preston approached Tulloch as he walked along the corridor. "Congratulations on your victory."

"Thank you," Tulloch said and walked on, with Preston nearly running at his side.

"No, I mean it, Tulloch. Look, we've never been the best of friends. Maybe we can alter that now."

"Goodbye, Preston," Tulloch said and strode on, leaving Preston glowering at him.

"What did he want?" Carlton asked.

"To be friends," Tulloch replied. "Rats leaving the sinking ship. I won't miss him when I leave Sandhurst."

"Nobody will," Carlton replied. He was quiet for a few moments. "We'll hear where we're bound for today."

Tulloch nodded. "Will you miss Sandhurst?"

Carlton was quiet for a few moments. "It's a place I'll always remember," he said. "I hated the first term."

"We all hated the first term," Tulloch agreed. "If we can survive that, we can survive anything."

Outerston ordered the final-year cadets to his office one by one to hear their fate.

"Tulloch," Outerston said when Tulloch stood before him. "You are being commissioned into the Lothian Rifles."

Tulloch shook his head as the disappointment grew. "I applied for the Argylls and the Royal Scots, sir."

"The Argylls have sufficient officers, and the Royals can be extremely selective," Outerston explained kindly. "Next to the Guards, they are arguably the most elite regiment."

About to say, "You mean my family is not good enough, sir," Tulloch bit back the bitter words. He had learned that in the army, one obeyed orders without complaint.

"Yes, sir. Thank you, sir."

"The Lothian Rifles are an excellent regiment and they're on your list," Outerston said.

"Yes, sir," Tulloch agreed. "I'll be proud to join them."

"You'll have seven days leave when you graduate from Sandhurst and then report to the Second Battalion."

"Yes, sir," Tulloch could say no more.

Outerston gave a small smile. "Do you know where the Second Battalion is based, Tulloch?"

"I don't, sir," Tulloch admitted.

"Peshawar," Outerston said. "Congratulations, Tulloch, you may be blooded in the reality of your profession quicker than you expected."

*Peshawar. That's a major garrison town near the Northwest Frontier of India. I'll research it in the library.*

"Yes, sir," Tulloch said.

"Dismissed."

Carlton was accepted into the Durham Light Infantry, while Masson joined the Royal Irish Fusiliers.

"Simpson didn't get into the Guards," Carlton said. "He's in the Norfolks, I think."

Tulloch nodded, thinking of the Lothian Rifles and Peshawar. "The RSM will bid us a fond farewell and welcome a new intake," he said.

---

PROUD OF HIS SERGEANT'S STRIPES, TULLOCH STOOD AT attention at the Passing Out Parade. He slid his eyes sideways to ensure the company were immaculate in their drill, remembered the strutting civilians who had strutted into Sandhurst eighteen months before and wondered how he could have been so foolish and naïve.

The senior cadets marched up the steps of the Old Building as so many thousand potential officers had done before them. Tulloch saw the surface shine of their boots and belts, heard the unified crash and knew the staff had done an excellent job. He briefly wondered how many of the marching officers would rise to general rank and how many would die of disease or enemy action in some obscure corner of the world. *Unless this Mussolini fellow, or even Hitler, stirs up trouble.*

Tulloch automatically kept in step as he thought of the present political position. He suspected Mussolini was the biggest threat, with his African empire alarmingly close to British possessions.

*Will I be fighting the Italians soon? Well, time will tell. Concentrate on today and let tomorrow take care of itself.*

The cadets thundered through the wide doors of the Old Building for the final time. Another significant doorway, Tulloch remembered leaving the Royal High School, except here was King George taking the salute with the Camp Commandant at his side.

Tulloch marched onto the gravel square for the last time and knew that in every ending, there was a beginning, and his military life was about to commence. He listened to the silver notes of the bugle sounding the Last Post over Sandhurst and knew he had never heard anything more beautiful. Tulloch took a deep breath, straightened his back, and strode to his room to pack up his kit.

# Chapter Five

*First out of Eidyn's bright fort, he inspired,*
*Faithful warriors who'd follow him.*
**The Goddodin**

"Where are you headed?" Carlton asked as they sat in the King's Head.

"India," Tulloch said. "The Lothian Rifles have two battalions, the First stationed in Scotland and the Second in India. They have a vacancy in the Second Battalion."

Carlton looked pensive for a moment. "Right into the deep end, then, Tulloch. When are you leaving?"

"On the next troopship," Tulloch said. He smiled. "Where are you bound for?"

Carlton laughed. "Aldershot," he said. "I know the way!" He held out his hand. "The best of luck to you, Tulloch."

"And you, Carlton." They shook hands, with Tulloch aware they may never meet again, or the army could post both regiments to the same base for years.

Tulloch turned and marched away, straight-backed and erect, a young officer striding to his future.

ALTHOUGH HE HAD READ DOZENS OF BOOKS AND SPOKEN TO the old sweats in Sandhurst, nothing prepared Tulloch for his first impression of India. The multi-crossed Union flag hung limply over the fort at Manora on top of the hundred feet high cliffs. Below the cliffs and floating on the heaving sea, listless seabirds watched the troopship steam into the harbour. The troops lined the rails as they approached Karachi, some pointing and talking excitedly, others quiet as they wondered what their future might hold in this alien land.

"It's hot," Lieutenant Harper, a fresh-faced officer also on his first posting out East, said.

Tulloch nodded. He had tried to accustom himself to the heat on the passage through the Mediterranean and down the Red Sea and the Indian Ocean, but it seemed to intensify as they approached Karachi. He thought the heat reached out from the land in pulses of unremitting savagery.

*Welcome to India.* Tulloch thought and smiled. He might not be in his chosen regiment, but he was arriving at a destination with the best chance of active service.

"Get ready for disembarking!" A colonel barked, and officers and men gathered their kit and clustered in formations. Tulloch stared at the jewel of the British Empire, seeing a confusion of shades of brown and dun, with crowds of people and vehicles of different types, from donkey carts and camels to horse-drawn carriages and steam-powered trains. An offshore breeze wafted an array of scents from the crowded city, and Tulloch realised he was smelling authentic India, a combination of sweet fragrances, spices and odoriferous slums. A group of tugs steamed out to escort the troopship into the harbour, allowing the officers and men on board time to view the city and the multitudes of dark-faced people who stared back at the ship.

The throb of the engines ended, the anchors descended with a splash and a noisy rattle, and men ran to secure the troopship

43

to bollards on the dockside. Tulloch became aware of the noise of the city. Everybody on shore seemed to be shouting; a gangway scraped into place, officers and NCOs bellowed orders, and a regimental brass band played martial airs that seemed incongruous in the Asiatic surroundings.

To protect them from the sun, the troops wore the heavy Wolseley helmets, named after General Sir Garnet Wolseley, a famous nineteenth-century soldier. Within minutes, Tulloch felt the sweat breaking out from his forehead to his legs.

*I'll have to get used to the heat; this is my life for the foreseeable future.*

The men clattered off the ship with the old India hands giving free advice to the youngsters who had never left Britain before.

"Don't give anything to the beggars, lads, or you'll never get rid of them."

"Don't drink the water unless you boil it."

"Keep your head covered against the heat, lads, or the sun will get you."

"Avoid the women, or they'll give you the pox."

The youngsters stared at this dusty city, so different from the exotic India of their imagination. People were everywhere, teeming multitudes, all seemingly intent on making as much noise as possible.

Military police, both British and Indian, helped move the disembarking soldiers onto the trains that took them to their various destinations, with dark smoke and puffs of steam adding to the confusion. Tulloch saw a tanned European civilian sitting on a stool carefully taking notes, wondered why somebody would want to waste his time on an Indian train station and stopped when a Military Police corporal threw a smart salute.

"Where to, sir?" The corporal asked Tulloch, with sweat running down his beefy red face.

"Peshawar," Tulloch told him. "I'm joining the Lothian Rifles."

"This way, sir," the corporal directed Tulloch to a train so he was sitting in a stifling hot compartment within an hour of leaving the ship, with other officers around him and noisy soldiers in the lower-class carriages. Other Ranks travelled in compartments that held six men and their kit, with two tiers of three bunks. The officers had slightly more space in the creakingly ancient carriages.

"I heard Bobs Roberts travelled in this train," A lean captain said as he lounged in a chair. "He complained about the age and condition, and it's only got worse since then."

Tulloch grinned. Roberts had died over twenty years before, which said everything about the age of the trains.

"Russell," the captain said, holding out a slender hand. Tulloch did not recognise his uniform and supposed it was an Indian regiment.

"Second Lieutenant Tulloch, sir."

"Just Russell when we're off duty," the captain said.

The chairs were of cane, with a trio of sashes in the window. Tulloch stepped to the window to watch the seething crowd outside.

"Careful now," Russell advised. "One sash is for the wire mesh to ensure half the insects of Asia don't invade us. You'll remember the plagues of Egypt? Well, when the beasts got fed up with spreading disease and irritation to the Pharaoh, they flew to India, as you'll soon find out. The second sash is for the shutters to keep out the sun; use the shutters, or you'll roast, and the third is for the glass to repel the dust."

"Thank you," Tulloch said.

Russell grinned. "You'll get used to India. Hello! We're moving at last! Settle down, Lieutenant; Indian railways are not renowned for their reliability or speed."

The train steamed steadily north until it pushed through a flat landscape of ugly desert punctuated by small trees battered by the heat. A smell of tamarind trees and ammonia entered the train.

45

"The Sind Desert," Russell said. "Welcome to the romantic East." He grinned. "Now you know why so many generations of Britons have given their lives for the glories of the Empire."

Tulloch smiled uneasily, unsure if the captain was serious. "It doesn't look very glorious," he said.

Russell laughed. "Don't worry; Tulloch, it gets worse when you go on the grim.[1]

Much worse. You're Scotch, aren't you?"

"Scottish," Tulloch corrected, more out of habit than irritation. "Yes, from Edinburgh."

"You'll fit in well here, then. The Celts always fare better and integrate more than the English. We're more conventional, you see."

Tulloch smiled and looked away, allowing his thoughts to drift. He had never thought of himself as Celtic before, but if his companion chose to believe that, he would not contradict him.

The train left a legacy of thick smoke hanging heavy over a plain that stretched forever. Tulloch stared out of the dirty window, noting the occasional village where people dressed in white congregated to watch them pass. Tulloch followed their progress on a map that seemed more colourful than accurate.

"Lie back, Tulloch," Russell advised. "You'll reach your destination eventually. Don't use British time here; this is the East, where tomorrow is like yesterday, and a millennium is only a word. Most of those people live as their ancestors lived, and a railway or a British officer more or less won't make much of a difference." His grin showed irregular white teeth.

Trains and dust, changing trains in a hectic station in a town Tulloch had never heard of, with British and Indian soldiers around him, Sikh policemen in splendid turbans and a convoy of camels from the northwest. Tulloch followed directions, feeling a long way from the serene austerity of Edinburgh's New Town. He moved jerkily northward, feeling the grit of dust between his teeth and awed at the sheer scale of the landscape.

Tulloch did not know when the atmosphere altered, but he

knew it had. The land outside the train felt different. The people walked with more confidence, the colours were different, and the air was brighter and sharper, yet Tulloch sensed a new tension.

"Ah," Russell had been dozing opposite Tulloch said. "You felt it too, did you?"

"Yes," Tulloch said. "Where are we?"

"Nearly at your destination, old man," Russell held Tulloch's gaze. "You'll either love it or hate it, but one thing's certain, Tulloch, Peshawar and the Frontier will change you forever. You'll never look at your fellow man the same way and never view yourself as you did before."

"Why is that?"

Russell gave a slow smile. "The Pathans, or Pashtuns to give them their real name, will test you like nobody else. You'll find what sort of man you are in the next few months." He held out his hand. "Good luck. We might meet you again up the grim."

"I hope so, Russell," Tulloch said.

"The army's a small world, Tulloch. We're bound to meet again."

"Thank you," Tulloch shook Russell's hand. They held each other's gaze for a second and parted. Despite Russell's words, Tulloch doubted they would ever meet again.

———

WHEN TULLOCH LEFT THE TRAIN AT PESHAWAR CANTONMENT Station, he was dusty and tired, with his head reeling from days of travelling. He looked around, seeing a vast British cantonment of dapper bungalows behind neat gardens, marching British troops beside British women and children, and a barrack block in the distance.

"Tulloch?" A dapper lieutenant with piercing eyes stepped forward.

"That's me," Tulloch admitted.

"Muirhead, Lothian Rifles." The lieutenant extended his hand. "You're joining us, I believe."

"Yes, sir," Tulloch snapped to attention and threw his smartest salute.

Muirhead grinned. "You're fresh from Sandhurst, then," he said.

"Yes, sir."

"Don't worry; we'll soon knock that nonsense out of you. My name's Muirhead; you only call me sir when we're on duty."

The British Cantonment at Peshawar was like a small slice of Great Britain within India, with barracks for the rank and file and bungalows and an Officers' Mess for the officers. The heat was less muggy than further south, Tulloch thought, thankfully.

"Why choose the Lothian Rifles?" Muirhead asked as he brought Tulloch into the Officers' Mess. The room was nearly empty except for the Mess Sergeant standing beside a small bar.

Tulloch thought quickly, unwilling to admit the Lothians had been his third choice. "I liked the idea of the independent thinking of the riflemen and the fact they operate in front of the line infantry."

"We," Muirhead corrected gently as he ordered two chota pegs [2] from the mess sergeant and ushered Tulloch to one of the tables.

"We?"

"You said 'they operate.' You're one of us now, so it's 'we operate in front of the line infantry,' or 'we used to anyway.'" He smiled over his chota peg. "We'll soon have you trained up."

Tulloch stopped to view the large picture of a battle that covered one wall, with a red-coated regiment holding a position while soldiers in blue coats attacked with flashing bayonets.

"The Battle of Alexandria, 21st March 1801," Muirhead explained. "Our first battle honour and, I believe, one of the first British victories over the French in the Revolutionary War."

"I read up on the regimental history," Tulloch admitted.

"I'm glad to hear it," Muirhead said dryly. "Now, if you've

recovered from your journey, get yourself washed, put on a decent shirt, and I'll take you to meet the colonel."

Colonel Pringle eyed Tulloch up and down, smiled, nodded, leaned back in his chair, and lit his pipe. Bald and moustached, his moustache was as grey as his eyes, while his row of medal ribbons included the Military Cross and half a dozen campaign medals. He eyed Tulloch for an uncomfortable few moments before he spoke.

"You've no military background, no experience, no history of soldiering, and yet you think you're good enough to join the best regiment in the British Army. Why?"

Tulloch thought quickly as Pringle filled his pipe. "I joined because the Lothian Rifles are the best, sir."

The colonel nodded slowly, puffing out aromatic smoke. "Yet you put us as your third choice. What do you think of the situation in Europe, Tulloch?"

*He already knows the Argylls were my first choice.* "I think it could escalate, sir. Both Mussolini and Hitler are dangerous men."

"Will that impact on us here?" Colonel Pringle asked with his level stare never straying from Tulloch's face.

Tulloch was not prepared for the question. "It could, sir." He was glad of the military history he had studied at Sandhurst. "In the last war, the Germans and Turks tried to bring Afghanistan into the fighting, and there's no reason to doubt they would not do the same again."

"How about the Congress?" Pringle asked, chewing on the stem of his pipe.

"They want us out of India," Tulloch said. "As does this Gandhi fellow." He thought hard, with the colonel's musing eyes probing into his thoughts. "If Mussolini or Hitler suborns them, things could get complicated."

"They could indeed," the colonel agreed. "What do you intend to do about it?"

"Me, sir?"

"You, sir," the colonel asked. "You're a British officer. It's your responsibility to defend the people of India. How are you going to do it? Quickly, man!"

"By doing my duty the best I can, sir," Tulloch gave the first reply that came to his head.

"And?" The colonel added more tobacco to his pipe.

"And by ensuring my men are trained and equipped to the highest standards, sir," Tulloch said.

"That's better, Tulloch." Pringle allowed himself a bleak smile. "You're a Lothians' officer now, and your priority is your men. Never forget that."

"I won't, sir," Tulloch said.

"We had some difficulty recruiting after the war," Pringle continued. "The depression ended that. We have nearly a full battalion here. A few are old sweats from the Great War; the majority are young men in their twenties forced into uniform by poverty and unemployment. They make excellent soldiers."

"That's good, sir," Tulloch said.

"I'm posting you to Four Platoon in 'B' Company," the colonel said. "Sergeant Drysdale's a good man; he's been in the regiment for decades. If you have any problems, ask his advice." He placed his still-smoking pipe on the broad desk. "Get to know your men, Tulloch. That's the first rule of a good officer."

"I will, sir," Tulloch promised.

"All right. Get settled in, learn the geography of the cantonment, and meet your men. Off you go, Tulloch, and welcome to the Lothian Rifles."

When Tulloch had his first parade, Four Platoon surveyed him through expressionless, stony eyes. Regular soldiers, most were in their mid or late-twenties, with a few older men who had seen service around the Empire. One tall man caught Tulloch's eye. He stood at attention without any tension and had intelligent eyes in a deeply tanned face. *That man has a story behind him,* Tulloch thought.

Medium height with a broad chest and a drooping moustache, Sergeant Drysdale boasted a chestful of medal ribbons and an inscrutable gaze that hid his feelings.

"Platoon ready for inspection, sir," he said with a salute that any Guardsman would have envied.

Taking a deep breath, Tulloch walked the length of his men, seeing only stubborn, closed faces. He knew they would become individuals in time, men with a history, personality, and characteristics, but at present, they were a homogeneous mass of expressionless soldiers in khaki drill. They stared straight ahead, some trembling with the effort of standing at attention, their uniforms immaculate, with Wolseley helmets all at the same angle.

"My name is Second Lieutenant Tulloch, and we're going to get to know each other very well," Tulloch began.

The men looked straight ahead. Nobody smiled. The tall man looked as if he were carved from granite.

Tulloch remembered his training. *Never allow the men to see you ruffled; keep calm at all times.* "We'll start with a route march," he said.

"We'll need rifles and bayonets, sir," Sergeant Drysdale said quietly. "Peshawar is close to tribal territory."

"Will they attack British soldiers?"

"The Pathans will attack anybody, sir," Drysdale said. "Particularly British soldiers."

"Thank you, Sergeant."

After only ten minutes, Tulloch realised that a route march in India was vastly different from a route march in Great Britain. Although they were only entering the Indian spring, the heat was intense while the dust was worse, rising from the ground and penetrating everything and everywhere. Tulloch coughed and choked as Four Platoon marched resolutely onward.

When the platoon left the cantonment, one saturnine man gave Tulloch a sidelong glance and began to sing.

*"I love a lassie,*
*A bonny black Madrasi,*
*She's as black as the ace of bloody spades.*
*She's got a beautiful smooth belly,*
*And her pa's a lord in Delhi*
*Parvati, my black best girl."*

Tulloch did not know the words, although he was to hear various versions of them hundreds of times in the future.

Other men joined in until the dust grew too dense, and the singing ended. Only the rhythmical thump of boots on the hard ground broke the silence and a wind that seemed like the blast from a furnace door. Tulloch kept level with the men, struggling to breathe in the dust and heat. He called a ten-minute halt after an hour and sat near the men, listening to their conversation. At first, he wondered what they were saying, with their talk a mixture of English, Scots, army jargon, and Urdu.

"We've got a *chokra* then," one long-faced man said, "a *chota-sahib*."[3]

"We've all got to learn," the tall private replied. "He'll turn into a *pukka-sahib* [4] eventually. Give him time, Brown."

Brown grunted. "I hope he learns quickly, then, Hardie. This Fakir is stirring up trouble with the Waziris."

Tulloch listened, took mental notes, and marched the men on, wondering who the Fakir was and what trouble he was making. He decided to return through Peshawar to look at the city, marching through Edwards Gate with its attendant bazaar and onto the teeming streets.

The population of Peshawar was different from Karachi, diverse and challenging, staring at the platoon of British soldiers. Tulloch saw camel caravans with tall, bold-eyed drivers, men with ringlets and a warrior's stance, and women wearing burkas that covered their faces so only their eyes were visible.

*I'm certainly not in Edinburgh now, but this place feels more like Central Asia than India.*

The population was not hostile, but nor did Tulloch find them friendly. They seemed to continue their lives as if the British were not present or important. Tulloch noted one man who seemed different, for he watched the platoon march past with some interest.

*I've seen that fellow before,* Tulloch thought. *He was at the station in Karachi, watching the trains. He's no native, but what's a European doing wandering about Peshawar in native clothes?*

When Tulloch dismissed Four Platoon and retired to his quarters, he still wondered about the stray European. His head pounded, full of images from the day, and he sighed when a smart corporal approached him.

"Sir!" the corporal saluted. "Major Hume requests your presence."

"Thank you, corporal," Tulloch said. "Where can I find him?"

"Adjutant's office, sir. I'll take you," the corporal said.

Major Hume was the adjutant and company commander, a man of forty with a finger missing from a near-forgotten skirmish somewhere on the Northwest Frontier. He walked with a pronounced limp from another wound and greeted Tulloch with a grin that revealed false teeth.

"So you're the new commander of Four Platoon," he said as Tulloch reported to him. "Very good, Tulloch. They're a great bunch of lads, a perfect combination of youth and experience." Hume spoke with the accents of Fettes and Edinburgh University, yet Tulloch could sense the steel beneath the smile that the wounds already suggested. "You'll learn a lot from them, Tulloch, and teach you how to be a leader."

Nobody in Sandhurst had told Tulloch that the men could teach the officers anything. He raised his eyebrows, remembering Dunn's advice at the boxing match. "Yes, sir."

"Lean on Sergeant Drysdale, Tulloch. What he doesn't know about soldiering isn't worth knowing." Hume smiled. "The NCOs keep the army together, not the officers. Oh, we give the orders, but men such as Drysdale ensure the men carry them out and prevent us from making too much of a fool of ourselves."

Tulloch nodded, unsure of this new aspect of soldiering.

"You'll think you're good at drill after Sandhurst," the major said. "And maybe you are. Now we'll teach you to drill the Lothian way. You'll learn drill with the lance corporals under RSM Watson."

Tulloch had learned never to question orders. "Yes, sir."

"You've got to show the men you can do it before you teach them," Hume explained. "Once you've settled into our way of doing things, we'll take B Company on a long route march, show the flag, toughen the men and let you see the countryside." He grinned again. "You'll like it on the Frontier, Tulloch. Or you'll hate it."

———

"WE'RE ON THE CUSP OF THE NORTHWEST FRONTIER HERE, Tulloch," Lieutenant Muirhead said as they halted B Company on a rocky ridge. "The map will claim that it's British territory, but don't you believe it. Everything you see ahead is Pashtun tribal territory, and our writ only extends as far as the range of our rifles, and then only if the Pashtun agree."

Tulloch looked over at the labyrinth of ragged hills that marked the end of British India and the beginning of Central Asia. The hills were grim, grey, and wild, a tangle of savage country peopled by intractable Pashtun tribes who had no desire to allow the British, or anybody else, a foothold into their territory. Behind the Pashtun tribes, at the far end of the passes, sat Afghanistan and, beyond that, independent Persia and the great mass of the USSR, nations which had no reasons to love Great Britain.

"We've tried every possible method of keeping the tribes in order," Muirhead said. "We've built a chain of outpost forts, recruited the Pashtun warriors into a frontier force, used political agents in tribal territory, and launched a hundred punitive expeditions." He grinned sourly. "This is our Hadrian's Wall, except this time, we're the Romans and the Pashtuns are the wild Caledonians."

"That's a thought," Tulloch said. "History is turning circles. New empires rise on the ashes of the old." He squinted through the shimmering heat haze towards one of the frontier forts, with its grey mud battlemented walls looking like something out of the Middle Ages, except for the incongruous wireless masts rising above the tower and the barbed wire entanglements intended to slow any rush by aggressive tribesmen.

"Will we ever subdue the Pashtun?" Tulloch asked the rhetorical question.

"Did the Romans ever subdue the Caledonians? Did they ever subdue us?" Muirhead retorted. "And here's another thought, Tulloch. Do we want to subdue them? Of all the peoples we've fought on the fringes of the Empire, we have the greatest respect for the Pashtuns. Oh, we all admire the courage of the Zulus and the Sudanese, but the Pashtuns have fought us to a standstill and always teach us something new."

Muirhead stood on the highest point of the ridge, silhouetted against the bright sky with his Wolseley helmet incongruously unwieldy and his pistol holster unfastened, ready for an instant reaction. Beside and below him, the men of B Company made themselves as comfortable as possible in the austere surroundings. Operating so close to tribal territory, Muirhead had posted picquets, men who watched for any incursions by tribal warriors. Tulloch knew it was unlikely, but the tribes had been restless recently, and it was always best to be careful.

Muirhead continued. "Although we don't admit it, these encounters along the Frontier make soldiering worthwhile. Otherwise, all we would do is aid the civil powers, which is the worst job in the world, march around to show the flag and mount guards for inflated dignitaries."

Tulloch smiled. "Unless *Il Duce* causes trouble in Europe."

"Unless *Il Duce* causes trouble," Muirhead agreed. He stood on the ridge for a few moments. "Well, there we have the Frontier, Tulloch. You'll have heard of the Fakir of Ipi, of course."

"I've heard something of him," Tulloch admitted cautiously.

"Learn more," Muirhead advised. "He's out there somewhere," he indicated the tangle of hills and valleys. "Encouraging the Waziris and anybody else to rise against us. In Europe, Mussolini and Hitler may be the threat, but on the Frontier, the Fakir of Ipi is every bit as dangerous." He grinned. "You might earn your spurs quicker than you expected, youngster!"

# Chapter Six

*This is the truth I tell you;*
*Of all things, freedom's most fine*
*Never submit to live, my son,*
*In the bonds of slavery entwined*
**Walter Bower**

Mirza Ali Khan, better known as the Fakir of Ipi, was a Waziri tribesman from the clan of the Khel Wazir. Tulloch was unsure of his age but guessed he was in his forties at least. The Fakir had been the imam of a mosque in Ipi, a small village between Bannu and the lower Tochi Valley near the Afghanistan border, not causing the British or Afghans any trouble. In 1936, he became involved in tribal politics.

The Fakir might have been destined to be one of the many unknown and anonymous imams of the Frontier if a woman-hungry Muslim student had not decided to abduct a Hindu girl. Kidnapping was not uncommon along the Frontier when some predatory warrior from the border tribes swooped into British-protected territory, grabbed a Hindu woman, and carried her back to his lands. The British had a recognised procedure for such cases, whereby the local political officer met a tribal *jirga*-gathering - to resolve the matter. In this case, the Waziri student had kidnapped a woman named Chand Bibi, the daughter of a Hindu merchant who lived in Bannu. When the kidnapper forced her through a Muslim marriage, her father took his case to court, despite many people claiming the woman had converted to Islam.

When local agitators incited the Waziri tribesmen to protest and delay the trial and return of the woman, the British authorities quelled the disturbance. The Fakir of Ipi was one of the principal agitators and continued after the father won his case, claiming the British government was increasing its influence in tribal affairs.

"This Ipi fellow seems to be a prime troublemaker," Tulloch observed as they sat in the Mess under the picture of the Battle of Alexandria.

Muirhead sipped at his whisky. "He is. He's stirred the Waziris up in a wave of religious fervour, and the entire Waziri tribe has risen against any infidel, especially us."

Tulloch felt a surge of excitement. Although he did not desire trouble and deaths on the Frontier or anywhere else, the prospect of using his military skills was exhilarating. "Do you think we'll be needed?"

Muirhead smiled. "Calm down, young warmonger. War isn't a game. You'll get your chance to shine. In the meantime, you have a regimental dinner to prepare for."

"I'm not looking forward to that," Tulloch admitted.

"More nerve-wracking than facing the Waziris, eh?" Muirhead said with a laugh. "Learn your part and speak slowly, and you'll be fine."

"Yes, sir," Tulloch said automatically.

Formed in 1793 at the beginning of the French Revolutionary War, the Lothian Rifles was not an old regiment by British Army standards. However, it had accumulated a great deal of tradition and an impressive collection of battle honours in its century and a half of existence. As well as being the only regiment to use the Border Pipes rather than the great Highland bagpipes, there was a regimental dinner on the anniversary of the battle of Alexandria.

As the regiment's senior lieutenant, Muirhead took Tulloch aside and quietly prepared him for his central role. Proudfoot, Tulloch's batman and company runner, helped him dress into his full regimentals with a stiff shirt and skin-tight trews that were so unsuitable for the climate. As a Lowland regiment, the Lothian Rifles did not wear the kilt, which had disappointed Tulloch.

The officers assembled in the Mess, with every man drinking one glass of claret and talking in low voices, discussing the coming dinner or the situation in Waziristan. As the most junior member of the Mess, Tulloch stood at the back, waiting for somebody to speak to him before he replied. Muirhead stepped to him. "Courage, *mon brave*," he murmured, "remember the regimental motto. *Gin ye daur* – if you dare."

Tulloch took a deep swallow of his claret, trying to dampen his throat. "Thank you, Muirhead."

After a few moments, the mess sergeant arrived and saluted the colonel.

"Dinner is served, sir."

"Thank you, Sergeant," the colonel replied formally and led the way into the dining room, with the officers following in order of rank. As they entered, the pipers played the regimental tune, *The Flowers o' Edinburgh*. When every officer was seated, the pipers altered the music to the *Lothians at Alexandria*, which was unique to the Lothian Rifles and only played on this occasion. Pipe Corporal Porteous composed the tune the evening before the regiment went into action at the Somme. Porteous had died in the first twenty minutes, but his music survived as a permanent reminder.

Nobody spoke during the rendition, and Tulloch sat, uncomfortable in his tight clothes. The officers termed the first course

First Toast, which was half a boiled egg served on a small square of toast. A fish course was next, straight from a tin, Tulloch guessed, followed by the main course of stringy beef, then a plum pudding and second toast. The officers ate in silence as a tribute to the men who had died at Alexandria. When they finished Second Toast, and the mess sergeant ensured the stewards cleared the plates, Colonel Pringle stood up.

"Now Mr Tulloch will read us a passage from the regimental history," the colonel said as the mess sergeant placed a decanter of Glenkinchie whisky and another of claret in front of him.

Tulloch stood as the mess sergeant handed him a leather-bound copy of the regimental history. He knew every officer was watching him as he read the passage that described the Lothian's part in the battle of Alexandria. His first words came out as a croak, and the colonel nodded.

"Bring Lieutenant Tulloch a glass of water."

"Thank you," Tulloch said, sipping the cold water before continuing. He spoke clearly and slowly, emphasising the part the Lothians had played in the battle and pausing when speaking any individual's name.

When he finished, the colonel nodded. "Well read, Tulloch," he approved, poured whisky into a large silver quaich[1] and passed it around the officers while smoke curled from a dozen cigars and cigarettes.

Tulloch sat down, acknowledged Muirhead's approving nod and relaxed a little. He felt like he had passed another initiation and would be accepted more into the Officers' Mess.

Being accepted by his platoon, Tulloch found, was more challenging. Men who were talkative and cheerful with each other became taciturn when he approached, and his attempts at humour met with stony faces and tight lips.

Sergeant Drysdale watched, as expressionless as the men, with his seamed and weather-hardened face never relenting, whether on the maidan – the drill square - the ranges or on the route marches Tulloch ordered.

He soon discovered that Private Anderson was the platoon sportsman and serial womaniser. Anderson played football for B Company and the battalion, ran the half marathon five minutes faster than his nearest rival and only replied to Tulloch with two-word answers: "Yes, sir" or "No, sir."

"You're a wee bit older than most of the men, Hardie," Tulloch said to the tallest man as they returned to barracks after a day at the ranges. "How long have you been a soldier?"

Hardie considered the question for a long ten seconds. "It must be twenty years now, sir," he replied slowly.

"Were you always in the Lothians?" Tulloch noted the faded medal ribbons on Hardie's chest, with one green medal edged with red he did not recognise.

"No, sir," Hardie said.

Tulloch nodded and stepped away, realising that Hardie was not inclined to reveal his past.

"Hardie?" Muirhead smiled when Tulloch asked later that day. "Now, there's a man with an interesting past. I've offered him promotion three times, Tulloch, and he's turned it down each time."

"What's his story?"

"Nobody's sure," Muirhead said. "I can tell you he has the East African campaign medal from the Great War if that helps."

"The green and red ribbon," Tulloch said. "He doesn't speak like a ranker, either."

"No, he doesn't," Muirhead agreed. "As I said, he's a man with an interesting past."

Tulloch found Brown to be the opposite of Hardie, a cheerful man who was always ready to break into song, often with obscene verses that made the other members of Four Platoon laugh. His favourite, and one of the most sung in the battalion, was *I Love a Lassie, a Bonnie Black Madrassi*, with verses that altered according to their circumstances.

"You're the battalion comedian, Brown," Tulloch said as

Muirhead arranged a battalion concert. "How would you like to show your talents to a wider audience than Four Platoon?"

Brown looked surprised to have an officer speak directly to him. "How do you mean, sir?"

"Lieutenant Muirhead's looking for volunteers for his concert, Brown, and you're a famous comedian."

Brown shook his head. "I wouldn't say I'm famous, sir."

"Well, now's your chance to rectify that, Brown. Get your act ready for a larger audience."

Brown tried not to look pleased. "Yes, sir."

When Brown appeared at the concert, Tulloch soon realised he had made a mistake. Jokes which were humorous when aimed at Brown's peers lost their humour when the butt was the colonel and senior officers. Tulloch watched and listened in horror as the evening wore on, Brown's jokes became more pointed, and the officers glanced at him and the colonel, who sat with a fixed smile on his face.

When the concert eventually ended, Colonel Pringle summoned Tulloch to his office.

"Who was that comedian, Lieutenant? Brown, wasn't it?"

"Yes, sir," Tulloch prepared himself for a stinging rebuke.

"Well, Tulloch, we can't have a private soldier making such jokes at my expense," Pringle said as Tulloch waited for the axe to fall. "Promote him to lance-corporal. Dismissed."

"Yes, sir," Tulloch said, wondering at this strange regiment he still did not understand.

"Do you hunt, Tulloch?" Muirhead asked later that day.

"No, sir," Tulloch replied.

"If you did, there is jackal hunting at Peshawar. Good sport if you don't mind jumping over irrigation ditches. Polo then. Do you play polo?"

"No, sir," Tulloch said again.

"Nor do I. It's a damned expensive sport. You'll have to join the football team, and the boxing team." He lowered his voice.

"One has to be social out here, Tulloch, and hope for a local war to alleviate the boredom."

"Yes, Muirhead," Tulloch said, unsure if the senior lieutenant was trying to help or rebuking him for being too insular.

---

"DID YOU HEAR THE NEWS?" SECOND LIEUTENANT TAIT, THE only officer junior to Tulloch, burst into the Officer's Mess with the top button of his shirt undone and his hair uncombed. "The Waziris have destroyed the Bannu Brigade!"

"What?" As Tulloch and the younger officers in the mess rose in unison, the older men looked up briefly and returned to their previous pursuits. Major Hume and Muirhead did not disturb their game of billiards, with the balls clicking cheerfully as a backdrop to the Mess.

"It was at Bichhe Kaskai in Waziristan," Tait spoke rapidly to the crowd that gathered around. "We were trying to overawe the Fakir by marching a column from our base at Razmak eastward to join up with another heading south from Mir Ali."

Tulloch only knew the names from the map, although most officers present could visualize these bases on the Frontier.

"The Waziris ambushed both columns, but the Razmut column reached its destination. The Mir Ali column had to withdraw, and the Razmut column joined them. We had over a hundred casualties, and the Waziris grabbed their weapons."

Major Hume potted a tricky shot and looked up, cue in hand. "There's more trouble ahead then. Rifles are the currency of the Pashtuns." He sipped at the whisky and soda that sat on a small table at his side. "Have any of you youngsters bothered to read the intelligence reports?"

As Adjutant, Hume always posted the current intelligence reports on the notice board in the Officer's Mess, with standing orders for the duty officer to read them. Very few officers spared the time from more important matters like polo, rugby, and looking after their men.

"I thought not," Major Hume said. "Read them. There's more to this affair than the usual tribal trouble. The Fakir of Ipi and the latest kidnapping are behind it, and we'd better keep our bayonets sharp." He glanced at Tulloch and Tait. "You two lads might see some real soldiering sooner than you expected." He watched as the junior officers scrambled to the notice board to read the intelligence reports, smiled, and returned to his game.

Tulloch had already scanned the report but now studied it with more attention.

The intelligence officer did not add much to Tulloch's understanding of the situation along the Frontier. Tulloch did not know who gathered the information, which reported that the Fakir appeared quiet but was suspected of hiding men who rebelled against tribal authority, accepting bribes, and using hired killers to dispose of his enemies and their families.

"Never neglect intelligence reports," Major Hume said as he finished his game, lifted a newspaper from the rack and retired to his usual chair. "You must always know what's happening on the other side of the hill." He scanned the first page without comment. "Having an efficient battalion is fine, lads, but knowing what's happening in the world and being prepared to act accordingly is also part of a soldier's armoury."

"Yes, sir," Tulloch said.

"We'll be on the march soon," the major predicted as he returned to his newspaper. "You lads best ensure your men are at their peak. We'll have a route march today, grenade practice and extra musketry drills. Tulloch and Tait, you'll find things a bit different from now on. Learn from the older, if not wiser, heads."

Tulloch disliked using grenades, although his short stints bowling cricket balls as a schoolboy had taught him how to throw with reasonable accuracy. Each soldier carried two Mills bombs – grenades – and Tulloch reminded himself how they worked. The grenades had a split pin that held an arm. By withdrawing the pin, the soldier freed a plunger that connected to a detonator of fulminate of mercury. The fuse was five or seven seconds long, giving sufficient time to throw the bomb and duck out of harm's way. When the grenade exploded, the iron casing split into lethal segments that could destroy any human life in a five-yard radius.

The Lothians proved proficient with grenades, so Tulloch spent little on them and hurried on to musketry.

Most of the musketry was with the Lee-Enfield rifle, but a week after the ambush of the Banu Brigade, a divisional instructor introduced the Lothians to Bren guns, a new pattern of light machine gun.

The sergeant instructor held a Bren up as he spoke.

"This is the Bren light machine gun," he said. "When there are sufficient available, every section of the British army will have one, so everybody has to learn how to fire and maintain this weapon."

The Lothians watched with their customary cynicism.

"The Bren fires .303 ammunition, the same as your rifles, and they come in a 30-round box detachable magazine." The instructor held one up and demonstrated how to load. "It's gas-operated and can fire between 500 and 520 rounds a minute, although, in practice, you won't get above 120. The maximum firing range is 1850 yards, with 600 being the effective range."

Tulloch liked the Bren. He had used the Lewis Gun and the Vickers Medium Machine Gun on the ranges at Sandhurst but considered the Bren a superior weapon. Easier to carry and less likely to jam, it was accurate, able to fire single shots or longer bursts, and the gunner's number two could easily replace the barrel when continual firing wore it out.

"When do we get ours?" Tulloch asked.

"Alas, not yet," the instructor replied. "But when they come, you'll be ready for them."

Tulloch ensured all his men were proficient with the Bren,

with Private Innes of Eight Section showing more skill than the others.

"You're a natural, Innes," Tulloch told him.

"Aye, nae bother," Innes said without changing his expression.

*Will these men ever accept me? Maybe I'm not meant to be an officer in this regiment.*

———

As Major Hume predicted, the situation escalated. The Fakir of Ipi incited trouble across Waziristan and beyond, with minor raids on small villages, attacks on Hindu shops and businesses and warriors sniping British bases and convoys. British intelligence reports said the Fakir raised a lashkar – a tribal army – in the Khaisora valley near the Lower Tochi Road deep in Waziristan.

"That's bad," Major Hume addressed the officers after a hard day's training. "From the Khaisora Valley, the Fakir can interrupt communications with our bases at Razmak and Bannu. Keep at it, boys, the local frontier force boys are fine at the daily irritants, but this looks like becoming a full-scale tribal rising."

The officers glanced at each other, and Tulloch noted the rising anticipation.

"Will we be called on, sir?" Tait asked.

"I'd say so," the major said.

Tait nodded and grinned. "My platoon is ready, sir."

Tulloch was not alone in feeling some excitement. "So is Four Platoon, sir."

"I'm glad to hear it," Hume said. "I'd hate to think all that training and the Sandhurst education had gone to waste."

"After all," Tait said. "We are soldiers. We joined up to fight, not to parade or stand guard."

Tulloch agreed, although he wondered how he would behave when the fighting began. He listened to his colleagues' stories about the Pashtun, their bravery, their skill at guerrilla warfare, and, above all, their cruelty.

"Don't leave any of your wounded behind," Hume reminded, "and for God's sake, don't let the Pashtun capture you. There's nothing they'd like better than a British officer to torture and murder."

Tulloch nodded. "I'll bear that in mind," he said.

"They won't catch me," Tait boasted. "I'm too good for them."

Hume gave a slow smile and said nothing.

"Other regiments are being called up," Tait complained. "Don't they want us?"

"By the time we get into action, the campaign will all be over," Tulloch agreed.

"In the army," Hume said from behind a newspaper. "Ninety-five per cent of the time, you are waiting for something to happen. Three per cent of the time, it happens, and you are too busy to think anything, and for two per cent, you wish to God it had never happened."

The colonel intensified the Lothians' training. The battalion improved in using the ground and cover when facing the enemy. He ordered company to compete against company with a crate of beer for the victor. He trained the men in field signalling, fire orders, battle formations, and platoon tactics.

"Each officer must know what his platoon can and cannot do, and every man should know his place, his duty, and what is expected of him in every situation!" Colonel Pringle said, holding his gently smoking pipe in his hand. "It is your duty, as officers, to ensure they do."

Tulloch sweated with the rest, learning the strengths and weaknesses of his men as every day, they expected orders to take them to the Frontier.

The senior officers explained the skills and art of patrolling, with Sergeant Drysdale giving tips he had learned in no-man's land in the Great War and on the Frontier. "Listen for anything unusual. Never move if you even suspect the enemy is watching. Patience, silence, and darkness are your friends; the Pashtun can lie for days just to take one shot at a British soldier, and we have to be better than them."

"We'll work at night as well as by day," Colonel Pringle said, watching everything, taking notes and passing on his observations to the officers.

Tulloch's first nighttime patrol was a disaster, with half his men disappearing until Sergeant Drysdale sighed and rounded them up.

"They'll get better, sir," Drysdale promised. "Better to learn here than in Waziristan when the Pashtun are watching and waiting."

The colonel trained them in withdrawals and attacks, timing everything, criticising and giving abrupt advice.

"The hardest manoeuvre is a fighting withdrawal," Colonel Pringle said. "Some of our worst disasters and most glorious annals have occurred when withdrawing in the face of superior enemy forces. Think of Mons or Corunna or March 1918."

"Were they not all retreats, sir?" Tait asked.

Colonel Pringle fixed him with a glare that Medusa would have envied. "The British Army never retreats," he said coldly. "We retire or withdraw."

The Lothians trained in attacking fixed positions, platoon against platoon and company against company, each day hearing news from the Waziri uprising and hoping to be called to the front.

"They've forgotten about us," Tait said as the summer eased on.

"They don't want us to show them up," Tulloch said with a wry smile. He saw Major Hume lift his head at his statement, stare at him for a moment and look away.

The colonel trained the battalion in defending sangars, with one company defending and three attacking, complete with blood-curdling screams and blank cartridges. When one assault ended in a free fight, one company against the rest, the colonel watched with an approving smile.

"A few black eyes and bloody noses will do no harm and prove our fighting spirit."

While the colonel observed his battalion, Tulloch watched his platoon. He saw that Hardie was a natural leader with as much tactical skill as any commissioned officer and offered him a promotion.

"Not for me, sir," Hardie refused politely. "I'm happy where I am."

"You're wasted as a private, Hardie," Tulloch said.

"No, sir," Hardie shook his head. "I'm better in the ranks."

Brown lost his lance-corporal's stripe when he brawled with a member of another platoon. He shrugged away the demotion and laughed as he rejoined his mates. Tulloch learned more about his men, realising that Hogg, medium-sized, with an equable temperament, was a street fighter with more underhand tricks than anybody he had ever met.

*I'm getting to know them, yet they're still wary of me. Will they ever accept me?*

With the Waziri campaign in full swing, the RAF loaned two Westland Wapiti aircraft to the regiment, and the Lothians trained in air cooperation, with most of the soldiers watching the flimsy biplanes soaring above them and swooping low to drop leaflets and dummy bombs.

"Aircraft were useful in the last war," Sergeant Drysdale said as the aircraft roared overhead. "I can't see leaflets defeating the Waziris, though. I doubt any of them can read."

The following month, two light Mark II tanks arrived at Peshawar. They were smaller than Tulloch had imagined and slower. He watched as one failed to negotiate a minor obstacle, and the battalion responded by towing it off with mules while a section pushed from behind.

"I'm not impressed with tanks," Tulloch gave his opinion after a single day's exercise.

Drysdale raised his eyebrows and said nothing.

"Did you see many in France, Sergeant?"

"Yes, sir," Drysdale replied. "They were useful in attack and flattening barbed wire defences for the infantry to follow. I've heard some people say that tanks will be the future of land warfare."

Tulloch pointed to one tank where the crew was working on a stalled engine. "That one won't!" He remembered the lectures at Sandhurst about armoured warfare and wondered if tanks would make infantry redundant.

Colonel Pringle gathered his officers together after another gruelling day of training. "Remember one basic rule, and you can't go far wrong. The primary law of tactics is to be superior at the point where you intend to strike the decisive blow. Hit them at their weakest when you are strongest, and always follow up your victory to make a triumph into a rout."

Tulloch added that simple pearl to his notebook.

The trouble in Waziristan continued. The Fakir was too wily for the British to catch, settling near the Durand Line, the official border between the tribal territory over which the British had nominal control and independent Afghanistan. Whenever a British column came close, the Fakir and his lashkar could slip over the frontier into Afghanistan.

The Waziris mounted raids into the British protected areas, murdering, burning houses, businesses and farms, kidnapping civilians, rustling livestock, and stealing or destroying lorries, while the British mounted punitive raids.

"We're trying to swat a fly with a cricket bat," Muirhead said. "The government hampers us with so many rules and regulations it seems they support the opposition."

"All we can do is keep fit and train," Tulloch said.

Every few days, Tulloch inspected the barracks. The other ranks called them bungalows, although they were long, high and held an entire platoon. Each man had a bed, a kit box, a mosquito net, and his thoughts. Privacy was unknown, and the boredom of garrison life was alleviated only by route marches, sports, a horde of servants, and the possibility of active service "up the grim." Rumours abounded, and every man knew his neighbour's business.

Tait was waiting for Tulloch as he marched his platoon back from the parade ground.

"The old man's called for a meeting at 16.00 hours, Tulloch."

"Do you have any idea why?"

Tait grinned and stroked the neat moustache he was attempting to grow. "I'm not sure, but my batman told me we were going to war."

"Your batman said we were going to war?" Tulloch said to Tait as his platoon returned to the barracks.

Tait drew on his cigarette. "He did. In this regiment, Tulloch, the sergeants have the superior mess and scrounge the best whisky, and the batmen know what's happening even before the colonel."

Tulloch wondered if Lightfoot knew more than he did, decided it did not matter, and smiled. "We'll soon know if your batman's information is accurate."

Colonel Pringle stood before his officers, faintly smiling as he held his pipe in his right hand.

"Gentlemen," the colonel said. "The government has tried to defeat the Waziris without us, and the government has failed. Gentlemen, the time for training has ended. The Lothian Rifles are going to war."

# Chapter Seven

*In peace the sons bury their fathers, and in war, the fathers bury their sons.*

**Francis Bacon: *Apothegms***

"War on the Frontier is different to anything you might experience elsewhere," Major Hume reminded. "The Rules of Engagement restrict us, while the enemy has no rules. We must wait until the enemy fires at us before we fire back, at least until we get inside Waziristan."

Tulloch nodded.

"Even inside, we can't fire unless the enemy is at least ten strong, carrying rifles and not on a path. We can't touch civilians or burn their villages or crops."

Tulloch frowned. "We would never touch civilians, sir."

Hume snorted. "Wait until you find the remains of one of our wounded after the Waziri women have castrated and flayed him alive," he said. "You might think differently then."

Tulloch nodded. "Perhaps, sir."

"We're going into Razmak Cantonment and eventually into the Shaktu Valley," the colonel said. "We established Razmak in

1923 between the Waziris of Razani and the Mahsuds of Makin. The two tribes were nearly permanently warring with each other, and our camp was an attempt to keep the peace. It's a permanent perimeter camp nearly seven thousand feet above sea level, with all the facilities you would expect, including a cinema, churches, a bazaar, sports pitches and so on."

"How long will we be there for, sir?" Tulloch asked.

"Until we've squashed the trouble," Hume said. "We've missed the early part of the campaign, so let's show the powers that be that the Lothians Rifles are the best in the business."

The Lothians travelled the first part of the journey by rail, jerking and rumbling towards the Frontier. Then they transferred into trucks, alternatively baking in the heat or coughing in the clouding dust as a troop of Crossley armoured cars motored alongside, turrets swivelling to cover the hills on either side of the track.

"We're taking this campaign seriously," Tait said. "The lads on the earlier expedition thought it was a peacetime stroll. That's how the Waziris ambushed them so easily."

When they reached the border of Waziristan, the Lothians debussed. Wearing their shorts and pith helmets, they looked around at the hostile hill country.

"The Tochi Scouts are on the hills," Colonel Pringle said, thrusting his pipe between his teeth. "Even so, I want picquets out, flank guards and a strong rearguard."

"Tulloch," Hume said. "Take Four Platoon to the front." He grinned. "You're our advance guard."

"With me, lads!" Tulloch shouted and trotted ahead. He could rely on Sergeant Drysdale to make the final details.

The Tochi Scouts waited for the Lothian Rifles. Tulloch had seen these men from a distance but never worked with them; now, he watched with admiration as they marched on either flank of the Riflemen. Tall and mobile; each man was a Pashtun from the Frontier, wearing khaki turbans and shorts with a grey shirt over a hard body. Tulloch knew his Riflemen were amongst the best marchers in the army, but the Scouts drifted past, lifting their feet high and ignoring the rugged terrain.

Tulloch felt a surge of elation as he pushed to the front of his men. After years of learning and training, at last, he was soldiering. He was marching at the head of his men through a hostile environment.

Ragged grey mountains reared on either side, dressed with scattered copses of trees and reamed with ravines and an occasional swift-running stream.

*Keep your eyes open at all times,* Tulloch remembered Muirhead's constant warnings. *The Pashtun are the best hillmen in the world. They can disguise themselves as a bush, hide under a twig and appear when you least expect it.*

They passed a Pashtun village, with the grey walls keeping out intruders and a high guard tower rearing above like the domain of some mediaeval robber baron. A youth herded goats and glared at the British column through kohl-rimmed eyes. The ancient rifle on his back had probably seen service with Queen Victoria's army half a century before, and his attitude mirrored the Pashtun who had originally stolen it from some unwary sentry.

*We're not only in a different country, we're in a different era,* Tulloch thought; *this boy is only the latest in a line of warriors. His ancestors probably fought Lord Roberts or even Alexander the Great.*

They marched on, with Brown trying to sing, but the words were hollow, flat under the brooding mountains. Tulloch thought of the quiet green slopes of the Pentland Hills and touched the reassuring weight of the Webley revolver in its holster at his belt.

"Welcome to Waziristan," Sergeant Drysdale murmured, lighting a cigarette. The smoke clouded around him, the aroma of tobacco distinctive as the bleat of goats sounding behind them. The youth was following at a distance, herding his animals and watching every movement of the Lothians.

Tulloch heard the distinctive crack of a Lee-Enfield rifle and the whistle of a bullet before he realised the Waziris were firing at the Lothians.

"Keep marching," Lieutenant Muirhead arrived at Tulloch's side. "Ignore the snipers." He sounded as calm as if he were on the maidan in Peshawar.

Newly aware of a prickle between his shoulder blades, Tulloch marched on, checking his platoon. The veterans plodded on, kicking up dust, while some of the younger men glanced nervously at the gaunt hills on either side.

"I love a lassie," Brown began, "a bonnie black Madrasi,

She's as black as the coals in deepest hell,

And she cannae fire a rifle,

Not even a wee bit trifle,

When we're marching in Waziristan."

Some of the others joined in with the sound puny amongst the vastness of the landscape. Tulloch added his voice, coughing as dust caught in his throat.

"Sergeant, best change the point man," Tulloch said quietly.

"Yes, sir," Drysdale said. "I'll put Hogg and Kelly up there. Kelly's as steady as the castle rock, and Hogg's as good a man as you'll find in a duffy."[1]

On their left flank, the Scouts drifted up the slope, extending their line as if by instinct, with the officer in charge giving orders in fluent Pushtu. Tulloch knew the British recruited the Scouts from across the Frontier, with the officers carefully selecting men for each area to ensure they had no tribal affiliations. Blood ties and blood feuds could transcend any oaths of loyalty.

Another rifle cracked out, followed by a third, and Tulloch saw the Scouts look for cover. One moment they were there, and the next, they vanished as though they had never been. The firing continued, growing in intensity.

"Tulloch!" Major Hume barked. "The Scouts have run into trouble. "Take your platoon up there and give them a hand. Lieutenant Tait, take over Tulloch's position."

"Yes, sir," Tulloch replied automatically. He felt a sudden mixture of fear, apprehension, and excitement.

"Come on, lads; we're supporting the Scouts. Get into an extended line; keep your distances." Tulloch headed for the slope, striding forward in the secure knowledge his men were following. He sensed the passage of the bullet that screamed past his head.

*Somebody's shooting at me!*

Tulloch visualised the Pashtun in his baggy clothes, a grey-bearded man sighting along the barrel of his rifle, working the bolt and aiming. He weaved automatically as if he were advancing on the rugby field and grunted as a bullet smashed into the ground at his feet, splintering a rock into fragments. He glanced behind him and saw Four platoon advancing steadily with five yards between each man.

"Come on, lads!" Tulloch shouted, more to encourage himself than his men. He realised his fear was gone and saw Sergeant Drysdale on the flank with his cigarette hanging from his lips and his rifle at the trail. He moved on, instinctively weaving, stumbled over a loose stone and saw the slope rising before him, grey rocks and brown rocks with the summit crest far above.

The firing increased, and a whiplash scored the ground beside Tulloch's feet. He saw the blue smear of lead on the rocks with more curiosity than fear. If he had not stumbled, that bullet would have hit him. *On such small hooks does a man's life hang.*

Tulloch heard the crunch of nailed boots on rock at his back and knew he could not hesitate, however many Pashtuns shot at him. He was a British officer; he had accepted the King's Commission, and his men depended on him to lead. Forcing back his fear, Tulloch took a deep breath of air that seemed to have come from a dusty furnace and pushed on, long striding.

"Lothians?" The voice came from the ground at his feet.

"Yes," Tulloch saw a Scout lying behind a rock, his khaki turban merging with the colour of the ground and his Lee-Enfield held in steady hands.

"Captain Bridie."

"Lieutenant Tulloch," Tulloch checked his men.

"You push ahead," Bridie said. "We'll cover you; find a spot a hundred yards in front and cover us."

"Yes, sir." It was a classic move that Tulloch's men had trained for a hundred times, but training without fear and acting under the fire of Waziri warriors were two different things.

Even when he was close to them, Tulloch found it difficult to see the Scouts as they merged so effectively with the landscape. He moved on, jinking from side to side with the hill rising above him and the musketry increasing. He heard his men gasping behind him and the irregular crackle of the Scouts covering fire and grinned sourly.

*The instructors at Sandhurst had taught fire discipline, making it a cardinal rule never to fire when friendly soldiers were between you and the enemy. Obviously, that rule does not apply on the Frontier.*

The hillside rose in a series of ridges, with the next fast approaching. Tulloch gave the command.

"Cover, Four Platoon, and let the Scouts come through us."

The platoon threw themselves down and began to fire, working the bolts of their Lee-Enfields as they aimed at an invisible enemy. The sound of musketry was no different from the ranges back in Peshawar, but the sensation was different, with small eruptions of dust where the enemy bullets struck back. Tulloch heard Brown humming under his breath and saw Hogg aiming each shot, his face set in concentration.

"Scouts!" Bridie shouted and rose, with his men following in a khaki wave, nearly soundless over the uneven ground.

Wishing he had brought a rifle rather than his revolver, Tulloch could only lie prone as the Scouts passed through the Lothians and moved further towards the contested crest. Tulloch thought they glided effortlessly rather than ran across the rough, rocky terrain.

The Pashtun bullets slammed around Tulloch, and he realised they had targeted him because he was an officer. He eased closer to his protecting boulder, saw that the Scouts had gone to ground, waited for a second and shouted.

"Right, Four Platoon! Through the Scouts!"

Tulloch was the first to rise and gasped as something tugged at his tunic. "Come on, lads!"

He ran forward, stumbling and sliding, feeling very isolated despite the platoon behind him and the watching Scouts. A scatter of shots greeted the advance; Tulloch saw two Pashtuns rise from cover as his men roared forward. He lifted his revolver and fired, feeling the kick in his wrist. He knew a running man had little chance of hitting his target, but the fact he was shooting made him feel better.

Tulloch crested the ridge and looked around. The ground sloped downward, with the reverse slope a mirror image of the hill they had climbed, a jumble of ragged rocks and an occasional tree, with the hard gleam of a river in the valley far below. He slid down a pace to ensure he was not on the skyline and saw his men around him, some laughing, most panting for breath.

"Any casualties?" Tulloch asked, reloading his revolvers, with the fat brass cartridges warm to the touch.

"No, sir," Sergeant Drysdale reported. "I only saw three Waziris."

"That's one more than I saw," Tulloch admitted.

Bridie hurried up with his Scouts. He had not even broken sweat. "Did we get any of them?"

"No, sir," Tulloch replied.

"Somebody did," the lieutenant pointed to a splash of blood on a rock.

Tulloch wondered if one of his bullets had ended a life. He saw Hogg crouched behind a rock, staring along the ridge, and Drysdale already posting picquets on the flanks.

*Typical Frontier encounter,* Bridie commented. *Using a sledge-hammer to crack an egg. I doubt there were more than half a dozen Waziris there, probably just young lads proving their manhood by having a crack at British soldiers.* He shouted an order in Pashtu, and a section of his men took position on the crest. "Thanks for your help, Tulloch. You'd best return to the column."

Tulloch felt his tension draining away. He had survived his first skirmish; he had been fired at without running away. He was now a soldier.

# Chapter Eight

*There is something in a woman beyond all human delight; a magnetic virtue, a charming quality, an occult and powerful motive.*
**Robert Burton,** *Anatomy of Melancholy*

Three Hawker Hart light bombers flew overhead, elegant with their sharp noses and tails; the Harts were one of the most successful biplanes Britain had produced, faster than some fighters but already obsolete as monoplanes edged into production.

"They're good enough for the Frontier," Muirhead said. "The Waziris don't have any aircraft or anti-aircraft guns. I think the Italian or German planes would eat the Harts for breakfast."

Tulloch watched as the three aircraft disappeared into the distance, with the sun reflecting on the metal bodywork. Muirhead followed them with his binoculars. "They'll be bombarding Waziri villages with leaflets warning the inhabitants to leave before the RAF drops bombs."

Tulloch grunted. "Is there any point in that?"

"No," Muirhead said. "Most people can't read, and the Fakir capitalises on the leaflets. He told his people his magic charms can turn bombs into paper, and every time they drop leaflets, the RAF proves him correct."

Tulloch laughed, unsure if Muirhead was joking or not.

"The Fakir is an astute man, using his people's superstitions and backwardness to further his cause."

"I heard that as well," Tait said. "We're fighting here with both hands and one leg tied behind our back."

The battalion marched on, joining the Scouts by placing pickets on each peak before passing, ignoring the odd shot from solitary snipers and beginning to get the feel of the Frontier. Supply trucks passed them, loaded with meal, rice, and other essentials, each with a guard of three or four soldiers, British or Indian.

"Why do they ride when we have to walk?" Private Aitken asked.

"Do you want to sit in the dust, with every Waziri in Waziristan taking a potshot at you?" Kelly asked.

"No," Aitken replied.

"Nor do they," Kelly told him.

"I love a lassie, a bonnie black Madrasi," Brown began.

"Stick your bloody Madrasi," Innes retorted, and the column trudged on, heads down, boots kicking up dust as they inched through the gaunt hills.

They passed the junction at Isha Corner and watched as a *kafilah* [1] of camels slowly plodded by from Bokhara or Samarkand.

"Stand aside, men," Colonel Pringle ordered, and the Lothians stepped off the pukka government-built road to allow the caravan to pass as they had for a thousand years or more. The camels sauntered, head to tail, with supercilious looks as they passed the intruders on their trail. As well as camels, there were sheep, donkeys and men with ragged turbans and long rifles. Women walked beside their men, with the sun catching the huge earrings that swayed, nearly touching their shoulders, and silver and gold rings on their fingers.

"Women," Aitken watched them pass.

"If you touch one of them, you'd be dead before tomorrow's dawn," Sergeant Drysdale said. "Castrated, blinded and probably flayed alive."

Tulloch watched the caravan fade into the distance on its journey to Peshawar, a timeless reminder that the British were only visitors in this ancient land. Wave after wave of peoples had passed through Afghanistan on their way to India; some had remained to merge with the indigenous population or create enclaves in hidden valleys.

"Move on," Pringle ordered, interrupting Tulloch's train of thought.

The Lothians continued their march with increasing military traffic as they crunched onto the baking Miranshah plain. The sun reflected from a million stones, burning the men's feet even through their boots as a trio of vultures wheeled and circled overhead. The aircraft were long gone now, a distant memory as they approached the cantonment of Razmak.

"There we are, lads," Sergeant Drysdale said. "We have three major camps in this area, Wana, Miram Shah and Razmak. Pray to your God that this war ends soon, for we're entering a government prison or the world's largest monastery if you prefer." He gave them a sour grin. "No women allowed. After a few weeks, you'll be glad of the chance to fight the Waziris, if only to break the monotony."

The British camp spread across the plain, with tents parading behind a triple row of barbed wire and a mud wall. Electric lights stood between the wall and the wire, ready to illuminate any tribesmen who attempted to infiltrate the camp. Half a dozen Indian pattern Crossley armoured cars stood in a row, separate from the infantry as if holding themselves aloof from the sweating foot soldiers. A dozen cursing mechanics toiled over their engines to keep them free of the ever-present dust.

Sentries, British, Gurkhas and Indians paced the wall or

manned machine guns, watching the Lothians march in without expression.

"We don't know how long we're here," the colonel said, "so get comfortable, acclimatise yourselves, keep your rifles clean and ignore the flies."

Tulloch found it hard to ignore the flies, which infested everywhere. They buzzed over every square inch of the camp, with the Officers' Mess their favoured spot.

When he ensured his men were safe within the stone barracks, Tulloch walked around the vast camp, looking through the wire at the mountains beyond the plateau and wondering if the Fakir was there. For a moment, he remembered the Pashtun's bullets hissing past, shrugged and returned to his quarters.

"Visitor!" Major Hume said as a tall Pashtun appeared outside the Officer's Mess. "See who that is, Sergeant."

The mess sergeant returned a moment later. "It's a Pashtun gentleman who claims to know the colonel, sir. Shall I allow him to enter?"

Hume frowned. "I suppose you may, Sergeant."

The officers watched as the Pashtun stooped into the Mess and looked around.

"Is this any way to welcome a guest?" he said in perfect English. "You could at least offer me a cup of tea."

"Who are you, sir?" Muirhead asked.

"Captain Russell, Intelligence officer," the man replied.

Tulloch raised his eyebrows as he remembered the helpful officer he met when he first arrived in India. Russell looked every inch a Pashtun, with his long hair, untidy, loosely tied turban with loops dangling around his neck, baggy, dirty trousers and sandals. The bandolier he wore across his shoulders was half full of cartridges, while the long knife at his belt looked ferociously dangerous.

"Have to look the part," Russell said. "And act the part, so I can't drink anything sensible." He nodded to Tulloch. "Evening

Tulloch. I said we'd probably run into each other on the Frontier."

"Good evening, sir," Tulloch replied.

"Do you know this fellow, Tulloch?" Muirhead asked.

"We met on the train from Karachi, sir," Tulloch said.

"I see," Muirhead eyed Russell for a moment. "Most intelligence officers I've met wear European clothes rather than dress like the Pathans."

"How many intelligence officers have you met?" Russell asked.

"One," Muirhead said bluntly.

"I'm not that type of intelligence officer," Russell explained with a small smile.

"What can we do for you, Russell?" Major Hume asked.

"Apart from a decent pot of tea," Russell said, "you can't do much, but I may be able to help you." He looked around, aware that every eye in the Mess was focused focussed on him.

Major Hume ordered tea from the mess sergeant and gestured to a chair. "Take a pew, old man, and tell us more."

Russell settled down with a sigh, looking suddenly weary. "You'll know all about the Fakir of Ipi," he said, "but I don't think he's acting alone, and I don't mean the other Waziris either."

When a mess waiter brought a cup of tea, Russell drank slowly with his eyes closed. "Keep them coming; there's a good chap."

"What do you mean by not acting alone, Russell?" Hume asked.

"I fear somebody's encouraging Mirza Ali Khan to stir up the tribes."

"Do you mean Gandi? Or the Congress fellows? They all want rid of us," Hume said. "And you can forget Gandi's peaceful protests; that's only for public consumption. He'd create riots and disorder if it suited him."

"Neither," Russell said, with his attitude altering from breezy nonchalance to sincerity. His eyes hardened. "We understand them and their desires. We don't like them, but we understand them. No, Major, there is somebody else."

"Who?"

"I don't know yet," Russell admitted. "I'm here to warn you to keep your eyes and ears open. I suspect a European connection."

"Russia?" Major Hume asked. "They've been interested in Afghanistan since the 1840s. Are they capitalising on the troubles in Europe and Africa to interfere here?"

"Maybe, although I don't think they've bothered with India since their Revolution. I'd think Germany," Russell said. "Herr Hitler has ideas above his station, and tying us up in a war in the Frontier would allow him the freedom to move into Czechoslovakia or elsewhere."

"We'll keep our eyes and ears open," Major Hume promised. "I'll pass it on to the officers."

"Let me know if you find anything." Russell's smile failed to hide his concern. "If you see anybody who doesn't seem to belong or hear anything that doesn't quite fit, let me know."

"How can we contact you?" Hume asked.

"Leave a note with Colonel Clark, my boss," Russell said. "He knows where I'll be." He lifted his second cup of tea. "Oh, and if you do happen to come across this fellow, be very careful; he'll be highly trained and dangerous. I'd like him as a prisoner rather than a corpse, for I have some questions to ask him."

Tulloch saw the steel behind the façade and guessed that whoever Russell questioned would have a very unpleasant experience.

"Naturally, if you can't capture the fellow, I'd prefer him with a bullet in the head than running loose around the Frontier."

Major Hume grunted. "If he fires at us, Russell, we'll return fire, but I am not ordering my men to shoot anybody unless they're a proven enemy." He lifted his chin to glare at the intelligence officer. "We're soldiers, not assassins playing some game of cloak and dagger."

Russell laughed. "I wouldn't expect anything else, Major." Finishing his tea, he stood up. "I'll spread the word. Best of luck to the Lothians."

Tulloch watched as Russell sauntered from the Mess. "Is that normal, sir? Do we often get involved in intelligence affairs?"

"Normal?" Major Hume shook his head. "I wouldn't say there is anything normal about the intelligence officers, Tulloch." He nodded after Russell. "They're all a bit suspect, and that one more than most. I'd walk wide of him if I were you."

"What should we do about this German chap?" Tulloch asked.

Hume shook his head. "Nothing, Tulloch. We are soldiers. Our job is to fight the king's enemies and protect our borders, not search for possible political agitators. That's a sordidly disgusting job we'll leave to the likes of Russell."

"What if I see him, sir?" Tulloch persisted.

"If you see him?" Major mused again. "I doubt you'd recognise him even if you did. He won't be wearing a label saying *German spy.*" He smiled at his attempted humour. "No, Tulloch, he'll be as well disguised as Captain Russell. However," he said. "If you do see such an apparition, shoot to kill. The world would be all the cleaner for his absence."

"Yes, sir," Tulloch said. He realised he had added something more to his military education and quelled the slightly uneasy feeling inside him. As Major Hume had said, his duty was to fight the king's enemies, and if a German agent acted against the peace of British India, he was an enemy.

Anyway, Tulloch told himself, the possibility of meeting such a man was so slight it was not worth considering. His prime concern was his platoon. With that thought, Tulloch left the Mess and marched across to the men's barracks. He heard the crack of a rifle without flinching and did not know where the bullet landed.

"WE'RE MOUNTING PATROLS FOR THE NEXT FEW DAYS," THE colonel said. "Learn from the Scouts and the Gurkhas; they're the best in the business."

Tulloch found the Gurkhas to be small-built, cheerful men with immense enthusiasm and a zest for life that transferred itself to the Lothian Rifles. Officered by some of the best men Britain could produce, they had given a century of loyal service.

"Whatever we do here," a young Gurkha lieutenant explained in an Irish accent, "the Waziri are watching. If we fall into a routine, they will know and lay an ambush, so always vary what you do. They lay mines or lie in dead ground, waiting for us." He grinned, "it's great fun if you don't weaken."

"And if the Waziri catch you?" Tait asked.

"Oh, then they'll hand you to the women for torture and a slow death," the grinning officer said. "Best not to get captured, old chap."

The Lothians listened and learned. In their short time at the British base, they learned how to patrol and never to drop their guard. They learned to watch the skyline for the enemy and guard against any nonchalance. The dry plain surrounded the British camp, with a series of stony ridges and dried-up water-courses, with scrubby vegetation, all of which afforded cover for Pashtun marksmen.

Tulloch was part of the first serious Lothian patrol, which moved along a river valley, accompanied by a company of Gurkhas and Scouts.

When the Gurkhas sent an advance party up the slopes, Tulloch and his platoon accompanied them, scrambling up the rocky hillside in the wake of the Gurkhas, who treated everything as a joke.

"Keep your heads down at night," the Gurkha officer advised, "build sangars around your camps, post strong piquets, and keep movement to a minimum. The Pashtun are out there, and they can shoot the legs off a fly."

The combined force marched ten miles into Waziri territory and camped on high ground. They remained a night without any alarms and marched back to Razmak, slightly disappointed but happy to return without casualties.

"You missed all the fun," Major Hume greeted them. "While you were swanning around the countryside on your wee jaunt, we had snipers firing into the camp. We lost an engineer and had a Sikh wounded."

"It's time we showed them the Lothians are here," Colonel Pringle said. "If the Pashtun can stay out at night," he said, "then so can we." He nodded to his officers. "Let's see if all our training has been worthwhile. We'll send out two reconnaissance patrols of thirty men, and each patrol will leave an ambush party of five men."

Hume grunted as Muirhead gave a dry laugh. "Play the Waziris at their own game, eh?"

"Exactly," the colonel agreed, with his pipe in his right hand. "Tulloch, you and Sergeant Drysdale pick three of your best marksmen and watch the northwestern side of the camp. Muirhead, do the same on the southeastern."

"Yes, sir," Tulloch agreed. He felt a leap of elation at the prospect of more action.

"No smoking, lads," Drysdale ordered the patrol. "The smell of tobacco lingers, especially at night. And don't take any heavy kit. Just your rifle, bayonet, water bottle and something to eat. You'll get hungry and cold, but that's part of the job."

Tulloch listened, aware that the sergeant was speaking as much for his benefit as for the more experienced privates.

"Don't fall asleep," Drysdale cautioned. "We'll need to rely on each other, for if the Waziris capture us, we'll be a long time dying."

The men nodded, with Private Brown shifting uncomfortably as he muttered details of the Waziris' treatment of prisoners.

"With your permission, sir," Drysdale said, "I think we should base ourselves there," he indicated a slight ridge where two stunted trees battled the heat. "We have a decent field of fire, and the trees will give us some cover. If you let the sentries on the wall know where we are, they'll be less likely to shoot us."

"I'll do that," Tulloch knew that Drysdale was taking command but also knew he would be foolish to ignore the veteran's advice.

"Also, sir, if you don't mind me saying, you'd be better with a rifle than a revolver. The enemy will try to pick off the officers first."

"Thank you, Drysdale," Tulloch nodded gravely. He remembered the sniping and wondered if a Waziri was watching, loading his Lee-Enfield, and eyeing this young British officer.

Night fell swiftly, immediately altering the atmosphere, magnifying every noise, and making innocent humps of rock appear as crouching Pashtun. Tulloch took a deep breath and lay still. Following Drysdale's advice, he had his men lying in a shallow beside the trees, each soldier facing a different direction with rifles ready. They breathed slowly and steadily, waiting, watching and sensitive to every breath of wind and nighttime noise.

*Now I can test myself against the best.*

Tulloch heard a whisper from the left and gripped his borrowed Lee-Enfield tightly. He swivelled his eyes in that direction, feeling the tension rise within him as he peered into the dark, seeing nothing.

Drysdale put a hand on his shoulder. "An animal, sir," he whispered. "Probably a jackal or a wild dog."

Tulloch's tension faded only slightly. He nodded and continued to peer into the dark, feeling the sweat drip from his forehead despite the chill. Twice he was certain he saw something move, only for the shape to dissolve when he concentrated his vision. He heard Brown shift slightly, the crunch of something on stone and then a high-pitched scream as a predator found its prey. Somebody swore softly, the obscene words coarse in the dark.

The night passed, with scudding clouds obscuring a scimitar moon and the stars intermittently brilliant in the high arc of the sky. When the moon emerged, its pale light reflected from the triple rows of barbed wire, reminding Tulloch that he was well outside the defensive perimeter. He wondered what the time was, decided that checking his watch would necessitate too much movement and fought the cramp in his left leg.

The noise of gunfire came suddenly from the other side of the camp. Tulloch heard the sharp bark of a rifle splitting the silence, followed by a harsh challenge.

"Halt! Who goes there?"

A double crack of musketry followed the single shot and then a fusillade, quickly dying away. Nobody answered the challenge, and Tulloch craned over his shoulder in an impossible desire to see what was happening.

The firing began again, punctuated by a single long scream, and one of the old-fashioned Lewis light machine guns on the wall added its hellish chatter.

The noise died away, save for somebody whimpering in agony. The lights around the camp illuminated the land behind the wire, throwing every undulation into harsh shadow and seeping slightly toward where the Lothians lay still. A flare soared skyward on the opposite side of the camp, and hoarse voices demanded to know what was happening. Tulloch listened for a while, his natural curiosity battling with his sense of duty compelling him to remain in position. He pushed the safety catch on his rifle forward, sensing somebody was nearby.

Another flare soared, and then Tulloch heard footsteps a few yards away.

"Sir!" Drysdale whispered and fired without shouting a challenge. Somebody fired back with the bullet screaming overhead.

Private Brown roared, "No, you don't, you bastard," fired and worked his rifle bolt, with Private Anderson also firing, the shots crackling through the night. Something hit a rock and ricocheted past the Lothians' position. Silence returned, frightening in its intensity. Tulloch smelled cordite in the air and Brown's harsh breathing. Somebody moved in the dark, stone clinking against stone, and Tulloch saw something flitting at the periphery of his vision, traversed his rifle and fired instinctively. He felt the rifle recoil into his shoulder, worked the bolt and fired again.

A flare hissed overhead, bursting into vivid light, and Tulloch saw the crumpled form of a man on the ground, lying still.

*I think I've killed a man.*

The thought brought instant elation, followed by horror. *I have ended somebody's life. That man was alive a second ago, and now he's dead.*

Tulloch half rose to inspect the body until Sergeant Drysdale grabbed his arm. "Keep still, sir! There will be more of them."

Tulloch slowly sank down, checked his rifle, and waited as the harsh light of the flare died away. The resulting darkness seemed denser than before, and Tulloch tried to restore his night vision.

He heard the soft slither of sandals on stone and shifted slightly to face his left. He saw only darkness and then a more solid shape.

"Halt!" Tulloch grated the familiar word just as Drysdale fired. The enemy retaliated, and Brown and Tulloch fired together, the twin reports merging into a single sound.

A bullet thudded into the ground beside Tulloch as he worked the bolt of his rifle and aimed into the silent dark. *How many of them are there?*

"Hold your fire," Tulloch hissed. He stared outward, trying to make out shapes and analyse noises. Something shuffled a few yards away.

"Over there, sir," Anderson whispered.

"Yes; shoot it," Tulloch replied, and three rifles fired.

The shuffling ended, and silence blanketed the picket.

Tulloch eased his rifle to the right and left, feeling very vulnerable in case the Waziris were watching him.

A flare soared from the camp, with the fringes of light only flickering around Tulloch's position. He saw a humped shape ten yards beyond his position, guessed it was a Pashtun warrior and aimed his rifle without firing.

*That man may be shamming, or he may be dead. I'll remain here until daylight and then check.*

The flare sank and died, and the night dragged on, with a fluctuating wind lifting the surface dust. Tulloch waited, shivering as the temperature plummeted.

Dawn was welcome, a grey sky streaked with pink, highlighting the harshness of the plain and outlining the mountains in rugged splendour. Tulloch eased cramped limbs and gazed around, seeing only empty ground and stark boulders.

"Where are the bodies? We shot two men at least."

"We did, sir," Drysdale agreed. "The Waziris must have moved them during the night."

"I didn't hear a thing," Tulloch admitted.

"Nor did I, sir," Drysdale said. "These lads could cross a field of crystal bells without disturbing a watchful angel."

Tulloch left his position and studied the surrounding ground. A host of insects feeding on blood told its story. "A man lay here," he said, "wounded or dead, I don't know. Somebody carried him away - see the deeper marks of the sandals?"

"There's another over here, sir," Drysdale said.

"We got two of them, then,"

"We did," Tulloch said.

*I helped kill a man. I am now a soldier.* Tulloch knew he should feel sorry for the warrior he killed, but instead, he felt only satisfaction. It had been a fair contest between the Waziri warriors and the Lothian soldiers, and, on this occasion, the Lothians had won.

*A mixture of guile and aggression is the answer, then. I'll remember that.*

# Chapter Nine

So all day long the noise of battle roll'd.
Tennyson: *The Passing of Arthur.* Despite Tulloch's
successful ambush, the Waziri night sniping continued.
The next night, they claimed another victim—a Dogra sentry
who allowed his head to protrude above the parapet. The
Dogras wanted instant retaliation and sent out a fighting patrol
that returned frustrated in the evening without seeing a single
Pashtun warrior.

The snipers returned that night, wounding a cook in the
early hours and sending a bullet singing from the body of an
armoured car.

"The trouble is," Muirhead said, "we don't know where
they're based. If we knew that, we could at least return fire."

Hume looked up from his newspaper. "Tracer bullets," he
said. "During the last war, we could see where the enemy
machine gun posts were when they used tracer bullets."

"The Waziri don't have tracer," Muirhead said.

Tulloch lifted a hand. "Could we not give them some, sir?
You know what expert thieves they are. Maybe one of our
patrols could lose some ammunition just by mistake, sir."

Hume considered for a moment. "You're a fly man, Tulloch. You've been mixing with the Jocks [1] too much."

"Yes, sir," Tulloch agreed.

"Take out your patrol, Tulloch. The Quartermaster will find you a dozen clips of tracer ammunition. Put the tracer in a haversack and leave it in a convenient place." Hume returned to his newspaper. "We'll make a soldier of you yet, Tulloch."

"Thank you, sir," Tulloch replied.

Tulloch picked a dozen men for the patrol, with Sergeant Drysdale, Hogg, and Hardie his first three choices.

"Us again, sir?" Drysdale raised his eyebrows.

"Us again," Tulloch agreed without explaining.

Drysdale nodded and gathered the men. Hardie showed no emotion at all, while Hogg stamped his boots, slipped a Kukri knife into his belt opposite his bayonet, and gave a slight smile. Brown sang the first line of an obscene song, cracked an even more obscene joke, and lit a cigarette.

"Are we going overnight, Sergeant?"

"Not this time, Brown," Drysdale said.

Tulloch led them on a five-mile march across the plain to the foothills beyond. Although the patrol had an ulterior motive, he followed the recognised procedure of advance and rearguards, with men on each flank.

"Maintain your distances," Tulloch ordered, leading from the front. He knew the Waziris were watching him and felt a slight tingling at the base of his spine at the thought of a tribal marksman placing him in the vee of his backsight. When he reached the edge of the plain, Tulloch stopped, posted picquets, and gave the men twenty minutes' rest. He removed the haversack of tracer ammunition, placed it beside a rock, and toured his men, exchanging brief pleasantries.

The heat intensified, with two vultures circling overhead. Tulloch glanced at his watch. He wanted to give any watching Waziri the impression he was working to a timetable as an excuse for leaving the haversack behind.

"Two minutes, men," Tulloch said.

"Don't forget your haversack, sir," Drysdale reminded.

"That's a present for the Pashtuns," Tulloch said quietly.

"I see," Drysdale understood immediately. He glanced around at the threatening hills. "Right, lads. Kelly and Aitken, take the advance guard; Innes, you and Hardie are on the left flank." He organised the platoon for the return march.

"We'll see if they take the bait," Colonel Pringle said when Tulloch returned. "At worst, we've supplied them with a few dozen more rounds of ammunition. At best, we can pinpoint the sniper's position."

"Yes, sir."

Pringle's smile was as evil as anything Tulloch had ever seen. "Then we'll give them a surprise."

"Yes, sir. Do you want my platoon ready to return fire?"

"Yes, Tulloch. We're replacing the Dogras on guard duty tonight. I want double picquets and every man on standby under the wall." Pringle began to clean the bowl of his pipe with a blunt pocket knife. "They'll love you for that, Tulloch."

"Yes, sir."

The night passed without incident, leaving the Lothians tired and frustrated. Lieutenant Tait took out a patrol the following day, and three Mark Two tanks clattered into the camp in the afternoon, with half the garrison crowding around to watch.

"Tanks in Waziristan?" Tait said, drawing on his cigarette and still tense from his patrol. "General Coleridge is treating this campaign seriously."

"We knew that when he called on us," Muirhead told him.

"Get your men ready for marching," Hume advised. "Something's in the wind."

"When do we march?" Tait asked.

"When General Coleridge orders," Hume said. "I'd guess in a couple of days."

The Lothians remained on guard duty that night, standing sentinel on one section of the long wall and making themselves as small a target as possible. Clouds covered the moon and stars, making it harder to peer onto the stony plain and the invisible mountains beyond.

"No smoking!" A hard-voiced sergeant ordered when a man lit a cigarette. "The Paythans can see a cigarette a mile away!"

As the corporal spoke, Tulloch heard the sharp crack of a rifle. He saw the brief red streak coming from the edge of the plain and smiled.

"There he is!" Tulloch shouted. "Fire!"

With the tracer indicating the source of the sniper, every sentry on that section of the wall opened fire, and a moment later, the mountain guns joined in. Tulloch grinned, knowing that Colonel Pringle had arranged for artillery support.

"Five rounds rapid!" Muirhead ordered, and the Lothians enjoyed the opportunity as the mountain guns fired three rounds each.

"Cease fire!" Muirhead ordered. The musketry ended, and the Lothians peered into the dark beyond the wire. "I doubt the Waziris will try that again tonight. Get back to barracks, everybody who is not on duty."

Tulloch grunted. "That was an expensive method of getting rid of one Waziri marksman."

Muirhead nodded. "Maybe so, but if it saved one British, Gurkha, or Indian life, it was worthwhile." He winked. "Are you the duty officer tonight?"

"No, sir."

"Then get to bed, young sir. I suspect we have turbulent times ahead."

---

THE COLUMN FORMED UP IN THE DARKNESS BEFORE DAWN, THE Lothians, a Sikh battalion, and a platoon of Tochi Scouts. They ate a hurried breakfast and marched out of the main gate of

Razmak with the huddled sentries watching them behind closed faces.

Tulloch remembered the hurried conference the previous evening when Colonel Pringle informed them of the plan.

"Coleridge has already sent the main column to flush out the Fakir of Ipi's lashkar. The Fakir has attracted stray warriors from half Afghanistan as well as his usual Waziris, so his rising could become general."

The officers had listened, nodding as they understood how dangerous a general rising along the Frontier could become.

"When he sees the main column, the Fakir will run towards the Durand Line. The Gurkhas and Dogras are already in position with mountain guns to block that move, so the lashkar will double back into the Khaisora Valley, where the Sikhs will harass them, and we provide the full stop." Colonel Pringle packed tobacco into the bowl of his pipe. "Or that's the general idea."

The officers dispersed to make the final preparations for the march. They caught up with the main column within two hours and joined the rear, with the men complaining about the dust.

"How long are we with this lot for?" Tait asked.

"About five miles," Hume replied.

The Scouts led the column and guarded the flanks, occupying the peaks as the British, Gurkhas, and Indians marched along the road. With armoured cars and tanks in the column and Scouts picquets taking control of the hills on both sides of the road, Tulloch did not anticipate any trouble as the column uncoiled slowly through Waziristan.

They moved slowly, with the sound of engines from tanks, armoured cars, and supply lorries alien in the near-primaeval hills. Tulloch viewed the surrounding hills, wondering how many Pashtun warriors were watching and how many agile youths were bringing news of their approach to the Fakir.

"These heavy columns will never catch such a wily warrior as the Fakir," Tait observed.

"That's not the idea," Tulloch said. "The main column is too powerful for the Fakir's lashkar to fight, so he'll run and split into smaller parties, which we'll deal with."

A flight of three aircraft passed overhead, with the biplanes looking very fragile. Tulloch watched them for a moment, wondered what it was like up in the clouds looking down on the tangled valleys of the Frontier.

Major Hume summoned his officers. "We're leaving the column in ten minutes, gentlemen. The Tochi Scouts and Dogras are keeping the L of C - Lines of Communication - open. Warn your men."

The Lothians trudged on until they came to a side valley when Colonel Pringle led them to the right, and they followed. The valley was narrow, with precipitous sides of rock and scree, with barely a suggestion of vegetation. The rocks multiplied the heat, so the men felt like they marched through a furnace. Sweat started immediately, and men looked to the right and left, where the gaunt slopes could hide a thousand Waziris.

"Tait," the colonel said, "take your platoon and secure the hill on the south. Tulloch, take the north; drive away any unfriendly Waziris."

Tulloch led from the front, gasping in the heat as he splashed through a fast-running river and zig-zagged up the slope. His nailed boots slid on the rock, which was seared by gullies and baking hot. The ridge was nearly a thousand feet above the river, knife edged at the top, so even Tulloch's platoon had to move in single file.

"Come away from the summit," Tulloch ordered. "We don't want to present ourselves as targets for the enemy."

Four Platoon followed Tulloch, with boots clattering on rocks and the occasional dislodged boulder rolling down the hill, gathering a retinue of small stones and dust on its passage. Brown slipped and skidded until Hardie rescued him with a strong right hand.

"Up you get, Broonie!"

Tulloch halted beneath the skyline, motioned for his men to keep down and cautiously crested the ridge.

The slope on the other side was equally steep, sliding down to a plateau a thousand feet below, with a blue-green river rushing into a small lake. At the side of the lake, a line of pine trees provided shade for the thousands of men who camped there, together with what looked like artillery pieces.

*That's the Fakir's lashkar. The main column has not disturbed him yet.*

Tulloch lay prone and watched, wishing he had a telescope or a pair of binoculars. He ordered his men to secure the ridge and not appear over the skyline, told Sergeant Drysdale to hold the position and slid back to warn Colonel Pringle.

"You look agitated, Tulloch." Pringle stood alone, stuffing tobacco into the bowl of his pipe.

"Yes, sir. The Fakir's lashkar is on the other side of the ridge."

The colonel smiled. "Good. I'm glad we've come to the right place."

"Yes, sir."

"Keep the ridge secure and scout the Iblanke Kotal," [2]Colonel nodded to a deep gash where the knife-edge dipped suddenly, causing a defile in ominous shadow. "Don't let the Fakir see you."

"No, sir," Tulloch said. "If he brings up his entire lashkar, it'll take more than a platoon to hold him."

"Let me know the minute anything happens," Pringle ordered, producing a silver lighter and putting the flame to his pipe. "You're our eyes and ears on the Iblanke Kotal, Lieutenant."

"Yes, sir."

Tulloch scrambled back, wondering if he had made a fool of himself. He led his section to the *kotal* and stared down at the lashkar on the far side. The *kotal* allowed easier access to the savage ridge but still ascended around five hundred feet from the valley floor on either side. There was no track, only a scree-covered slope that rose in a series of steps, with a handful of trees clinging precariously to patches of thin soil. On the far side of the pass, in a valley that ran parallel to the ridge, the Fakir's lashkar spread over the ground.

Tulloch saw the men under tribal banners of black or green, some with Persian script on the silk, which he guessed contained quotes from the Koran. "They're not all Waziri, sir," Sergeant Drysdale said. "I can see Mahsud and Bhittani tribesmen there, so we might be facing Khonia Kel."

"I don't know the name," Tulloch admitted.

"He's a bad man from way back," Drysdale said quietly. "The sort of man who has kept the Frontier alight since long before our time. He could write a manual on irregular warfare if he knew how to write."

Tulloch saw a battery of small field guns with the lashkar and scores of men on horseback. "It's like something from the Middle Ages."

The wind increased as Tulloch sat just beneath the skyline, with the knife-edge ridge stretching on either side. He looked across the valley to a parallel ridge, knowing that if the Waziris occupied that in numbers, they could make life very difficult for his small force. "Get half the men into defensive positions, Sergeant," Tulloch ordered. "Build sangars and ensure each man has a good field of fire."

"Yes, sir," Drysdale said.

"I expect Coleridge will push the main column against the Fakir soon. If he stays to fight, we can hit him on the flank. If he cuts and runs, we'll block his retreat over the *kotal*." Tulloch realised he was talking too much. "I'm taking the rest on a patrol along the ridge."

"Very good, sir," Drysdale said.

The far side of the pass was rougher, with jagged, broken rocks that slid under the soldiers' boots and a pair of patrolling eagles that resented the human presence in their territory. After twenty minutes, Tulloch knew not to expect the enemy to approach from that direction.

*A few snipers might get a foothold here, but that's all.*

The men were in position, waiting behind sangars, staring down the pass, cleaning their rifles and talking in low voices.

Tulloch heard the artillery first and saw the bright flashes as the shells exploded around the Fakir's lashkar in the valley below. The sound and sights were strangely unwarlike, as if he were watching an exercise or some child's game.

"That's it started, sir," Sergeant Drysdale reported calmly.

"It can't be far off dusk," Tulloch said. "Surely the Waziris will know the area better than our men in the dark."

"Yes, sir, but the Fakir will know that as well. He won't expect a night attack."

Tulloch nodded. He was learning a lot from Sergeant Drysdale.

From their position on the *kotal*, the platoon had a bird's eye view of the unfolding battlefield. Tulloch saw the artillery explosions crashing down for five minutes, followed by the staccato rattle of light machine guns and musketry. He heard the rumble of tanks and listened to the crack of their guns, with the Pashtuns heading towards the British attack.

*It's strange to be up here, knowing only a couple of miles away, men are fighting and dying, and here we are in safety like the Gods on Mount Olympus looking down on humanity.*

"Evening, Tulloch," Muirhead said, panting with exertion. "I brought up Tait's platoon to reinforce you. Do you know what's happening?"

"General Coleridge is attacking the Fakir," Tulloch said. "That's all I know."

Muirhead grinned, with his teeth showing white in the gathering gloom. "Let me enlighten you, dear boy. The general allowed his men to be seen in daylight so the Fakir knew what force was against him. Normally, when a large column enters Waziristan, the Pashtuns melt into the hills, so Coleridge appeared clumsy, enticing the fakir to stay put, thinking he could easily escape when our lads lumber in at night."

Tulloch nodded. "I see." He wondered how much Muirhead knew and how much was pure conjecture.

"The Waziris would feel quite relaxed, knowing they would slip away at first light, and then Coleridge has upset all their plans with a dusk attack. He'll use the artillery to hold them, then attack with the tanks and infantry."

Tulloch stared into the gloom. "The tanks and infantry are already in action." He could see the tanks lumbering forward, occasionally firing, with the flash of their guns bright against the dark. The staccato hammer of musketry was plain now, and the mechanical rattle of machine gun fire.

"The Fakir will split his forces then, and we'll be in action. Take a section down the *kotal*, Tulloch and see what's happening." Muirhead sounded casual. "Try not to get caught."

Tulloch nodded and called on Eight Section. They were tired after their night on the ridge but keen to see what was developing.

The *kotal* was stark, rising to a summit and a steep descent to the Fakir's side. Tulloch extended the section across the width of the pass, with the dark bringing a rising wind and emphasising the flashes of explosions and sounds of constant gunfire.

"Don't stray," he ordered, "and don't get separated from each other."

"Yes, sir," Brown answered for the men.

"We'll be a hundred yards behind you," Lieutenant Muirhead said. "Don't fire unless you have to, Tulloch. The colonel wants to bring them into our ambush. If the Waziris press too hard, fall back on us.

"We'll do that," Tulloch promised, stepping forward and downward.

As the night closed in, dark, stark and dangerous, the firing became more extensive. When the British artillery fired volleys, the Waziris pieces replied, allowing Tulloch to see the explosions on both sides with a continuous rattle of musketry.

"Sir," Brown said, "I think somebody's coming up the pass."

"Let them come," Tulloch said. He felt surprisingly calm, even detached, as if he was not part of what was happening. "I'll have a look." Keeping low, he moved down the slope, moving from cover to cover. After a couple of hundred yards, he heard noises beneath him and crouched behind a rock, lifting his rifle. He eased forward the safety catch and waited, peering into the dark.

The footsteps were hurried, unlike the usual Pashtun long, measured stride. Tulloch squinted downward, waiting for the oncoming man to appear in his backsight. He froze as he realised somebody was above him, blocking his passage back to his platoon.

Fragments of memory thrust into Tulloch's head, stories of the cruelty of Pashtuns to British prisoners, and he resolved to die rather than surrender. He peered around him, hoping his night vision was as good as the prowling Pashtun. The battle continued below, with the British artillery pounding the Waziri lashkar. Tulloch lifted his head slightly to save his night vision and saw movement above him.

*That's unlike the Pashtun. We don't usually see them unless they're out of range or don't care.*

Tulloch saw the man quite clearly, squatting amidst a cluster of rocks with binoculars in his left hand and a pistol in his right. Although he wore the clothes of a typical Waziri warrior, Tulloch sensed something was wrong.

*A Waziri doesn't sit like that.*

The man shifted position, raising himself onto the rock and lifting the binoculars to his eyes.

*I've never seen a Pashtun using binoculars before. Who is this fellow?*

Tulloch rested his rifle on a rock, wishing the light was stronger. He allowed his night vision to take over, watching as the man slid behind a boulder, put down his binoculars and scribbled a note on a small pad.

*A Pashtun who can write?* Tulloch remembered what Russell had said. *I'd wager that this fellow is the German spy.* Tulloch started as a memory struck him. *I've seen that man before! He was at the dockside at Karachi when the troop ship arrived, taking notes, and again in Peshawar.*

Moving as quietly as possible, Tulloch left the sanctuary of his rock and slithered toward the spy. The man finished writing, lifted his binoculars, and returned to his position, staring upward at the pass.

*Got you, my friend!* Tulloch lifted his rifle and aimed. "You there! You're my prisoner!"

The man turned at Tulloch's first words, rolled closer, ducked beneath the barrel of the rifle and landed a solid punch. Tulloch doubled over, gasping, as one of his men roared out a challenge.

"Hello down there! What's happening? Is that you, sir?"

The spy grabbed Tulloch's rifle, snarling. Tulloch glimpsed a swarthy, thin face with brown eyes, held onto his weapon and swung hard with the butt. He felt the thrill of contact as the rifle butt cracked onto the spy's shoulder, but the spy dodged away. For a second, he was face-to-face with Tulloch, wrestling, with his teeth bared in a black hole of his mouth.

"Down here," Tulloch roared and heard the clumsy crunch of British ammunition boots on the rocky surface. He twisted the rifle, hoping for a clean shot, but the spy was strong, wiry and very agile.

"Brown! Hogg! Hardie!" Tulloch shouted, struggling to hold his opponent.

"Coming, sir!" Brown replied, with his boots sliding over the scree to send a small avalanche of broken stones downhill.

The spy muttered something and rammed his knee upwards, catching Tulloch in the inner thigh, and scrambled away. Tulloch gasped, doubled up to protect his genitals and swore, grabbing for his rifle.

"Sir!" Brown knelt beside the reeling Tulloch. "Are you all right?"

"Get that man!" Tulloch gestured down the slope. "Don't let him escape!"

"Which one, sir?" Brown lifted his rifle, fired, worked the bolt, and fired again. "There are hundreds of them, sir!"

"Best get back to the sangars, sir," Hardie was kneeling beside Tulloch. "It's not safe here."

Hogg had run downhill after the fleeing spy but returned with his mouth open and his rifle at the trail. "He got away, sir, but these other buggers are coming."

The main British attack had broken the fakir's lashkar, and the Pashtuns had scattered in a dozen different directions. Hundreds were swarming up the pass, some carrying banners over their shoulders. One of the Royal Artillery guns fired a star shell, with the sudden harsh light illuminating a mass of fleeing warriors.

"Back to our positions, lads," Tulloch said, saw the spy's binoculars on the ground and scooped them up as he withdrew. Hardie fired a final shot, worked the bolt and retired, with Hogg at his side, swearing mightily.

"Oh, I love a lassie," Brown said, sliding behind a sangar in a shower of stones. "A bonnie black Afghani!"

"Aye," Hogg said. "And she's brought all her relations to get you, Brownie!"

The platoon was waiting for Tulloch, glancing up from beneath their pith helmets, wide-eyed and tense.

"Can we fire now, sir?" Drysdale asked, squinting down the barrel of his rifle.

Tulloch slid behind a rock. The star shell was already fading, showing a mass of men advancing up the *kotal* without any formation or obvious leadership.

"Fire!" Tulloch ordered.

"We were waiting until you returned safely, sir," Drysdale said, firing into the mass.

"Fire!" Tulloch repeated, firing, working the bolt and firing again. With the light gone, he could not aim but fired where he had seen the mass of men running towards him. "Aim low, boys; remember your shooting downhill!"

Four Platoon fired with the sound of their rifles echoing from the surrounding hills. Some Waziris slid into cover and fired back, with bullets pinging from the rocks or whining overhead. Others continued upward, their shapes becoming more apparent as they closed.

"Come on, lads," Innes shouted. "The closer you come, the easier it is to shoot you."

"They'll try to outflank us," Drysdale warned, reloading with calm precision.

"Take the left flank," Tulloch ordered. "I'll take the right."

"Sir," Drysdale hurried away as the leading Waziris tried a rush, and the platoon replied with rapid musketry.

A British shell exploded on the lower part of the *kotal*, the sudden flare damaging Tulloch's night vision. More Waziris rushed forward, and the musketry increased. Bullets whined around the sangars and raised dust clouds and jagged chips of rock from the ground. Private O'Hara grunted, rose slightly, and slumped to the ground with blood spreading from a hole in his chest.

"Withdraw to the next position," Tulloch ordered. "Odd sections first, then even." He had practised staged withdrawals around Peshawar, but moving under fire was different, with some men ducking or returning fire to the danger of their comrades. "Take O'Hara back!" He would not leave a wounded or dead man for the Pashtuns.

As the platoon withdrew, the Waziris erupted from the left flank, screaming as they charged. Tulloch did not need to order the men to fire and joined in.

"I thought you could use a hand," Lieutenant Muirhead said as his men joined the section. "Lovely evening for a brawl, don't you think?" He emptied his revolver at the men on the flank and reloaded, thumbing the cartridges home.

Tulloch took a deep breath as Muirhead's men lay down to begin rapid fire on the Waziris. "Couldn't be better, sir."

"Time to withdraw a little, Tulloch," Muirhead decided. "We can't let you have all the fun, can we?"

Tulloch ducked as a bullet whined overhead. He noticed that Muirhead had not flinched. "Oh, I don't mind sharing, sir."

"We'll withdraw by platoons," Muirhead ordered. "The Paythans are in front and on both flanks. Take your boys back first."

Tulloch called back Four Platoon, counting the men as they passed him. When he reached the summit of the *kotal*, Colonel Pringle was there with the bulk of the battalion. He nodded as both sections arrived at his position.

"How many Waziris, Muirhead?"

"I'd say about five or six hundred," Muirhead said.

"Tulloch?" The colonel looked directly at Tulloch.

"I think more than that, sir," Tulloch said with an apologetic glance at Muirhead. "And a spy, sir."

The colonel started. "A spy? What makes you say that, Tulloch?" He glanced down the *kotal* where the Pashtuns were gathering for another rush to break through the British line. "Tell me after we've dealt with these fellows."

Pringle roared out orders that saw the battalion Lewis machine gunners fire. They were positioned to rake the path in a vicious crossfire that scythed down the leading Waziris. The colonel had positioned a company on either flank, and they opened rifle fire on any warrior they saw. Within ten minutes, the Waziris had recoiled in disorder and returned down the pass.

"Major Hume, follow them with A and C companies. Don't give them time to settle," Pringle ordered. "The rest, sit tight. Tait, take out a patrol to the left flank, RSM Watson, do the same on the right." He waited until Hume and the patrols were away before returning his attention to Tulloch.

"Now, Tulloch, tell me about this spy." Colonel Pringle led Tulloch away from the other officers and listened to what had happened.

"Did you get a clear look at him?" Pringle said.

"Yes, sir," Tulloch described the spy.

"And you're sure you saw the same man in Karachi and Peshawar?"

"I am sure, sir," Tulloch said again.

"I'll pass your information onto the Intelligence Bureau," Pringle said. "They might wish to talk to you. Was there anything else?"

"Yes, sir. The spy dropped these," Tulloch handed over the binoculars.

"Did you say he was German?" Colonel asked with a wry smile.

"Captain Russell, the intelligence officer, suggested he might be German, sir."

"Well, the intelligence officer was wrong," the colonel said. "Look at this," he showed Tulloch the maker's name on the binoculars. "*Filotecnica Salmoiraghi*. These are Italian Army binoculars, Tulloch. I'd say the man you tangled with was one of Mussolini's boys, reaching out towards India."

"Was he the man Captain Russell believes is stirring up the Fakir against us?"

"Quite possibly, Tulloch," Pringle said. "I can think of no other reason for an Italian to be with the Fakir's lashkar and taking notes of our troop trains."

"I failed to capture him," Tulloch said.

Pringle nodded. "That's to be expected. Men like that will be experts at avoiding capture, and you were a little busy with a horde of angry Waziris attacking you. Now, write a report for Captain Russell, mention your earlier encounters with this fellow, and then grab some sleep. You look just about all in. Dismissed."

# Chapter Ten

*"There is no place where espionage is not possible."*
**Sun Tzu**

"Lieutenant Tulloch!" Captain Russell stood outside Tulloch's quarters in Razmak. Dressed in a stylish light-grey suit, washed and shaved, he looked a different man, except for the deep intelligence in his eyes and the dark tan from months living outdoors.

"Sir," Tulloch stepped aside to allow Russell access.

"Tell me about this man you saw." Russell stepped inside and sat on the only chair in the room as if he owned the place. He listened while Tulloch gave details.

"You've seen this man three times in total," Russell confirmed when Tulloch finished. "Are you sure it was the same man?"

"I've been giving that some thought, sir," Tulloch said. "I am sure."

"Was he disguised as a Pashtun?" Russell asked.

Tulloch thought for a moment before he replied. "He wore Pashtun clothing, sir, but he had no beard. I don't think he was trying to pass himself off as a Pashtun."

Russell grunted. "That could mean the Fakir knows who he is. Let me see the binoculars." He held out his hand, took the binoculars and examined them minutely. "Yes, Italian army standard issue. You have a fine prize there." He took a silver cigarette case from his pocket, extracted a cigarette, and offered the case to Tulloch.

"No, thank you," Tulloch said.

"You don't smoke?" Russell raised his eyebrows. "You might find a cigarette helps in stressful situations, but probably a good idea not to smoke when dodging Waziris along the Frontier."

Tulloch nodded, wondering what else Russell wanted. He leaned against the wall, saying nothing.

Russell drew on his cigarette and exhaled a long ribbon of blue smoke. "Did you get a good look at this Italian fellow?"

"I was face to face with him, sir," Tulloch said. "As close as I am to you."

"Would you recognise him if you saw him again?"

Tulloch pondered for a moment. "I would, sir. His features were nothing special; I mean, he would not stand out in a crowd, but there was something about him. Maybe it was his eyes, but he had a presence that one could not mistake."

Russell leaned back in his seat, contemplating Tulloch through eyes that looked old for his age. "That's interesting," he said. "Nobody in the Intelligence Bureau has seen him. Indeed, we had only heard rumours and speculation. You're unique."

"I've given you a description, sir," Tulloch said. "That might help."

"Yes. You said the spy's features were nothing special. A man of medium height and average build, strong and wiry, with intense brown eyes. How do you think that will help us identify him on a Frontier this size? Or if he slips into India to help Congress or Gandhi?"

Tulloch nodded. "I see what you mean, sir."

"I'll need to speak to your commanding officer," Russell said.

He finished his cigarette and flicked the stub into a basket in the corner.

"About what, sir?" Tulloch asked.

"About you, Tulloch," Russell said softly. He stood up with all the grace of a hunting cat and smiled. "There's no time like the present, Tulloch. Come with me."

Tulloch looked down at his old, now sadly battered uniform. "I'm hardly dressed to see Colonel Pringle, sir."

"I'm sure he's seen worse," Russell said, adding an edge to his voice. "Come with me, Tulloch. That's an order!"

Colonel Pringle was on duty in his office, with the light attracting moths and various insects. He shouted, "Come in," when Russell knocked on the door and indicated that Tulloch should follow. Tulloch stood at attention inside the door as Russell addressed the colonel.

"I have spoken to Lieutenant Tulloch," Russell said. "He is the only man capable of identifying the Italian spy."

Colonel Pringle leaned back in his chair, with the light casting hard shadows on his face. He lifted the pipe from his desk. "That may be correct," he allowed.

"It is," Russell said. "Lieutenant Tulloch's various encounters have already furthered our investigation by identifying the European agent as Italian rather than German."

The colonel nodded, looking from Russell to Tulloch and back. "Yes," he said. "Gathering intelligence is your department, Captain Russell. We deal with the military side of things."

"The two are often connected, Colonel," Russell said.

Colonel Pringle nodded without a word. He began to stuff tobacco into the bowl of his pipe.

"I'd like to borrow Lieutenant Tulloch for a while until we lay this fellow by the heels," Russell said.

The colonel grunted and lifted his silver lighter. "My wife gave me this lighter," he said. "On our tenth anniversary. It's been with me ever since." He applied the flame to his pipe. "If I loaned you Lieutenant Tulloch, it would leave me with an officer short," he said, puffing from the side of his mouth. "Lieutenant Tulloch is proving himself a capable man, and we still haven't captured the Fakir."

"I'm aware of that, Colonel," Russell said. "I am sure you can find another regimental officer, while his information is more valuable to us than any mere lieutenant."

"None of my officers are mere," Colonel Pringle said mildly. "Nor are any of my men. They are all part of the fabric of the regiment. The loss of one diminishes us all." He clenched the pipe between his teeth. "What does Lieutenant Tulloch say?"

"I haven't put it to him yet," Russell said, holding the colonel's stare.

"What do you say, Tulloch?" Pringle puffed blue smoke into the room.

"I'm a Lothian Rifleman, sir," Tulloch replied immediately. "I'd prefer to stay with the regiment."

The colonel nodded. "Then there's your answer, Russell. Tulloch remains with us. Good day to you." He nodded to the door.

"Good day to you, Colonel," Russell replied calmly. "You'll make better progress in the Intelligence Bureau than in regimental soldiering, Tulloch." He grinned. "I haven't given up on you yet."

"I'm a Lothian Rifleman," Tulloch repeated.

"For now," Russell said, threw a casual salute to Pringle and strode away.

Tulloch was unsure what to think when Russell left the office. His youthful dreams of soldiering had not included hunting spies among the tangled mountains of the Frontier, but the world had changed since Colin Campbell had led the 93rd Highlanders at Balaclava.

"Is that it, sir?" He asked.

"It is as far as I am concerned," Colonel Pringle replied. "I don't know what power Captain Russell has, but you're one of my officers, and I'm damned if the Intelligence Bureau will take you against your will." He added more tobacco to his pipe. "Intelligence gathering is a dirty business at any level, Tulloch, and one you'd best steer clear of."

"Yes, sir," Tulloch said. "I plan to."

He returned to his bungalow in the lines, aware of Robert Burns' words that the best-laid plans of mice and men aft gang agley yet confident that Colonel Pringle was on his side.

"What was that about, Tulloch?" Muirhead asked after Tulloch had put his platoon through an early morning parade. "That intelligence fellow took you to the old man last night."

"He wanted to borrow me for the Intelligence Bureau," Tulloch said.

Muirhead shook his head. "I hope you turned him down, Tulloch. Once these people get their claws in you, they never let go."

"I turned him down," Tulloch confirmed.

"Good man," Muirhead said.

Tulloch pushed Russell's request to the back of his mind. He took his platoon out on road protection details, guarding the convoys of lorries that brought supplies and ammunition into Razmak. The Lothians were veterans now, ignoring stray snipers and judging to the inch whether a rifle shot was sufficiently close to cause concern.

"Where are we going today, sir? Sergeant Drysdale asked as Tulloch led his platoon out of the main gate and past the triple row of barbed wire.

"We're escorting a bunch of Sappers who are inspecting the roads," Tulloch said. "The Waziris have taken to laying mines and cutting the telephone wires."

Drysdale grunted. "I prefer a stand-up fight to this sort of campaign, sir," he said.

"So do I," Tulloch admitted.

A cheerful engineering captain named Field commanded the engineer detachment and greeted Four Platoon with a smile and a wave.

"Have you chaps met any mines yet?"

"Not yet," Tulloch admitted.

"You've been lucky," Field said. "The Waziris are clever devils. At the beginning of the campaign, they tried using spent cartridges filled with explosives and a detonator. Then they graduated to cylinders like this," he showed a metal box about three inches long and an inch in diameter. "Bigger than the cartridges and more lethal. Our intelligence wallahs think some European fellow helped improve the Waziris technique."

Tulloch lifted his head. "I believe an Italian agent is working with the Fakir," he said.

"Is that so?" Field said. "Well, I wish he wasn't. From these cylinders, the Paythans have moved onto old cigarette tins, with explosives at the bottom and filled with pebbles and nails, a poor man's shrapnel but just as deadly." He raised his voice to enable the entire platoon to hear. "If any of you chaps see a cigarette tin lying on the ground, let me know. It's probably a booby trap."

"Do they leave them lying around for our men to lift?" Tulloch asked.

"Sometimes," Field said. "More often, the Waziris bury them just under the surface of the road at places our infantry walk in single file. Either that or they hide the mines under a scattering of dung, which the explosion also blows into the victim's body."

"Nice," Tulloch said.

"You can blame your European friend for the mines," Field said, "but the dung and subsequent blood poisoning is a hundred per cent Paythan."

"Do they cause casualties?" Tulloch asked.

"Yes, men and animals," Field confirmed. "One of my men had to shoot a mule a few days back when one of these infernal things blew off her leg."

With this new example of the Italian agent's work in his head, Tulloch was in a thoughtful mood as he escorted the engineers on their patrol.

*This Italian agent is dangerous if he's causing casualties to our men. I know nothing about the intelligence side, but the military side involves me.*

Escorting engineers was a slow job, walking in the sappers' wake, watching for ambushes. The engineers examined every inch of the road in painstaking detail, probing into corners, poking at piles of cattle and camel dung, and making technical observations that Tulloch did not understand.

"What are you doing?" Tulloch asked when the sappers began to lay gun cotton around the stay wires of a telephone pole.

"The Pashtuns like to cut the wires," Field said cheerfully, "so we're booby-trapping them. Not enough to kill, but we might blow off a finger or two."

"I don't agree with that," Tulloch said. "You might injure some innocent herd boy."

Field's face darkened. "Once you've been out here longer, Lieutenant, you'll realise that nobody is innocent. What you think is an innocent herd boy one minute can take a message to the insurgents or plunge a knife in your back the next."

"Maybe so, Field, but I still don't agree with waging war on civilians. We're meant to be above such things."

Field shook his head. "Life out here is not the same as in civilised Edinburgh, Lieutenant. There are different rules; Allah smiles on the strong and the devious and grinds the weak and hesitant underfoot."

Tulloch looked up at the gaunt mountains. He knew what sort of men lived there, yet still could not reconcile himself to making war on possible civilians.

"I see movement up the hill, sir," Drysdale murmured, pointing with his chin.

"Very good, Sergeant," Tulloch had been concentrating on the opposite side of the road. "Send up a section to have a decko."

"Sir!" Drysdale nodded. "Corporal MacBride, have a look at that spur. It might only be a goat or a Waziri with a grudge."

"Yes, sir," MacBride said.

The explosion took them all by surprise. Short and sharp, it came from the side of the road. A long scream followed, and Private Anderson writhed beside a small crater, staring at the bloody stump where his foot had been.

"Anderson!" Tulloch ran to the injured man.

"I've got you, Willie!" Kelly was there first, applying a tourniquet to Anderson's leg to stop the flow of blood.

"Mine," Field said, pointing to the remains of a metal box that lay beside the wounded man.

"Kelly, Aitken, Innes, take Anderson back to Razmak!" Tulloch said, with a new understanding of the dangers of mines. He waited until they had gone before lifting the metal box, still hot from the explosion. Although it was twisted and torn, Tulloch could make out the design. There was an image of a woman in green and black, smoking a white cigarette, with the name *Modiano* written above.

"Modiano?" Tulloch repeated the name.

"Italian cigarettes, sir," Hardie said. "I've knocked about the world a bit, and the Italians love their cigarettes. Their men like to pose with them, and the women think smoking makes them look sophisticated."

"Thank you, Hardie," Tulloch said. That was the longest voluntary speech he had heard Hardie make, and wondered anew about the taciturn man's background. He nodded to Field. "Carry on, Field, and lay these gun-cotton charges on the wires."

*Anderson won't be running any more half marathons or playing football for the battalion. Maybe I should help Captain Russell.*

# Chapter Eleven

*"I have been a stranger in a strange land."*
**Exodus 2:22**

"Well, Tulloch, I have some news for you," Colonel puffed furiously at his pipe. "Captain Russell has pulled strings, and the powers-that-be have obtained a transfer for you from the regiment to the Intelligence Bureau." He shook his head. "I don't want to lose a promising young officer, but the word of a mere regimental colonel has little weight, I'm afraid."

Tulloch took a deep breath. "How long for, sir?"

"How long is a piece of string, Tulloch?" Colonel said. "We'll be sorry to lose you, and I hope you find your way back to the battalion. The best of luck, Tulloch."

"Thank you, sir."

Tulloch knew that military life was a series of arrivals and departures, but this one seemed very abrupt. He said farewell to his platoon and brother officers, who were equally surprised as he left.

*After losing Anderson to that Italian mine, I can see the point in hunting down the agent, although I hope it's only a short assignment. I am not made for an intelligence posting.*

When a utilitarian fifteen-hundredweight truck picked Tulloch up the following morning, a cheery Baluchi driver transported him in a dusty ride to a nondescript building within the British cantonment in Peshawar. Captain Russell welcomed him with a smile and a handshake.

"We need you, Tulloch," Russell said. "We'll put you through some intensive training and then set you loose on the Frontier with a few picked men."

"What will I be doing, sir?" Tulloch asked.

"Searching for Mussolini's agent," Russell's smile did not fade. "You're the only man who might recognise him."

"That's a tall order, sir, given the size of the Frontier, unless the local Pashtun will want to help."

Russell laughed. "Oh, they'll cut your throat in a second if they get their hands on you. That's why we're going to train you first." He smiled as if he had said something vastly amusing. "We're sending you on a special intelligence course for three months. The Intelligence Bureau in the Home Department of the Government of India runs these courses in the security intelligence responsibilities it shares with the military. They're normally in Simla, but you'll have to make do with Quetta. I've tailored the course to your requirements naturally."

"Oh, naturally," Tulloch agreed.

"The language faculty is part of the Department of Military Training," Russell said, leaning forward. "Are you ready?"

Tulloch grinned as the novelty of the experience suddenly appealed. "I am," he said.

"Good man," Russell said, handing over a buff envelope. "Your travel documents are enclosed."

After a tedious journey by rail and road, Tulloch arrived at the Staff College at Quetta, where he found a score of intense instructors and even more officers. Quetta was in Baluchistan, near the Afghan border and the road to Kandahar, with views of high ragged hills.

"You are Lieutenant Tulloch," a beaming academic with shining spectacles and a grip like a wrestler said. "Come in and learn, my boy, come in and learn."

Most students were senior in rank to Tulloch and avoided him as they concentrated on their studies. After the satisfaction of command, Tulloch found the college restrictive, if interesting.

"What's your name?" An intense instructor with piercing eyes asked.

"Tulloch, sir."

"I'm Colonel Montgomery. I haven't seen you in my classes. Why are you here?"

"To learn Urdu and Pashto, sir, and whatever else I can pick up."

Montgomery nodded, with his head tilted slightly to the side. The medals on his chest told of active service in the Great War. "Ah, going to the Frontier, are you?"

"Yes, sir."

"You're from the Lothian Rifles," Montgomery said. "They're based at Razmak. Why have you come to the Staff College when your unit is on active operations?"

"I was sent here, sir. I didn't have a choice," Tulloch said, resenting the implication.

"I see." Montgomery eyed Tulloch up and down. "You'd better learn a European language as well. The next war will be in Europe." He marched away with his shoulders back, jaunty and confident.

The training was as intense as Russell suggested, cramming Pushtu and Urdu into Tulloch's head and teaching him advanced fieldcraft and more small arms weapons training.

"Have you ever read Kipling's book *Kim*?" The bespectacled instructor asked.

"When I was at school," Tulloch replied cautiously.

"Welcome to the reality," the instructor replied. "Grow your beard, Tulloch. It will help disguise your face on the Frontier."

The self-defence training left Tulloch aching all over, and an instructor had him running over hills by day and night while teaching him about Pashtun culture and the Islamic religion.

"Family, feud, hospitality and religion," the instructor pushed home his lessons. "You must know how the tribesmen think and act, or you'll give yourself away, which won't be pleasant."

"No, sir," Tulloch agreed.

"You're not going to pretend to be a Pashtun," the instructor reminded. "You will be in the background, part of the scenery, but you must ensure you don't stand out from the crowd."

"I'll try to blend, sir," Tulloch promised. He worked harder even than he had at Sandhurst until he lived, thought, and dreamed of the Pashtun culture.

Despite its proximity to Afghanistan, Quetta did not share the same tense atmosphere as Peshawar, and Tulloch saw some British women moving around the bazaar. One tall, dark-haired woman caught his eye, and he found himself staring at her for longer than was polite. When she realised he was looking, the woman frowned, smiled and turned away. She waved to him behind her back, just a small flutter of her fingers, and Tulloch wondered if she was inviting him to talk. Before he stepped closer, the intense Montgomery appeared.

"Don't neglect your studies, Lieutenant," Montgomery said, and when Tulloch looked again, the woman was gone.

After Tulloch had spent three exhausting months in Quetta, Russell arrived at the college and stood before him in his tiny room.

"You're not ready yet, Tulloch. You'll never be fully ready, but we don't have time to waste and don't know what trouble this Italian fellow may be stirring up. I'm giving you an escort of a section of Scouts."

Tulloch sat on the only chair in the room. "Nobody has told me what I am supposed to do, sir? Wander around Pashtun territory on the off chance that I might meet this Italian fellow?"

Russell gave his easy smile. "Didn't I say? I'm coming with you, Tulloch. You won't get rid of me as easily as that."

Tulloch nodded, not sure whether to be relieved or annoyed. On his own, he could make the decisions, while a senior officer would cramp his style. On the other hand, Russell knew the Pashtun people better than him and could keep them safe. "Yes, sir."

"I thought you'd be pleased," Russell said. "Get ready; we're moving in two days."

"That will give me time to inform the regiment where I'm going," Tulloch said.

Russell shook his head. "You can't tell anybody. Anything written can be read, and anything spoken can be overheard. From today onward, you say nothing to anybody."

"Yes, sir," Tulloch said.

---

THEY ENTERED THE KHYBER PASS ON A CARAVAN OF CAMELS, with an escort of four Scouts in Pashtun clothes. The British sentries eyed them through suspicious eyes.

"Rough-looking lot," one man growled in a Cumbrian accent.

"Look like Waziris to me," his companion agreed. "Probably the Fakir of Ipi going to rally the troops."

The Cumbrian glowered at Tulloch. "If I had my way, I'd put a bullet in you, mate."

Tulloch walked on. He had a momentary fear he might meet a detachment of the Lothians who would recognise him, then reasoned that such a scenario was unlikely. Dressed in Pashtun clothes and with an unruly three-month beard, it would be an observant soldier who would see through his disguise.

As soon as he entered the pass, Tulloch felt the atmosphere alter. He experienced the familiar tension and looked around at the British and Indian soldiers and the travellers through the narrow sword slash through the hills that was the Khyber.

"March on, fellow Pashtun," Russell encouraged in Pashtu.

Tulloch found that living as a Pashtun was vastly different from living as a British officer, although he mixed as little as possible with the indigenous natives. The British and Sikh soldiers treated him with studied suspicion; most other Indian soldiers avoided his company, while the ordinary Pashtun and Afghan villagers were hospitable to travellers.

Over the next few weeks and months, Russell left the talking to Russell and the Scouts as he scrutinised every face in his hunt for the Italian agent. He grew used to Pashtun food and living beside campfires, to hearing Pashto spoken in place of English or Urdu, and to the sudden changes of weather so typical in the hill country.

They drove their camels through the valleys to the Afghan frontier, where a stark notice stated: "It is absolutely forbidden to cross this border into Afghan territory."

"What now?" Tulloch asked.

"Now we trade," Russell told him. "We make camp at the side of the road here, with Indian soldiers half a mile away on one nation and Afghan soldiers on the other, and we watch the world go by." Russell gave his slow grin. "We're hiding from both in a place neither will suspect, yet half the traffic of Afghanistan passes this way. If the Italian agent comes, you will recognise him."

"I'll try," Tulloch said.

"In the meantime, I'll send out a couple of Scouts and wait until my spies report to me." Russell was quite at home in this troubled borderland with his bearded face relaxed and the Lee-Enfield a fixture across his shoulders. Tulloch thought of the long line of adventures out here, from Alexander Burnes to John Nicholson, and knew that Russell would have fitted perfectly well into that company.

"Do you have spies along the Frontier?" Tulloch asked.

They spoke in Pashtu, with Russell chewing betel nuts and stroking his fine brown beard. "We operate with a network of informers," he said. "We pay them, and they gather information for us."

"Can you trust them?" Tulloch asked.

Russell laughed. "As much as I can trust any Pashtun. Some are probably working for me and the other side."

"Will the Italian fellow know about us?"

"He'll know as much about me as I do about him," Russell said, suddenly serious. "That's where you come in, Tulloch. He doesn't know about you, which gives us an advantage."

Tulloch frowned. "Are you using yourself as bait, Russell?"

"I am," Russell admitted and tapped his rifle. "That's why I carry this." He put a hand on the long knife on his belt. "And this. If any Pashtun comes for me, I'll find out who sent him, and we'll have the Italian."

"That's a dangerous game," Tulloch said.

"It's worth it," Russell replied, spitting betel juice onto the ground. "If the Italian kills me, I depend on you to square the account."

"I only came here to identify the man," Tulloch said. "I'm not an assassin."

"A general Pashtun rising could tie up tens of thousands of British soldiers for months or years," Russell reminded. "If Congress decided to join in, Britain would be too busy in Asia to become involved in Europe. Think of a second Mutiny, Tulloch."

"Colonel Montgomery advised me to watch Europe," Tulloch said.

"I've met Montgomery," Russell told him. "An intense sort of man." They looked up as one of the Scouts appeared at the edge of the ring of firelight.

"Yes, Nazo?" Russell asked.

Nazo glanced at Tulloch.

"You can talk freely, Nazo," Russell told him.

Nazo squatted beside the fire. "I heard there are foreign agitators in the Hurmaz Valley," he said.

Russell nodded. "Thank you, Nazo," he said. "We'll leave before dawn, leaving the camels here. The drivers will care for them."

———

RUSSELL CROUCHED BENEATH THE SKYLINE, LOOKING DOWN AT the narrow Humaz Valley with patches of cultivated land beneath the brooding hills. Tulloch lay on one side and Nazo on the other, all three ignoring the rain that wept from bruised clouds that concealed the peaks of the highest mountains.

Tulloch removed his Italian binoculars from beneath his clothes and scanned the landscape, careful not to allow any stray light to reflect from the lens. "It all looks perfectly normal to me."

Three villages sat on the valley floor, surrounded by fields and with a central river running cold at the side.

"And to me," Russell said. He glanced back to the remaining three Scouts, who were their constant companions. "We'll move closer."

They eased down the hill, with Tulloch using all his training and the experience of the months searching the Frontier to move silently and unseen. He knew he would never be as expert as the Scouts but was more silent than most British soldiers and did not dislodge any loose stones on his descent. Russell held up his hand to stop them at a transverse ridge halfway down the slope and checked again.

The valley was narrow, and Tulloch studied the three walled villages, each with its watchtower. Small fields abutted each village, with crops and fruit trees, while sheep and goats grazed on the lower slopes of the hills. Tulloch traversed his binoculars left and right, searching for anything unusual. The rain showed no signs of easing, hammering down on the huddled goat herds and the flat-roofed houses within each village.

"I can't see anything untoward, Russell. Did your spies tell you anything you haven't told me?"

Russell smiled. "You're learning, Tulloch. No, they didn't say much. They told me a foreigner was in the valley, moving from village to village and spreading anti-British propaganda."

Tulloch studied the closest village, where a watchman stood on the tower with a Lee-Enfield on his shoulder, trying to shelter from the rain in a corner of the chest-high wall. "So, this foreigner may or may not be our man, sir, and he may or may not be in any of these villages."

"That's correct," Russell said. "We'll sit here and watch for movement. The Pashtun are a very patient people, and we must emulate them."

Tulloch settled behind a tuft of rough grass and fixed his binoculars on each village in turn. After an hour, the women began to return from the fields, with the sound of their voices and laughter distorted by the rain and clouds.

Towards sunset, Azeem, one of the Scouts, gestured with his head as the great gate of the central village opened, with the watchman peering down from his perch.

Tulloch focussed his binoculars on the gate as five men rode out. The two outriders were broad-shouldered, with bandoliers of ammunition across their chests and Lee-Enfield rifles protruding from their shoulders. The three central men rode in a V formation, with the leading man riding a sturdy Kabul pony. Tulloch watched him for a moment, studying his bearded features and casting his mind back to the man with whom he had wrestled on the stony ridge.

"I think that's the man I saw, sir."

Russell glanced sharply at him. "You think? Aren't you sure?"

"No, sir," Tulloch said. "I'll have to get closer to be sure."

Russell eased forward his rifle, worked the bolt, and aimed at the leading man.

"He's too far away, damn the man." He lowered the weapon without firing.

Tulloch watched the riders trot down the valley. "They're going into that last village, sir," he said as the gate swung open.

Russell nodded. "Then so shall we," he said quietly. "Was that the man you saw or not?"

Tulloch considered for a moment. "I am not certain, sir, but I think it was."

"Our lives are on the line here, Tulloch. If it was, it's worth our while going after him. If not, we'd be putting ourselves in pointless danger entering that Waziri village."

Tulloch nodded. "Yes, sir, I am aware of that."

"Well then, man?"

Tulloch knew the fate of the patrol, and perhaps the entire mission depended on him. "We go in," he decided, forcing a smile. It was better to make a wrong decision than to be indecisive.

Russell looked at him. "As you say," he agreed quietly.

They waited until night when darkness clamped down on the valley, and the sound of the central river was loud in the still air, and then Russell gave the order to move. Tulloch took a deep breath and eased down the slope, stopped when he dislodged a stone and waited for three achingly long minutes before continuing. The silence seemed to press on him, stiflingly oppressive, as if the surrounding hills were listening to his movements and thoughts.

The watchman on the tower was alert, but save for Tulloch's single stumble, the men were experts and moved slowly and silently towards the village.

Russell watched the watchman. When he turned away to peruse the far side of the valley, Russell silently mouthed "Now," and Tulloch and the others climbed the rubble and mud wall, easing into the village and crouching until everybody was present. Russell was last and counted his men, his eyes gleaming in the dark.

"We'll get rid of the watchman first," he spoke in Pashtu, which Tulloch now understood. "Wait here."

The tower had a small wooden door at the bottom with internal stairs, and Russell climbed rapidly and quietly. He returned within five minutes, wiping his knife.

"You two get ready to open the gate," Russell ordered two of the Scouts. "The rest come with me. The agent will be in the headman's enclosure. This way."

They moved silently through the village, with each self-contained home behind mud walls, where the man and his family lived in relatively secure isolation. When a dog barked further up the valley, the raiders slid into the shadows and remained still, invisible to any casual glance. The barking rose to a crescendo and ended, so only a slight breeze disturbed the silence.

The headman lived at the end of the village furthest from the watchtower, with the ubiquitous mud wall and heavy wooden door. Russell slid into the shadow of the wall and nodded to Nazo and then to the wall.

Without a word, Nazo eased into the headman's compound, and within two minutes, he removed the bar inside the door and pulled it wide enough to permit access but not sufficient to attract the watchman's attention. Russell led the others inside.

"Keep the door ajar," he murmured. "We might have to make a hasty exit."

When a dog within the village started barking, they froze in the shadow of a wall until somebody quietened the animal with shouts and what sounded like a brutal kick. Tulloch took a deep breath to control his breathing and realised that Nazo was shaking. Strangely, that helped steady Tulloch. *If even a Pashtun feels the strain, there is nothing wrong with me being nervous.*

They waited another five minutes before Russell moved again, heading for the largest compound. Tulloch heard the murmur of voices inside and a high-pitched male laugh, followed by a deep voice.

Russell nodded to Nazo and Azeem, who took up positions

outside the buildings with their rifles ready. "You Scouts stay outside and grab anybody who tries to escape. Come in if you think we need help." He gestured to Tulloch to accompany him.

"You're the only man who can identify the spy."

Tulloch nodded, fighting his nerves. He remembered the blast of the mine and Private Anderson staring at the bloody stump where his foot had been.

"On the count of three," Russell said, drawing his revolver. "One, two, and three!" He booted in the door and ran inside, with Tulloch at his heels.

Five men lounged on low couches around a Bokhara carpet, with rifles leaning against the wall behind them. Three were undoubtedly Waziris, while Tulloch immediately recognised a fourth. Despite the man's beard and Pashtun clothing, he had a presence that made him stand out from his companions.

"That man!" Tulloch shouted, pointing to the Italian agent. The Waziris reacted by reaching for their weapons, with one grabbing his rifle and another drawing the long knife at his waist. The knifeman threw himself forward, snarling as he thrust at Russell, who fired first. His bullet hit the Waziri in the chest, knocking the man backward onto the floor. Tulloch ducked as the second Waziri fired, then squeezed the trigger of his rifle and saw the bullet spin the man around. He worked the bolt and fired again, hitting the Waziri in the face, blowing half his head off in a spray of blood, bones, and brains.

The Italian drew a small pistol from inside his clothes and fell to his knees, shouting something Tulloch did not catch. One of the other men glanced around and dived for the door. Russell spun around and fired, catching the escaping man in the leg. The man yelled and collapsed, writhing on the ground as bright blood spurted from his leg.

Tulloch fired at the spy, aiming to wound rather than kill, but the Italian was a moving target. Tulloch's bullet missed and hit the third man, who crumpled to the ground with his mouth wide open in shock.

"Hold him!" Russell shouted, aiming at the Italian without firing. Tulloch jumped on the man, only for the Waziri he had wounded to take hold of his leg and bite into his thigh. Tulloch grunted and kicked the warrior away, saw he was drawing a knife and shot him in the chest.

While the wounded Waziri distracted Tulloch, the Italian took a snapshot at Russell, missed and ran through the door, with Tulloch and Russell firing at him. Nazo grabbed at him, but the Italian elbowed him in the throat, dropped to the ground, rolled away, rose, and ran faster than Tulloch believed possible. Russell scooped up something from the floor and stuffed it inside his jacket as the wounded man crawled for the door, trailing blood, until one of the Scouts grabbed him.

"Well done, Azeem," Russell shouted. "Put a tourniquet on his leg and take him with us. Did the Italian get clear?"

"Yes, sahib," Nazo replied, looking over his shoulder with his rifle ready to fire.

The shooting had roused the village, with men emerging from their houses, carrying rifles, and searching for the source of the noise.

"That's a pity, but it can't be helped," Russell said. "Time to get out. Run for the gate and take the prisoner with us."

When the captive protested, Russell thrust his pistol into his mouth. "You're not a Pashtun!" He said. "You're European!"

"Come on!" Tulloch said as a group of Waziris moved purposefully towards them. "Azeem! Nazo! Bring the prisoner!"

The Scouts half-carried and half-dragged the captive towards the far-too-distant gate, ignoring his whimpers and yells.

"If anybody looks aggressive," Russell ordered. "Shoot them. There's too much at stake to worry about niceties."

Azeem grinned in complete acceptance. They moved quickly, ignoring the villagers' demands for information until one of the Waziris levelled his rifle.

Nazo fired first, and within a few moments, the raiders were dodging bullets and firing back at the Waziris.

"Come on, you!" Tulloch grabbed the prisoner's shoulder and dragged him, protesting loudly, past the compounds. A dozen dogs were barking at once, a woman was screaming, and somebody had let loose a herd of goats, which ran between the houses, creating more confusion.

"Keep moving," Russell ordered, firing his revolver at a dimly seen man. One of the villagers brought a flickering torch, so yellow light danced between the compounds, allowing the Waziris to discern friends from foes. Other villagers followed his example, and Russell cursed when a bullet kicked up a fountain of dust at his feet.

"They're getting closer!"

Tulloch agreed, although at least the woman had stopped her high-pitched screaming. He saw a man dart behind the corner of a house, released the prisoner, knelt, fired, worked the bolt of his rifle and fired again. He fancied he saw a spurt of dried mud where one of his bullets had landed. The tribesmen ducked back, and Tulloch grabbed the prisoner again.

"The Scouts are at the gate," Russell put his arm around the limping captive to help him, but as they approached the gates, two Scouts pushed them shut.

"Open the gates!" Russell roared. "It's us!"

The Scouts lowered their rifles to point at the raiders. One man knelt and took deliberate aim at Russell.

"Turncoats!" Russell said and shot the kneeling Scout. The second man knelt and fired, with his bullet crashing into Russell's stomach. He grunted and doubled over, still holding his revolver, as an ominous red stain crept over his clothes.

"Shoot him!" Russell gasped, "For God's sake, shoot him!"

Tulloch and Azeem fired simultaneously. The Scout crumpled, kicking, and Azeem worked the bolt of his rifle, took deliberate aim, and fired again. The bullet smashed into the turncoat, throwing him back. "That was my cousin," he said and spat on the ground.

Russell pushed himself upright. "Get out," he ordered. "Get the prisoner back to Peshawar."

"Come on, sir," Tulloch hesitated. He pushed the prisoner towards the gate and held Russell's arm. "You can make it."

"No," Russell groaned. "I'm gut shot. Tulloch!" He raised an agonised face. "Take this!" He handed over the sheaf of documents he had lifted from the headman's floor. "Get it to Peshawar. Colonel Clark."

"Yes, sir," Tulloch tucked the documents away. "Come on, sir; don't give up!"

Russell shook his head as his voice rose in panic. "Don't leave me here. Shoot me! For God's sake, shoot me!"

"What?" Tulloch hesitated. "I can't," he looked at the open gate, where the Scouts had dragged the wounded prisoner outside. Nazo was waiting, firing his rifle at any villager who showed himself. The dog's barking persisted as a background to everything that happened, and the goats continued to roam, watching proceedings through their yellow eyes. The villagers were out in force, creeping closer as they fired their rifles. A bullet whined past Tulloch's head, ruffling his turban. Nazo fired back.

"Come on, sahib! There are too many of them!"

Russell glanced over his shoulder. "For God's sake, shoot me!" Tulloch had never seen such naked fear as on Russell's face. "They'll flay me alive!" Russell screamed, lifted his pistol to his mouth and squeezed the trigger. The hammer fell on an empty chamber, and he tried again, with the same result.

The villagers were running from their houses, men and women together, crowding closer. Tulloch fired, worked the bolt of his rifle, and fired again. He heard Nazo and Azeem firing and saw spurts of dust rising around him.

"Tulloch!" Russell screamed. "Don't let them take me alive!"

"God forgive me," Tulloch prayed, aimed his rifle at Russell's head and fired. He felt the weapon's vicious kick and fired again, seeing Russell's skull explode. "God forgive me," Tulloch whispered again as nausea rose in his throat. *Now I am a murderer. I have murdered a British officer.*

"Sahib!" Azeem shouted and fired into the approaching Waziris. Tulloch ran from the village, feeling sick but aware he had committed an act of kindness rather than murder.

"Where to, sir?" Nazo asked as they scrambled away from the village, dragging the wounded prisoner. Tulloch took the rear-guard, turning every few seconds to watch the village. He realised that with Russell dead, he was in command and had to make the decisions.

"The first thing is to get away from these Waziris," Tulloch said as the pursuers erupted from the village behind them. He took a snapshot into the mob, worked the bolt and followed Azeem.

# Chapter Twelve

*Everyone is ready to speak ill of a stranger.*
**Aeschylus: *The Suppliants***

"Up the hill," Tulloch ordered. "Carry the prisoner if he won't walk!"

They scrambled up the slope, with Tulloch in the rear, turning to fire his rifle when a Waziri bullet smashed into the rocks beside them. One of the Waziris still held a torch, which gave Tulloch a mark to aim for, so he sprayed bullets around the light. When he ran out of ammunition, he stopped to load, cursing the time the procedure took, and rolled a couple of large boulders down the slope in the hope of causing a small avalanche.

"Sahib!" Nazo hissed. "We must keep moving!"

Tulloch heard the villagers pursuing, fired another clip and reloaded before scrambling back uphill. Nazo and Azeem were waiting for him at the ridge they had occupied previously, with Nazo pressing a hand over the prisoner's mouth.

"Keep moving," Tulloch ordered. "The further away from here we are by daylight, the better."

"How about him?" Nazo a thumb toward the prisoner.

"We'll take him with us," Tulloch said. "He's not badly hurt." He knew he sounded callous, but the well-being of a foreign spy who was aiding Pashtuns to kill and maim British soldiers was not important. Tulloch thought of Russell's death and looked away. "Come on!"

They moved on, dragging the wounded prisoner with them despite his protests and whimpers of pain. Even in the dark, the Scouts found their way, and after his weeks living with them, Tulloch kept up. Rather than retrace their route, he ordered them to find the closest British base.

"Any base, sahib?" Azeem asked.

"Any base," Tulloch agreed.

He heard shouting behind them and knew the Waziris were still following, no doubt waking the countryside to search for the infidels.

"Don't stop," Tulloch ordered, driving his men relentlessly, with the prisoner sobbing with a combination of weariness and pain. "How far to the nearest British base?"

"Not far," Azeem said, which, Tulloch knew, could mean anything to a Pashtun. "Tomorrow, sahib, or the next day."

They slogged across knife-edge ridges where eagles screamed beneath them, and the treacherous scree slithered underfoot, and they crossed rushing rivers of bitter-cold water. Twice Tulloch hung back to ambush their pursuers and fired long-range shots at dimly seen men. On one occasion, Azeem entered a village to improve the dressings on the prisoner's leg, and with the famed hospitality of the Pashtuns, the villagers helped with no questions asked.

"They'll spread the news," Tulloch said.

"Yes, sahib," Azeem agreed, "but the prisoner will live."

Tulloch tried to question their captive, speaking in Urdu, Pashto, and English. The man said nothing, shaking his head to every question as if he were either dumb, deaf, or stubborn. When Nazo offered to loosen his tongue with his knife and the red-hot embers of a fire, Tulloch refused.

"We don't do that sort of thing."

Although Nazo did not argue, Tulloch could see the Scout thought him a strange man, and perhaps he was. Every hour, Tulloch remembered how he had shot Russell and knew the memory would haunt him for years, if not forever. He remembered how Russell had warned him the Frontier would change him and smiled sardonically as they negotiated yet another gaunt mountain with a rain-swollen stream hammering down the slope.

As an aircraft droned above, seemingly belonging to a different world, Tulloch wondered if clean sheets still existed somewhere or if he had only dreamed of tram cars and radios, flushing toilets and the soft voice of a Scottish woman.

"Come on, lads," Tulloch encouraged as he dragged the stubborn prisoner up the slope, with a small herd of goats watching from a distance. He recognised the shape of the hills, with a distinctive cleft he had studied through his binoculars and could almost smell British soldiers. "Not long now."

Nazo grinned, keeping watch on the left flank, with Azeem on the right, Scouts with whom Tulloch knew he could dare anything.

"Not long now, Sahib," Nazo agreed and laughed.

They topped the ridge, keeping low, and looked ahead to see another valley beneath, with the ubiquitous Pashtun walled villages surrounded by small fields. Beyond the valley, the land rose in tortured, savage hills.

"When Allah made Afghanistan," Azeem said, "he laughed at the joke he played on mankind."

Tulloch laughed with him. "Not long now," he said.

---

EVEN FROM A DISTANCE, TULLOCH KNEW THE ENCAMPMENT was British. There was a regularity in its construction that seemed unnatural, imposed on the landscape, while the lights on the tall stands reflected on the strands of barbed wire that stretched around the perimeter. "Keep back just now," Tulloch ordered his Scouts. "Some of these sentries aren't used to the country yet."

"Yes, sahib," Azeem said, looking around as Nazo thrust the prisoner into the shelter of a rock.

Tulloch stepped into the middle of the track and approached slowly to prove he was not attempting to sneak in. When he saw the pith helmets of a British regiment on the walls and the flash of light on metal, he spread his arms wide with his rifle slung across his back.

"Who goes there?" The challenge came immediately. "I see you!"

"Friend!" Tulloch shouted, stopping where he was. "Lieutenant Tulloch of the Lothian Rifles with two Tochi Scouts and a prisoner."

"Advance and be recognised!" The voice was pure Northumberland. "Come closer, or I'll shoot!"

Tulloch stepped forward into the arc of light and stood still with his arms outspread. He could see his shadow looking like a crucifix and hoped he would not be sacrificed on the altar of mistaken identity.

"Who did you say you were?" The Northumbrian asked again.

"Lieutenant Tulloch of the Lothian Rifles," Tulloch repeated.

"You don't look like a Jock," the sentry sounded suspicious. "Stand there!"

Tulloch stood still with the Scouts supporting the prisoner. "Not long now," he murmured, and Azeem laughed.

"Maybe not long for this world, sahib," he said. Nodding to his left, where two British soldiers trained a Lewis gun on them. "Allah is waiting to welcome us."

"Sergeant!" The sentry bellowed. "There's a Paythan here claiming to be a Jock. Should I shoot him?"

"Not much difference between them," the sergeant joined the sentry and glowered at Tulloch. "Only shoot him if he is a

Jock, Glendinning. The Paythans are more civilised. Come closer, you, so that I can get a look at you."

Tulloch took a step forward, keeping his head up and his hands away from his rifle.

"Ugly looking blighter, isn't he?" the sergeant said pleasantly. "Who did you say you were, mate?"

"Lieutenant Douglas Tulloch, of the Lothian Rifles, Sergeant," Tulloch found difficulty thinking in English after weeks of speaking Pashtu. "With two Tochi Scouts and a prisoner."

"You sound a bit Scotch," the sergeant allowed. "You're a long way from the Lothians, though. Come here and move slowly, or you'll be going back to Jockland in a wooden box."

Tulloch took another step closer, aware that half a dozen rifles and a light machine gun were pointing at him.

The sergeant walked from the perimeter to study him. "Who commands the Lothians?" He kept his rifle trained on Sturrock's face.

"Colonel Pringle, Sergeant, with Major Hume as adjutant, and you call me sir," Tulloch used his best cut glass accent.

The sergeant stiffened to attention and saluted. "Sorry, sir. You can't be too careful on the Frontier."

"You're quite right to be cautious, Sergeant," Tulloch said. "Now, let my Scouts and my prisoner in, and tell the duty officer I am here."

"Yes, sir," the sergeant replied. "Open the gate for the officer, lads! What the hell are you waiting for? Jump to it!"

———

CAPTAIN HARPER NODDED AS TULLOCH SAT OPPOSITE HIM IN his quarters, with a map of Waziristan pinned on a board behind him and a pile of papers on the desk in front. "You think your prisoner may be an Italian spy? What do you intend to do with him, Tulloch? Remember that Italy is ostensibly a friendly country."

Tulloch sat back, luxuriating in the environment. "I don't honestly know, sir. I'll hand him on to higher authority as quickly as possible, write my report and return to my regiment." The thought of being back in the Lothians, even in Razmak, was like going home.

"You'll hand him to somebody higher than me, I hope," Captain Harper said. "We expect a supply convoy tomorrow. Stay here tonight, and you can leave when it returns. Take your prisoner with you." He grinned. "I don't want him here in case he attracts unwanted attention."

Tulloch hitched a lift in a fifteen hundredweight truck with his silent prisoner and the Scouts beside him. They rattled to Razmak to find the Lothians had departed, and there Tulloch said goodbye to Nazo and Azeem, who returned to their parent regiment. Handing the prisoner and the documents Russell had recovered to the Military Police, Tulloch waited for orders in Razmak, playing billiards and developing a taste for whisky before eventually crossing India by rail and road to arrive in Simla at the foothills of the Himalayan mountains.

"Report to Lieutenant-Colonel Clark at Army Headquarters in Simla," the orders had said, with no other details.

Tulloch knew that the Army Headquarters and the Government of India moved from Delhi to Simla in the summer, as they worked better in the cool hills rather than the sultry heat of the plains.

"Who?" a smiling major asked when Tulloch requested directions. "Simla is bristling with colonels of all sorts and varieties," he said. "I don't know a Colonel Clark." He stepped to the filing cabinet at the back of his office and raked through his folders. "Give me a minute, Lieutenant. Oh, here we are; Colonel Andrew Clark, Intelligence Bureau, Home Department. That's why I don't know him. I don't have many dealings with the intelligence wallahs. They're a queer lot, you know."

"So I've heard, sir," Tulloch agreed.

"Ah, there we are," the major handed over an address. "Best of British, young sir, and don't let him cajole you into anything you don't want to do."

"I'll try not to, sir," Tulloch said.

Colonel Clark was undoubtedly the untidiest officer Tulloch had ever met. He operated from a large bungalow on the northern edge of Simla, with a pair of cord trousers on his lower half and an ancient, patched khaki top above. His hair was over his ears, and he wore a broad silver wedding ring.

"Tulloch!" The intensity of Clark's eyes immediately dispersed any idea that the colonel was merely a harmless eccentric. "Glad you could make it. Come in," he ushered Tulloch into his abode and nodded to the tall Sikh on guard. "Thank you, Amar. Please ensure we are not disturbed by anybody."

"Sahib!" The Sikh saluted and stepped back outside.

Colonel Clark sat on a padded leather chair behind a cluttered desk and gestured for Tulloch to sit opposite. "Well, Tulloch, I read your report. You had fun, didn't you?"

Tulloch removed a small dog from the seat of a second leather chair before he sat. "We lost Captain Russell, sir, and the Italian agent escaped."

"I know." Clark lifted a document Tulloch recognised as his report. "The Italian agent escaped."

"I'm afraid so, sir."

"And Russell got shot," Clark said, leaning back in his chair.

"Yes, sir. It's in the report," Tulloch said as the dog settled on his feet.

"You'll be blaming yourself for shooting him," Clark fixed Tulloch with a look that could have cracked glass.

"Yes, sir," Tulloch admitted.

"Well, don't," Clark said. "You did him a favour. The Pashtuns would keep him alive and in unbearable agony for days. You did the right thing, and Russell knew that."

"Thank you, sir," Tulloch knew the memory would continue to haunt him.

"I'm surprised that a couple of the Scouts batted for the opposition," Clark continued. "That's highly unusual; they're normally true to their salt."

"Maybe the Fakir got to him," Tulloch said.

"Maybe. You brought back your patrol and a prisoner," Clark continued. "That's a success. You also brought back this." He held up the packet of documents Russell had retrieved from the village, now badly stained with Russell's blood. "I take it you did not try to read them."

"No, sir," Tulloch said. "I was too busy trying to remain alive."

Clark's smile looked genuine. "I may be cold-blooded, but the contents of these documents were worth a life, even that of Captain Russell."

"What do they say, sir?"

Clark pondered for a moment. "What I'm about to tell you will go no further, Tulloch. Understood?"

"Understood, sir," Tulloch said.

"You may know that the present Amir of Afghanistan, Zahur Shah, is as pro-British as any Afghan ruler can be and still retain his position."

Tulloch nodded. "I don't take much interest in politics, sir."

"You should, Tulloch," Clark rebuked him. "The military is only an arm of the politicians. Anyway, the Italians, and probably the Germans, wish to depose Zahur Shah and replace him with Ammanullah, who was a previous Amir and presently resides in Rome."

Tulloch sat straighter. "This affair is deeper than one agent stirring up the Waziris, then."

"As I said, Tulloch, you should take more interest in politics. Ammanullah has settled nicely in Rome and found himself an Italian mistress and some very highly placed Italian friends." Clark shuffled the documents. "I strongly suspect that

Ammanullah's girl is a very close friend of the Italian foreign ministry."

"Do the documents confirm your suspicions, sir?"

Clark nodded. "Yes, Tulloch," he said. "Pietro Quanoni, the Italian minister in Kabul, is fermenting trouble along the Frontier to keep us busy here." He tapped the documents. "With a great chunk of our army and air force tied up on the Frontier, Italy will have an easier job if they move against Egypt or the Sudan."

"Is that in the documents Captain Russell retrieved, sir?" Tulloch asked.

"The documents you brought back hint at the possibility," Clark told him. "Now we know Quanoni is sending agents to the Fakir of Ipi."

"Was the man who escaped one of them, sir?"

Clark nodded again. "He was, as was the man you captured. A couple of my more unscrupulous colleagues are interviewing him even as we speak." He opened a drawer of his desk, removed a file and passed it over to Tulloch. "Do you recognise any of these men?"

The file contained a mixture of photographs and line drawings of men. Tulloch leafed through them, shaking his head. "No, no; not him." He stopped at one grainy photograph. "That's the lad I brought in."

"Antonio De Luca," Clark said. "We have him on file, and we'll soon find out what he knows."

Tulloch leafed through a couple more images and stopped again. "That's the man!"

Clark took the black and white drawing. "Are you sure?"

"Yes, sir. He has a face you would not notice in a group of three, but I sensed something powerful in that man."

Clark turned the image over. "That is Francesco Giorano," he said. "The name will mean nothing to you, yet he's one of the most dangerous men in Europe, one of Italy's best agents. We've never managed to get a photograph of him, and we didn't know for sure he was on our Frontier." He looked up at Tulloch. "Well done, Lieutenant."

"Can we counter them, sir?" Tulloch asked.

Clark's smile was slow and welcome. "Now we know for certain that they are here," he tapped the documents, "and what they're doing, yes. They're pushing Fascism to the Fakir of Ipi." Tulloch did not anticipate his laugh. "The Italians don't know their man. We'll spread counter propaganda that Fascism is a godless doctrine, which will destroy any hope the Italians have of persuading the devoutly Muslim Fakir." He sighed. "That's not your concern, Tulloch, unless you wish to transfer to the intelligence bureau?"

"No, thank you, sir. I'm happier as a regimental soldier."

Clark grunted. "I'll keep your name in mind for the future. Francesco Giorano is as slippery as an oil-slicked eel. Let's hope something nasty happens to him before he returns home to Mussolini. With the Italians now ensconced in Libya, Ethiopia and Somaliland and their fleet powerful in the Mediterranean, they're getting a bit too dangerous for my liking."

"Yes, sir. I wish I'd caught him."

"Next time," Clark said and shuffled the papers on his desk. "All right, Tulloch. Your battalion has sailed for home, so you'd better join them as soon as the next ship sails. In the meantime, enjoy the fleshpots of Simla. You'll have a few days to recover. I've had your possessions brought here and found you a bungalow."

"Thank you, sir," Tulloch said.

"Just one thing, Tulloch," Colonel Clark said. "Remember, what you've been doing remains with you. Don't discuss it with anybody."

"Yes, sir."

"That's all. Dismissed."

Tulloch left the bungalow with a sense of relief. He did not dislike Clark, but he was apprehensive the colonel might ask him to remain in the intelligence service.

# Chapter Thirteen

For the lips of a strange woman drop as a honeycomb, and her
   mouth is smoother than oil,
But her end is bitter as wormwood, sharp as a two-edged sword.
**Proverbs 5:3.4**

Tulloch could appreciate why the army and the government chose to spend the summer months at Simla. At an altitude of seven thousand feet, the climate was refreshingly cool, and the local mountain walks provided free exercise and expansive views over the Himalayan mountains. With time to spare, Tulloch joined the United Services Club, an entirely male environment that could have been transported from Queen Victoria's latter years with a smoking room complete with deep leather chairs in dark red.

"You must be Tulloch," the Sikh officer had a Connaught accent and bright blue eyes. "I'm MacBride."

Tulloch shook his hand.

"I've seen you stalking the hills and wearing out the library books," MacBride said. "You need company, my man, and not of the masculine variety. There's a Viceregal Ball tomorrow night, and you're invited."

"Am I?" Tulloch asked.

"You am," MacBride told him. "Wear your best bib and tucker, and if you don't have one, I can make arrangements to get you dressed to kill and pretty as a Parisian picture."

Tulloch felt something sink inside him. He had no desire to meet anybody else, let alone a woman.

"The fishing fleet is still here,"[1] MacBride said with a slow smile as Tulloch walked into the ballroom. He lifted his glass in salute. "They must have been waiting for you."

"I'm sure they were," Tulloch was ill at ease back in civilised company after so long in the wilds. He looked around the room with the officers in their dress uniforms and the women in bright colours sipping cocktails and looking elegant and unapproachable. He glimpsed himself in a mirror with his weather-darkened face, flint-hard eyes and a uniform that was now at least two sizes too large after the weight he had lost. *I don't fit in here,* he thought, excused himself to MacBride and headed for the exit.

"You look a little lost." The woman was tall, dark-haired, and carried an aroma of expensive perfume.

Tulloch started. He had not expected a woman to talk to him. "A little," he admitted, hoping she did not wish him to indulge in prolonged conversation.

"Me too," the woman said and held out a hand. "I am Amanda." Her lips curved in a smile that reached her sparkling grey eyes.

"How do you do? I am Douglas Tulloch." They shook hands, with Amanda's grip firmer than Tulloch had expected. He stood for a moment, unsure what to say. After so long speaking Urdu and Pashtu, even forming words in English was a struggle, while he had never been comfortable in female company.

"I've seen you before, I think," Amanda said, with a slight frown that quickly cleared. "Yes, in the bazaar in Quetta!"

Tulloch blinked, remembering the glimpse he had enjoyed before Montgomery had interrupted. "That's right," he agreed. "You waved to me."

Amanda smiled. "I hoped you might come with me," she said easily, as if she had known him for years.

"One of the senior lecturers arrived," Tulloch explained.

"Ah, I wondered." Amanda gestured to a waiter and lifted two glasses of wine from his tray. "You do drink, I presume?"

"A little," Tulloch said cautiously.

"Try everything in moderation," Amanda said, handing a glass to him. She sipped at her wine and screwed up her face. "Not that this stuff would encourage you to drink. It's awful!" She laughed. "Did you like Quetta?"

"I didn't see much of it except the college and some of the surrounding hills," Tulloch admitted. "I liked what I saw. It seemed a lively yet safe place."

"Did you cross the border into Afghanistan?" Amanda asked.

"No," Tulloch shook his head.

"I did," Amanda said. "My father had some sort of diplomatic mission to Kandahar. That is a fascinating city, Douglas. You'd love it. Did you know that Gaspar or Caspar, one of the three wise men, was said to have founded Kandahar?"

"No," Tulloch allowed Amanda to prattle on, which saved him the trouble. She was vaguely attractive, he thought, watching her. Certainly not a classical beauty, but there was something alluring about her.

"Shall we dance?" Amanda suggested. "The next one is a waltz, I believe." She tactfully removed Tulloch's glass when he moved towards the dance floor. "I'd best take this." She placed their glasses on the side table as the small orchestra began to play.

Tulloch had learned to dance as a youth but lacked practice, while Amanda moved as smoothly as an expert. He placed a hand on her back and felt her slide her palm into his.

"You have very hard hands," Amanda told him and smiled as Tulloch immediately relaxed his grip. "That was a compliment, Lieutenant Tulloch," she said. "I don't like men with soft hands."

"Thank you," Tulloch tried to think of a reciprocal compliment as he concentrated on keeping in step. Amanda guided him while making it appear as if he had led.

"You're very good at this," Tulloch said as the music ended, and they found seats at the side of the room.

"You're not," Amanda said, smiling to ease any sting. "When did you last dance?"

Tulloch thought back. "Many years ago," he admitted.

"What's your regiment? British or Indian Army?" Amanda glanced at his insignia. "Lothian Rifles. I thought they were back in Britain."

"They are," Tulloch said. "I got left behind." He was unsure how much he should admit.

"That was rather careless of you," Amanda said, smiling again.

"It was," Tulloch agreed. He signalled to a waiter, who brought Amanda champagne while Tulloch sipped a disappointing whisky.

"Thank you," Amanda said, cradling her champagne. "Where were you to get left behind?"

Tulloch smiled. "Nowhere special. What brings you to Simla?"

"Nothing special," Amanda placed a slender hand on Tulloch's forearm. "Does your colonel dislike you that he wants you to remain in India?"

"You're a very inquisitive lady," Tulloch kept his smile, although he wished he had left the room before Amanda approached him.

"And you're giving nothing away, Lieutenant Tulloch," Amanda replied.

Tulloch shook his head. "I was on duty, Amanda." He realised he did not know Amanda's surname.

"Not with your regiment," Amanda continued.

"I'll be with them as soon as possible," Tulloch told her.

Amanda nodded and finished her champagne. "Another dance, Douglas?"

"I'd love to, and I'll try not to trample your feet this time," Tulloch replied.

"That would be kind of you," Amanda said and lowered her voice. "You weren't that bad, Douglas; I was teasing."

About half the younger officers present were dancing when Tulloch and Amanda stepped onto the floor. Tulloch tried to copy the required steps and caught the rhythm. He realised Amanda was scrutinising him, shaking her head slightly when he made a mistake and nodding encouragement when he was successful.

"You're getting better," she said, holding his arm as they returned to their seats. "Now, you were telling me about your time in Quetta, I think?"

Tulloch smiled. "You were telling me about Kandahar and the magi."

"That's right," Amanda said. "I know one of us was telling something. You should smile more often, you know, Douglas. It suits you. Did I tell you that Baluchistan also had Biblical associations?"

"You did not," Tulloch replied. He liked the shape of her lips as she spoke as if she was rolling each syllable around her mouth.

"Ah," Amanda leaned closer with her eyes bright with the pleasure of imparting knowledge. "There's a mountain called *Takht-i-Suliman*, which means Solomon's Throne."

"I didn't know Solomon was in Baluchistan," Tulloch said, trying to remember his Bible. "I thought he married the Queen of Sheba."

Amanda patted his sleeve. "Listen and learn, Douglas. You see, according to the Pashtun people, Solomon was lonely, so he flew his magic carpet to India to find a wife. The ruler of India was impressed with this wise man from the west and found him a suitable lady, who he placed on his magic carpet and carried away."

Tulloch raised his eyebrows. "Oh?" He relaxed with the easy flow of her words.

Amanda continued. "Solomon was a happy man with his new bride, but she was not. She cried when she left India, so Solomon landed his carpet on a handy mountain to allow her a final view of India. That mountain has been known as Takht-i-Suliman ever since."

"I did not know any of that," Tulloch said as Amanda finished her story. "Folklore opens the door to the soul of a people." They sat in silence for a few moments, with Tulloch throwing sidelong looks at her. He decided that she was growing on him and wondered if she were one of the fishing fleet, trawling for a husband. "You didn't tell me why you are here." Tulloch reminded.

"Oh, I live in Simla during the summer," Amanda said. "My father's stationed here, you see." When she smiled, she looked younger than Tulloch had first imagined. He had estimated her age at about twenty-five, but now she looked about twenty-one or two.

Tulloch began to relax more, with the exit losing its appeal. "What's it like to live here?"

Amanda screwed her face up, which further reduced her age. "It can be very romantic, with balmy nights of bright, bright starry skies and a round white moon, with those high hills stretching to infinity. On a good day, I can have rickshaw rides with handsome young officers like yourself and all to the background of exotic Eastern aromas." She stopped and looked sideways at Tulloch. "That's one side of it. On the other side, we keep meeting the same people, so when I saw you, all shy and unsure and mysterious, I had to find out more."

Tulloch did not swallow the hints but allowed Amanda to continue, which she did.

"The residents in Simla share the same conversations, gossiping about each other's lives and affairs. You know the sort of thing, who is going out with who, who was at whose party and who was not invited, that sort of thing."

"It sounds a bit like the Officers' Mess," Tulloch said solemnly. "Men can gossip too."

"It can be so boring here," Amanda told him. "You're new blood, somebody interesting. The Lothians were at Peshawar and on the Frontier recently, weren't they? Up the Grim, as the swaddies would say."

"We were," Tulloch admitted.

"Were you involved in anything exciting?" Amanda asked, smiling into Tulloch's eyes.

Tulloch considered his reply. "That depends on what you call exciting," he replied.

Amanda narrowed her eyes. "Tell me what you did, Douglas. I seldom meet officers who have been on the Frontier, real soldiers, rather than poodle fakers."

"India is full of real soldiers," Tulloch said. "The Lothians had a skirmish or two with the Waziris. No more than any other regiment."

"Handsome young officers are meant to woo ladies by boasting of their prowess," Amanda said, teasing him with a subtle flick of her hair.

"I didn't have anything to boast about," Tulloch said, remembering Russell's face as his bullet hit him. He closed his eyes as the shame and self-loathing returned in full measure. "Nothing at all." He stood up. "Excuse me, please, Amanda." Placing his drink on the table, he left the ballroom and stumbled through the careless crowd.

Standing outside, Tulloch allowed the evening air to cool him down. He tried to push away the image of Russell's face and the terror in his voice as he pleaded for Tulloch to shoot him.

"Douglas?" Amanda had followed him. "Are you all right? Did I say something to upset you?"

Tulloch nodded. "I'm all right, thank you. Sorry, Amanda. Bad memories." He forced a smile.

"Do you want to share them?"

Tulloch wondered what this smiling young woman would say if he told her he had deliberately killed a wounded British officer. "Best not," he said. "Thank you."

Amanda stood beside him with their shoulders nearly touching. "It's a beautiful evening," she said, staring at the view. "I told you it was one of the advantages of living in Simla."

Tulloch took a deep breath, cursing himself for thinking bitter thoughts when an attractive young woman was talking to him. "You were entirely correct," he said. "It is beautiful here." He shifted closer so his left arm brushed against Amanda's shoulder. Pushing away his dark memories, he returned her smile.

"Well, Amanda?" Colonel Clark appeared from behind them with a pipe in his mouth. "How did Lieutenant Tulloch shape up?"

"He didn't say a word," Amanda stepped away from Tulloch.

"What?" Tulloch began, straightened to attention, and would have saluted until he remembered he was not wearing his hat. "Sorry, sir, I didn't see you there."

"Good," Colonel Clark replied to Amanda. "I didn't think he'd say anything." He nodded to Tulloch. "Well done, Tulloch." He removed his pipe, added tobacco to the bowl and puffed contentedly for a few moments. "It's a grand vista," he said. "I'll leave you young people alone." Winking at Amanda, he turned on his heel and stalked away.

Tulloch stood still for a moment, staring at the hills without seeing anything. "Were you testing me with all your questions?" He heard the edge in his voice.

"I'm sorry," Amanda did not face him. "Father asked me to."

Tulloch shrugged. "It doesn't matter." He remained still for a few moments as the music and laughter from the ballroom increased. He thought of the man he had shot. "We all do things we don't want to."

Amanda touched his arm. "I didn't like fooling you," she said.

"No," Tulloch replied and repeated, "It doesn't matter." Stepping away from the ball, he walked into the night, leaving Amanda alone on the balcony with the coolness of the night wrapped around her. Tulloch did not look back.

# Chapter Fourteen

*East and West, Home is best.*
**Charles Spurgeon:** *John Ploughman*

The troopship docked at Southampton, with the khaki-clad soldiers swarming down the gangplank into the welcoming British rain, joking about football, beer, and women.

With no regimental responsibilities, Tulloch caught his train for the long, tedious journey from the south of England to Scotland. His mood lightened as they crossed the Royal Border Bridge at Berwick-upon-Tweed, and he gazed out of the window with rising anticipation. Scotland had never looked more beautiful or peaceful, with the long green Border hills, the well-tended farms, and neat little towns and villages under their pall of smoke.

*Home again,* Tulloch thought and pushed away the memories of the Northwest Frontier, the mine blowing off Anderson's foot, and the recurring vision of his bullet killing Russell. *Put that behind you, Douglas. Reliving the past is unhealthy.*

Coming into Edinburgh was always a delight as the train steamed under the great Castle Rock and into Waverley Station, with the station announcer's voice echoing under the glass roof and the busy porters scurrying through the crowds. Tulloch breathed in the atmosphere of mixed smoke and steam, listened to the Scottish accents, collected his hand luggage, and walked up the Waverley Steps to Princes Street. He did not realise how much he missed his home city, where the Scott Monument reared skyward, and the busy trams pushed beside the dignified row of shops.

*Now I am undoubtedly home again.*

He spent a couple of nights with his parents, surprising them with his sudden appearance.

"You've lost weight," his mother said, examining him at arm's length the moment he stepped in the door. "And you're tanned dark with the sun. Tell us your adventures."

His father viewed him from a distance, looking pale and old behind his neat moustache, with his dark suit as neat as ever and his tie perfectly knotted.

"You've decided to visit, then," Father said. "Your regiment has been in Scotland for weeks."

"I was delayed in India," Tulloch said, surprised and a little pleased that his father followed the Lothians' movements.

"Well," his mother interrupted, throwing a frosty look at her husband. "It's good to have you back, Douglas. I'll put the kettle on."

Tulloch found his childhood house smaller than he remembered, with the serene streets of the New Town quiet after the hectic bustle of India and the tension and bloodshed of the Frontier.

As they sat around the old familiar table with the crisp white tablecloth and the green tea cosy over the best china teapot, Tulloch told them an edited version of the past years. He left out the horror and dwelled on the comradeship and sights he had seen. His mother watched him through concerned, knowing eyes, assessing the changes in her son and making allowances for his new maturity.

153

"You've got a medal!" Mrs. Tulloch pointed to the green-white-and-red ribbon on his chest.

"Only the Indian General Service Medal," Tulloch said. "Everybody gets one."

"Have you had sufficient soldiering now?" His father asked. "Are you ready to come to your senses and join the firm?"

Tulloch contemplated a lifetime of sitting in an office with the clock regulating his movements, dealing with house sales, family squabbles, and the petty bureaucracy that kept solicitors in employment.

"Not yet, Father," he said. "I'm an officer in the Lothian Rifles, and I think there's trouble brewing with Mussolini and that German fellow, Hitler."

"That will blow over," Father said, with his Royal Doulton teacup held in his slim white hand. "Mussolini's done a good job in Italy, getting the trains to run on time, and Hitler is putting Germany back on its feet. We could do with somebody like him here."

"Could we?" Tulloch asked.

"Get the unemployed back to work," Father said. "Lazy shirkers, the lot of them."

"You'd need to create jobs for them first," Tulloch knew that many of the other ranks had only joined the army because they were unemployed. Serving king and country was not a lure for them.

"They can find jobs if they look," Father said. "They must be prepared to make sacrifices."

"Douglas did not come here to argue," Mother tried to make peace in what threatened to become a major argument.

"No," Tulloch said, happy to end the discussion amicably. "I didn't. I must report back to the regiment in two days."

"Two days," the disappointment on his mother's face was painful. "Well," she said. "We'll just have to make the best of it."

It was strange to lie in his old bed, with youthful things around him and pretend the horrors of the Frontier had never happened. All his old possessions remained, with the rugby ball he had used and the old maps of the Pentland and Border Hills. Tulloch walked the Edinburgh streets, welcoming the washing rain and the street lamps through the gloom, the familiar, homely sound of Edinburgh accents and the gurgle of the Water of Leith beneath the towering Dean Bridge. He enjoyed his mother's homemade lentil soup, "always your favourite," she reminded him with a sad smile of times gone past, and he showed his appreciation with a rare hug.

"No need for that," Father said gruffly.

Mother lingered for a significant second before releasing herself and dusting her hands down her hips. "I'd better be getting on," she said.

All too soon, Tulloch's leave was over, and he had to return to his second home, the regiment.

"Take care, Douglas," Mother put on a brave face, although Tulloch could see she was fighting tears. "Come home safe to us."

"I'll do my best," Tulloch promised, feeling a little emotional yet guilty that he wanted to get away.

---

THE LOTHIAN RIFLES WERE IN BARRACKS OUTSIDE DALKEITH, with the Midlothian countryside spreading around them, interspersed with the bings and industrial architecture of the coal mines. The sentry at the gate presented arms with a flourish, and Tulloch walked in, announced himself to Major Hume and breathed a sigh of genuine relief.

Four Platoon welcomed him with shy smiles. "We thought you were deid," Brown told him. "What happened, sir?"

"I got left behind on the Frontier," Tulloch explained.

"We heard you were on some intelligence-gathering mission," Lightfoot said, and Tulloch remembered it was impossible to hide things in the Lothians. "Like Gary Cooper."

"Nothing as dramatic as that," Tulloch said, shaking his head. He looked over his platoon with renewed affection. "You're all looking soft and fat. We'll go for a route march tomorrow and get you back in trim." He grinned at the expected barrage of abuse as he left the barrack room. It was good to be back.

The officers knew little more than Four Platoon and greeted him with raised eyebrows and curious smiles.

"You were away a long time," Muirhead said in an unspoken question.

"Too long," Tulloch told him. He felt guilty about being more comfortable in the Officers' Mess than at home. Although he missed his parents, he knew he had outgrown them; he had put away childish things and embraced this new life.

"You can't tell us all that happened, can you?" Tait asked hopefully.

"No," Tulloch sat on a chair with a whisky in his hand and the buzz of the mess around him. At the side, Major Hume played billiards with Captain Forsyth, a long-faced man with a ready laugh, and the cheerful click of the balls provided a musical background.

"I hope you can stand the boredom of routine regimental soldiering after your adventuring around the Frontier," Muirhead said.

Tulloch laughed. "I'll do my best." He accepted another whisky from the mess waiter and looked around the room. Although he had been a Lothian Rifleman for three years, this was his first time in the regiment's headquarters. He nodded to the familiar picture of the Battle of Alexandria, smiled at the collection of memorabilia from subsequent wars and campaigns, and immediately relaxed.

"This Hitler fellow needs taking down a peg," Muirhead said. "He's been busy in Europe while you were gallivanting with the Pathans."

"So I hear," Tulloch said. "But he got the trains to run on time."

"That was Mussolini," Muirhead corrected. "You'll have to get your dictators sorted out, Tulloch."

"I knew it was one of them," Tulloch said, sipping at his whisky. "I dare say we'll have to sort them both out before we're done." He thought of Colonel Clark's warnings about Mussolini and clamped his mouth shut.

"I dare say," Muirhead agreed. "The world usually despises us in times of peace and runs to us for help when things get sticky." He shrugged. "We'll see if our old allies, the French, help."

"Time will tell," Tulloch said.

Muirhead eyed him thoughtfully. "What happened on the Frontier, Tulloch? You've changed."

Tulloch swallowed his second whisky without effort and signalled for another, seeing Russell's pleading face and feeling the pressure of his finger on the trigger. "It was a bit rough," he said.

"Did you succeed in what you were trying?" Muirhead asked. "I believe a foreign agent was operating with the Fakir of Ipi."

"That's correct," Tulloch agreed. "We didn't catch him."

Muirhead nodded. "That's a shame. The world is getting more unsettled by the day, and these fascist states are a bit uppity." He signalled to the mess sergeant for another drink. "Our government has, at last, wakened up to the new threats and has begun to modernise the armed forces, and about time, if you ask me."

Tulloch sipped at his recharged glass, remembering the military history classes at Sandhurst.

When the Great War ended in 1918 after four years of horrendous slaughter, Britain immediately dismantled what was probably the most efficient army in the world. Men returned to civilian life, often to find themselves unemployed or working for less wages than in 1914. A wave of anti-war sentiment washed over the country as the much-reduced army returned to its pre-war role of policing the Empire. Winston Churchill, sitting in government, passed the "Ten Year Rule," which stated all three services should plan with the assumption there would not be a major war for ten years.

Never keen to spend money on the army, the Cabinet grasped the pacifist straw and neglected the nation and the Empire's defences for the best part of twenty years. For most regiments, training was restrictive and repetitive, musketry, digging trenches, marching, and square bashing on the parade ground. The only chances of active operations were in Ireland in the early 1920s, with the RAF in Iraq, Palestine, and the Northwest Frontier. Apart from that, the army aided the civil powers, which was a thankless, squalid task of policing riots and acting as targets for stone-throwing mobs who were frustrated with politicians the soldiers also despised.

Successive British governments neglected defence, with what money they spent poured more into the air force and the navy. The army was a much-neglected third force. Simultaneously, the nation's leaders buried their heads in the sand and refused to contemplate the triple growing threats of a resurgent Germany, an aggressively fascist Italy, and a militaristic Japan.

The Government, secure in their belief that the RAF and Navy could defend Britain and the vast empire without the expense of a modern army, virtually ignored the German and Italian efforts during the Spanish Civil War. They hoped the League of Nations could stop Italy from invading Ethiopia and turned a Nelsonian eye when Germany reoccupied the Rhineland in 1936, and Japan attacked first Manchuria and then China. The League proved to be a paper tiger, and the fascist powers, encouraged by other nations' non-intervention, continued their military progression.

Not until 1937 did Britain wake up and try to put right their somnambulism of the preceding nineteen years. By then, it was nearly too late, with threats across the Empire and Europe. In India, Gandi and Congress clamoured for independence. Further east, Japan cast a formidable shadow across a swathe of territory from New Zealand to Malaya and Burma. Italy threatened Suez and the Red Sea, and Germany was a resurgent power in Europe.

Tulloch thought of the Lothians in India, with Great War vintage Lewis Guns rather than the modern Bren guns.

"What's Herr Hitler been up to while I've been on the Frontier?" Tulloch asked.

"Oh, he's been a busy little Nazi," Muirhead said. "You know he's occupied the Rhineland, of course."

"I do," Tulloch said. "That was a few years ago, now."

"And he's merged Germany with Austria," Muirhead watched as Tulloch finished his third glass of whisky and signalled for more.

"The Central Powers of the Great War coming together," Tulloch said. "Is Hitler hoping to reform the old Holy Roman Empire?"

"That at least," Muirhead murmured. "Go easy on the whisky, old man. Major Hume rather likes Glenkinchie, and you're knocking it back as if there's a race."

Tulloch glanced at his glass, realised it was empty again, and placed it on the table at his side. "I wouldn't wish to drink Major Hume's whisky," he said.

"No," Muirhead agreed. "Especially when he's losing at billiards." He placed his glass beside Tulloch's, smiling. "A disgruntled Major Hume can be as dangerous as Hitler, who has moved into Czechoslovakia, not only the German-speaking parts."

"I heard about Chamberlain's 'Peace for our time' piece of paper," Tulloch said. "We virtually handed Czechoslovakia to Germany."

"What else could Chamberlain do? We're in no position to help," Muirhead pointed out. "Czechoslovakia is a landlocked country, so the Royal Navy isn't much use, and our aircraft don't have the range to fly so far and return." He gave a wry smile. "Anyway, I doubt that dropping leaflets on Germany would work."

"We might have different rules of engagement in Europe than on the Frontier," Tulloch said.

"I should hope so!" Muirhead said hotly. "Do you realise that the Treaty of Versailles allows Germany an army of 100,000 men, yet Hitler now has a hundred and five divisions, that's around a million bayonets, including ten motorised divisions and six Panzer – that means tank – divisions."

"That's bad," Tulloch agreed. "We have three armoured divisions, one in Egypt and two in the UK, and one of these has no tanks yet. You see? I have done some homework." He grinned, eyed his empty whisky glass, and looked quickly away.

Muirhead caught the look. "Aye, and thanks to Chamberlain's astute diplomacy, Hitler has added the Czech army to his own, and the Czechs are bonny fighters. Add that to Austria, and Hitler has the best soldiers of the old Austrian Empire in his army and no Russian or Italian front to distract him if we go to war."

"The Italians may join Hitler," Tulloch said quietly.

"They may," Muirhead said. "They could strike at Egypt from Ethiopia or Eritrea. Our second battalion's just been posted to that part of the world."

Tulloch nodded. "It will be a grim struggle if we face Italy and an enlarged Germany with our half-equipped army. Back to the trenches, then?" He watched the mess sergeant pouring whisky into Major Hume's glass, closed his eyes and saw his bullet crashing into Captain Russell.

"Maybe," Muirhead said slowly. "The French have the largest air force in the world and some superb tanks, so hopefully, between the two of us, we'll win. It depends on Mussolini to an extent. He has a large army and air force, and his navy will keep the French and the Royal Navy occupied in the Mediterranean."

Tulloch grunted. "The Italians may also cause trouble in India if they join Hitler."

Muirhead raised his eyebrows. "Is that why you were on the Frontier so long?"

Tulloch realised he had said too much. "It's only a possibili-ty," he said.

Muirhead smiled. "Hopefully, the politicians don't do anything completely stupid until we're at least half prepared for a European, let alone a global war. Our tanks are primitive, and half our infantry are only trained to march and drill."

Tulloch nodded. He knew the army had two types of tanks, the heavy 'I' tanks, designed to cooperate with slow-moving infantry and the faster cruiser tanks with thin armour. "Looking for sense from a politician is like looking for a virgin in an Alder-shot brothel."

"Unfortunately, I agree with you," Muirhead said. "The future looks bleak, Tulloch."

"Every day makes us stronger," Tulloch said. "The longer the politicians delay, the better equipped and trained we get."

"Here's to a prolonged peace," Muirhead signalled to the mess sergeant and ordered two more whiskies, ensuring they were not Glenkinchies. "And more optimists like you."

Tulloch smiled bleakly. "I'm no optimist," he said, "but I'm damned if I'll give up before the fighting starts."

"What happened to you on the Frontier, Tulloch? You've changed."

Tulloch sipped his whisky, aware that Muirhead had already asked that question. "Have I?" He thought of the man he had shot and finished his drink.

# Chapter Fifteen

*The laws are silent in time of war.*
**Cicero: *Pro Milone***

"Lothians! Lothians! Show them your cap badge, Lothians!"

Tulloch heard the drunken roar as he walked along Dalkeith High Street towards Eskbank. He swore softly and increased his pace, hoping he was mistaken in identifying the voice.

As he approached King's Park, he saw a score of soldiers and civilians engaged in a brawl. He looked for an NCO or some of the provost staff - the regimental police - realised there were none and swore again. Officers tried to avoid becoming involved with quarrelling other ranks in case a drunken private attacked them, which was a serious offence.

"Enough!" Tulloch shouted, hoping his presence alone could bring the Lothians back to their senses. He sighed when he recognised Brown and Hogg in the middle of the affray. Brown wrapped his belt around his fist and used the buckle as a knuckleduster, while Hogg had neatly disposed of a civilian with a savage head-butt.

Tulloch calculated there were seven Lothians, four from Eight Section and three he did not know, and a dozen civilians, possibly miners from the local pits. As the noise escalated, a small crowd gathered, most cheering on the civilians.

"Go on! Give these swaddies what for!" One shapely young woman shouted, adding some anatomical details.

"Kick their heids right in!" A middle-aged woman in a head scarf encouraged. "Send them back to their barracks! They've no right to mix with decent folk."

Tulloch strode forward and pulled away one of the battling civilians. "Enough! You men get back to your homes!"

A leering civilian faced him and swung a wild punch that Tulloch easily avoided. "Get back home," he said and sighed when the man tried again. "Go home! You're too drunk to beat me, and if you were sober, you would not try!"

Hogg stepped closer. "It's Mr. Tulloch! Are you all right, sir?"

"Yes!" Tulloch shouted above the noise. "Break off the fight and get back to barracks before somebody is hurt!"

When the civilian tried a third swing, Tulloch sidestepped and landed a right cross that landed on the point of the man's jaw, sending him to the ground.

"Nice punch, sir!" Hogg approved.

The middle-aged woman pointed to Tulloch. "Here! I saw that," as a police sergeant arrived with two constables at his back.

"I'll take the soldiers away," Tulloch volunteered as the police momentarily looked helpless.

"Who are you?" The sergeant asked.

"Lieutenant Douglas Tulloch."

"Oh, sorry, sir. I thought you were one of the soldiers." The sergeant touched his cap in sudden respect.

"I am one of the soldiers," Tulloch replied.

"I mean one of the rabble," the sergeant indicated the still battling privates.

Tulloch felt his indignation rise. "What rabble?" he asked

quietly. He remembered Brown in Waziristan, Hogg calmly firing when the Waziri bullets were kicking up the dirt, and Anderson screaming when the mine tore off his foot. "These men are keeping you secure!" Tulloch had always been of equable temperament, but now his temper rose. "Get your bloody civilians under control, sergeant, and I'll see to my men!" With his anger driving him, Tulloch strode into the middle of the struggling mob. Shoving aside the civilians, he prevented Brown from strangling a tousle-haired youth.

"Get back to barracks, Brown! And you, Hogg! Kelly! Put that man down and join Brown!"

A snarling civilian tried to kick Tulloch, who lifted his foot, stamped on the man's leg, and scraped the edge of his shoe down the shin. "Get out of my way!"

When police reinforcements arrived, most of the civilians and one of the soldiers fled, making it easy to round up the rest.

"I want to arrest your men," the police sergeant said, pointing a finger at the truculent Hogg.

"I'll take care of them," Tulloch grated. "Your civilians jumped my men. If you want to arrest them, you'd best take me too because I fought one of the civilians."

The sergeant hesitated, wondering how his superiors would view him arresting an officer. "I'm sure there's no need for that, sir."

"Good man, Sergeant. I'll take my rogues off your hands, and you can concentrate on the civilian element. Good evening to you."

When the sergeant replied, "Good evening, sir," Tulloch hurried away his Lothians before the police changed their minds.

"Come on, lads," Tulloch shouted. "Heads up and quick march! Get in step there, Brown!"

He marched them through the barrack's main gate and onto the parade ground. "That was a disgraceful display," he roared at his platoon and told them they were a disgrace to their uniforms before dismissing them.

Tulloch watched them run to their barracks, wondered if the police sergeant would report him, decided he did not care whatever happened and walked into the Officers' Mess.

"Whisky, please," he ordered from the mess sergeant and saw the light catch the purple pips on the chaplain's shoulders. "Good evening, padre," Tulloch said evenly.

"Good evening, Lieutenant Tulloch," Renwick, the chaplain, replied and ordered a brandy. "I'm glad you managed to join us again. How was the Frontier?"

Tulloch sat down with the chaplain opposite, watching everything he did. "It was all right," he said.

"I heard a rumour a man died," Renwick said quietly and raised a hand. "It's all right, Lieutenant; I keep things to myself. How did Captain Russell die?"

About to avoid the question, Tulloch found the chaplain's quiet eyes disturbing. "I shot him," he said, expecting outrage, accusations of murder and horror.

Instead, Renwick replied with a one-word question. "Why?"

"Because he asked me to," Tulloch said. "And to save him from being tortured to death."

Renwick nodded. "Was there another option?"

Tulloch finished his whisky and signalled for another. "Make it a double," he said, and the sergeant gave him a third of a gill, with the light shining through the dark amber fluid and reflecting from the pattern of the crystal.

"Was there another option?" Renwick repeated quietly. "Could you have saved him?"

Tulloch considered the question. Gut shot and hardly able to walk, Russell would not have managed to escape from the Waziri village. Tulloch and the two Scouts could not have carried him and still managed to escape, while Russell would have probably died that same night or the next day.

"No," Tulloch said. "I could not have saved him."

Renwick nodded, with his gentle eyes probing deep into

Tulloch's soul. "I think you saved that man from a great deal of suffering," he said.

"Thank you, padre," Tulloch replied. He knew the chaplain's words had not taken the pain away; the memory would always be there, but they had helped.

Renwick stood and patted Tulloch's shoulder. "If you want to talk about it, Douglas, you know where I live."

When he stood to go, Tulloch followed. The whisky remained where he had left it, untouched in its crystal glass.

---

"He's one of us, boys," Hogg said. "I heard him stick up for us. He said, if you want to arrest them, you'll have to arrest me too, and I'll fight every one of you civilian bastards."

"He never said that," Aitken said. "I dinnae believe it."

"Are you calling me a liar?" Hogg's voice rose in disbelief that somebody could challenge him.

"No," Aitken denied at once. "I'm no' saying that. I just cannae believe that Tully threatened to fight the polis. I mean, he's an officer."

"Aye, I ken he's an officer," Hogg said. "But he's on oor side."

Tulloch lingered at the barrack room door for a moment, listening to the conversation, smiled, and walked on. The little confrontation at King's Park in Dalkeith had helped the platoon to accept him. If the taciturn Hogg said something, few of Four Platoon would argue. For the first time since Russell's death, Tulloch felt some weight lift from his shoulders.

---

"We're being transferred to the 3rd Division," Muirhead said. "Our divisional commander is a strange wee man called Montgomery, who is currently sick and running the division from a hotel in Portsmouth."

"Montgomery? I met him in the college in Quetta," Tulloch said, hoping he was not giving too much away. "Since then, I've heard he did some useful stuff in Palestine."

"That's the fellow," Muirhead agreed. "He's a bit of a maverick, I've heard. Mad keen on training and won some sort of medal early in the Kaiser's War." He shrugged, sipped at his whisky, and peered at Tulloch over the edge of the glass. "Now that Russia and Germany have signed a non-aggression pact, Poland is looking vulnerable. The Soviets want their old territory back, and Germany wants *lebensraum*, space to expand."

"We've signed a mutual assistance treaty with Poland," Captain Forsyth said soberly, "although how we're meant to assist each other, I don't know."

"We can only assist them by declaring war on Germany," Tulloch said.

"It will be an expedition to the Baltic, then," Muirhead said. "That will be a change from Peshawar and Razmak." He swirled the whisky in his glass as if hoping to see the future in the amber liquid. "We'll have to sail through the Kattegat and past the German naval bases at Bremen, Wilhelmshaven, Kiel, and Hamburg." He shook his head. "Remember Jutland, gentlemen? We could see a major naval engagement at the start of the war."

"As long as we control their submarines," Tait said. "That's a sneaky way to fight a war, hiding underwater to murder merchant seamen."

"I think we'll declare war if Germany invades Poland," Forsyth walked over to the billiards table and tried a trick shot. "We've been too patient with Herr Hitler, and now it's time to cry halt to end his nonsense." He lined up a ball and hit it straight into a corner pocket.

"Let's hope that Hitler has more sense than to start a war," Tulloch replied.

"He called our bluff in the Rhineland, Austria, the Sudetenland and Czechoslovakia," Muirhead watched Forsyth at the billiard table. "He'll think we're a paper tiger and call it again."

"Then it will be a full-scale war," Forsyth said, pocketing three balls in a row and missing a fourth.

Forsyth was correct. On the First of September 1939, Hitler's armies invaded Poland. Two days later, at eleven in the morning of the Third of September 1939, Britain declared war on Germany. At five o'clock that same day, France joined Britain.

"We're at war with Germany," Major Hume announced to a crowded Officers' Mess.

"It's round two of the same war," Captain Forsyth said without looking up from the billiard table.

Tulloch nodded without saying anything. He lifted his whisky glass to his lips and wondered what the future would hold while he felt his heartbeat increase. He looked up as the door opened, and Colonel Pringle stepped into the Mess. Everybody fell quiet, and Captain Forsyth stood beside the billiard table with the cue at his side like a rifle.

"The Lothian Rifles will be part of Montgomery's 3rd or Iron Division, in 2 Corps," Colonel Pringle announced. "Despite the many rumours, we are not sailing to the Baltic but are heading to France to defend Western Europe from an expected German invasion."

The collected officers nodded thankfully. Nobody had looked forward to negotiating the passage through the Kattegat, past the German coast with its warships and aircraft, to reinforce the Polish army.

Pringle continued, speaking quietly and with a minimum of emotion. "Lord Gort is in overall command of the British Army, with General Ironside CIGS."

Tait glanced at Tulloch. "Gort's never commanded anything larger than a brigade. That doesn't bode well."

Pringle allowed the murmured comments to fade away. "I'll leave you gentlemen to take whatever steps you think best. We will be getting new kit soon, including a consignment of Bren guns and Bren gun carriers. Ensure your men are ready for war.

That's all." He withdrew without a further word, leaving the Mess buzzing with speculation.

"Germany," Tait said, ordering a double whisky. "I never thought we'd be fighting them again."

Tulloch grunted. "Our duty is to fight the enemy wherever he may be, Tait. The colonel will make the battalion as efficient as possible, and we must do the same with our men. The better trained they are, the better they'll fight and the more chance we'll have of survival."

Tait grunted. "You're different, Tulloch. What happened to you on the Frontier?"

"I realised what soldiering is all about," Tulloch told him. "Excuse me." Standing up, he walked to the rifle range for extra practice, aware that Tait and Muirhead watched him leave.

The Lothians readied themselves for war. They took delivery of Bren guns and Bren gun carriers and hastily trained the men in their use.

"We have two types of carriers," a harassed instructor shouted to a gathering of officers and senior NCOs, "the Bren Carrier and the Scout Carrier. The Bren Carrier, as the name implies, is armed with a Bren gun. Both are lightly armoured against small arms fire and can carry supplies or a small number of men."

Tulloch listened, happy that the Bren gun carrier increased the mobility of the battalion while offering a minimum of protection for its crew.

"The carrier has a range of one hundred and fifty miles, with a top speed of thirty miles an hour," the instructor said. "By the end of this year, every infantry battalion will possess ten of these little beauties," he patted the ten-millimetre-thick armour affectionately. "Use them well."

While the platoon commanders were teaching their men the basics of the Bren gun carriers and the Motor Transport officers were puzzling over the intricacies of the engines, the battalion prepared for a European war. The adjutant ran himself ragged with the administration, snapped at officers senior and junior to him and aged ten years in as many days. The colonel snarled at majors, who growled at captains and lieutenants, who barked at NCOs, who passed on the stress to private soldiers. The quarter-masters checked and rechecked their stores, mechanics laboured over spare parts and stubborn engines, and cooks fretted about how to feed men when the food chain was unreliable.

Tulloch trained his platoon in patrol work, ensured their marksmanship was up to standard, and they could all fire the Bren gun.

*"Oh, we're no awa' tae bide awa',*
*And we're no awa' tae leave ye,*
*We're no awa, tae bide awa',*

We'll aye come back and see ye," Private Brown sang, to the dismay of his colleagues, who pleaded with him to keep quiet with undisguised threats.

"*Chibberow,* [1] you croak-voiced bastard!" Aitken yelled.

"Away and learn to sing, for Christ's sake," Kelly shouted as Hardie sat in a corner, smiling quietly.

Tulloch said nothing, leaving Sergeant Drysdale to keep peace in the platoon.

"We're getting there," Muirhead said, in a rare moment of peace between bouts of frantic activity. "This Hitler fellow has a lot to answer for, invading Poland and causing me all sorts of bother."

Tulloch agreed.

There were three infantry brigades in the 3rd division, the 7th, 8th and 9th, with three field regiments of Royal Artillery and an anti-tank company, all based in the south of England. The Lothians travelled by road and rail, joining the 3rd division a few days later, and immediately found that General Montgomery believed in intensive training, with weapons training, digging training, signals training and patrol training.

The Lothians excelled at patrol training, passing on tips they had learned the hard way on the Frontier, although they were not so good with the new Bren gun carriers or the mortars and had to work hard to catch the other units. Tulloch immersed himself in regimental life, reacquainted himself with his colleagues and his men and tried to forget the horror of shooting Russell.

"Do I know you?" Montgomery asked when he toured the Lothians. "Yes, you're Tulloch. You were at the college in Quetta, bound for the Frontier."

"That's right, sir," Tulloch agreed.

Montgomery nodded. "I see you survived."

"Yes, sir," Tulloch agreed as Montgomery walked away with his head slightly to one side; *he looks like a bird*, Tulloch thought.

Montgomery ordered that every man, including the recently added reservists, was experienced in firing their weapons and had thrown at least three grenades. When the order filtered down to the Lothians, most of the off-duty men of the rifle companies arrived at the ranges to watch the cooks and clerks.

"That's the way, master gyppo," Brown encouraged the surprisingly slender head cook. "Hold the rifle steady now! It's no' a ladle."

"Leave him alone," Innes said. "He's the most dangerous man in the battalion."

"Him?" Brown asked incredulously. "How him?"

"Have you never tasted his cooking?" Innes laughed. "He tries to poison us every day."

On the 19th of August 1939, King George VI inspected the division, with the Lothians spick, shiny and nervous. The king toured the battalion at a walking pace, spoke to the colonel and Major Hume and left.

"Well, lads," Tulloch said to his platoon. "You can all say you've seen the king."

"Yes, sir," Brown said, "and the king can say he's seen us."

"I'm sure he's deeply honoured," Tulloch said.

# Chapter Sixteen

*If the trumpet gives an uncertain sound, who shall prepare himself to the battle?*

**1 Corinthians 14:8**

In September 1939, the division prepared to leave for France. Troop trains carried them to Southampton, with the long files of khaki-clad men embarking on the ships from half past ten in the morning while seagulls screamed around them. A crowd of spectators gathered to see them leave, some waving handkerchiefs or saying farewell to husbands, sons, brothers, or boyfriends.

The Lothians, fresh from India, accepted the discomfort with hardly a comment, while other regiments had been based in the United Kingdom for years and speculated about this new adventure.

"The poor buggers don't know what they're in for," Brown said, waving to a young woman, who looked surprised but returned the greeting with exuberant enthusiasm.

"Neither do we," Hogg replied. "Fighting the Germans won't be the same as patrolling the Frontier."

"Better food, French wine, and hundreds of French women,"

Brown stepped onto the already crowded deck. "No mosquitoes, no malaria or Delhi Belly, no hot season when you cannae breathe or monsoons when the rain comes down in solid chunks. France will be paradise compared to bloody India."

The troops crammed into the ships, filling every space with sweating, often nervous men who laughed, told coarse jokes, and spoke loudly to hide their unease.

"The Germans better not bomb the ship," Aitken said.

"Nah, the RAF and the Navy will see to them." Innes gestured to the sleek grey-painted warships who waited to escort the convoy, the seamen watching the long files of khaki soldiers through curious eyes. The two services could have belonged to different worlds, Tulloch thought as he organised his platoon.

They left the harbour at midnight, with the long convoy of transports between busy Royal Navy ships. Tulloch stood at the rail and watched the navy, admiring their sleek efficiency as they shepherded the merchantmen without fuss into the chopped dark water of the Channel.

"You didn't get much time at home, Tulloch," Muirhead joined Tulloch at the rail.

"I'll blame Hitler for that," Tulloch said. "I doubt he'll apologise, though."

Muirhead smiled. "I think that's highly unlikely. My father crossed the Channel in 1914, going to the Kaiser's War, and now it's my turn. I wonder if my son must do the same."

"Maybe we'll finish the job this time," Tulloch said. "We should never have allowed the Germans to get their strength back."

Muirhead looked sideways at him. "Some people believe the Versailles Treaty was too harsh."

"So I've heard," Tulloch said. "I don't believe in allowing bullies the tools they need to continue bullying." He watched the lights on the other ships in the convoy, with the phosphorescence of a score of wakes gleaming through the dark.

Muirhead nodded. "Maybe you're right, Tulloch. Come on; we'd better get to bed; the next few days could be lively."

They arrived at Cherbourg the following morning without losing a single man and without sighting the enemy, which Tulloch put down to the skill of the Royal Navy.

*"Fair stood the wind for France,*
*When we our sails advance,*
*Nor now to prove our chance,*
*Longer will tarry;*
*But putting to the main,*
*At Caux, the mouth of Seine,*
*With all his martial train*
*Landed King Harry.*

Tait quoted, surveying the unlovely waterfront through a dank grey mist.

"In Michael Drayton's time, France was the enemy," Muirhead murmured. "I wonder how he'd feel with France as an ally."

Tait smiled. "I just liked the poem."

Shortly after the division disembarked to a few greetings from dispirited-looking Frenchmen, news filtered that the division's transport had landed at Brest, where the dockers had forced the boot of every officer's car and stolen the contents.

"They broke into the laundry vans as well," Muirhead passed on the information. "They're worse thieves than the Pashtuns!"

"I thought the French were our allies," Tait said as the division scoured Cherbourg for transport.

"Waterloo still rankles," Tulloch said.

"So does bloody Agincourt," Tait grumbled.

Scraping together every piece of transport they could hire, steal, or borrow. The division moved on, some by train, others on creaking cars and the unfortunate on foot. On the first of October 1939, they arrived at Evron, west of Le Mans, expecting more training before they moved to the front. The division bedded in barns, public halls and farm outbuildings, sleeping on straw and visiting the local estaminets for comfort and company. Two days later, they were moving again, this time to a position south of Lille.

"March, march and bloody march," Tait said. "War in Europe is not about fighting the enemy. War is about marching and travelling."

"Well, here we are," Tait said when the Lothians settled into their new positions. "With nothing between us and the Germans except a few fields and a shallow anti-tank ditch."

Tulloch looked over the French countryside, with neutral Belgium beyond.

"The Belgian army might not agree with that," he said. "They fought well in the Kaiser's War." He looked forward. "You're right about the defences, though. We'd better do something about them."

The French had built an impressive defence line along their border with Germany. Known as the Maginot Line after Andre Maginot, the French Minister of War, the series of concrete forts was intended to prevent any German attack. However, the French decided not to complete the Maginot Line to the sea to avoid offending neutral Belgium. That meant Northeastern France, bordering Belgium, was less heavily defended and more vulnerable to invasion.

"A five-year-old child with a balloon on a stick could break in here," Colonel Pringle said when he reviewed the defences. "I want the ditch deepened and lengthened, minefields laid with our artillery covering funnelling gaps. I want triple layers of barbed wire, two-man rifle pits behind and in front of the main trenches and dog-leg pits for the Brens."

The officers nodded. The older men recognised much of the procedures from the previous war.

"I want anti-tank obstacles and emplacements erected and our anti-tank guns concealed and ready to strike." Pringle pointed out the best positions for the anti-tank guns. "Have these blasted carriers arrived yet?"

The Lothians had been working with their open-topped Bren gun carriers, which, being tracked, could operate across country as well as on the roads.

"Not yet, sir," Forsyth, the Motor Transport officer, said.

"Immediately they arrive, I want patrols out to see what's in front of us," Pringle said, "Until then, I want foot patrols. Rotate the officers and men so everybody learns the countryside."

"Yes, sir," Hume scribbled notes in a small black book.

While they waited for the supposedly inevitable German advance through neutral Belgium, the Lothians, and the other units in the division, laboured to increase their security. Except for the British base at Razmak, Tulloch's only experience with defensive warfare was entirely theoretical. Now he saw the practical reality at first-hand.

The engineers laid minefields, with areas deliberately left weak to invite enemy tanks onto emplacements where camouflaged two-pounder anti-tank guns waited in hopeful ambush. The engineers unstrung rows of barbed wire, with mines in between and weak points luring an attacker towards concealed machine guns.

*As Private Dunn told me, aggression alone is not sufficient. We need guile as well.*

As the engineers worked, the Lothians sent out patrols to probe the enemy positions and to examine the British Observation Posts and defences from the German point of view.

"Tulloch, you've got more experience of patrolling than most. Take out the junior officers and NCOs and pass on your skills," Pringle ordered. "Remember, the Belgians have denied us permission to cross their border. They'll intern you if you break their laws."

"Yes, sir," Tulloch said solemnly. After dodging the Waziris in their homeland, he was not concerned about Belgian policemen or military. "I won't cross the border, sir."

"We don't want an international incident, Tulloch," the colonel said. "The Belgians are standing firm on their neutrality."

"Will Germany invade Belgium, sir?" Tulloch asked.

"Of course they will," Pringle snapped. "They won't lose men by throwing them against concrete gun emplacements when they can go round the flanks. They'll invade, we'll advance to meet them, and we'll have an encounter battle somewhere inside Belgium."

"Yes, sir. In that case, why are we making defences here?"

"If the Germans push us back, we have a settled line to stop them," Pringle said.

"I see, sir." Tulloch realised he still had a lot to learn.

Tulloch spent the next few weeks on patrols as summer drifted into autumn, and the line remained peaceful. He became thoroughly familiar with the local topography, taking his Bren gun carrier to within a few hundred yards of the Belgian border and waving to the sentries on guard.

"What's the point in this, sir, if we're entering Belgium when the Germans invade?" Aitken asked.

Tulloch had long since ceased to wonder how the other ranks obtained their information. "Practice, Aitken, and ensuring we know the land better than the Germans if ever we have to fight here."

"Yes, sir," Aitken replied.

With every motorised patrol, Tulloch's platoon became more expert with the carriers and more confident in moving around France at night. After two weeks, Colonel Pringle allowed limited leave in Lille, with strict orders not to cause trouble.

"That means you, Hogg," Tulloch warned. "And you, Brown. This isn't Dalkeith, and I don't want to rescue you from the provost sergeant or the local gendarmes."

"We'll be fine, sir," Brown promised and jumped into the back of the fifteen hundredweight lorry that carried the men into Lille.

Tulloch turned away, trusting the provost sergeant and his

men to keep order in the battalion. He stepped into the Officers' Mess and ordered a mug of tea.

The chaplain joined him and eyed the mug without commenting. "How are you, Lieutenant?"

"I'm fine, padre, thank you," Tulloch replied.

"No nightmares?" Renwick asked casually.

"Not even one," Tulloch lied.

"That's good." Renwick gave his gentle smile. "Many men have nightmares after an experience like yours. I still have them from the Somme and Ypres."

Tulloch glanced at Renwick's chest, which was bare of medal ribbons.

"I don't wear my medals," Renwick said quietly. "I was a very young man then, and I saw far too many even younger men die." He stood up. "The nightmares you don't have won't go away, Douglas, but they'll get less frequent in time. Find something to distract you. A woman is a good idea." The chaplain grinned. "She might drive you to distraction, though."

Tulloch met Renwick's smile, although he had no conception of finding a woman. "Thank you, padre. I think the Germans might provide sufficient distraction over here."

"Perhaps so, Douglas," Renwick replied sadly. "Let's hope the politicians may yet find a peaceful solution without any more deaths."

"Yes, Padre," Tulloch agreed. "But if we do, that will still leave Hitler with a large army and a history of successful aggression. He'd only bide his time and attack somewhere else. Somebody has to stop him, and we're the only nation man enough for the job."

The chaplain sighed. "Unfortunately, Douglas, you may be right. Appeasing a bully only encourages him." He stood up. "I'm glad you're feeling better, and I still advise you to seek some cheerful company."

Tulloch watched the chaplain leave, knowing the current war situation would make it difficult to think of anything except his duty. The officers knew that the Germans had concentrated troops on the Belgian border and saw the RAF Fairey Battles dropping leaflets on Germany and the French air force operating high above. Still, not a single German bomb fell on the Lothians, and the troops began to wonder if the war was real.

"If we were facing the Waziris," Tait said, "they'd have raided us half a dozen times by now."

"All of Belgium lies between us and the Germans," Tulloch reminded him.

"They would still have raided," Tait insisted. "This is a phoney war that will soon blow over." He walked beside Tulloch in the slow rain. "Have you heard the latest song?"

"Song? No," Tulloch said, and Tait began to sing.

*"Mother dear, I'm writing you from somewhere in France,*
*Hoping this finds you well.*
*Sergeant says I'm doing fine, a soldier and a half,*
*Here's a song that we'll all sing, it'll make you laugh!*
*We're going to hang out the washing on the Siegfried Line,*
*Have you any dirty washing, mother dear?*
*We're going to hang out the washing on the Siegfried Line,*
*'Cause the washing day is here."*

Tait laughed. "That's what this war is like," he said. "We dig trenches and patrol in friendly territory, and the Germans move their units about hundreds of miles away and growl menacingly towards us. Folk are right; it's a phoney war."

While the British sang comic songs about the German Siegfried Line, the French continued to rely heavily on their Maginot Line. In common with many British officers, Tulloch took advantage of some free time to view the Maginot. He found them an impressive array of concrete forts built between 1930 and 1935, with smaller casements in between. While each fort had a garrison hundreds strong plus heavy artillery, the casements held lesser numbers, machine guns and a 47-millimetre anti-tank gun. In front of the forts were advanced warning posts, barbed wire, minefields, and anti-tank obstacles.

"The Maginot Line is a formidable obstacle," Tait said when they returned and toured the Lothian's minefields and sloping horizontal barbed wire aprons.

"Yes," Tulloch said. "How would the Waziris overcome it?"

"Oh, they wouldn't," Tait said. "They'd go round the flanks."

"So will the Germans," Tulloch predicted.

"Belgium is neutral," Tait reminded.

Tulloch nodded. "Do you think that will stop Hitler from invading?"

Tait considered for a moment and shook his head. "No. Hitler doesn't seem like a man to respect anybody's neutrality."

"We'll be moving into Belgium then," Tulloch said.

"We're aware of that, Tulloch," Major Hume had joined them. "Yet the Belgians won't allow even a single British observer enter their country to reconnoitre possible positions in case it compromises their neutrality. We'll probably be fighting with our left flank open as well, as the French Sixteen Corps are not in position yet."

"That's comforting," Tulloch said.

Tait shook his head in disbelief. "Have you seen the French, sir? Most of their men don't want to fight at all. They are slovenly, ill-disciplined, and low in morale."

"That doesn't mean they can't fight," Tulloch defended their allies. "The Waziris didn't dress like the Brigade of Guards, but they are no slouches when it comes to warfare."

"The French are trained in one form of defence," Major Hume said. "When the Germans attack, the French will hit them with concentrated artillery and machine guns. If the Germans penetrate the French line, they'll slow them with local reserves, then counterattack in superior numbers." He ran a hand over a strand of the Lothians' barbed wire and peered towards Belgium. "In other words, gentlemen, they're still fighting the last war while the world has moved on."

Tulloch listened without offering his opinion. Everybody looked up as a squadron of French aircraft flew overhead, keeping inside French airspace.

"You'll all be aware of Helmuth von Moltke's words," Hume said. "No plan of operations will ever extend, with any sort of certainty, beyond the first encounter with the hostile main force."

Tulloch remembered von Moltke's words from Sandhurst. "Yes, sir."

"Von Moltke was saying armies need to be flexible. The French tactics are rigid," Hume said. "I think we could end up fighting alone, gentlemen."

"What are our plans, sir?" Tait asked.

"Montgomery will soon tell us," Hume said with a small smile. "He's not backwards in coming forwards."

Rather than accept the French doctrine of copying First World War tactics, General Montgomery began an intensive training program that pushed his division. They practised moving forward as a division, delaying an advancing enemy, and crossing bombed bridges or other obstacles. They trained in digging in new defensive trenches and in a fighting withdrawal.

With each exercise, the division improved its efficiency, and Montgomery began to whittle away at the officers. He inspected each unit and removed any officer who lacked the necessary drive and skills. Even senior officers found themselves taken away from fighting units and placed miles behind the lines, organising the railways or working on mundane administrative tasks.

"I see you're still with us, Lieutenant Tulloch," Montgomery stood before Tulloch.

"Yes, sir," Tulloch was surprised that Montgomery remembered his name.

"You'll find fighting the Germans a bit different to the Waziris," Montgomery said.

"I expect so, sir," Tulloch agreed.

"I've got my eye on you, Tulloch," Montgomery said and moved away to talk to Colonel Pringle.

"What did that mean?" Tait asked later that day.

"God knows," Tulloch said.

"It sounded ominous," Tait glanced over his shoulder as a staff car parked beside Colonel Pringle's quarters. "I'll give you some free advice, Tulloch. When senior officers take notice of you, it's time to make yourself invisible."

Tulloch nodded. "Sage advice, Tait," he agreed. "Sage advice." He followed the direction of Tait's gaze and saw a scruffy officer and an equally untidy civilian leave the staff car.

"Who's that?" Tait asked. "Or rather, what's that? They're dressed like drunken tramps."

"The military man is Colonel Clark of the Intelligence Bureau," Tulloch replied quietly. "What the hell is he doing here?"

"How do you know him?" Tait asked quickly, but Tulloch had taken his advice and disappeared.

The following day, Colonel Pringle called Tulloch into his office. "How's your French, Tulloch?"

"Schoolboy level, sir," Tulloch said, "at best." He remembered Colonel Clark's visit and hoped this interview was not connected.

Pringle made a note on a small pad on his desk. "Do you have any other languages?"

"Passible Urdu and Pashto, sir, with a smatter of Italian. Not much use here."

"Probably not," Pringle agreed. "Brush up on your French, Tulloch. You might need it."

"Why, sir?" Tulloch asked.

"We'll be working closely with the French army, Tulloch, and maybe operating in Belgium, where French is also widely spoken. I want my officers to be able to liaise with our allies."

"Yes, sir," Tulloch felt relieved the colonel did not mention Clark as he left.

The training continued as autumn eased into winter, with Colonel Pringle supervising the men with the .8-inch Boys anti-tank rifles. Germany continued to move its divisions to the Belgian border, and aircraft from the RAF regularly flew overhead, still avoiding Belgian airspace.

"There are the Brylcreem boys again," Tait jerked a thumb at the sky. "Do you know they're still only dropping leaflets on Germany? Can you believe it? We're meant to be at war with them, and we bombard them with bits of blasted paper."

"And what does our beloved Prime Minister think?" Captain Forsyth said. "Chamberlain told Montgomery he doesn't think the Germans intend to attack us."

"Why are we here if the Germans aren't going to attack?" Tait grumbled. "This isn't a war; it's Much Ado about Nothing, and we're actors. Hang up your washing on the Siegfried Line? The way we're acting, we'll be sharing a laundry with the Germans."

"Don't worry about it, lads," Major Hume said. "We're off to the Saar to gain some experience facing the Germans."

"When?" Tulloch asked.

"In two days," Hume said. "Gort wants every unit to have some experience of facing the Germans rather than manning the Belgian frontier, so pack up your parrots and monkeys and get ready to move."

Tulloch nodded. "Yes, sir." *Wherever we go, I want to be as far away from Colonel Clark as possible.*

# Chapter Seventeen

*Now it is fearsome to look around,*
*When blood-stained clouds are drawn across heaven;*
*The sky will be stained with men's blood,*
*When the battle-women know how to sing.*
**Njal's Saga**

Tulloch crouched in his newly dug trench as the sleet slithered down from a grey sky. He looked over Four Platoon with their weather-tanned, inscrutable faces. Sergeant Drysdale waited, with the inevitable cigarette dangling from his lower lip and his eyes busy checking his men. Eight Section was closest to Tulloch. Innes carried the Bren, which provided the section's main firepower, with Kelly as his number two while the others had their Lee-Enfield rifles. Hogg looked ready to commit murder, Brown was humming a popular song, and Hardie appeared as calm as if he were on holiday. Lightfoot, Tulloch's batman and the section runner, tapped the kukri he had thrust in his belt in case the patrol ended in close-quarter fighting.

"Eight Section," Tulloch said. "You know what to do."

The men nodded. Hogg stamped his boots on the frozen mud, preparing for the patrol.

*I led these men into Waziristan, and now we're in front of the Maginot Line, about to probe the German positions.*

"Follow me," Tulloch ordered and waited until the wind pushed a cloud across the demi-moon before rolling over the parapet and sliding free of the trench. The men followed, trusting in his leadership, all of them old sweats, experienced in patrolling the Frontier. They carried the minimum of equipment, with their bayonets smoke-darkened to prevent moonlight from reflecting on the blades and a bullet up the spout of each rifle.

Tulloch moved in a crouch, heading for the dark patches between the drifts of wet snow. Somewhere ahead, the Germans were waiting, probably putting out patrols exactly like his, with junior officers eager to prove their suitability for higher commands by killing British or French soldiers.

"The French suspect the Germans of using a farmhouse as an OP – Observation Post," Major Hume had said. "The French have sent two patrols out without success, but I think we can do better. Use your Frontier experience, Tulloch, and show them how to do it."

"Yes, sir," Tulloch said. He knew he should be scared but instead felt a surge of mixed excitement and anticipation. He wanted to see how his Waziristan veterans fared against European opposition.

"The French are watching everything we do," Colonel Pringle said quietly. "They seem a little reluctant to fight. Let's encourage them."

"We'll do our best, sir," Tulloch promised.

An abandoned farmhouse stood directly in front of the British positions, forlorn in the gloom of the night, with starlight reflecting from what glass remained in the windows. Tulloch led his patrol to within a hundred yards of the house and placed them in a shallow depression. The men sunk down, peering into the dark, with their breathing harsh in the night.

"Two men face the rear, one each flank, and the rest watch the farmhouse. If the Germans come this way, they'll expect us to occupy the farm."

The men settled down. After service on the Frontier, they were accustomed to extremes of climate and understood the need for silence. Nobody smoked. Nobody spoke. They waited with the patience of veterans as the night wore on, with a biting wind alternating with sleet showers.

Tulloch lay still, accustoming himself to the night sounds and the tricks the dark played with his vision. He watched a bush for a moment, nearly sure he saw it move, studied it carefully and decided only the wind stirred the branches. He kept still, knowing the Germans might be scanning the ground.

A cat ran past, probably a stray from one of the already-abandoned farms, early victims of the war. None of the men moved. The cat halted to examine them, decided they were neither a threat nor a source of food and continued its hunt.

Tulloch felt something tap the side of his boot. Hardie had kicked him gently and nodded to the right of the farmhouse. Tulloch passed on the message until every member of the section knew something was happening. He pushed forward the safety catch on his rifle and waited, ignoring the intermittent sleet showers.

Within three minutes, Tulloch saw a darker shadow slide through the night and heard the distinct thud of a boot landing on stone. He looked sideways, expecting to see more than a shadow. He peered along the barrel of his rifle.

The wind shifted, revealing the moon, which gleamed on the snow-streaked ground. Tulloch saw something move, then stop. He lifted his Italian binoculars and focussed on the area.

*Two men standing still, both carrying weapons, and a third is emerging from the farmhouse.*

Tulloch realised he was looking at the first German soldiers he had seen. They were tall and looked fit, with grey uniforms and rounded steel helmets, while one carried what looked like a submachine gun.

*I could fire now and kill these three or wait and hope for a better target. I'll wait.*

Tulloch watched as clouds returned to obscure the moon, and the three German soldiers began to move again. Others left the farmhouse to join them until Tulloch counted eight men under a man with a pistol, whom he guessed was an officer. The German patrol eased around the house and returned, with each man covering the next.

Waiting until they were all inside the farm, Tulloch tapped Hardie's boot. "Cover me," he whispered and crawled forward over the cold ground.

Aware the Germans would be watching from the farmhouse window, Tulloch moved with as much care as he had on the Frontier. He slid from cover to cover, hugging the dead ground and watching for movement from the building. He saw moonlight reflect from the steel helmet of a man at an upper window and heard the low murmur of voices from the ground floor.

*The man upstairs is the danger; the men below are the target.*

Easing behind the brick garden wall, Tulloch pulled the pin from two grenades, took a deep breath, stood up, and threw both through the lower window before immediately dropping down. The sentry on the upper floor reacted a second too slowly, so the first grenade exploded with an ugly crump before he gave his warning shout.

Innes's Bren gun stuttered as the second grenade crashed out, and Tulloch lay flat as his section plastered the farmhouse. Only one man attempted to return fire, leaning from the upstairs window, and a blast from the Bren finished him. Tulloch saw fragments of stone and a cloud of dust and wood from the window frame as Innes sprayed his target.

"Cease fire!" Tulloch ordered, and his section obeyed, so silence descended, broken only by a terrible moaning from inside the house. He waited for a moment, watching for movement from the unseen German positions. "Cover me!"

Rising to a crouch, Tulloch zig-zagged forward to the walls of the now smoking building. He glanced in the ground floor window and saw three dead men and one writhing with his legs mangled and blood over his face. Tulloch climbed in the window and discovered which of the dead men was the officer. Careless of the splintered bones and warm blood, Tulloch removed the officer's insignia and all the papers he was carrying, then did what he could for the injured man.

"Your friends will be here soon," Tulloch said gruffly before climbing out of the window and running back to Eight Section. He froze as a star shell exploded above the farmhouse.

"When that fades, it's back to base, lads," Tulloch said as he slid to his previous position.

"How many did we get, sir?" Brown asked, avoiding looking at the bright light overhead.

"I saw three dead and one wounded," Tulloch replied, "and the lad upstairs makes four dead. There should be another three Germans."

"They ran," Hardie said quietly. "When Innes was hammering at the top window, they ran out the back door. I might have got one of them." He tapped his rifle.

"Well done," Tulloch said. He knew that Hardie was one of the best shots in the battalion. The star shell faded away, and a single artillery round screamed down to explode on the opposite side of the farmhouse. "Come on, lads, before it gets dangerous here."

As Tulloch spoke, a salvo of mortar shells arrived to explode around the farmhouse in tall fountains of white smoke.

"The Germans don't know that one of their own wounded is inside there," Lightfoot said.

"Oh, they know all right," Hardie said. "They just don't care."

More artillery shells landed, destroying the farmhouse and

the surrounding garden walls as Tulloch led Eight Section in a rapid withdrawal.

———

COLONEL PRINGLE NODDED IN SATISFACTION WHEN TULLOCH handed him the captured documents and regimental insignia. "You're beginning to make a name for yourself in the battalion, Tulloch. Don't take too many chances out there."

"I won't, sir," Tulloch said.

"I'll get these documents back to Intelligence," Pringle said. "They might prove useful, or they could be the weekly rations." He tapped the stem of his pipe on his desk. "The regimental insignia will tell us who our immediate opposition is, at any rate. You've been out on patrol three nights out of seven, now Tulloch. What do you think of the Germans as soldiers?"

"Very well disciplined, sir, but not great at night."

"No?" The colonel gave a brief smile. "What makes you say that?"

"They make too much noise, sir, and follow the same routine. We knew they occupied that farmhouse, and Hardie heard them from a distance."

"Our Waziristan experience is coming in handy, then," Colonel Pringle said. "I'll pass on your observations as well. Now get some rest, Tulloch. Tomorrow could be another busy day."

The Lothians were based a quarter of a mile in front of the Maginot Line, with three lines of newly dug trenches and dugouts. Tulloch collapsed onto his canvas-and-wood camp bed, checked his revolver was handy in case of any nighttime emergency and fell asleep in seconds.

"For God's sake, shoot me!" Tulloch had never seen such naked fear as on Russell's face. "They'll flay me alive!"

Tulloch moaned in his sleep, reliving his Waziristan experiences. He woke with a start to hear distant machine-gun fire, remembered where he was and realised he was soaking with sweat. Instinctively, he reached for his revolver.

*I'm all right. Nobody except the chaplain knows, and it was a work of mercy.*

Tulloch closed his eyes and tried to sleep.

"Tulloch!" Moustached and burly, Major Hume glowered at him from above the camp bed. "The colonel wants you."

"Sir." Tulloch scrambled to sit up and guiltily replaced the revolver in its holster. He had never worked Hume out. The major was never ruffled and seemed to know what to do in every situation.

"Get dressed, Douglas, and bring your revolver," Hume said, leaving the dugout.

The day was still young, with faint stars in the grey sky as Tulloch hurried to the colonel's quarters. He halted outside to straighten his uniform, took a deep breath, and pushed inside.

A civilian stood beside Colonel Pringle; medium height and slightly shabby, he examined Tulloch as he entered.

*I've seen you before,* Tulloch thought, still groggy from being awakened so abruptly.

"Tulloch. This gentleman is Mr Prentice." The colonel made a curt introduction.

"Mr Prentice," Tulloch held out his hand.

"Lieutenant Tulloch," Prentice's grip was firm and cool as he continued to assess Tulloch. "I believe you saw Francesco Giorano in Afghanistan."

*This man doesn't beat about the bush.* "I saw him in Waziristan, on the Northwest Frontier," Tulloch corrected. "I did not see him in Afghanistan."

Prentice nodded. "Would you recognise him again?"

Tulloch felt instant dismay. "I believe so, Mr Prentice." *This man is the civilian I saw with Colonel Clark. I thought I had left the espionage behind when we left the Frontier.*

"We think Giorano is in Belgium," Prentice said, "consulting with German agents and calculating the relative strength of the

British, French, German and Belgian armies." He spoke slowly and precisely as he held Tulloch's gaze. "We want you to enter Belgium and identify him so we can prevent him from doing any more damage."

Tulloch glanced at Colonel Pringle for support.

"It's your decision, Tulloch," Pringle said, holding his pipe in his left hand. He began to clean inside the bowl with a stubby-bladed knife.

"I'd prefer to remain with the regiment, Mr Prentice," Tulloch said at once.

"The army has many eager young regimental officers," Prentice said quietly, "but only one officer who can identify a very dangerous enemy agent. You have already proved your worth in Waziristan, Tulloch. Those papers you brought back helped us nullify a threat from Afghanistan and the Pashtun tribes."

"Lieutenant Tulloch has made his decision," Colonel snapped.

"I hope he reconsiders," Prentice said. "Francesco Giorano has already cost us one of our best agents." He fixed Tulloch with a steady stare. "Charles Russell was a dedicated officer and a personal friend of mine."

*God forgive me,* Tulloch prayed, aimed his rifle at Russell's head and fired. He felt the weapon's vicious kick and fired again, seeing Russell's skull explode. *God forgive me,* Tulloch whispered again as nausea rose in his throat. *Now I am a murderer. I have murdered a British officer.*

"Russell found the documents in Waziristan," Tulloch reminded. "Not me. That was his blood staining them."

Colonel sat back in his chair and began to fill his pipe. "How long will this operation take, Prentice?"

"Only a few days," Prentice said. "We take Tulloch into Belgium, identify Giorano or not, and take him back. Three days if everything goes smoothly, maybe five if we meet a hitch."

"I'm not a spy," Tulloch said, pushing away the memory of Russell's death.

"Nobody's asking you to spy," Prentice reassured him. "Only to identify a dangerous enemy agent."

The colonel struck a match and applied it to the bowl of his pipe. "I hadn't heard that we were at war with Italy," he said, with his weary, humorous eyes shifting from Tulloch to Prentice and back.

"Not yet," Prentice said. "Mussolini's biding his time until he knows who will likely win. Removing his agent may help convince him to back the better horse."

"I see," Colonel puffed blue smoke into the air. "What do you think, Tulloch?"

Tulloch heard Russell's final words ringing in his ear. "I'd prefer to remain with the regiment, sir, but I think my duty is to find Giorano. I want to avenge Captain Russell."

"It's not a personal vendetta," Prentice reminded. "You'd need to be professional."

"I'd like to avenge Captain Russell," Tulloch repeated.

"There's no vengeance," Prentice said quietly. "You'll be dressed as a civilian and won't need a weapon. All you do is identify the man we think is Giorano and leave the rest to us."

# Chapter Eighteen

*At the door of life, by the gate of breath,*
*There are worse things waiting for men than death.*
**Algernon Swinburne: *The Triumph of Time***

Crossing the border into Belgium was easier than Tulloch had expected as he sat in the passenger seat of the Peugeot 402. Dressed in civilian clothes, Prentice stopped at the simple barrier, where a smartly uniformed guard approached them. Prentice handed over their forged French identification papers, joked with the guard, and drove into Belgium.

"Let me do the talking," Prentice said casually. "You have only one job to do, and that's to identify Giorano."

"That's all I'll be doing," Tulloch said. "Get into Brussels, point out Giorano, out again and back to my unit and hope Hitler doesn't invade in the meantime."

Prentice grunted. "If he does, we'll be the first out of the country, Tulloch, and that's a promise."

They drove along quiet, well-maintained roads, with Tulloch marvelling at the peaceful appearance of the country when three rival armies were gearing up for battle on its borders.

"Stick your head under the sand, little ostrich," Prentice murmured. "Maybe that way, Hitler will ignore you, and the troubles will all disappear."

Tulloch tapped the revolver in his inside pocket. "Let's hope Belgium's faith in human nature is justified."

Tulloch had expected Brussels to be wary, with soldiers everywhere and air raid defences on street corners. Instead, the city bustled with life, with many more civilians than military and women laughing as they continued their daily routine.

As in Edinburgh, the town centre was ancient, but unlike Scotland's capital, many of the old buildings were well-maintained. A ring of tree-enhanced boulevards surrounded the centre, providing shade in summer and shelter in winter. Prentice drove slowly to their hotel.

"It's only a small place, the *Palatiale*," Prentice said. "I don't wish to draw unwanted attention by living anywhere like the *Metripole Hotel*, and anyway, we're on a tight budget."

Tulloch nodded. "Whatever it is, it'll be better than sleeping in a muddy trench."

Once they booked in, Prentice handed Tulloch a bundle of money, a map of Belgium, and took him on a walking tour of the city. "That's the British Embassy," Prentice said and pointed out the significant buildings.

"You'd best familiarise yourself with the layout before we do anything," Prentice said. "If anything goes wrong, you have the choice of running into the British Embassy as a DBS or trying to make it across Belgium to rejoin the army."

"What's a DBS?"

"Distressed British Subject," Prentice informed him. He pointed to an elaborate station. "That's the railway station. You could catch a train to the French frontier from there." He glanced over his shoulder. "Keep watch all the time, Tulloch. If we got into Belgium without difficulty, so can the Germans or Italians."

"Do you anticipate anything going wrong, Prentice?"

"It's always best to have an escape route, Tulloch." Prentice stopped at a street corner and gave a brief history of Brussels. "The Flemish speakers think of Brussels as their city and often dislike French speakers, so be careful."

Tulloch nodded. "I'm not here as a tourist," he reminded. "Let's find Giorano."

Prentice nodded. "As you wish." Buying a newspaper, he handed it to Tulloch before taking him through a doorway in a shabby tenement that boasted four storeys and a frontage of multi-paned windows. "Second floor up, Tulloch, and the second door."

The flat was small and untidy, with two rooms and a primitive bathroom. Prentice stepped to the window. "Now, Tulloch, this is where you earn your corn."

"What do you want me to do?" Tulloch glanced at the busy street below and the building opposite.

Opening a drawer, Prentice produced two pairs of binoculars. "I want you to watch those windows across the road." He pointed to a tenement building similar to the one where they were. "That's where we've seen our suspect. Remember, all you do is identify him and don't let him see you."

Tulloch looked around the room. It was sparse in furniture, with only a couple of chairs, a table, and a small chest of drawers. He dragged a chair to within a few feet of the window and sat down with the binoculars in his lap.

"Keep back from the window," Prentice advised. "If you see Giorano, let me know, and I'll do the rest."

"What rest?" Tulloch asked.

"That's not your concern," Prentice replied. "Once you've positively identified your man, you've completed your job, and you can return to your unit."

Tulloch nodded. He did not want to be involved in any type of espionage.

"I'm going out," Prentice said. "I'll be back in a couple of hours."

Tulloch nodded. "I'll be here," he said. Leaning back in the straight-backed wooden chair, he lifted the binoculars and focussed on the window across the road.

The suspected agent's room was well-furnished, with leather armchairs, a bookcase, and half a dozen wine bottles and associated glasses on the table.

*Our Francesco Giorano likes his home comforts. What a contrast from life on the Frontier.*

Time passed slowly as Tulloch sat on the chair with his binoculars fixed on the opposite window without anybody appearing in the room. After two hours, Prentice returned with brown bags full of bread and cheese. He sat on the other chair and began to eat. "Our men are still following the suspect."

"Can't they take a photograph of him?" Tulloch asked.

"Not without raising suspicions," Prentice said. "The Belgians are a bit nervous with half the German army massing on one border and us and the French on the other."

Tulloch nodded. "That's understandable."

Prentice stepped over, still chewing. "I'll take over. Eat something first, and you'll find a bed in the next room. Get some rest, and I'll wake you in four hours."

The bed's elderly springs creaked under Tulloch's weight. Placing his pistol on the small bedside table, he lay with his mind whirling with images of the Frontier and France. The memories combined in a kaleidoscope that kept him awake for half an hour before he eventually drifted into a dreamless sleep.

"Somebody's there," Prentice sounded tense as he shook Tulloch awake. "See if it's your man."

"Right."

When Tulloch reached for his revolver, Prentice pushed him towards the door. "We haven't got time for that! Giorano might leave at any second! Come on!"

The street lamps were on as Tulloch entered the front room. He peered across the road with the binoculars, seeing the back of a man's head. "He's sitting at the table, facing the other direction," Tulloch said. "Wait until he turns around."

The suspect poured himself a glass of wine and drank it maddeningly slowly as he read a document.

"He's reading something," Tulloch said.

"Can you see what?" Prentice asked.

"The print's too small," Tulloch replied. "It might be the German order of battle, and it could be the football pools."

Prentice stood at the opposite side of the window with his binoculars raised. He glanced down at the street below, and for a second, Tulloch saw a man in a long coat standing underneath a lamppost. *I'll wager that's our agent.*

Prentice swore. "Turn around, man! I haven't got all day!"

Both men started when somebody kicked open their door, and three men burst into the room.

"What the hell?" Tulloch asked, turning towards the door. Two intruders held pistols while the third shouted, "Surrender!"

"Get out, Tulloch!" Prentice yelled, falling to the floor and drawing a revolver from a shoulder holster. "Run, man!"

Tulloch swore and threw his binoculars at the leading gunman, who ducked and fired, with the bullet crashing into the far wall. Prentice fired, hitting the leading man, with the force of the bullet sending him staggering back against the door. The second gunman fired, hitting Prentice in the chest. He reared back, spouting blood, and the gunman fired again, drilling a bullet through Prentice's head and spraying blood and brains against the wall.

With his revolver still in the bedroom and faced by two men, Tulloch knew his best chance was to run. Feinting left, he broke to the right and dived through the open door before the attackers realised what was happening.

*We thought we were so clever following Giorano; he knew all about us.*

Tulloch heard the two men follow him into the common stair, with their rubber-soled boots thumping on the ground as he raced into the street outside. About to shout to the man underneath the lamppost, he realised he was standing unnaturally still.

*He's dead. Probably knifed from behind.*

A man emerged from the tenement opposite, and for a moment, Tulloch stared straight at him. The man met his gaze, narrowed his eyes, and pointed.

*That is Francesco Giorano, and he recognised me.*

Tulloch lengthened his stride and hurried along the dark street, trying to avoid the yellow light the lamps pooled. He heard footsteps behind him and increased his speed. He ran towards the car, saw all four tyres were flat and swore.

*The enemy has sabotaged the car. I'm a soldier, not a blasted spy. What the hell am I doing here? My Waziri training is no good in a city.*

Brussels' streets were darker than Edinburgh's, and Tulloch's limited French prevented him from asking for help. He heard the thump of footsteps behind him and ran aimlessly, wondering if it were better to stay on broader streets with more people or on side streets where he could evade his pursuers.

*Where is the British Embassy? If I get there, I should be safe.*

The footsteps behind him seemed louder. Tulloch glanced over his shoulder and saw two men following, one tall and burly and the other average height, yet both looking dangerous. He thought they might be the men who shot Prentice, but things had happened so quickly he was unsure.

*What do I do now? Stand and fight? Or run?* He swore softly, turned a corner, and saw a broad boulevard open before him, bare-branched trees swaying slightly in the breeze and half a dozen people walking. Tulloch increased his pace, hoping his pursuers would not shoot him in front of witnesses.

A car roared past with a white-faced passenger glancing at Tulloch without interest. He lifted a hand to attract the driver's attention, glanced behind him, and saw his pursuers were still there.

*If I fight them, I might get arrested and then what? Will the Belgians intern me for the duration of the war?*

Tulloch swore again and increased his speed, hearing the footsteps behind him. He hated running from the enemy but could see no alternative.

*I'm not going to run. I'll stand and fight and damn the consequences.* Tulloch looked for a wall to stand against, confident he could make a good account of himself against a couple of foreign agents, either Italian or German.

He heard the rumbling noise a moment before he recognised the source. *That was a train,* he told himself. *Prentice showed me the railway station. Where?*

Tulloch looked around, increasing his pace as hope increased within him. He recognised the building, strolled past it, then turned and ran inside. Tulloch's sudden burst of speed surprised his pursuers, so he gained a few yards when he entered the station. Two policemen paced across the main concourse glanced at him without interest and looked away.

A uniformed clerk was on duty at the booking office and looked up when Tulloch lunged at the counter.

"Tournai," Tulloch remembered the name of a town near the Belgian border with France. He recalled his French. "A ticket for Tournai, please."

The clerk frowned and replied in a language Tulloch supposed to be Walloon or Dutch. He took a deep breath, forced a smile, and repeated the question in French. The clerk shrugged.

"Do you speak English?" Tulloch asked.

"Yes," the clerk replied slowly.

"A ticket for Tournai, please," Tulloch said, handing over all the money he had. He knew his pursuers were waiting a few yards behind him, one with a hand suggestively inside his jacket. The patrolling policemen paced past with their hands behind their backs.

"Your train leaves in ten minutes, sir," the clerk said, handing over a ticket. He sorted through the money, extracted two notes, and returned the rest with a smile.

"Thank you," Tulloch selected the highest denomination note. "Please delay the two men behind me," he said and lowered his voice. "I think they are French agents."

The clerk accepted the bribe without a qualm. "Yes, sir," he said.

Tulloch turned away, deliberately brushing against one of his pursuers. When the man reacted with a push and angry words, both police turned in his direction, as Tulloch had intended. He hurried towards the Tournai train as one of his pursuers followed, and the other tried to buy tickets.

Tulloch leaped on the train, checked his watch, and saw he had six minutes to wait until it left the platform. He hoped the clerk could delay the agents, so they missed the train and watched the platform anxiously.

Four minutes to go, and still no sign of the agents. Tulloch silently thanked the nameless clerk. He heard the engine hiss out steam and guessed the driver was preparing to depart.

Two minutes. Tulloch began to relax a little. The train was juddering now as the steam mounted. He swore when he saw his pursuers striding towards the train, breaking into a run when they realised the time. The guard on duty also saw them and shouted something, with the words lost in the increasing noise of the train.

The agents were racing now as the guard held the train. Tulloch cursed as they reached the back of the train and jumped on board before it picked up speed. He knew there was nowhere to hide on the train, and it was a journey of ninety-five minutes to Tournai, so his pursuers were bound to catch him.

"Guard," Tulloch tried the direct approach. "These two men are foreign agents."

The guard looked Tulloch up and down. "Are you Belgian, sir?"

"No, I'm British," Tulloch admitted.

"Then you are also foreign," the guard said.

"They are Belgium's enemies," Tulloch knew the words sounded stilted.

"Belgium is neutral, sir. We have no enemies."

"Not yet," Tulloch said. "I'd be careful." He moved up the six-wagon train, unsure what to do but trying to put as much distance as possible between himself and the two pursuers.

"How far is it to Tournai?" He asked one of the few fellow passengers, a stout gentleman with a luxuriant moustache.

"Ninety-seven kilometres, sir," the man answered promptly. "We'll be there before midnight."

"Thank you," Tulloch said. He moved on. Nothing in his army training had prepared him for such a situation. *Ninety-Seven kilometres, that's about sixty miles, which is too far to walk.*

The idea came to Tulloch as he moved further up the train towards the engine. Sitting down, he took off his socks, and as he closed each connecting door behind him, he jammed them shut, tying the handles together with his socks. He knew such a simple stratagem would not delay the enemy for long, but every minute helped.

When Tulloch came across an abandoned leather bag, he rummaged inside, found a pair of man's boots, and deftly removed the laces. That tied the next connecting door, and Tulloch realised the train was slowing down and the guard was shouting something.

"Ath! We are stopping at Ath!"

Tulloch groaned. An influx of passengers would undoubtedly remove his simple defensive precautions. He saw a dozen people on the dimly lit station, most moving towards the train. Tulloch waited until they were boarding, then opened the door and jumped onto the platform. He ran under the lights to make himself visible, then quickly doubled back in the shelter of the crowd. Running in front of the stationary train, he strode down half the length and re-boarded as it eased away.

Keeping back from the windows, Tulloch looked over the

platform and saw his pursuers searching frantically for him. One was at the booking office, and the second turned to stare at the train as it departed through a great bank of steam.

*Catch me if you can!* Tulloch thought. *I'll sit here until we reach Tournai, then walk across the frontier and over to the British positions. The mission was not a success.*

# Chapter Nineteen

*Boldest men at their posts, staunch under stress,*
*May their souls be, after the battle,*
*Made welcome in heaven's land, home of plenty.*
**The Goddodin**

Tulloch staggered through the dark, with moonlight glinting on the tangle of barbed wire ahead. He kept to the centre of the road, hoping the engineers had not planted more mines since he had been here last. Somebody murmured close by, with the distinctive shape of a British steel helmet rising from a two-man rifle pit.

The Lothian sentry pointed his bayonet-tipped rifle at Tulloch. "Halt and identify yourself! Who are you, you bastard?"

Tulloch stopped at once, knowing how nervous a man on stag could be. "Lieutenant Tulloch of B Company, Lothian Rifles!"

"Step forward, sir!"

Tulloch stepped forward with his hands wide, remembering the same scenario when he had returned with the Tochi Scouts on the Northwest Frontier.

"Stay on the road, sir," the sentry warned. "The verges are mined."

"Thank you," Tulloch said. He waited until a sergeant beckoned him forward, staring suspiciously at his muddy civilian clothes.

"Take me to the colonel," Tulloch said.

"He'll be in bed, sir," the sergeant reminded. "He might not like to be disturbed."

"Take me anyway," Tulloch ordered.

Colonel Pringle wore his trousers and a revolver when Tulloch reported his arrival. "You're safe then, Tulloch," he said. "Get some sleep, and you can make your full report tomorrow. I'll notify Colonel Clark that you're back. Goodnight to you."

"Good night, sir," Tulloch said as Lightfoot, his batman, appeared magically at his back.

"This way, sir. You're back in your old quarters with everything ready."

---

PRINGLE AND COLONEL CLARK VIEWED TULLOCH ACROSS THE width of the desk, with a map of northeastern France spread over one wall and a map of Belgium on the other. Clark looked up when Tulloch gave his verbal report.

"You're sure it was Francesco Giorano?"

"Yes, sir. I'm positive."

Clark pursed his lips. He wore a uniform jacket with the insignia of his rank, worn corduroy trousers and a pair of black boots with brown laces. "And Prentice is dead."

"Shot twice, sir, once through the head."

Clark swore softly. "That's two good men Giorano has cost us. You're lucky to have survived, Tulloch."

"The devil looks after his own, sir," Tulloch said. "And Giorano's men killed our other agent, sir, the man who tailed him."

"He was a local man Prentice hired," Clark said. "I don't know his name. I've put two men on Giorano, and with your positive identification, Tulloch, we no longer need you."

"Thank you, sir. I'll be glad to return to regimental soldiering."

"You'll probably be safer," Clark said. "It's a bit sobering that the *Servizio Informazioni Militare*, SIM, the Italian Military Information Service, is working so closely with the Germans in Belgium. We rate them very highly, far higher than the *Abwehr*, the German equivalent."

"I had never heard of them until the Waziri campaign, sir," Tulloch admitted.

"No," Clark said. "They don't poke their heads above the parapet very often. Mario Roatta, their head of operations, has directed some notable assassinations, including King Alexander of Yugoslavia and Louis Barthou, the French Foreign Minister." He looked at his hands, palms up. "We got our hands on Roatta's latest report on the Italian armed forces, which is accurate and quite scathing, but his own department is extremely formidable. His aid enabled Franco to win the Spanish Civil War and stopped the supply of arms to Haile Selassie in Ethiopia."

"I didn't know that, sir," Tulloch said.

"Aye, a duck looks serene when it swims, but its feet paddle like mad. More happens underwater than on top in the world of espionage, Lieutenant Tulloch. Be thankful you have only scraped the surface."

"I am, sir," Tulloch said. "I don't intend to dig any deeper."

"That's all, Tulloch," Colonel Pringle growled. "Dismissed."

"Sir," Tulloch rose from his seat, saluted and left the office.

While Montgomery's 3rd Division watched the quiet Belgian border and continued to train, British units serving on other sections of the line experienced sporadic bouts of action. At the beginning of March 1940, the Germans raided the Duke of Cornwall's Light Infantry, killing two NCOs and capturing sixteen men. The Lothians trained, waited, and discussed the progress of the war.

"Have you heard the news?" Tait asked. "The Russians and Finns have made peace."

Tulloch nodded. "Thank goodness. Churchill had some wild idea of sending British help to Finland, so we'd simultaneously be at war with Russia and Germany."

Major Hume looked up from his appraisal of the Lothians' participation in the latest 3rd Divisional exercise. "Nothing would be more likely to bring Italy into the war," he said, "and encourage the Germans to attack here. We don't have the manpower or resources for a war on two fronts, as well as defending the Empire."

While all of Europe waited for the Germans to invade, the units on the front line engaged in patrol activity. Towards the end of March, a six-man patrol of the Lancashire Fusiliers ambushed ten Germans, killed five and captured one. Above the lines, French, German, and British aircraft exchanged fire, with casualties on both sides.

"The Norwegian affair is not going well," Muirhead said.

On the Ninth of April 1940, Germany invaded neutral Denmark and Norway. Denmark surrendered the same day, and German troops and aircraft poured into Norway. France and Britain sent small, ill-equipped forces to help defend the country, but the Germans were well-prepared and won a series of victories. The Royal Navy showed its teeth with victory at the Second Battle of Narvik, sinking eight German destroyers and a U-boat.

"The Navy is doing its stuff," Tulloch replied.

"Thank God for the Royal Navy," Muirhead said. "According to our intelligence officer, the Germans thought the Norwegians would throw in their hand with Hitler as Austria did. He believes the Norwegian resistance is delaying the German invasion of the Netherlands and Belgium."

Tulloch nodded. Ever since the British Expeditionary Force had landed in France the previous year, rumours had swept them with speculation when the Phoney War would end, and the real war begin. So far, except for minor patrol operations, the army had been quiet in France, and only the Royal Air Force had engaged the enemy.

"We'll see when it happens," Tulloch said.

At three o'clock in the morning of the Tenth of May 1940, the Germans invaded Luxembourg, the Netherlands and Belgium.

---

# 10th May 1940

A frantic barrage of anti-aircraft guns woke the 3rd division. Officers and men tumbled from their beds as they realised hostile aircraft were ahead. Some of the more optimistic privates fired their rifles at the unseen attackers while others dived into the bottom of shelter trenches, holding their steel helmets in place.

"Take your positions!" Colonel Pringle emerged from his quarters with his tunic undone and his pipe in his hand. "Anti-aircraft gunners, get to work!"

Immediately the order passed from man to man, months of training kicked in, and they ran to their posts, unsure what was happening. Men looked skyward in anticipation, clutched their rifles and either prayed or cursed, depending on their natures.

"Cease firing, Brown; you too, Kelly," Tulloch ordered. "You're wasting bullets, and we don't know if the RAF is up there." He knew the psychological advantages of fighting back, but his austere mind rebelled at the thought of wasting bullets.

Brown lowered his rifle, glowered at the sky, and spat on the ground. "About time they bastards came, sir. We've been waiting long enough."

"We may not have to wait much longer," Tulloch told him. He remained with his platoon as dawn rose ominously red in the east, silhouetting a long line of alder trees. He watched the trees for a moment as the news came from above.

"Six hours' notice, boys. The Germans are on the move. We're all on six hours' notice."

An hour later, the news the Lothians had long expected arrived.

"The Germans have invaded Belgium and the Netherlands!"

"Here we go, boys!" Sergeant Drysdale sounded almost relieved. "We knew it was going to happen; now let's show Hitler he cannae meddle with the Lothians!"

"Gin ye daur!" Innes shouted, and a few others repeated the regimental motto. Others were silent while Hardie tested the edge of his bayonet with a slight smile on his face.

At eleven that morning, General Montgomery ordered the commanding officers of every unit in the Third Division to report to his headquarters. With Colonel Pringle away, the officers crowded around the radio in the Mess, with the seniors at the front and the juniors elbowing for space at the back.

Major Hume repeated the news for the benefit of those who could not hear.

"The Germans have invaded Belgium, Luxembourg, the Netherlands, and France!"

"So much for Belgium's neutrality!" Tait said.

"That's the real war started then!" Forsyth smoothed a hand over his hair. "We'll be facing the panzers soon."

Hume shouted the following announcement. "The King of the Belgians has formally requested Allied assistance."

Tait shook his head. "It's a damned shame the Belgian king didn't allow us to recce the ground first or even use aerial photography to find the best defensive sites."

Tulloch was unsure which feeling predominated in the mess, elation, apprehension, or relief that something was actually happening. The army had waited for months, with alerts of imminent action followed by cancellations, exercises, and training.

At midday, Colonel Pringle returned.

"Plan D will come into immediate effect, and General Montgomery asked us to impress on the troops that is the real thing and not an exercise."

Pringle looked over his officers. "We are about to face the most professional and indoctrinated army in the world," he said. "Let's show them that we are their masters. The Third Division is the best-trained division in the British army, and we're the best battalion in Three Div. At 14.30 hours, forward units of 3 Division will cross the frontier into Belgium. That means us, gentlemen."

The senior officers in the division had been aware of the German intentions, if not the invasion date. The 3rd Division left their carefully prepared defensive positions and led the advance of the British 2 Corps into Belgium.

Tulloch gauged the mood of his men. Some were tense, others excited, some talked incessantly while Brown sang, and Hardie sat in the back of the fifteen hundredweight lorry, watching the French countryside roll by. Tulloch wondered what Hardie was thinking and then concentrated on leading his platoon. He sat in the leading Bren gun carrier, baking in the sun as the Lothians moved forward with a piper playing in the second carrier, and the men keyed up and ready.

*This is what I imagined when I viewed the picture of the Thin Red Line,* Tulloch realised. *This is soldiering.*

As they approached the border, a Belgian frontier guard stepped in front of the leading carrier and demanded that the division stop and produce its formal authority to enter the country.[1]

"Tell that silly bugger to stand aside, Tulloch!" Colonel ordered. "You speak French!"

"Stand aside, monsieur," Tulloch shouted. "We're here at the request of your king!"

"Show me your authority!" The guard repeated.

"Oh, for God's sake," Tulloch said. "Drive on, Aitken, but don't hit the fellow!"

"Yes, sir!" Aitken gunned the engine, circled the border guard, and crashed through the striped wooden pole that marked the frontier. The wood splintered under the impact, the guard jumped back in amazement, and some of the Lothians cheered.

Tulloch glanced over his shoulder and saw the regiment following him, most sticking to the road but others circling the frontier post. He hid his smile.

"The Lothian Rifles are going to war." He realised that the frontier guard's action was the last symbolic action of Belgium at peace. From that day onward, war would ravage Belgium, and things would never be the same again. He remembered Colonel Pringle's words as he gave the officers their final briefing.

"The 3rd Division will seize a defensive line on the banks of the Dyle, from Wavre to Leuven," the colonel had said and outlined on a map the position the Lothians would hold. "After that, we're in the lap of the war gods. It all depends on how the tactical situation develops." He thrust his empty pipe between his teeth and grinned at them. "Off we go, gentlemen."

As the Lothians advanced across the Belgian countryside, the civilians left their houses to greet them with cheers and flowers. A few waved small flags, mostly Belgian with a scattering of British, presumably left over from the 1914-18 War.

"You'd think we'd already defeated the Germans," Brown said.

"In the eyes of the Belgians, maybe we have," Hardie replied. "The older ones will remember the trenches of the last war, and the further we advance, the less chance they have of being in the front line." He did not often speak, and Tulloch wondered anew about his history.

Kelly laughed. "Advancing in Europe is much easier than campaigning on the Frontier. If Belgium were Waziristan, we'd have a dozen snipers shooting at us by now." He smiled and waved to an attractive dark-haired woman who threw a small bunch of flowers at him. "Keep it warm for me, hen!"

"Leave the bints alone, Kelly," Aitken said. "We haven't met the Germans yet."

"No, and they haven't met us."

They rumbled through Brussels as the clock hit five, with the fifteen hundredweight lorries bumping over the cobbled streets and what seemed like half the population throwing sweets, fruit, and flowers to the British soldiers. The Lothians waved back, blew kisses to anybody who looked even vaguely feminine and gave the thumbs-up sign to the men. The piper continued to play the Border Pipes, and Tulloch thought every mile they travelled was another mile the Germans would not occupy.

With a flower garland around his neck, Brown waved to the crowd while Kelly placed the stem of a flower down the barrel of his rifle.

"Where are the German planes?" Tulloch asked when they halted to refuel and feed the men. "As Private Kelly said, the Waziris would have had a field day sniping at us. Why have the German aircraft not attacked? We're a perfect target for them."

Tait nodded, examining the sky where only a few fleecy clouds marred the unbroken blue. "Maybe the RAF have chased them away, or perhaps they're too busy fighting the Belgians and French."

"Maybe," Tulloch said doubtfully. "If this were the Frontier, I'd say the Waziris were allowing us to walk into an ambush."

He thought of Private Dunn at Sandhurst and his advice to temper his aggression with guile. This blind advance into Belgium seemed too easy, like a blindfolded man walking towards the edge of a cliff.

"Keep alert, men," Tulloch warned his platoon. "We don't know what's happening out there. Listen for enemy aircraft."

The bright afternoon faded into dark as the Lothians approached the River Dyle, finding their way in the gloom and camouflaging their vehicles and camps as best they could.

211

"The Germans might send spotter aircraft over," Colonel Pringle said. "I want the Bren guns ready as a low-level anti-aircraft defence."

"It's gone very smoothly," Major Hume said. "We're a few miles east of Louven and not a whiff of the Germans by air or land."

"That's a bit worrying," Muirhead observed. "The Germans are meant to be very efficient."

Leaving the officers to their discussion, Tulloch ensured his men were fed and posted picquets. "Two-man rifle pits, lads, two-hour stags. Don't fall asleep, and keep alert for the Germans."

"The Belgians are between us and the enemy, sir," Brown pointed out.

"Maybe so, Brown, but pretend they are not and keep alert." Tulloch grabbed two hours' rest before he awakened to tour his platoon's defences. The men were awake and reported everything quiet.

"Don't check on them too often, Tulloch," Muirhead gave quiet advice. "You've let them know you're here; now, leave Sergeant Drysdale to get on with it, or the men will think you don't trust him."

Tulloch nodded. "Yes, sir. I feel that something is about to happen."

"It is," Muirhead replied quietly. "And that's even more reason for you to get some sleep. A tired officer can make mistakes that lead to men getting killed."

The sound of musketry reached the Lothians a few minutes after dawn.

"Here we go!" Tulloch shouted to his men as he crawled out of his blankets. "Stand to!"

Mainly composed of Frontier veterans, the Lothians needed no more warning and were already at their defensive positions with rifles and Brens ready to repel any German attack. Aitken held a Boys rifle, a hand-held anti-tank weapon and stared into the distance, waiting for the Germans.

"Where's the firing coming from?" Tait asked, standing on a small ridge as he swept his binoculars from left to right and back. "I can't see a damned thing."

"It's from the north," Muirhead replied. "The Middlesex Regiment."

"The Middlesex are a machine-gun battalion," Tulloch reminded. "I can't hear any machine guns replying."

Muirhead swore. "Something's wrong," he said. "The Middlesex should be eager to fire back." He nodded to Tait. "Go and see what's happening, Tait, but keep your head down in case the Germans are fooling around."

Tulloch watched Tait for a moment, then returned to scrutinising the terrain in front of his platoon. He saw an elderly farmer driving a small herd of cows for early morning milking and a young couple slipping into the side door of a cottage.

"No Germans there, sir," he reported to Muirhead.

"I can't see any, either," Muirhead agreed.

Tait returned with the news that a battalion of Belgian infantry had fired on the Middlesex, and the local Belgian commander refused to move, saying his king had ordered him to defend Louven.

"Bloody idiot!" Muirhead shook his head. "Firing on your allies is no way to fight a war."

While the British and Belgians argued, the Germans advanced into Belgium and quickly captured the bridges across the Albert Canal.

"They're moving quickly," Muirhead said. "The Belgians could have defended the Albert Canal for days if not weeks."

"Maybe the Belgians won't fight until the Germans reach us," Forsyth said.

"Working with allies always creates difficulties," Major Hume said wearily. "Everybody thinks they know best, and the loudest voice defeats the soundest counsel. We always fight better when we fight alone."

"I don't think we would have won the last war without the French," Muirhead said. "They took up much of the German strength, as did the Russians, of course."

"We would still have won," Hume said. "The war would have taken a bit longer and assumed a different shape, that's all. No long line of trenches to defend France, costing hundreds of thousands of lives. The French army mutiny forced Haig to prolong the Passchendaele battle to divert the German attention, for example."

Muirhead grunted, unhappy about being contradicted but unwilling to argue with a superior officer.

Hume continued. "Rather than wait for higher command to settle the issue of who will defend Louven, Montgomery volunteered to place himself under Belgian command."

"Montgomery did that, sir?" Tait said. "I don't like having a Belgian in charge of us. "What happens when the Germans reach here? Will we have to do what the Belgians say?"

Major shook his head. "Not according to my source," he said. "I think Montgomery will place the Belgian general under arrest and take command."

"Thank God for small mercies," Tulloch said. "This is the strangest war I've ever heard of."

"All wars are strange," Muirhead murmured. "Whoever begins them thinks they'll go according to their plan, but they create their own dynamics, and chaos ensues."

"Wars are an opportunity for men to show at their best," Forsyth spoke loudly. "Bravery, glory and comradeship."

"Sordid mass slaughter; legal murder," Hume said. "Yet we have all chosen soldiering as a career and must make the best of it."

"It was the best of times; it was the worst of times," Tait said with a sardonic smile. "Whatever it may be, we're in the middle of it now."

Tulloch thought of his recent adventures in Brussels and the death of Prentice. "Politicians and rulers steer us all towards wars," he said bleakly. "And we follow the idols of national glory and prestige while the devil makes merry at our expense." He realised that everybody was looking at him and closed his mouth.

"Come on, gentlemen," Hume said. "We all have our duty to do."

# Chapter Twenty

By war's great sacrifice, The world redeems itself.
**John Davidson: *War Song***

Reacting to Montgomery's decision, the Third Division withdrew behind the Belgians and formed a second line of defence.

"Digging again," Aitken groaned. "If I had wanted to dig, I'd have become a miner at the Lady Victoria, with better money and nobody trying to shoot me."[1]

"You a miner?" Innes scoffed. "You'd be scared of the dark!"

"I'll show you scared, you windy bastard," Aitken replied. "You only carry the Bren because you think it protects you better than a rifle."

Tulloch walked past, satisfied that his men were happy. If British soldiers ever stopped grousing, he would know something was wrong.

The engineers and pioneers were busily laying barbed wire when Colonel Pringle summoned the officers to his temporary quarters in the kitchen of a substantial house.

"If the Germans come," Pringle said baldly, "the Belgians will retreat. Their morale is poor from top to bottom."

216

"Will we stop them from retreating, sir?" Tulloch asked.

"No," Pringle said. "We'll let them go. They won't strengthen us, and they might unsettle the men. We'll fight better without them."

The officers nodded and planned for any retreating Belgians to pass through their men without hindrance.

"If you see a mob of frightened men running past," Tulloch told his platoon. "Don't shoot. They'll likely be Belgian soldiers."

"Our allies, whose country we are defending," Aitken said softly.

Tulloch nodded. "We do our duty, Aitken," he said, putting an edge in his voice.

"Windy buggers," Kelly said as Hogg shook his head and Hardie shrugged and cleaned his rifle.

As more German aircraft appeared overhead, news of further German advances in Belgium reached the Lothians.

"The Germans are pressing the Belgians and Dutch hard," the rumours came. "The Germans have broken through at Maastricht."

The Lothians dug deeper rifle pits, laid more mines, and strengthened their barbed wire defences. Anti-aircraft guns fired in intermittent retaliation to the German aerial attacks. The anti-tank gunners selected their positions and hoped to show their expertise, while Brown altered the words of his song.

"I love a lassie, a bonnie Belgian lassie,

She's as braw as my lassie fac Lochend,

But she's only got one problem,

A teenie-weenie problem,

She runs so fast I cannae catch her up."

"Shut up," Brown," Innes shouted. "Any woman with some sense would run away from you with a singing voice like that!"

The officers supervised the NCOs, who chased the privates, who exchanged black humour and sweated over the new defences.

"We'll be fighting soon," Colonel Pringle said as the latest reports came in from the front. "Don't depend on the Belgians for support; they're pulling back all along the line."

Tulloch looked up as he heard aircraft. He saw a dozen black dots high above the clouds and discounted them as no threat.

A harassed NCO ran to Colonel Pringle. "Sir! The Belgians are withdrawing!" He threw a belated salute. "We have a message from General Montgomery, sir. The Belgian commander wants his tired troops to rally and rest behind us."

"Let them through," Pringle told his officers. "I want no jeering or catcalls. Make that an order."

"Yes, sir," The officers strode to their respective companies, trying to hurry while retaining a calm appearance.

The Lothians watched in silence as the Belgian soldiers withdrew in good order, with Tulloch wondering how he would feel if higher command ordered him to withdraw through Scotland in the face of a German advance. *How many of my men would obey, and how many would slip away to fight on their own accord? He watched his men's faces, with Brown and Aitken not disguising their contempt, Hogg carefully sharpening his bayonet on a stone, and Hardie making minute adjustments to his backsight.*

When the Belgians were finally away, Colonel Pringle walked the length of the Lothians' line with his pipe between his teeth, stopping to talk to officers and men.

"Watch that house in front, Smith. You have the Boys Rifle. If I were a German, I'd park my panzer there."

"I've got the range, sir," Smith said.

"I thought you would have," Pringle said with a grim smile and moved on.

"Ah, Tait, how are your men today?"

"Grand sir, thank you. "We have a clear field of fire in front now."

"Good show, Tait. Keep it up."

"We will, sir!"

The colonel approached Sergeant Drysdale. "It's like the old days, isn't it, Sergeant?"

"Yes, sir," Drysdale replied. "Waiting for the enemy to come."

They exchanged a few memories of Arras and Ypres before Pringle walked on. Although he was in his mid-forties, he moved with all the spring of a young man. He knew his battalion was on the front line, and the Germans could attack any time, but he had positioned his men with all the skill his experience had given him.

"It's in the lap of the Gods now, Tulloch," Colonel Pringle said.

"Yes, sir. I can imagine Mars throwing his dice to decide which way the battle should go."

"Let's hope the dice lands on Hitler's head and splits it open," Pringle said and stepped away, seeing everything without apparent effort.

Tulloch watched the sun set, blood-red and ominous, and heard the sinister squeak and rattle of a tank in the far distance. He glanced around, saw the anti-tank two-pounders were ready and tried to relax.

"Things are going to get busy, men," he said to his platoon. "Keep alert."

"We will, sir," they replied.

That night, the 14th of May, the Lothians heard cheering and firing to their right, where the Coldstream Guards held the line.

"The Coldstreams have caught some Jerries, then," Hume said. "God help the enemy."

Tulloch nodded as the firing died away and checked his men were awake.

"We're waiting, sir," Kelly said and pushed forward the safety catch of his rifle.

The night passed without further incident, and the next day the Lothians discovered the Germans had been Belgian stragglers from the 10th Division.

"The Coldstreams shot them down like rabbits," Kelly said. "They shot ten Belgians."

"Poor buggers," Brown shook his head. "Running from the

Germans only to get killed by their allies. Personally, I'd prefer to face the Jerries than the Guards."

"Aye, hard bastards, the Coldstream. They'd shoot you and make your corpse stand to attention," Innes gave his opinion.

Refugees began to appear, frightened Belgian civilians running from the advancing Germans. The Lothians let them pass through, some men wishing them luck.

"Look at them," Brown said. "They're absolutely terrified."

Aitken nodded. "Aye; the Germans don't have a good reputation."

Hardy watched them without expression, took his bayonet from its sheath and began to sharpen the already sharp blade.

Tulloch established Observation Posts well in front of his platoon, led a section-strong patrol, found only frightened civilians and stray animals and returned to hear more bad news.

"The Dutch have packed in," Colonel Pringle informed the officers, "which will free more German units to attack Belgium and France."

"It took the Germans only five days to conquer the Netherlands," Hume said. "And German bombers flattened the centre of Rotterdam. Take note, gentlemen, we are not fighting men who obey the rules of civilised warfare."

"Nor did the Waziris," Tulloch responded quietly.

Hume continued. "The Germans thought they would only meet the French and Belgian soldiers here. I think we have surprised them by sitting tight."

The officers grinned, with one or two stamping their feet. "The lads are champing at the bit," Forsyth said. "They want to meet Jerry face-to-face."

Tulloch agreed. Ever since his men had seen the frightened refugees fleeing from the advancing Germans, they had wanted to take revenge. The refugees always looked scared, often carrying all their personal possessions, entire family groups, old women, mothers, and children, all fleeing from the advancing Germans.

"Who's on our left flank? The Belgians?" Colonel Pringle grunted. "They'll break at the first serious German thrust, gentlemen, so the Germans may outflank us. If so, we'll have to fight on two fronts simultaneously."

The Lothians strengthened their defences, tightened their belts, spat on their hands, and waited for the inevitable confrontation.

"Tulloch," Pringle said. "You're our patrol specialist. Take a patrol forward and see what's happening. I want information rather than confrontation, but if you see an opportunity, don't hesitate."

Tulloch nodded. "I won't, sir." He knew his men were eager to test the Germans.

Tulloch selected his old Waziristan hands of Eight Section and pushed them carefully forward, listening for any sounds.

"Extended order," he said, knowing his veterans did not need further instructions. After dodging Pashtuns, they would not give themselves away to a less skilled European enemy. The patrol advanced across settled farmland, with prosperous farms and neat fields, stopping every few yards to reconnoitre and inspect anything that might hide an enemy.

Tulloch sniffed the air, stopped, and lifted his hand, with the patrol halting at once. He whispered, "I smell tobacco smoke," to Sergeant Drysdale.

Drysdale nodded and signalled to the men, who sank into cover, waiting for whatever came out of the dark. They heard the ominous squeak and rumble of what they thought were tanks and hoped their anti-tank defences were adequate.

Tulloch signalled for the patrol to remain static while he scouted forward. He knew that Sergeant Drysdale would ensure the men returned safely. He crawled forward, waited in the shelter of a wall for a moment and raised his head slowly, using a patch of weeds to shield his movement.

The adjacent field was empty, with a boundary wall dimly seen in the dark. Beyond the wall, Tulloch saw the upper turret of a tank, with a single sentry sitting on top, casually smoking a cigarette.

*They've had things too easy so far,* Tulloch thought, *with minimum opposition from the Dutch and Belgians.*

Lifting his binoculars, Tulloch studied the tank, trying to recall his tank recognition classes. *A light tank. Our Boys anti-tank rifle can take care of it.* Rolling carefully over the wall, Tulloch inched across the field, hoping to see if there were more than one tank. The murmur of voices stopped him, and a loud laugh instantly subdued. Tulloch heard a sharp order, and the sentry stubbed out his cigarette and dismounted from his perch.

Tulloch waited another five minutes and withdrew, crawling backwards through the field. He watched a relieving sentry take a position beside the tank, with his head and shoulders clear above the wall. He waited until the man looked in the opposite direction, slid over the wall, and returned to his patrol.

"Back we go, boys."

Colonel Pringle listened to his report.

"One tank only," he repeated.

"I only saw one, sir," Tulloch said. "There might have been more. The sentry was very lax, but his officer, or maybe his NCO, was more alert."

"Did they see you?"

"No, sir. I didn't see any sign of an OP or any patrols. The Germans seem to shut down for the night as if they're confident there's no threat from us."

"Or from the Belgians," Pringle agreed. "Thank you, Tulloch. We'll alert the anti-tank boys." He smiled, "I might even ask the division artillery to have a stonk on that part of the world just before dawn. The Germans will be on standby then."

"Yes, sir," Tulloch agreed.

Twenty minutes before five the following morning, Three Division's artillery opened up, with every piece firing three shells in a concentrated barrage that targeted the German position

Tulloch had highlighted. As his platoon watched from their trenches, the storm of fire and steel landed.

"Poor buggers under that lot," Aitken said.

"Rather them than me," Brown replied.

Hogg sat on the edge of his trench, watching without comment.

When the shellfire died away, the Germans retaliated, aiming for the British guns rather than the Lothians. Their barrage lasted precisely three minutes and stopped, leaving a cloud of dust and smoke.

"That was all your fault, Tulloch," Muirhead commented casually. "I hope you're proud of yourself." He winked and turned away.

On the 15th of May, with Montgomery's 3 Division still in firm control of Louven, the retreating Belgians claimed the Germans had captured the town, which made some of the Lothians laugh out loud.

"We must be German, then," Brown said and adopted what he believed was a German accent. "We haff come to take your country, no?"

"You're gonga, [2]you are, Broonie," Hogg told him. "That sounds more like a drunken Portuguese with a stutter."

"It's all right, lads," Tulloch addressed his platoon. "Some idiot learned of the Grenadiers shooting the Belgian stragglers, added two and two and made five. Brown, you can stop trying to be German now."

Before the Lothians had time to digest the fiction, news filtered from the right of the British Expeditionary Force that the Germans had broken through the French front south of Dinant. Colonel Pringle called the officers to his headquarters, and Hume gave a succinct address. "They've made inroads at Sedan and Mezieres, too," Hume said, "and they're pressing the French 1st Army on the Wavre-Namur gap." He moved his pointer around a large map of France, showing where the

Germans had advanced. "We can expect the Germans to attack us any time, gentlemen."

"What do we do, sir?" Forsyth asked.

"We sit tight until ordered to attack or retire," Colonel Pringle said.

When Tulloch returned to his platoon, the men were aware something had happened. "Are the Germans coming, sir?"

"Probably, Brown," Tulloch replied.

"The waiting is the worst part," Lightfoot said. "I don't like the waiting."

"Windy bastard," Kelly said, ignoring Lightfoot's threatening gestures.

The Germans did not threaten the Lothians' position the next day but pushed forward minor advances to test Three Division's defences. Montgomery held firm in Louven, defeating every German attempt to enter.

The Lothians heard the firing and saw the smoke as the Royal Ulster Rifles held back an attack until massively superior numbers and heavy artillery shelling pushed them back.

"The Germans have penetrated as far as Louvain Station," Tait shouted, looking over his shoulder.

"The Ulstermen won't like that," Tulloch replied. "They'll counterattack."

The Lothians listened to the stammer of Bren guns and hammer of musketry as the Ulsterman regrouped and surged back into the attack, throwing out the Germans during a morning of savage fighting. At one point, the station's glass roof collapsed on the Ulstermen while Second Lieutenant Garstin crossed the subway with a Bren and took the Germans in the flank. The Ulsters, supported by the King's Own Scottish Borderers and 7th Field Regiment, threw back the attackers with bayonets and grenades.

Hogg grunted and showed misshapen teeth. "Bloody Germans. Did they think we'd cave in like the Belgians?" He stamped his heavy boots on the ground and nodded in the direction of the Ulstermen. "I met some of the Ulstermen on the Orange marches. They're not boys you want to argue with."

Tulloch did not comment. He knew Hogg supported Heart of Midlothian, but the extreme Protestant connection with the Orange Lodge was new to him.

After their repulse at the railway station, the Germans resorted to a sustained artillery bombardment and attacked the Coldstream Guards at half past one that afternoon. Despite their losses to the barrage, the Guards held firm and pushed the Germans back in a bloody encounter.

"You're not doing very well, are you, Hitler?" Aitken jeered.

"They're coming again," Tait shouted as the Germans mounted another attack on Louvain.

"Come on, then," Aitken invited, sighting along the barrel of his rifle.

Aware that their nerves were suffering, Tulloch toured his men, encouraging them where he needed to and sharing jokes with the Frontier veterans.

"Sir!" Drysdale pointed to the field immediately in front of Four Platoon. "I saw a German head pop up behind the dyke."

"If you see a German, shoot him," Tulloch said.

Brown gave a high-pitched laugh. "Holy Moses, I am dying,
Just one word before I go,
If you see a German soldier,
Stick a bayonet up his
Holy Moses, I am dying."

"There's another," Drysdale snarled and fired, with the crack of the rifle disturbing Brown's song. Eight Section joined in with Innes's Bren stuttering and raising dust and chips of stone from the wall. Kelly, Innes's number two, handed over a spare magazine.

· · ·

Tulloch peered over at the wall, saw half a dozen Germans hastily withdrawing, borrowed Kelly's rifle, and fired, bringing one down.

"Well done, boys," he said, handing back Kelly's rifle. "They were just probing our defences. Don't wait for orders, fire on sight."

With their initial attacks repulsed the Germans resorted to their artillery, hammering at Three Divisions' positions with light and medium guns as the British took cover in their trenches and waited.

"We didn't have this on the Frontier," Tait said, holding his steel helmet in place as dirt and stones spattered down.

"Welcome to civilised warfare," Tulloch replied.

In common with the other regiments in the division, the Lothians took casualties, with the cry of "stretcher bearers!" becoming horribly familiar as the day wore on. Tulloch tried to ensure the wounded were moved quickly to a field hospital and the dead decently buried.

"Men like to know they'll be cared for if they're hit," Major Hume said. "Nothing affects them worse than having wounded comrades screaming or moaning beside them."

"According to the latest news, the French are rattled on our right," Forsyth commented, "and the Belgians on the left are about to break."

"We'll hold out," Hume said as the artillery eased. The sudden silence was deafening as men poked their heads from their rifle pits, shook themselves to see if they were still alive, exchanged dark humour with their oppos and peered forward.

"Aye," Tulloch said. "We'll hold out, but will our allies?"

# Chapter Twenty One

*Our wearisome pedantic art of war,*
*By which we prove retreat may be success.*
**Robert Browning: *Luria I***

On the 16th of May, the Germans again pushed at Louvain, with an intense artillery barrage causing more casualties to the Coldstream Guards. The German infantry attacked without armoured support, and the British repulsed them. However, despite the success, Viscount Gort realised the Germans were about to surround the British and ordered a withdrawal to the Escaut Canal.

"What for are we withdrawing?" Aitken complained. "Every time they attack, we beat them!"

"The Frogs are running," Brown said. "And the Belgique are panicking again."

"So? We can win the war without them!"

Brown smiled. "Maybe later. We'll have to consolidate our position so they cannae outflank us."

*Maybe later,* Tulloch repeated Brown's words as the Lothians packed up and withdrew with the rest of the division. He saw

Montgomery briefly, a man who seemed calm despite the gravity of the situation.

They withdrew that same afternoon, with British armour on the left flank and rear to cover the infantry, and the divisional artillery hammering at the German positions. The Lothians acted as rearguard to the 8th Infantry Brigade, already accustomed to the intermittent German shelling. Thanks to Montgomery's insistence on constant training, every officer and man knew his part, and the withdrawal was smooth, despite the enemy's attempts to interfere.

The British withdrawal plan was simple, with the two front-line brigades gradually thinning themselves out before retiring through the third brigade, which held a reserve line. The system was replicated down to platoon and section level, with every man heading for a pre-designated rendezvous point.

"Come on, lads!" Tulloch encouraged.

"Get fell in!" Sergeant Drysdale shouted. "Brown! None of your singing! Lightfoot, you've left the spare Bren barrel behind. Come on, you idle buggers; we're heading back towards France and decent vino!"

Tulloch shepherded his men from their forward positions into waiting fifteen hundredweight trucks and grunted as a battery of twenty-five pounders fired a final salvo before limbering up.

"We can't win a war by retreating," he said.

"Tell that to the French," Forsyth replied. "They seem to be in a race with the Belgians to see who can put the most distance between themselves and the Germans."

"What happens now?" Tait asked.

"Four Div is on the River Senne," Major Hume said. "We pass through them and reform on the Dendre. Then Four Div will withdraw through us."

Tulloch nodded. When Montgomery had insisted they practice retiring under enemy pressure, he had thought it a waste of time. Now he saw how difficult a procedure it was, he blessed the general's forethought.

The Lothians were thoughtful as they drove through Belgium. Civilians who had cheered them on their advance now watched solemnly, with some women in tears. Nobody threw flowers or chocolate. Some were packing up to join the steady flood of refugees fleeing from the Germans. The Belgian civilians did not know their destination or how long they would be on the road; they only knew they didn't want to live under German occupation.

"Poor buggers," Brown gave his considered opinion. "We're leaving them in the lurch."

"Aye," Aitken agreed. "If their army had fought harder, they could have stayed at home, but they'll blame us."

Innes snorted. "We're always to blame, aren't we? And always the first they ask for help when things go wrong."

Tulloch listened. The joking had ended now as men endured the frustration of a retreat after they had defeated the enemy in battle. He understood how his men felt.

"The Coldstreams lost a hundred and fifty men, mainly from shelling," Forsyth said. "They'll be thirsting for revenge."

"Their time will come," Hume said. "The Gods of War will roll their dice more than once in this war."

The 3rd Division passed through the 4th, motored to the Dendre, and watched Four Division come through.

"They're a bloody shambles," Forsyth gave his opinion as the division came toward them with little order, units jumbled together and men looking tired. One of Four Division's armoured regiments, the 15th/19th Hussars, had performed heroics in defence, but German armour and anti-tank guns had destroyed many of their tanks. The Lothians watched the survivors limp back, quiet now, without any of the usual name-calling when two British regiments met. The Gordon Highlanders and Inniskillings had also met the Germans face to face, losing men and vehicles as they gave a good account of themselves. However, faulty communications and an over-hasty Belgian withdrawal left them dangerously exposed, so the Germans infiltrated between the Inniskillings' tanks, causing casualties.

"This war won't be easy to win," Forsyth said soberly.

"The units didn't support each other," Tulloch surmised.

"From what little I've heard," Major Hume said quietly, "the Hussars charged anything and everything. British cavalry has always been known for two things; their bravery and their lack of discipline."

Tulloch grunted. "We didn't have much use for horsed cavalry in France and Flanders in the Kaiser's War. Now it seems the Germans have perfected armoured cavalry's use, and we have not. We'll have to improve if we're going to beat them."

As the British Expeditionary Force shifted their positions, the RAF fought a heroic war in the skies. British airmen in the single-engine light bomber, the Fairey Battle, found themselves lacking in firepower and speed but still pressed forward with their attacks on advancing German columns. In the initial six days of the German invasion, the RAF lost sixty-seven aircraft and many valuable men.

Unaware of the sacrifices the RAF were making on their behalf, the Lothians took over their new quarters at the Dendre River and waited for further orders or a German attack. On the first day after their arrival, Tulloch watched aircraft overhead, knowing they were German and hoping they did not attack. They passed Three Division and headed south, leaving Tulloch with an uneasy feeling that the war in the air was also going badly. With the disintegration of their allies on either flank, the British began to wonder what would happen next.

"Did you hear about General Barker of One Corps?" Muirhead asked, lighting a French cigarette and calmly shaking out the match. "He heard engines on his flank, thought they were German tanks and sent a dispatch rider to General Brooke asking for help."

"Were they Panzers?" Forsyth scanned the skies for enemy aircraft.

Muirhead laughed and drew on his cigarette. "They were only motorcycles," he said. "Barker's an old woman. He won't last long."

"Trust a battle to show up the weak links in the army," Hume said. "Whatever happens in Belgium and France, the army will be stronger afterwards. Perhaps not in men and equipment, but in experience and higher command. The useless and weak will be weeded out, mark my words."

"Aye, and far too many good, experienced NCOs and men," Muirhead reminded.

After a smooth beginning, the British withdrawal became patchy, with divisions working toward different agendas. The Lothian officers kept their battalion together and listened in growing frustration as the retiral continued.

"Did you hear Barker's latest?" Muirhead asked. "He asked Brooke's permission to stand and fight, changed his mind, and withdrew too early, leaving a gap for the Germans to exploit. The man's an idiot, not fit to command a section, let alone a corps!"

"The men are fighting well," Forsyth said. "If only the senior officers understood their job better."

"Did somebody once say we were lions led by donkeys?" Tait asked.

"That was Erich Ludendorff, the German chief of staff in the Great War," Tulloch remembered his military history from Sandhurst.

"I thought we'd improved since then," Tait murmured. "I hope I have."

"Montgomery seems all right," Tulloch said. "He seems to know what he's doing."

Muirhead grunted. "Maybe. He's a bit of a maverick. He's efficient, though, which we need to defeat the Germans."

"As long as the Italians keep out," Tulloch said. "We'll be stretched if we have to fight in Africa and maybe India as well."

"The Italians?" Muirhead asked mildly. "Do they think Mussolini will step in?"

"I hope not," Tulloch said.

Muirhead leaned back in his seat. "You know more than you're saying, Lieutenant Tulloch." He smiled, closed his eyes, and fell asleep.

As the situation unfolded, Montgomery and his neighbouring general, Harold Alexander of the 1st Division, sent out their armour to cover the gap Barker's actions had created.

"We're spread very thin," Muirhead said as the British moved steadily toward the French border, with Bren gun carriers and anti-tank companies acting in place of tanks to cover their withdrawal. The Royal Horse Artillery moved out with élan, the men cheering as they moved forward.

"Out you go, Tait, and you too, Tulloch," Pringle said. "Act like a troop of tanks."

"Yes, sir."

Tulloch sat beside the driver, with three carriers under his command. They motored forward over the well-cultivated Belgian countryside, with the sound of battle all around and aircraft a constant presence above. Shellfire from both sides whistled overhead and exploded in great brown fountains of flame and earth as the carriers moved to give some protection to the soft-skinned transport.

"What do we do if we meet a panzer?" Innes manned the Bren, peering through a slit in the thin armour.

"Run like hell," Tulloch told him cheerfully. "Our Bren won't even scratch their armour. We're after their infantry."

"We could ram them, sir," Aitken, the driver, suggested.

"We'd crumple like cardboard," Tulloch said.

A shell exploded to their right, so close that the dirt descended into the carrier, and stones rattled off the thin armoured sides.

"Try to avoid the explosions," Tulloch advised.

"I'll do my best, sir," Aitken said, ducking as another shell exploded nearby. "These lads have got our number, sir!"

"Move towards them!" Tulloch signalled to the other carriers. "Let's rummel them up a bit!"

When the RHA officer barked orders, two guns unlimbered on their right flank, firing into a small wood where they suspected the Germans might be. The bark of British guns and the crump of explosions were reassuring as Tulloch's carriers moved forward, lurching over the uneven ground. Tulloch lifted his binoculars to examine the wood, now half hidden by smoke and shattered trees.

"Germans, sir!"

Tulloch saw the group emerge from the wood as the RHA shells exploded. "Engage them!" He ordered his carriers to advance in line, with the Bren guns opening fire as they found a suitable target.

After days of retirals, the Lothians were glad to have the opportunity to strike back. Innes crouched behind the Bren, took careful aim, and pressed the trigger, with the controlled hammer of the light machine gun adding to the noise of battle. Two field-grey-coated men fell at once, and the remainder scattered, evidently not expecting to be attacked.

Tulloch did not see who fired as the German artillery responded, with two more shells landing close to the carriers. He ducked as something screamed above his head, and stones clattered from the carrier's armour plate.

"Evasive action!" he ordered, and the three carriers weaved across the field.

The Brens continued to fire in short, aimed bursts. Some of the Germans fell, others fled or returned fire, with their bullets rattling unpleasantly from the carrier. More German artillery shells landed, throwing up dirt and rocks twenty yards away.

"They're getting our range," Tulloch said. "Spray the woods,

Innes; we might hit some of the gunners. Aitken, weave like buggery!"

"Yes, sir!" Aitken said, throwing the carrier into an irregular zig-zag pattern to confuse the gunners.

Tulloch heard more of the RHA shells rushing past to explode in a welter of fire, smoke, and shattered branches in the wood.

"Enough!" Tulloch judged they were so close to the trees they were in danger of being hit by the RHA shells. "Break off the engagement and withdraw to the neighbouring field."

The carriers weaved back across the field, avoiding the smoking shell craters as the German infantry reacted by increasing their fire. The men who had retreated rallied and joined their companions, encouraged by the carriers' withdrawal. Bullets hissed over the carriers and rattled from the steel plates.

"Now! Circle back!" Tulloch ordered. "Full speed ahead, Aitken! Innes, shoot these men!"

The carriers turned, catching the German infantry by surprise. Two were standing to fire on the Lothians, and a single burst of Bren fire cut them down. Another man fell, wounded and writhing, and the remainder fled, with bullets kicking up the dirt around them. The carriers withdrew to the next field as the RHA fired another salvo that exploded above the copse, spreading shrapnel into the trees.

"Sir!" Innes shouted above the clatter of the engine. "One of the gunners is waving to you!"

"Take us towards them, Aitken," Tulloch ordered, and the three carriers roared towards the guns.

"We've plugged the gap!" A cheerful RHA captain said. "Pull back to Three Div, Lothians."

Tulloch waved an acknowledgment and ordered his men back, with one carrier covering the others, firing short bursts with the Bren to keep any inquisitive German quiet.

They took position on the battalion's right flank, watching for the Germans and wary of any attack from the air. The men were bright after the minor success over the enemy, exchanging banter and reminiscences.

"Did you see that sergeant jump when we returned to get them? He looked like he was having a fit!"

"I nearly topped the carrier when we hit that hole! These Belgian farmers arenae much good at ploughing. They left a great dip in the field; two rainy days, and that will be a quagmire and ruin the crop!"

"The column's halting, sir," Aitken shouted.

"We'd best do the same," Tulloch said and watched as a messenger ran alongside.

"Colonel's orders, sir," the messenger was a lance corporal, with his face strained and a bloody bandage on his left hand. "You've to attend a meeting tonight as soon as we stop."

"Thank you, corporal," Tulloch said. "You'd better get a medico to look at that hand before it gets infected."

"Thank you, sir. I'll be fine." The man saluted and ran to Five Platoon, where Tait spoke with his sergeant.

"The French are on the point of collapsing," Colonel Pringle looked as trim as ever as he spoke to his officers, "and the Belgians are worse; I doubt they'll hold out for more than a couple of days. We'll be alone here, gentlemen, with both our flanks turned, so prepare for a dash to the coast."

Tulloch nodded. He thought of other British expeditions to the continent which had ended similarly, with Moore's retreat to Corunna strong in his mind, or the Walcheren Expedition.

"There is some good news," Major Hume told them. "Chamberlain's no longer Prime Minister. Churchill has taken the reins of office."

Tulloch absorbed the information. At that moment, he did not care who occupied Ten Downing Street. British politics seemed a world away from this life of shelling, retiring, and the anxious, scared columns of terrified refugees. The advancing Germans were the only thing that mattered, and how the Lothians would cope with them.

"The Luftwaffe is playing merry hell with the French, who don't know the difference between their own tanks and the Germans and are firing on their own men."

"The war is not going well, then," Tulloch said.

"We always start badly," Forsyth nearly echoed Tulloch's thoughts. "We like to give the enemy a chance, you see. It's more sportsmanlike."

"We're holding them every time we turn to fight," Tulloch said. "We're as good as they are."

"We have Alan Brooke as corps commander and Montgomery as divisional commander," Hume said. "They're probably the best senior officers in the army."

"Others are not so good," Forsyth gave his opinion.

"No defeatist talk," Colonel Pringle stuffed tobacco into the bowl of his pipe. "Especially not in front of the men."

"The men know what's happening, sir," Muirhead said quietly.

"Sorry, sir!" The bandaged lance corporal intervened. "Signal from the brigadier, sir, and we're on the move again."

"Right, gentlemen," Pringle said, ramming his pipe between his teeth. "Back to your men." He forced a smile. "This is only the first round, remember!"

Despite the resistance of the Third Division, the British continued to withdraw as the threats on their flanks increased. The Germans had pushed a salient deep into the French lines, with fourteen armoured or motorised divisions plus an unknown number of infantry divisions. While many French units fought furiously, others disintegrated under German pressure.

Even while retreating, Montgomery insisted on offensive patrolling in front of the division. Once again, Tulloch found himself with Eight Section in the disputed no-man's land between the British and German armies. He had studied a map of the area before leaving the battalion and decided to lay an ambush on a section of road close to the German headquarters.

*I want to rattle them. Rummel them up!*

"We're a fighting patrol," Tulloch reminded his men. "If you see anything that looks German, let me know." He grinned, always happier when fighting back. "We're better than them!"

"Yes, sir," Sergeant Drysdale said as the patrol moved carefully through a scared village of closed doors and across the dark fields. Drysdale carried a Boys anti-tank rifle, effective against anything smaller than a medium tank. At over five feet in length, the Boys was clumsy and heavy, but Drysdale hefted it easily.

"It's not perfect," he said, "but it's the best we've got against their vehicles."

Tulloch nodded. "As long as you're happy, Sergeant."

Shellfire lit up the horizon as both sides fired hopefully into the dark, and occasionally the hectic chatter of a machine gun or the steadier bark of musketry sounded as patrols clashed or nervous sentries fired at shadows.

Tulloch was more cautious than normal, for on the 24th of May, a much larger British raid ended in disaster with over a hundred casualties.

"We're not going to probe deep this time," Tulloch told Eight Section. "We'll use Waziri tactics. We'll find a nice little spot overlooking a road and wait for a juicy target." He knew that was not quite the offensive patrolling Montgomery expected,

but fighting the Waziris had taught him the art of ambushes. Drysdale, a veteran of the Great War and twenty years of subsequent campaigning nodded approval.

"I'll set up the elephant gun, sir." He patted the tripod. "And we'll remind the Germans that the Lothians are here."

They moved cautiously on, keeping to the shelter of walls and fences and moving from cover to cover, with the light from a burning farmhouse giving an ugly glow to the landscape. An owl hooted, the sound melancholic yet reassuring, a reminder that the natural world still existed beyond humanity's mad game of war.

An aircraft droned above, British, French, or German, Tulloch could not tell. He led his men on, listening with every step. He heard the low murmur of voices and signalled his men to sink down. A strong German patrol marched past, with the flames from the burning house reflecting from their round helmets and the sour smell of cooking emanating from their uniforms.

*The Waziris would have you on toast, boys,* Tulloch thought. He saw Innes aiming the Bren and shook his head. If Innes fired now, the patrol would be compromised, and they would have to return to the battalion. Tulloch wanted more than a sergeant and half a dozen clumsy infantrymen.

With the German patrol moving northward, Tulloch pushed on, keeping to the field boundaries and ready to sink into the accompanying ditch at any sign of German soldiers.

They passed a company-strength German encampment, and for a moment, Tulloch was tempted to spray them with the Bren.

*We might kill ten or a dozen, but they'd invariably outflank and wipe us out. I am to survive this war, not die a hero in France.* He shook his head. *That's not entirely accurate. I want to make the bastards pay for these refugees and bombing unprotected towns.*

Tulloch led them a quarter of a mile past the German camp, listening to the intermittent growl of traffic on the road. Reasoning that the Germans would feel safer so far behind their forward troops, he positioned his men in a suitable spot for an ambush.

They lay behind a banking with a few straggled trees on top. Beneath them, the road was straight between two bends and on an incline to slow any vehicles.

*That will do. We can play merry hell here and withdraw into the night if things get too frantic.*

"Wait for my signal," Tulloch ordered. He saw the men settle down, with Innes behind the Bren and Drysdale setting up the tripod and ensuring he had a good field of fire for the Boys. Hardie was as self-contained as always, tucking himself into a hollow in the ground and placing a loose branch over the barrel of his rifle as camouflage. Tulloch knew he could rely on these men and issued no more orders.

He felt quite calm. He had done all he could, he was working with professionals who knew their job, and the night would take care of itself. As Colonel Pringle said, it was all in the lap of the war gods.

They heard the rattle of armour, and three tanks passed, looking dangerous in the fading light of the dying fire. Sergeant aimed his Boys hopefully until Tulloch shook his head. He did not know how effective the Boys would be against a heavy German Panzer and doubted if Sergeant could load, fire, and destroy three quicker than the Germans would react, even if he put a couple of tanks out of action.

Drysdale shrugged philosophically and resumed his position, waiting with the patience of decades of military experience.

Tulloch heard the clopping of horses' hooves and rumble of iron-shod wheels, and a German artillery unit passed, with horses pulling the guns and men sitting on the caissons. He said nothing and Eight Section held their fire, waiting for Tulloch's order. Brown looked over his shoulder, silently urging his officer to move.

The time dragged on, passing midnight and on to the small hours. Tulloch realised the road was empty and wondered if he had lost his chance and should have struck at one of the earlier targets. *No, something has brought me here, and a better target will appear.* He checked his watch, considered having a swipe at the German infantry company on his return and stopped as he heard a car engine, accompanied by the snarl of motorbikes.

A car could contain anybody, an officer returning from checking his unit, even a local dignitary trying to escape the German advance, but the motorbike escort suggested somebody more important. Tulloch gestured to his men to maintain their positions.

The car was powerful and fast-moving, with the driver taking the bends at a speed Tulloch could only admire. The headlights probed ahead, flickering through the trees, and gleaming on the dark tarmac, a double-eyed monster roaring through the ravaged countryside.

"This one, lads, and then we'll clear out." No civilian driver would move that quickly in an occupied country, and the accompanying motorcycle only augmented Tulloch's hunch that the car contained a senior officer.

Drysdale adjusted the Boys' tripod and squinted along the barrel. The heavy .55-inch cartridge would tear through any thin-bodied vehicle, especially at its most effective range of a hundred yards.

The headlights glared around the bend, dazzling the Lothians, so some momentarily averted their eyes. Tulloch swore, knowing he should have anticipated the sudden flare.

"Sir?" There was urgency in Drysdale's voice.

"Fire," Tulloch ordered, blinking away the dazzle. He heard the solid thump of the Boys and the nearly simultaneous crash of the explosion. The snarl of the motorbikes increased, and Tulloch realised there were three. Drysdale released the second of his five-round magazine as Innes fired two short bursts from the Bren. The stuttering light machine gun fire ripped up the road as Hardie fired a single shot that threw the rearmost rider off his bike. The other rifles cracked out, with men firing into the carnage.

Tulloch saw the two Boys' rounds lift the car into the air and dump it back down, with the driver smashing headfirst through the windscreen. The only surviving motorcycle outrider slewed his bike to a halt and sprayed the ambushers with machine gun fire until Innes fired an accurate burst with the Bren that spun the man backward. He fell beside his companions, already dead.

"Cease fire!" Tulloch shouted. "Sergeant Drysdale, watch for Germans." Rising, he ran down to the burning car, hoping the petrol tank did not explode.

Aware the Germans would soon send somebody to investigate the firing, Tulloch ignored the dead motorcyclists sprawled across the road and concentrated on the car, approaching with his revolver in his right hand. Flames roared from the rear, and the driver's body hung through the shattered window.

As Tulloch approached, a man burst from the rear window, bloodied from a cut to his head. He saw Tulloch, snarled, and drew a pistol from his belt. Tulloch heard somebody shout and the crack of a rifle ducked and saw the bullet smash into the car an inch from the man.

*That's Francesco Giorano! What's he doing with the German army?*

"Surrender!" Tulloch shouted the first thing that came into his head. He levelled his revolver. He could shoot but knew the Italian agent would be more valuable alive than dead.

Giorano fired and ran, with the Lothians' bullets following him, kicking up fragments of tarmac and knocking chips from the trees.

"Don't fire, you bloody fools! You'll hit the lieutenant!" Drysdale snarled. Eight Section ceased fire as Giorano scrambled up the opposite banking, with Tulloch three yards behind and gaining.

"Sir!" Sergeant Drysdale shouted. "Get out of there! Something is coming up the road!" He altered his tone. "Innes, cover the road to the right. Kelly, go with him. Brown, take this!" He threw across the Boys and took Brown's rifle. "Move!"

Tulloch realised he could not catch Giorano without endangering the section, fired a couple of speculative shots at him and glanced inside the staff car. He saw two dead bodies in smart uniforms and a briefcase lying on the floor in the back. Ignoring the flames, Tulloch reached inside and grabbed the case, gasped as the heat singed his hand and quickly withdrew. He heard the growl of an engine on the road and saw the probing double beam of headlamps.

"Sir!" Sergeant shouted as Tulloch ran across the road to the section.

"Pack up, boys, and head back," Tulloch ordered. "Sergeant, take point, I'll take the rear."

The section moved at once, marching at rifleman's pace across the country while the blazing car lit up the sky behind them.

*Francesco Giorano again. Fate has dictated that our paths should cross.*

# Chapter Twenty Two

*Who durst defy the omnipotent to arms?*
**John Milton: *Paradise Lost***

Colonel Pringle took the document case from Tulloch. "You've done it again, Lieutenant. You seem to sniff out these things. Have you looked inside the case?"

"No, sir," Tulloch replied.

Pringle snapped open the catch and leafed through the contents. "How's your German?"

"Non-existent, sir," Tulloch admitted.

"As good as mine, then," Pringle said with a faint smile and lifted out a folded piece of stiff paper. "We can both understand this map, though," he passed over a map of northern France and Belgium, showing the disposition of German and allied troops and several coloured arrows.

"Yes, sir," Tulloch said.

"And this," Pringle said, showing a wallet of documents, "appears to contain the German Order of Battle, plus what looks like tactical plans for the German 6 Corps to unfold a pincer movement to outflank the BEF by sweeping the Belgians aside. If they do that, they can roll us up from the north."[1]

"Yes, sir," Tulloch said again. *What was Giorano doing with such detailed plans of the German advance?*

"I'll send these documents to General Brooke, who will undoubtedly pass them on to GHQ. After that, it's in the hands of God and General Gort." Pringle continued. "I dare say we'll see more movement due to your ambush, Tulloch, and you'll get precious little thanks for it."

"I'm not looking for thanks, sir," Tulloch said. "It was pure luck the staff car showed up when it did."

"Your other news is also important," Pringle said. "If you saw Giorano at the front line, we can almost certainly assume that Italy will join the party."

"I thought that was a given, sir," Tulloch said.

Pringle grunted. "One is never sure which way people like Mussolini and Franco jump. I think it depends on how the wind blows or how they feel when they get up in the morning. However, if Italy joins Germany, she will seriously threaten our position in Northeast Africa and the Suez Canal. I'll attach a note to that effect when I pass on these documents." Pringle began to fill his pipe with his musing eyes on Tulloch. "It was fortunate you commanded that patrol, Tulloch, for nobody else could recognise Giorano. A guardian angel is hovering over us, like the Angels of Mons."[2]

"I'd like to think so, sir," Tulloch agreed. "We need all the help we can get."

When Tulloch returned to his quarters, news filtered in from along the front. A British armoured counterattack at Arras had stunned the Germans without halting their main offensive, but a major French assault from the south failed. The Germans had captured Boulogne and threatened Calais, only twenty-odd miles across the Channel from the English port of Dover.

"It doesn't look good," Tulloch said as Tait relayed the bad news.

"If the Belgians collapse, as the boys from Four Div think they will," Tait said, "we'll be in trouble. The Germans have pushed Two Corps toward Ypres, which could separate us from the sea and our main supply line for ammunition, stores, and reinforcements."

Tulloch was aware of the situation. "We don't want to get trapped with the Germans between us and the coast," he said. "Particularly if the French collapse." He had seen the RAF making parachute supply drops to the BEF, which was already on reduced rations. He grunted. "We should have retained control of the Channel ports rather than entrust them to somebody else."

"Aye; we'll know next time," Tait said, lighting a cigarette. "When the Belgians and Frenchies collapse, we'll be alone. Twelve British divisions, two of which are only armed with shovels to dig trenches, against the entire German army."

Tulloch leaned back with his head spinning. "I'd rather have a British division with shovels than a Belgian one with machine guns and tanks. At least they'd fight."

"I wonder what General Gort will do next?" Tait said. "By entering Belgium, we've walked right into Hitler's trap." He drew on his cigarette and slowly released a ribbon of blue smoke. "Will Gort take us south with the French and further away from the coast and our supply line, or will he realise the French are a broken reed and make for the sea?"

"The minds of generals and politicians passeth all understanding," Tulloch said. "Let's hope for some sense before it's too late."

The same question occupied the battered British army as they heard the constant flow of news from their disintegrating allies. Men began to look over their shoulders, wondering what the future held.

"If the French pack it in, we'll be stuck here," Aitken said.

"That's right," Brown agreed.

"The Germans might put us all in the bag," Aitken continued. "The last war lasted four years. I dinnae fancy four years in a prisoner-of-war camp. What do you say to making for the coast if we give up?"

Brown nodded. "Aye. I'm game. Only if Gort surrenders, though."

"Aye, only if Gort surrenders," Aitken agreed.

Tulloch heard the conversation and walked on. He agreed with their sentiments yet could not see a couple of privates who spoke only English could walk through France to the coast.

He was still contemplating the privates' chances of success when Colonel Pringle called another officers' conference.

"I won't keep you long, gentlemen," Pringle said. "I have only two related items to mention. You may be aware that one of our patrols recently captured some documents from the enemy." He paused while some of the officers glanced at Tulloch. "The intelligence boys have analysed them, and they say the Germans intend to make Three Division front a holding front while they hit the north."

Forsyth grunted. "They know they'll get a bloody nose if they attack us," he said. "They want an easier target."

"That may be so," Pringle agreed. "We've certainly managed to deal with everything they've tried so far. However, we can't make as much use of that intelligence as we'd like because the Belgians and the French 1st Motorised Division to the north of the BEF have withdrawn."

The Lothians' officers responded with grunts, groans, and sighs. Muirhead glanced at Forsyth, raised his eyebrows, and said nothing.

"In response to our allies' withdrawal," Pringle said, "General Gort has ordered Three Div to move north to guard the British flank." He paused for a moment. "The Belgians have lost any desire to fight, gentlemen. They are giving way, and the BEF will retire to the Channel ports of Dunkirk and Nieuport."

"So now we know," Tait said. "We came, we saw, we returned to the coast." He shook his head. "I never thought I'd see the day."

"It's only the first round," Tulloch reminded.

"Maybe," Tait said. "It took us four years to defeat the Germans last time, and that was with the French and Russians fighting alongside us. This time we could be alone."

"Not quite alone," Tulloch said quietly. "The Empire is with us, and I'd rather have the Sikhs, Rajputs, and Gurkhas beside me than anybody else in the world." He smiled at a distant memory. "I visited the Hodson's Horse Officer's Mess once," he said. "That's an Indian cavalry regiment with a mixture of British and Indian officers."

"I know of Hodson's Horse," Tait said.

"So you should," Tulloch said. "I memorised a scroll they have on the wall that a long-gone British officer wrote. It says:

*Lord, make me worthy*
*Of the men I serve*
*Worthy of their loyalty*
*And devotion to duty;*
*Their wondrous willingness*
*And ready laughter;*
*Their great humility*
*That asks so little*
*And gives so much,*
*So readily, without complaint.*
*Grant them their simple wishes, Lord*
*And bless them, please,*
*For in this world,*
*No better soldiers breathe than these."*

Tulloch finished his recitation. "I thought that was quite comprehensive. With soldiers such as India provides, we are never alone."

Tait opened his mouth, closed it again and nodded. "Yes, that's true."

"Then there's Canada, Australia, New Zealand and the African colonies," Tulloch reminded. "We're certainly not alone."

The men were not happy when they heard the news.

"Running away? What for? We've beaten the buggers every time we've fought them!" Brown seemed to have forgotten his earlier plan to escape to the coast.

"The French havenae beat them," Hogg looked up from sharpening his bayonet, with the eighteen inches of polished steel looking deadly in his hands. "The Jerries have beaten the French and the Belgians."

"Oh, bugger the French and the Belgians," Kelly said.

"We don't have to," Innes reminded, with a grim smile. "The Germans have already done that for us."

On the night of the 27th of May, Three Division pulled behind the British line and headed to the left flank to support the hard-pressed Four Division. With Montgomery as Divisional commander, the complicated movement was smooth, with the route marked out and guides in position to direct traffic and radio contact between each unit.

Twice during the night, Tulloch heard aircraft overhead and once the steady thump-thump of distant artillery around Mont Kemmel. The Germans had been pushing at the British all the previous day and were only three thousand yards distant.

"We'd better complete this move before dawn," Tait said worriedly. "If the Luftwaffe finds all the divisional transport moving at the speed of a one-legged snail on these wee roads, they'll bomb us flat."

"We'll get there," Tulloch tried to sound more confident than he felt.

Nobody disturbed the battalion as they followed the narrow roads and the directions of the military police.

"First time I've seen a redcap I didn't want to punch," Aitken said.

Brown grunted:

*"I love a lassie,*
*A bonnie redcap lassie,*
*She's as pretty as a monkey at the zoo,*
*And she kisses like a navvy,*
*With lips like broken gravel,*
*Aggie, my redcap, too."*

"That was bad, Broonie," Aitken said. "That was really bad."

Tulloch hid his smile, glad to hear his men joking despite their precarious position.

The Lothians arrived in their new position at seven in the morning of the 28th of May and began digging in, positioning the machine guns, and sending patrols to probe towards the German lines.

"Take Eight Section again, Tulloch; you know them best, but don't go too far," Major Hume advised. "We just need to know the immediate neighbourhood." He lowered his voice. "The King of the Belgians has packed in and surrendered his entire army to the Germans."

Tulloch swore as the implications hit him. "What happens now, sir? We're fifteen miles from the coast, and if Belgium has packed in, we've no friendly soldiers on our flanks."

Hume grinned. "Now, Tulloch? We do what we're trained to do. We fight."

Tulloch saw the steel behind the smile. "Yes, sir. May I assume any soldiers we meet are hostile?"

"Assume nothing, Tulloch. Inform me of everything you see."

"Yes, sir," Tulloch agreed.

Tulloch's led his patrol cautiously, moving from farmhouse to farmhouse, knowing the Allies and Germans had fought over this ground in the previous war. He was thankful his patrolling had nearly always been in open country rather than villages or towns.

"Here we are again, sir," Drysdale said. They crouched beside a farmhouse wall with a faint wind rustling tall grass and banging a door open and shut while rainwater wept from a broken gutter. A litter of clothes and other possessions on the yard outside told of a hasty flight from the advancing Germans.

Behind Tulloch, Three Division was digging in along the canals and rivers running north of Ypres to shield Four Division's retreat towards Dunkirk.

*At present, there's no allied soldier between us and the Germans. We're the tail-end of the rearguard; we're shielding the British army, yet I feel nothing except sadness for the plight of the civilian refugees.*

"Look ahead, boys," Tulloch sank into the shelter of a raised bank as he peered through his binoculars.

"Germans," Sergeant Drysdale murmured as Eight Section sunk into cover. Innes aimed his Bren hopefully, smiling.

"Hundreds of them," Brown said.

In field grey or ominous black uniforms, the Germans moved steadily forward and occupied two farmhouses as Tulloch watched. Most were on foot, with some on horse-drawn carts that jostled and jolted along a farm track.

"They'll come here next," Drysdale said. "Who's on our flank, sir?"

"A hodge-podge of artillerymen, sappers and some French stragglers," Tulloch said, watching Drysdale's experience-schooled lack of expression. "We'll hold here for a while and calculate the enemy's strength."

"Heads down, boys," Drysdale said. "Hardie, you and Hogg watch the left flank; Aitken and Brown, take the right."

The Lothians cradled their weapons and watched the enemy with tension so tangible that Tulloch could nearly taste it. He looked upwards, blessing the torrential rain and heavy cloud that shielded them from the Luftwaffe. Maybe the colonel was correct, and a guardian angel protected the British army, for German dive bombers would have an easy target with the army retreating along narrow roads.

"Thank you, God," Tulloch breathed and focussed his binoculars on what seemed to be a main road. He saw the carts pull to the side as a dark staff car appeared. "Let's hope that's Adolf coming to inspect his troops."

The hammer of heavy machine guns sounded from along the British front, together with the angry bark of artillery.

"They're coming, sir," Innes warned, with his cheek nestled into the stock of his Bren. He looked around, hopefully.

"When you get a decent group, let them know we're here," Tulloch ordered. He had brought a rifle with him and sighted toward the nearby farmhouse, where the black-uniformed Germans were gradually approaching. For a moment, he remembered the black-uniformed Uhlans at Waterloo and wondered if these modern soldiers carried the same sinister reputation.

Innes nodded. "Yes, sir."

"Ready, lads," Tulloch said. "When they reach that tree," he indicated a lone tree at the edge of the field beside the farm. "Let them have it and then withdraw, evens first and then odds. Sergeant Drysdale, you take the evens, and I'll take the odds. Innes, when the firing starts, put a couple of bursts through the farmhouse window and try for some of these black uniforms."

"Sir," Innes altered the angle of his Bren gun.

Brown fired first, with the others a second later. Innes's Bren shattered the farmhouse's windows and kicked dust from the walls. Tulloch aimed at a burly sergeant, dropped his man, and worked the bolt to reload. The nearest Germans dropped, immediately returning fire as Eight Section gave them everything they had.

"Now, Sergeant," Tulloch ordered, and Drysdale withdrew with the even-numbered men.

Tulloch fired again as the Germans replied, with an MG 34 chattering, throwing bullets towards the British position. Tulloch swore at the speed of the German reaction, glanced behind him, saw Drysdale was ready and gave the order to withdraw.

"Come on, lads! Innes! Don't linger!"

The Germans saw the movement, stood, and advanced

straight into the fire of Drysdale's men. Tulloch wished he had two Bren guns.

"Back to Sergeant Drysdale," he ordered.

The men retired, with a few bullets kicking up dirt, and Innes halted, crouched, and fired his Bren from the hip. The Germans did not try to follow.

"Back," Tulloch ordered when he slid beside Sergeant Drysdale. "We've stopped their infantry, so they'll either come in platoon strength or order up tanks."

As soon as the patrol began to withdraw, German artillery targeted their positions, hammering down shells in a series of explosions that smashed down trees and spread fire and devastation all around.

*The Germans are very quick in reaction, and their artillery is accurate.*

"They don't like us, do they?" Aitken asked, lying with his hands over his head.

"They'll probably report back to Adolf that they've pushed back a British counterattack and destroyed an entire battalion," Brown said.

"I don't mind the shelling," Kelly said, cowering in the bottom of a ditch. "At least we can't hear Broonie's singing!"

---

COLONEL PRINGLE LISTENED TO TULLOCH'S REPORT. "Germans in black? That will be an SS battalion," he said. "You're the third patrol to encounter them; Tait saw them earlier, and Muirhead shot up a patrol last night. Now, grab something to eat for your men but don't settle because I don't think we'll be settling here for long."

"Why not, sir?"

"The Germans have reached Nieuport, which was a port we wanted to use," Pringle said dryly, "and a group of French deserters murdered Montgomery's Chief of Staff, Marino Brown."

Tulloch closed his eyes. He had not known Marino Brown, but the man's reputation was as a top-class soldier. "He'll be a loss, sir."

"He will," Pringle agreed. "We'll hear more details later."

News filtered to the Lothians as they held the Germans on their defensive line and worried about their exposed flanks.

"I heard that French cavalrymen were killing their horses and throwing away their guns although the Germans were still twenty miles away. I can't see them lasting much longer than the Belgians." Forsyth gave a crooked grin. "We'll be on our own, lads."

"Better that than having unreliable allies," Muirhead said. He looked up as a squadron of RAF Fairey Battles roared overhead to bomb the Germans. Even as the Lothians watched, German anti-aircraft fire erupted around the British aircraft, bringing down one.

"That's no way to die," Tait said as the stricken Battle spiralled out of control, with one man falling free, turning end over end as he plummeted downward. The aircraft landed in a massive explosion, with a column of dark smoke rising. The remaining Battles flew on, keeping in a tight formation.

"I heard the RAF is losing dozens of planes," Forsyth said soberly. "The Germans are shooting them out of the sky and bombing the airfields."

"Thank God for the Navy," Muirhead said.

"It feels like the end of civilisation," Tait commented.

"It will be the end of civilisation if Hitler wins," Muirhead replied. "We have to fight for the sake of a free world."

Tulloch saw the worry in Muirhead's eyes and knew that, whatever happened, Great Britain would have to continue the fight.

"We're withdrawing again!" the news filtered through as four

German divisions pressed Three Division, and the British army painfully withdrew towards Dunkirk.

After the previous orderly and well-organised moves, Tulloch found this latest retiral much different. With the Belgian surrender freeing more men, the Germans pushed hard on the rearguard and infiltrated into the gaps between units. The Lothians found abandoned lorries and equipment blocking the road, with groups of sullen French and Belgian soldiers glaring at the British and muttering muted insults.

"What was that?" Brown asked. "Say that again, Frenchy, and I'll ram your teeth down your throat!"

"They're blaming us for their defeat, the windy bastards," Aitken said. "Come up to me, son, if you fancy a square go!"

"Ignore them!" Tulloch ordered. "Our enemy is the German army, not French deserters. Save your energy for them."

"Aye, right, sir," Brown said, glowering at half a dozen Belgian soldiers who spat on the ground as the British marched past.

The Lothian Rifles remained as rearguard, moving back in a series of leapfrogs with Germans pressing on front and both flanks.

Tulloch looked up when he heard aircraft engines and saw two Fairey Battles limping back to the British lines. One was trailing smoke and trying to avoid the anti-aircraft fire that erupted around it.

"There were twelve Battles this morning," Sergeant Drysdale reminded quietly.

"Aye," Hogg said and spat on the ground. "There's no' twelve now."

"Where are the Fusiliers?" Forsyth asked, standing in the back of his Bren carrier and peering ahead. "We've to pass through them and form the next defensive line."

"They're meant to hold the next village, sir," Muirhead said.

"I can't see them! Where the hell are they?" Forsyth lifted his binoculars. "There's the village and no sign of the bloody Fusiliers. Have we come the wrong way? Or have they got lost?"

As Forsyth spoke, a German machine gun opened up, slicing into a marching company of Lothians. Three men fell, with another staggering, holding his leg and shouting.

"Get down!" Forsyth roared. "Get into cover!"

Colonel Pringle took in the situation with a glance and gave rapid orders to his men.

"A Company, see what's happening out there, extended order. D Company, support A." He raised his binoculars. "Forsyth, take your carrier and locate that damned machine gun!"

An artillery shell exploded beside the road, overturning a Bren gun carrier and crushing its driver beneath three tons of steel. The other occupants managed to scramble clear and sat on the road for a moment, dazed and confused.

"The Germans are looking for us now," Aitken said, licking his lips.

"That's because they knew we're the best," Kelly replied, pushing forward the safety catch on his rifle.

"B Company! Take the rearguard!" the colonel shouted. "Keep these Germans back!"

"Sir!" Lieutenant Muirhead took over as Captain Forsyth was scouting in his carrier. "Come on, lads!"

Tulloch brought over Four Platoon, ducking as German bullets and shells howled overhead. The men ran with their rifles at the trail, Brown singing under his breath and Aitken swearing in a constant monotone, repeating the same copulative adjective. Hardie's expression never altered, as though nothing bothered him or mattered.

The Lothians were on the outer fringes of a village, with a trio of abandoned and burning lorries at the side of the road and a farm cart and a dead horse further back. Tulloch spread out his platoon, with Innes already busy with his Bren.

"Three yards apart, boys," Tulloch lifted a rifle from one of the Lothian casualties, checked it was loaded and pushed forward the safety catch. "On my mark!"

The Germans advanced in disciplined rushes, moving from

cover to cover, with machinegun fire cracking overhead to disrupt the Lothians' response.

"Keep your heads down," Tulloch said. "They must cross the road to reach us, and the Germans increase their covering fire a couple of seconds before they leave the shelter of the buildings. As soon as they increase their fire, retaliate."

"Sir," Innes said.

"On my word," Tulloch repeated, surprised at how calm he felt. He heard the German covering fire increase and counted to three. "Fire! Five rounds rapid!"

Four Platoon opened up, with Innes firing the Bren in controlled bursts and the men firing like demons, glad of the chance to retaliate. Tulloch heard screams and German curses. He fired, worked the bolt, and fired again, willing his bullets forward into the invaders before he ordered, "cease fire!"

When the firing stuttered to a stop, Tulloch poked his head above the wall. Three black-uniformed men lay still on the road, and one was writhing, holding his stomach, and alternately groaning and screaming. Two men in field grey lay, with one moaning as he feebly tried to crawl away.

"Shift positions," Tulloch ordered. "Withdraw twenty yards and keep your heads down! The Germans will hammer this site in a minute."

Four Platoon retired at speed, running into the outlying houses of the village. They had barely slid into cover before a German battery targeted their old position. A dozen shells crashed down with the Germans' usual accuracy, throwing up dirt and fragments of stone amidst the flames and smoke. Tulloch waited until the fury had subsided, ignored the ringing in his head from shell fire concussion and spoke again.

"Now return to our previous positions," he ordered. "Quickly!" He led them, throwing himself down behind cover to aim his rifle. As he suspected, German infantry had already begun to cross the road. He fired, missed, worked the bolt, took a deep breath, and fired again as the platoon joined him. He saw some of the attackers drop, but a Spandau opened fire on his position, throwing chips from the stones and hitting one of his men.

"They're still coming!" Kelly shouted, reloading his rifle.

"Then stop them!" Tulloch shouted. He heard yelling from his right, wondered what was happening and knew he had to concentrate on the Germans in front. They had moved back into the farmhouse and were firing with rifles and machine guns. One man threw a stick grenade, but it landed far short and exploded harmlessly on the road.

"You couldnae hit a bull's arse with a banjo!" Aitken gave the inevitable response.

Hardie crouched behind a fragment of shattered masonry, firing without haste and aiming each shot. Tulloch saw him take deliberate aim at a black-uniformed NCO and shoot the man through the head. The Spandau fired again, its rapid chatter sending stone splinters into the air, and then what seemed like hundreds of German soldiers charged to the right of Four Platoon.

Innes lifted his Bren, but the Spandau fired again, forcing the platoon to keep down. Hardie and Drysdale found gaps in the wall for their rifles, firing rapidly without stemming the attack.

"They've broken in!" Somebody shouted from the right. "The Germans are in our lines."

# Chapter Twenty Three

*Close-ranked, stubborn, the warhounds fought.*
**The Goddodin**

"Then throw them out!" Tulloch retorted. "Innes, keep that Spandau quiet. Odd numbers, stay here with Sergeant Drysdale. Even numbers, come with me!" Keeping low, Tulloch propped up his borrowed rifle against a rock, drew his revolver, and bounded forward with his men at his back.

Five and Six Platoons were engaged in bloody hand-to-hand combat, with bayonets and rifle butts, and gasping, swearing men. Dead soldiers in bloodied khaki lay on the ground where German bullets or shells had found them, with a swathe of prone men in black or field-grey outside the slender perimeter.

Tulloch launched himself at the flank of the German attack, firing his pistol. He shot one man, missed another, and saw his platoon throwing themselves forward. Brown rammed his bayonet deep into the stomach of a tall German, shouting something incomprehensible.

"Push them out!" Tulloch roared. He saw Hogg rear back from a burly SS man, then smash forward with his head. The steel rim of Hogg's helmet sliced into the German's face, breaking his nose and opening a gash from cheek to cheek. Hardie, grey-haired and quiet, used his eighteen-inch bayonet with frightening skill, slicing open the throat of a tall German.

"They're breaking!" Kelly shouted. "Push them back to Berlin, boys!"

Four Platoon's attack on the German flank turned the tide. The Germans withdrew, running back as the Lothians jeered.

"Tell Adolf he cannae beat the Lothians!" Brown shouted. "Gin ye daur, you square heided bastards!"

"Where's your officer?" Tulloch asked a panting private, reloading. He realised his revolver was empty, although he could only remember firing three shots. The private shook his head, gasping.

"He's dead, sir," a steady-eyed sergeant wiped dark blood from his bayonet.

"You're in charge then, sergeant," Tulloch told him. "Naesmyth, isn't it?"

"Yes, sir." Naesmyth began to issue orders to his platoon. "Clean this shambles up. MacDonald, get on the Bren! O'Hara, you're his number two. Pass over any spare Bren magazines, boys!"

Leaving the capable Naesmyth in charge, Tulloch returned to Four Platoon.

"They've withdrawn, sir," Drysdale said, thrusting a Woodbine between his lips. "They're mustering behind that ridge there."

Both men looked up when a flight of Stuka dive bombers roared past, but they flew over and screamed onto another unit half a mile to the rear.

"Things are hotting up," Drysdale said, lighting his cigarette with steady hands. He did not flinch as a salvo of shells exploded over Four Platoon. "They'll try here next, sir."

Tulloch nodded. "Let's get ready for them." He checked the

platoon, ensuring each man was in position, and looked up when a man ran from Five Platoon.

"Sir!" A gasping corporal threw himself beside Tulloch. "Captain Forsyth's dead, sir. You're the senior officer for D Company."

"Where's Lieutenant Muirhead?" Tulloch asked.

"Wounded, sir. He's on his way to the Dunkirk perimeter in an ambulance."

"Right, Corporal," Tulloch thought rapidly, wishing Muirhead was still in charge. "Where's Lieutenant Tait?

"He sent me to you, sir. He's still in charge of Five Platoon."

Tulloch nodded, thinking rapidly. "Where's Sergeant Naesmyth?"

"Dead, sir. The same shell that killed the captain nearly cut him in two."

Tulloch swore. "Sergeant Drysdale," he said, "Take over Six Platoon. Captain Forsyth is dead."

"Yes, sir," Drysdale replied as calmly as if Tulloch had asked him the time.

Tulloch ran to take over the company, stopped when a mortar crumped down a few yards away, rose and continued. The Germans were closer to the Lothians' defensive wall here, with a platoon of SS throwing grenades that landed only yards away. Tulloch assessed the position, wishing he knew these men better.

"Who's the best grenade man here?" Tulloch asked.

"Me, sir," a stocky private said. "Private Connington." He had the blue seams of a miner on his neck and a stubborn chin.

"Can you throw further than those German lads?"

"Aye," Connington said after a moment's thought. "If I had any grenades left."

Tulloch raised his voice. "Does anybody have any spare grenades? Toss them here!"

The mortars landed again, two, three, four, raising tall fountains of dirt and smoke. Tulloch realised he had thrown himself to the ground, rose sheepishly, saw everybody else had done the same and dusted himself down.

"Grenades!" He ordered and four men and tossed their grenades over. Tulloch noted that blood covered one and nodded to the private. "Are you wounded?"

"No, sir," the man was slender, with wide, nervous eyes. "That's Captain Forsyth's blood."

"All right." Tulloch passed the grenades to Connington. "There you go, Connington, do what you can."

Connington lifted the first grenade, weighed it carefully in his hand, and took a deep breath. He extracted the pin, poised, swivelled, and threw, with the grenade arcing through the air. Tulloch watched its flight, and the second grenade was airborne before the first landed. He saw the explosion, and then the second grenade landed and the third, each within a five-yard radius.

"Fire into the explosions, boys!" Tulloch ordered and heard the steady hammer of the Bren and the staccato crackle of musketry. "Now, get your heads down!"

The Germans replied with machine guns and mortars, sending the Lothians into cover. Tulloch saw an explosion lift one man bodily in the air and shred another to bloody gobbets. He hugged the damp earth, fighting his fear.

When the mortaring stopped, Tulloch forced himself upright. "They'll come again, now!" he shouted.

The SS infantry charged silently and efficiently, running from cover to cover. Tulloch fired, hearing his men follow suit as the screaming wounded added another level to the horror. The German attack faltered as men dropped.

"They've lost hope," somebody shouted.

"They cannae lick the Lothians!"

"Come on, you Jerry bastards! We're waiting for you!"

The mortaring began even as the SS men retired, thumping in and around the Lothians' positions.

"They'll come during the mortaring!" Tulloch said. He grabbed a lance corporal. "What's your name?"

"Darnley, sir," the lance corporal said.

"Find Lieutenant Tait, Darnley," Tulloch ordered. "Tell him the Germans will advance as they mortar and warn him to guard his flanks. Move!"

"Yes, sir!" Darnley said, running at a crouch, diving behind a half-demolished wall as the mortar shells rained on the Lothians.

Tulloch shuddered as something exploded a few yards away, covering him with dirt and stones. Somebody screamed close by, the sound rising to a crescendo before fading to a hopeless whimper. More bombs landed in a steady crump-crump-crump around the Lothians' position, keeping the defenders pinned down as the SS battalion advanced.

*These Germans know their stuff. They're well-trained.*

Tulloch heard musketry on his right and hoped his messenger had reached Tait.

"They've outflanked us!" somebody shouted as a couple of men ran past, braving the falling mortars.

Tulloch swore. The mortaring ended, and he moved to the right flank, from where the firing was increasing.

"What's happening here?" He did not have to ask as the remnants of the right flank Five Platoon were retreating, firing as they came.

"Armoured cars and infantry!" Lance Corporal Darnley shouted. He staggered and fell, with blood seeping from a wound in his chest and his eyes wide.

"Stand firm!" Tulloch shouted. He saw an abandoned Boys rifle beside a dead man, slung his rifle over his shoulder, and lifted the anti-tank weapon. Checking the Boys was loaded, he moved forward. A young sergeant and a section of three men crouched behind a wall, firing at what appeared to be dozens of German infantry. The armoured car stood proud behind a tree thirty yards in front of the Lothians, spraying the British positions with machine gun fire.

"We can't hold them for long, sir," the sergeant said, ducking as a bullet propelled splinters over his face. He swore, wiped at a wound that wept blood into his eye, and fired again. "Whenever we show ourselves, that armoured car hammers us!"

"Who's best with the Boys?" Tulloch asked.

"Me, sir!" a lanky private looked around. Tulloch estimated him to be eighteen, with his helmet askew and his mouth drooping open. "Mackay, sir."

"Then kill that damned car, Mackay," Tulloch ordered.

"My pleasure, sir!" Mackay swapped his rifle for the Boys and settled down behind a shattered piece of masonry. He aimed, ignoring a burst of machine-gun fire that screamed overhead. "Right, you bastard," he said, pressing the trigger.

The Boys was a clumsy weapon but useful in the hands of an expert. Tulloch saw the heavy projectile hit squarely on the side of the armoured car, saw the vehicle rock sideways, and a man rise in the air, and then the other occupants bail out as the Lothians fired at them. Two Germans fell; one lay still while the other crawled away, wailing.

"The Germans are behind us, sir!" Private Cummings shouted. Stocky and fair-haired, he was usually quiet. "We're surrounded."

Tulloch swore. "Look after the Boys, Mackay," he said, moving to the rear of the company position. Lifting his binoculars, he saw field-grey and black uniforms in the field behind them and a pall of smoke in the near distance showing where the BEF was conducting their fighting retreat to Dunkirk.

*Where are the rest of the battalion? The Germans have cut us off, and unless we leave soon, they'll put us in the bag.*

"We're moving out, lads! Stretcher-bearers, carry the wounded."

Leaving Six Platoon as rearguard, Tulloch organised his company. They filed through the already shattered village with Six Platoon firing as they retired and found open country beyond. Two British fifteen hundredweight trucks sat at the side of the road, both smashed, and one with the driver dead at the wheel.

"We're in full retreat now, sir," Drysdale said.

"It seems so," Tulloch agreed. He saw Tait with his helmet on the back of his head and his revolver in his hand.

"Take over the rearguard, Tait. Hold them as long as you can, then come through me. I'll have Four and Five Platoons."

Tait nodded, wild-eyed. "Yes, sir." He pointed his pistol at the Germans, who advanced steadily through the village, dodging from cover to cover. "Come on, men!"

Tulloch pointed to a farmhouse two hundred yards distant, with stone walls all around.

"Head for that farmhouse, boys. We'll hold them there until dark. Sergeant Drysdale!"

"Sir," Drysdale's tunic was ripped, and a bloody bandage covered his left wrist.

"You take point. I'll command the rearguard when Six Platoon comes through us." He shouted for Four Platoon. "With me, lads! I want an extended line; hold the ground for Five Platoon to come through!"

Drysdale nodded to the remnants of the company as Tulloch shouted orders that saw the company form up with the stretcher-bearers in the centre. Four Platoon waited in folds of the ground or behind whatever cover they could as Tait broke off contact with the enemy and withdrew. One man fell, yelling as Tait led his men through Tulloch's new rearguard. A second private stooped and grabbed the wounded man, only for the Germans to kill both.

Tait stumbled past with the fifteen survivors of Six Platoon.

"Head for that farmhouse," Tulloch ordered, "sections covering sections and platoons covering platoons." He ducked as a mortar shell exploded twenty yards away. "Shoot any German that stands in our way. Gin ye daur!"

"Gin ye daur!" some of the Lothians replied.

"Four Platoon! You're with me!" Tulloch shouted. "Come on!"

It was hard to leave the dead behind, but Tulloch knew the Germans would treat them decently. He formed a screen of riflemen with two Bren guns for additional firepower. "Right, lads, on the count of three, open up and give the rest a chance."

The men looked at him through tired eyes. Their faces were filthy, their battledresses torn and stained, and some were wounded, but they would fight.

The German artillery started again, supported by mortars and machine-gun fire, as the German infantry waited at the fringes of the shattered village. A lone armoured car struggled up the single street, shouldered aside one of the burning British trucks and opened fire.

"Does anybody have a Boys?" Tulloch asked. Nobody had, but a couple of German mortar shells fell short, landing between Four Platoon and the armoured car. The vehicle withdrew hastily as half a company of Germans left the village and charged forward.

Acting without orders, Five Platoon opened fire, with the stutter of the Bren a reassuring sound. They hugged into whatever cover they could find, aiming and firing with professional aggression that hammered the advancing men. Tulloch waited until the attackers were twenty yards away before he fired, hitting a tall man. The mortaring stopped as the rearguard and the Germans contested the open ground until the attack failed, and the surviving Germans retreated, leaving their casualties where they lay.

"Right, lads," Tulloch said. "We're out of here."

He ushered the survivors away, with a section from Five Platoon providing covering fire, and ran across the field towards the farmhouse. Tulloch heard the noise behind him as the Germans occupied the Lothians' old positions and skidded to a halt behind Tait's Six Platoon.

"Get back," he shouted. "Get to the farmhouse!"

With the Germans celebrating their capture of the Lothians' previous position, the Company was relatively undisturbed as they occupied the farmhouse and surrounding outbuildings. The men looked at each other, wondering that they had survived and counting the dead and wounded.

"Settle in, men," Tulloch said and pointed out where he wanted the Bren guns to go. "Have we still got the Boys?"

"Yes, sir." Private Cummings held it up.

"Good man," Tulloch said. "Where's Mackay?"

"Wounded, sir," Cummings said. "He's lost an arm."

Tulloch grunted. "How are we for ammunition?"

"Only three rounds left for the Boys, sir."

Tulloch frowned. "Not great if they send armour against us. How about for the Brens and rifles?" They had three full mags for each Bren with thirty rounds for each rifle.

"Spread them out so each man has the same," Tulloch ordered. "If anybody is wounded and can't fire, take his ammunition as well." He raised his voice. "Aitken, you're a born scrounger; find whatever food you can and distribute it. Water, too; we'll all die of thirst before the Germans come."

The men moved on Tulloch's orders, with each platoon checking their casualties as the battle entered a momentary lull. Tulloch ran to the upper storey of the farmhouse and scanned the surrounding area. The Germans surrounded the farm and had pushed the BEF a couple of miles towards the coast. Tulloch could see shells exploding and hear the steady rattle of musketry and machine guns.

"What should we do, sir?" Tait asked.

"We hold out until nightfall and break through to our lines," Tulloch said. "Take the north and west perimeter, and I'll take the south and east. Shoot any German that comes close."

Tait nodded. "Yes, sir. Do you think the colonel will try to relieve us?"

"I think the colonel has enough to worry about," Tulloch said. "We're on our own, Tait."

"Yes, sir," Tait moved away to defend his section of the steading.

The men of D Company found their firing points, so they covered all approaches to the farmhouse with at least one Bren and half a dozen rifles. Aitken located what food the house contained, and Sergeant Drysdale distributed it fairly.

"We'll hold out until dark," Tulloch said. "The Germans don't like to fight at night, so we'll leave then and march to the British perimeter." He tried to sound confident, although he knew that nothing in war ever went according to plan.

Drysdale nodded, with the Woodbine cigarette seemingly glued to his bottom lip. They watched as a flight of Stukas passed overhead, and then a squadron of Heinkel HE III bombers headed for the coast. A lone Stuka appeared and circled the Lothians' position, but rather than scream down with its bomb, it dropped a packet of propaganda leaflets and flew away, followed by bullets from frustrated British soldiers.

"What does it say?" Drysdale asked as Brown lifted one of the black-and-white leaflets.

Brown read out the well-formed words, adopting a mock German accent to lighten the message.

"British soldiers

Here is your true situation!

You are completely surrounded!

Lay down your arms!"

Tulloch expected the resulting jeers and obscene comments from his men. He did not need to add anything.

"I'd like to see the RAF," Kelly watched the German aircraft pass in the direction of Dunkirk.

"I'd like to see the bints at the Cages," Innes said, referring to the red-light district of Bombay.

"I'd like to see Ensign Ewart's," Brown mentioned a famous pub near Edinburgh Castle, a haunt for generations of the garrison. "And the barman holding up a pint of McEwans."

"Aye," Kelly said, "And you'll expect me to pay for the round, I suppose."

"Well, it is your round," Brown said. "You're always short of money when the pubs are open." He lifted his rifle, aiming at the distant village, only to lower it when a German patrol marched in the opposite direction.

Tulloch toured the defences. Until now, he had been too busy to consider their position, but the lull in German attacks enabled him to ponder. The Germans had defeated Luxembourg, Belgium, and the Netherlands within days and had pushed the French and British back. Now the BEF was in a headlong fighting retreat to the sea, hopefully for the Royal Navy to evacuate as many as possible. Tulloch thought of other abortive European expeditions, such as Corunna and Walcheren, where the navy had rescued the British Army. However, the army had been much smaller then, and the enemy without tanks and aircraft.

*More to the point, how am I going to get D Company even close to the Dunkirk perimeter with half the German army between us and the BEF?*

Tulloch could hear the constant grumble of artillery and the rattle of machine guns toward the coast while German aircraft roared overhead. *If the Germans leave us alone for even one hour, we can recover and make this place defensible.*

"Sir!" Sergeant Drysdale saluted. "The Germans are gathering to attack again!"

"Thank you, Sergeant," Tulloch said and raised his voice. "Man your posts!"

The farmhouse had a wooden barn and two separate outhouses, with a stone wall surrounding a once-neat garden. Tulloch had posted Bren guns to cover the main approaches while he ordered Private Cummings to wait with the Boys in the centre, ready to respond to a threat from any side.

"Tanks, sir!" Drysdale said.

Tulloch swore. "Where?"

"Somewhere in the village, sir," Drysdale said. "I can hear them."

Tulloch directed his binoculars. He saw three six-wheeled

armoured vehicles, each armed with a 20 mm cannon. "Panzer-spähwagen," he said, scraping in his memory for their name. "An armoured car rather than a tank."

"Bad enough, sir," Drysdale said.

"Bad enough," Tulloch agreed and called for Private Cummings and the Boys. "Pick whichever one is easiest," he said, "and kill the bastard."

Cummings nodded solemnly. "I'll do my best, sir." He lay prone with the Boys ready.

Here they come!" Brown shouted as the armoured cars left the shelter of the village and rumbled along the track to the farm with half a company of infantry behind them.

Cummings waited a moment, aimed, and fired, with his first shot glancing off the leading vehicle to crash into a house wall. Cummings swore and reloaded, fumbling the heavy ammunition as the enemy approached. He fired again, hitting his target square-on and stopping it dead. The Lothians followed up with concentrated musketry as the German infantry spread out, finding cover as the crew bailed out of the armoured car.

Some men looked up at the sound of aircraft engines. Most did not, for a rumour had spread that a human face shone whitely against the ground, encouraging the Luftwaffe to attack.

"Only one round left, sir," Cummings loaded with concentrated savagery, adjusting the tripod to alter his angle of fire.

"Don't fire until you have a clear shot," Tulloch ordered.

The Lothians waited for the Germans, with only Brown's singing disturbing the tense silence. When the sound of engines increased, Tulloch focussed his binoculars on the village.

"Hold!" Tulloch put a hand on Cummings' shoulder. "The second armoured car isn't coming this way." He felt Cummings relax. "It's withdrawing to the village."

*It's a distraction, something to take our attention.*

"These are coming our way, sir!" Innes pointed to the half dozen Stukas that peeled from the sky above the farmhouse.

The aircraft came in a near-vertical dive with the howl of

their descent battering at the defenders' eardrums. Tulloch saw many of his men fall to the ground and cover their ears or hold their helmets close to their heads.

"Come on, you bastards!" Innes shouted, resting his Bren on the perimeter wall to fire upward at the aircraft.

The sound was terrifying as the Stukas screamed toward the defenders. The men were more used to air assault now and knew the sound was worse than the results. While most shrank into whatever cover they could find, others copied Innes and returned fire with rifles and Bren guns.

The leading Stuka dropped its bomb, completed its dive, and zoomed back up so close that Tulloch could see the goggles on the pilot's face. The bomb exploded squarely on top of the farmhouse, with the concussion throwing Tulloch to the ground. He lay there for a moment, trying to recover his senses as the second Stuka dropped its five-hundred-kilogram bomb. The explosion was outside the farm steading, yet still sufficiently close to shower the defenders with stones and dirt. Tulloch heard men screaming as he struggled to his feet, and the third Stuka released its bomb and rose again with the hideous wail battering at the men's ears.

Tulloch lifted his rifle and fired blindly, with little hope of hitting anything.

The remaining Stukas dropped their bombs and flew away, job completed and without losing a single aircraft.

The farmhouse and immediate surroundings were a smoking mess, with five-foot-wide craters and three separate fires burning. One man was screaming with both legs blown off, and others were dead, hideously mangled by the bombs.

"Stretcher bearers!" Tulloch shouted, with dust and smoke making his voice hoarse. He saw the two men struggle towards the wounded man, who looked piteously at them for help.

Tulloch looked at what remained of his company, knowing the German infantry would attack while the British were still recovering. "Tait!" he croaked. "Give me a roll call."

"Mr Tait's dead, sir," Sergeant Drysdale said quietly. He stood with blood on his face. "I'll get the roll."

"Thank you, Sergeant," Tulloch said.

*Should I give up? Or keep fighting. If the Germans attack now, we have little to offer in defence.*

As he pondered, he heard somebody singing and saw German infantry approach through the smoke.

# Chapter Twenty Four

*I saw savage men in war-bands,*
*And after the morning's fray, torn flesh.*
*I saw hordes of invaders dead.*
*Joyous, wrathful, the shout one heard.*
*The Battle of Gwen Ystrad.*
**Taleisen**

It was Private Brown who started the singing. Private Brown, who had run the gauntlet of Waziri fire in the Shahur Tangi defile on the Frontier and had a habit of telling bawdy jokes at inappropriate moments. Now, when Tulloch looked across to him, he saw that Brown was dying. He lay behind the remnants of the farmhouse wall, a desperately wounded man within a shattered building.

"Oh, we're no awa' tae bide awa,'
And we're no awa' tae leave you."

Brown sang softly through broken, swollen lips, spitting out blood with every word. One by one, the other members of Four Platoon of B Company joined in, some growling the words defiantly, others using the old familiar song to hide the fear that none would admit they possessed.

"We're no awa tae bide awa
We'll aye come back tae see you."

Tulloch shook away the memories and the songs as he readied himself for the next move. The night was gathering as dark clouds mustered above, easing the possibility of further air attacks.

"We're moving in half an hour," he said. "Diamond formation. Sergeant Drysdale will take point. I'll take the rearguard with Eight Section."

The men nodded, accepting their fate. Some had already given themselves up as dead or prisoners, while most still looked defiant, although shocked by the intensity of the recent fighting.

The Germans remained in the village as if they thought they had done sufficient. Tulloch knew they did not like to fight at night, which gave him an opportunity to slip away. He studied the ground around B Company's position, noting the scatter of German dead and wounded.

*The Germans are pushing the BEF out of France, but we're making them pay for their victory.*

Tulloch toured his defences. Brown was dead, his mouth still open in song, and only four men remained of Eight Section. Forty men of B Company were unwounded, shaken, and scared but still carrying their weapons, capable of fighting.

"We'll have to leave the badly wounded," Tulloch told them. "The Germans will look after them."

The men nodded, recognising the realities of the situation. The stretcher bearers visited each man, giving rough sympathy, morphine, and what help they could. Mackay lifted his remaining arm, grinning through his pain.

"Give me a Bren, sir, and I'll take some of them with me."

Tulloch knew the man was dying. "The Germans will look after you better than we can," he said and turned away to hide the betraying tears in his eyes. He could do nothing more for these men who had given everything for an ungrateful nation.

"Why don't the Germans attack at night?" Sergeant Drysdale asked. "They could swamp us if they tried."

Tulloch shook his head. "I don't know. Just be thankful."

"I am, sir," Drysdale said.

Hogg stamped his feet and settled his steel helmet on his head, carefully avoiding the sharpened brim that had done so much damage in his last encounter with the Germans.

As artillery continued to grumble in the background, Sergeant Drysdale counted the ammunition, spreading it out so each man had an equal amount. The Brens were down to two magazines each, with no cartridges left for the Boys.

"I thought we had one shell left," Tulloch said.

"I fired it at the Stukas, sir," Cummings admitted.

Tulloch nodded, understanding. "Break the Boys," he ordered. "Ensure the Germans can't use them against us."

"They wouldn't want the damned thing," Cummings said. "It's a beast." He said a last farewell to the clumsy weapon, removed the firing pin and smashed the Boys against the wall.

They slid out as darkness fell, saying their last goodbyes to the wounded. "See you later, chum. God bless."

"Jerry will look after you, Wullie. You'll be all right."

Some of the wounded were too far gone to care. Others were desperate to remain with their comrades.

"Don't leave me, sir! I can fight if somebody helps me! Just give me a hand, for God's sake!"

Tulloch steeled his heart to the cries. Being an officer was a hard thing at times like this.

"Come on, B Company. Take the point, Sergeant."

They marched into the night, heading for the distant rumble of guns that marked the defended perimeter of Dunkirk and leaving the wounded behind. In his head, Tulloch heard one man sobbing long after all other sounds died away,

———

"THE GERMANS ARE EVERYWHERE, SIR," LIGHTFOOT REPORTED as they headed northwest, moving across the country and avoiding the roads where the Germans congregated.

"So I see," Tulloch agreed. He used Lightfoot as a runner, carrying messages between Sergeant Drysdale and himself.

As was their habit, the Germans had halted for the night, with their camps spread across the route Tulloch's company had to cross. Tulloch was surprised at the volume of horse-drawn transport the Germans used and the casual way they camped. Although each camp was laid out in the same efficient pattern, the Germans spoke loudly as if they were so confident they did not need to take precautions.

"These lads would not last a day on the Frontier," Drysdale gave his professional opinion.

Tulloch agreed.

"Can we not rummel them up a bit, sir?" Private Elliot of Five Platoon was a Selkirk man, a product of centuries of bloodshed and reiving. The familiar phrase nearly brought a smile to Tulloch's mouth. "We can let their horses go and maybe set a wee fire in their ammunition stores."

Tulloch contemplated the suggestion. It would be immensely satisfying to cause upset to the German army, but his duty was to get what remained of B Company home safely. That meant keeping the Germans quiet while he threaded through their camps.

"Not this time, Elliot," Tulloch said regretfully. "Although I appreciate your suggestion." When Elliot watched the German camp, licking his lips at the thought of spreading mayhem, Tulloch knew the Germans might find winning this war harder than they presumed, despite their runaway start.

The sound of singing came from one German infantry formation, drowning the steady thump of British ammunition boots as the Lothians marched past. Tulloch grunted at the martial song with its rousing chorus, wondered what the words meant, and pressed on.

"Don't stop, lads." He ushered his company past the Germans, moving in sections and covering each other as the German singing rose to a crescendo before dying away.

"Tanks, sir!" Lightfoot reported. "We can hear them ahead."

Tulloch gestured for his men to lie down as he scouted in advance of the company. He passed a downed RAF Blenheim, with one engine riddled with machine gun fire and the pilot a charred horror in the burned-out cockpit and sunk into dead ground to look ahead. The Germans had parked their tanks in neat rows, with their crews sleeping at their sides and a dozen bored sentries slouching around the perimeter, smoking and talking.

Tulloch felt a surge of anger that the victorious Germans could act so casually.

*They know they are in no danger,* Tulloch told himself. *They've already broken the French, and we're in full retreat.* He saw four batteries of anti-aircraft guns amidst the parked tanks and grunted. *This war is different from anything we've fought before, and we're not prepared for it. We expected a static war like the last one, and the Germans have trained for a war of movement, emphasising tanks and aircraft.*

The Lothians moved on, so close to the German positions they could hear the sentries talking and smell the drift of their cigarettes and another sour aroma that Tulloch did not recognise.

*Germans,* he told himself. *That's the stench of Germans.*

As they progressed towards Dunkirk, the volume of abandoned British equipment increased. They came across two more wrecked RAF aircraft, one still smoking, with the pilot and navigator lying neatly at the side. The other was scattered over a hundred yards of field, with a double row of bullet holes across the roundels.

"At least we know the RAF is fighting," Cummings said.

"Keep moving," Tulloch ordered. "We can't do anything here."

Twice they passed encampments of scared refugees, with terrified civilians fleeing the war, cowering from both armies in their efforts to remain alive. Other refugees blocked the roads, with women, old men, and children predominating but also a trickle of younger men, some wearing Belgian or French army uniforms.

"Poor buggers," Innes said.

"Aye, let's hope the Germans don't invade Britain," Hogg replied sourly. "I don't fancy seeing my ma like that."

"I didn't know you knew your ma, Hoggy," Innes replied. "I thought you Orangemen were born true blue bastards." He moved away quickly before Hogg could respond.

Aitken viewed the long column of refugees. "Well, there's nothing much to stop the Germans from invading except the Navy," he replied. "They've smashed the French and kicked us out smartly enough."

"We're no' beat yet," Hogg said.

"Cut the noise," Tulloch ordered. He glanced at the sky. The short summer night was ending, with dawn fast approaching. He calculated the distance they still had to travel and swore, knowing they would not make the perimeter before daylight. Artillery fire sounded fitfully ahead, with the occasional flash of an explosion lighting up the sky and silhouetting trees and houses.

"Halt here, lads," Tulloch said and scanned the countryside while the men formed a diamond shape, facing outwards with their rifles ready. The roads were congested with shattered British vehicles, thousands of refugees, and advancing German columns, so Tulloch's only choice was to continue across country. He had to find somewhere to hide for the day and make a dash for Dunkirk the following night, provided the Germans did not find them. He checked his watch, cursing when he saw the glass was smashed, and the hands stopped at ten past twelve.

"I don't fancy spending the rest of the war in a Prisoner of War camp, sir," Drysdale said.

"Nor do I," Tulloch agreed.

They found a straggling wood, with three copses of trees in the lee of a ridge, and dug in. A couple of rutted fields separated the trees from a shattered farm, with a burning British lorry in between and the corpses of a British soldier and two civilians.

"The Germans are not as skilled as the Waziris at spotting us," Tulloch said. "But don't take chances. Don't talk, and keep any movement to a minimum."

"The men know what to do," Drysdale said. "I wish we had more ammunition."

"So do I," Tulloch agreed. "We'll have to make do with what we have." He posted sentries, ordered the men to dig rifle pits and hoped the Germans would bypass them as they pressed on the Dunkirk perimeter, only eight miles away.

"I want four men on sentry duty. Two hours stag each," Tulloch said. "Everybody try to grab some kip."

The men complained at the extra labour of throwing up trenches, and some were asleep even as their companions mounted stag. Tulloch understood their fatigue yet still forced them on.

"If any German aircraft come nosing," he said. "Don't be tempted to fire or look up. Keep your heads down."

The men nodded. They knew how dangerous German dive bombers were and had no desire to invite a return attack.

Stepping outside the perimeter, Tulloch critically examined the position, looking for anything a passing German may notice. Only when he was satisfied did he return. He lay in the two-man rifle pit Lightfoot had dug and closed his eyes, with images from the previous few days flashing through his mind. He dozed for a couple of hours, waking every few moments through stress and worry to ensure the sentries were alert. Nightmares haunted two young soldiers, so they thrashed around, disturbing the others.

"Sir," Drysdale woke him, speaking quietly. "We have neighbours."

The SS arrived in a convoy of trucks, black-uniformed men moving in disciplined silence as an officer barked at them. They parked two hundred yards from B Company, with the officer posting sentries at each corner of a sodden field. A large wooden barn stood against the boundary fence, dim against the waking dawn.

"German is a truly ugly language, sir," Drysdale said, "but they're efficient; I'll grant them that."

"Shhh!" Tulloch warned and hefted his rifle as a dozen soldiers ran to the third truck in the convoy and dragged back the cover. A burly NCO shouted orders, and a dozen bewildered British soldiers scrambled out with one tall officer at the back.

"Norfolks," Drysdale whispered.

"And one of them's an officer," Tulloch added. His stomach lurched with memory. "Lieutenant Simpson."

"Do you know him, sir?" Drysdale asked.

Tulloch remembered Simpson's mocking, sneering face as his fists came towards him in the boxing ring at Sandhurst. "Yes, I know him."

The Lothians watched tensely as the SS soldiers shepherded the British prisoners into the barn, pushing or kicking any who seemed reluctant. More SS arrived, sinister men in black uniforms marching like automatons.

"This doesn't look good, sir," Drysdale commented, pushing his rifle forward.

Tulloch agreed silently. He glanced over his men. Although some had wakened to watch what happened, many were still asleep through sheer weariness. Others lay with their eyes sunk into bottomless pits, their minds anywhere but here. All were unshaven and dirty, with torn uniforms and muddy boots, yet all retained their weapons; they were still soldiers.

Tulloch held the binoculars to his eyes and focused on the barn. He saw the SS soldiers push their prisoners inside at gunpoint, with a tall officer snapping orders. When a dark staff car eased into the field, the officer sprang to attention. He shouted something to his men, who jumped to immediate attention as the car drove slowly past, kicking up clods of earth.

"What's happening, sir?" Drysdale asked.

"I'm not sure," Tulloch replied. He watched as the SS officer approached the staff car. The passenger rolled down the window, and the two men spoke for a few moments before the officer straightened up, saluted, and returned to his men.

"I wonder who's in the staff car, sir," Drysdale said. "Some *burra sahib,* that's for sure."[1]

Tulloch tried to focus on the car, with the rising sun reflecting on the windows to block his vision. "It could be Hitler for all we know."

When the prisoners were inside the barn, the SS officer gave an order. Three of his men unhooked stick grenades from their uniforms, opened the barn door and casually threw them inside.

"Jesus Christ!" Drysdale blasphemed as the grenades exploded, unseen. "The Jerries have murdered those poor bastards!"

Tulloch watched, appalled. He would have expected such actions from the Waziris but not from a supposedly civilised people. *Civilised? They used poison gas in the Great War and bombed civilians in Belgium. They machine-gunned columns of refugees and invaded neutral countries. We cannot consider this a war against a civilised nation; we're fighting a war for civilisation.*

"Sir!" Ingles lifted his Bren. "Sir! Permission to fire, sir?" He stared at the SS men with hatred in his eyes. "I'll get the officer, sir, and these murdering bastards!"

Tulloch put a hand on Ingles' arm. "No. You'll get them, and then the whole battalion will be on us. I want to get us home, Ingles." Although he spoke the truth, Tulloch understood Ingles' anger. He wanted to destroy these black-uniformed savages.

As Tulloch watched, the SS officer and a dozen men moved into the barn, shooting. The staff car remained where it was while a score of SS soldiers walked casually to the barn and peered inside. The sound of their laughter drifted over to the Lothians.[2]

Tulloch realised that most of B Company were watching, some with fingers curled around their triggers, others trembling with barely suppressed anger.

"Sir?" Aitken had his safety catch off. "When can we fire?"

Even the imperturbable Hardie was waiting for the order to fire, lying prone with his rifle cuddled into his shoulder. Tulloch considered again, weighing his desire for vengeance against the needs of his men.

Forty British soldiers stuck behind German lines with only what they carried, and limited ammunition would have little chance of battling through to the British lines. Even if they succeeded in wiping out the entire SS battalion, the noise would alert other German units in the area.

"No. Hold your fire!" Tulloch said. It was another hard decision he had to make, like shooting Russell and leaving the wounded behind. He thought of Simpson again, wondering how many more good officers and men would die in this ill-starred campaign.

The SS left the barn, casually reloading their weapons. Some were laughing, while others lit cigarettes. On an order from the officer, they jumped to attention, dropped their cigarettes, and ground them out underfoot.

"Aye, aye, what's happening here?" The staff car moved again, rolling up beside the SS officer. With the alteration of angle, Tulloch noticed two flags fluttering from the bonnet. On the left wing was the sinister German swastika, while the right wing boasted the more colourful Italian flag.

The staff car came to a smooth halt in the centre of the field, with a platoon of SS men forming as a guard of honour. The SS officer saluted as the door opened, and a civilian emerged. Tulloch knew without looking that it was Francesco Giorano, right at the heart of a case of mass murder. He watched as the SS officer took Giorano inside the barn. There was the sound of a single gunshot, and they emerged a few moments later, with the officer holstering his pistol.

"That bastard just shot one of the Norfolks," Drysdale sounded suddenly old.

Tulloch nodded. "I know." He focussed on the officer,

committing his face to memory. The man was tall, slender, and gaunt, with wide eyes. *I'll know you if I see you again, son,* Tulloch thought.

"Bugger this! I'm taking these bastards!" Inglis aimed his Bren and prepared to fire until Tulloch put a hand on his shoulder.

"If you fire, Inglis, we'll all be dead within the hour," Tulloch explained quietly. "There are forty of us and at least three battalions of Germans within half a mile radius, plus tanks and armoured cars. I aim to get as many of us as possible home alive."

"Yes, sir, but," Innes looked up with frustrated anger in his face.

"Keep silent and keep alive," Tulloch said.

The Lothians watched in seething anger as Tulloch wondered at the connection between Giorano and the SS. He wrote down the location of the murders and tried to fit a description of the staff car.

Giorano elegantly lit a cigarette, and the SS officer took him on a tour of his unit, stopping to speak to a man here and there. He revisited the barn, leaving with his cigarette held in a languid hand.

"Look at that bastard," Innes said.

"We're looking," Hogg said.

It was mid-morning before Giorano returned to the car, with the SS again lined up as a guard of honour, presenting arms as the staff car drove out of the field.

"I hope our wounded are all right," Drysdale said quietly.

"So do I," Tulloch knew that worry would burden him until he learned what happened to the men he left behind. Only a few miles away, the steady grumble of artillery continued, and the Luftwaffe flew overhead in a constant flow to pound the British positions. Occasionally, an aircraft would head back inland trailing smoke, and twice, the Lothians saw one descend in flames.

"Got you, you bastard!" Aitken said.

Tulloch repressed the Lothians' incipient cheer in case the SS heard.

The day passed slowly, with the Lothians still angry and frustrated over the murder of the British prisoners.

"Do you think the artillery is further away now?" Tulloch asked as the day closed with flickering gunfire from the direction of Dunkirk.

"Yes, sir," Drysdale replied. "They're pushing us towards the sea."

"That's what I thought," Tulloch said. "We'll have to break through the cordon tonight, Drysdale, or we might be too late."

"Yes, sir," Drysdale agreed. "Do you know what the date is, sir?"

Tulloch tried to count back the days. "The third of June, I think, Sergeant. Maybe the fourth. I've lost count."

"So have I, sir," Drysdale said. He glanced over his shoulder. "The boys are about done now."

"They are," Tulloch agreed. "The more sleep they get, the better." He looked at the barn, feeling a surge of hatred for the SS officer and Giorano.

*I doubt I'll meet you again, Giorano, but if I get the chance to kill you and that SS officer, by the living Christ, I'll take it.*

# Chapter Twenty Five

*The great Dragon, most loathsome, terrible, and ancient; the slippery serpent, more cunning than all the beasts and than all the fiercer living things of earth, dragged him down with a third of the stars into the pit of infernal places.*

**Attributed to St. Columba**

Tulloch led B Company away from their trees half an hour after dark. They moved quietly, with most of the men hoping for an opportunity to avenge themselves for the murder of the Norfolks. Tulloch felt a new savagery in them; *they may be professional soldiers, but now they're warriors wanting to kill. God help any Germans who get in our way. The men are in the mood to take on Hitler's entire army.*

Tulloch eased them past the SS camp and on for a quarter of a mile before he halted. "Where's Hogg?"

"He was here a moment ago," Drysdale said. "He must have lost his way in the dark."

*Hogg's a veteran of the Frontier; he knows not to lag.* Tulloch swore, wondering if he should press on, wait, or look for the missing man. "Wait here for ten minutes, Sergeant. If I'm not back, take these lads to Dunkirk and get them safely over the Channel."

"Yes, sir," Drysdale said. "Maybe I'd be better looking for Hogg, sir."

Tulloch knew that Drysdale was correct. The senior officer should remain with the majority of his men, but he was also aware he was better at moving silently. "Give me ten minutes, Sergeant, then take them home."

"Yes, sir." For the first time since Tulloch had known him, Drysdale had some doubt in his voice.

Tulloch slid into the dark, surprisingly aware of a feeling of relief to lose the responsibility of command, if only for a few moments. He moved quickly, hearing the distant stutter of artillery as background noise without being aware of any threat. He heard somebody breathing ahead and dropped to the ground, watching intently. A man appeared, walking nearly casually, with a rifle slung over his shoulder and the distinctive shape of a British steel helmet on his head.

Tulloch waited until the man was three yards away and then rose, pointing his rifle. Hogg stopped at once with his bayonet in his right hand.

"Where the hell have you been?" Tulloch hissed.

"I got lost, sir," Hogg said, cleaning his bayonet. He held Tulloch's eyes in a nearly murderous glare.

"What happened to your bayonet?" Tulloch asked.

"I met a German soldier," Hogg's lips curled in a sneer. "One of they murdering bastards dressed in black."

Tulloch saw the cold hatred in Hogg's eyes. "You just happened to meet him, did you?"

"Yes, sir," Hogg slid his bayonet into its sheath.

"That was fortuitous," Tulloch replied. "I hope it was the officer."

"No, sir. I couldnae find him," Hogg admitted calmly. "Only the loud-mouthed sergeant."

Tulloch nodded. "Get back with the company. You've held us

up, so you can consider yourself on a charge when we return to the regiment."

"Yes, sir," Hogg hurried through the dark with Tulloch a few steps behind.

The company moved on faster now, finding more evidence of the retreat, with wrecked British vehicles blocking the roads and piles of abandoned equipment beside smouldering farmhouses.

The irregular crackle of musketry continued ahead, interspersed with rattling machine guns.

"There's less firing now," Drysdale said. "The artillery's stopped."

Tulloch nodded. "You're right," he said, pushing his tired men harder so they stumbled along, depending on the light from burning vehicles and houses to guide them.

"How do we get through the lines?" Drysdale asked as they skirted a German artillery unit, with the horses in neat lines and yawning men standing nonchalant guard.

"Listen!" Tulloch held up his hand. "The firing has stopped."

They heard the rattle of a single machine gun and then three sharp cracks from a rifle, then silence; a single shot and then silence again. One of the horses whinnied, the sound lonely in the devastation of the night.

"What the hell does that mean?" Drysdale fingered the safety catch of his rifle.

"We've either packed in, or there's nobody left to fight," Tulloch said. "It can't mean anything else."

"Jesus," Drysdale breathed. "What do we do now? Do you think Churchill has thrown in the towel?"

The idea appalled Tulloch. He considered it for a moment and shook his head. "No," he said firmly. "Churchill would not surrender, and Britain will fight on, whatever happens, and whoever else gives in. It's not in our nature to give up."

Drysdale looked at him, with his eyes granite hard set in dark pits. "I didnae think we would, sir. What's happened at Dunkirk, then?"

Tulloch contemplated for a moment, aware his men were listening, hoping for a straw of hope. "I think the evacuation has finished, Sergeant."

Drysdale took a deep breath. "Does that mean we cannae get picked up at Dunkirk then, sir?"

"I'll have a look and see," Tulloch told him. Glancing around, he pointed to a small group of trees. "Take the men to that wood and stay until I return."

"Yes, sir."

As Tulloch eased closer to the front line, the number of German units thickened until he knew he could go no closer without the Germans catching him. He saw troops of tanks parked close together and thought them a lovely target for RAF bombers.

*If we had dive bombers like the Stukas, we could wreak havoc here.*

Thick oily smoke polluted the air as Tulloch eased into the outskirts of Dunkirk. He saw line after line of wrecked and abandoned British vehicles, with the occasional dead body lying at the side. The streets were bullet-scarred, with German soldiers on sentry duty at crossroads and a few British prisoners huddled in groups of collective misery.

*The Germans have comprehensively defeated us,* Tulloch thought. *Walcheren, Corunna, and Mons were nothing compared to this. Has the Navy managed to get anybody across the Channel?*

Tulloch stepped into the angle between two buildings as a body of German infantry shepherded a column of British prisoners past.

"Shoulders back!" A young British sergeant ordered, nursing a wounded arm. "We're not beaten yet, lads!"

Most prisoners responded, straightening their backs and marching like soldiers. One man, limping from a leg wound, staggered to keep up until a lance corporal put an arm around his shoulders.

"Come on, mate. I'll help you!"

Tulloch felt sick when he saw the German guards jeering at

the wounded man. One burly German ran across and landed a hefty kick on the man's unwounded leg. The lance corporal turned on the German, fists clenched until two more Germans joined in with rifle butts and heavy boots.

Tulloch watched with increasing anger. *Enjoy your victory while you can, you Nazi bastards. We'll be back to get you.*

"We'll not be leaving by Dunkirk, lads," Tulloch informed B Company of what he had seen. "The Germans are rounding up stragglers, the wounded and the rearguard."

"Well, they're no' getting us," Aitken said truculently. "We all saw what the SS did to the Norfolk lads."

Tulloch agreed. He had no intention of surrendering. "We'll make for the coast south of Dunkirk," he said. "I don't know where the Germans will be, but we'll try and find some sort of boat."

*The sensible thing would be to join the nearest French unit, but from what I've seen of the French, that would only postpone the inevitable, and I don't want to get stuck deep inland. We're an island nation, and I feel happier near the sea.*

"We'll have to keep marching, lads. If we find any habitation without Germans, we'll look for food. No hoarding; we'll divide it into equal shares. The same goes for ammunition. Any abandoned British equipment is ours."

The men hitched up their trousers, shouldered their rifles and moved on. Weary, unshaven, and hungry, they looked around warily, passing scores of wrecked British lorries and hiding from marching Germans. The Lothians watched as a dozen Germans escorted a long column of French soldiers to the north.

"The sooner we're back home, the better," Innes said. "Then we can prepare to return."

Hogg nodded. "And kill more of these bastards."

Tulloch could feel the anger in his men, mingled with iron hatred he had never experienced with British soldiers.

"It might pass," Sergeant Drysdale said. "It was the same after Second Ypres when the Germans used chlorine gas. I'll never forget that horrible green mist or those poor devils dying in unutterable agony. That was the worst battle I was ever in, worse than the Somme or Passchendaele. That's the only time I've seen British soldiers kill the enemy wounded, we were so scunnered at the gas." He paused for a moment. "I hope the man who invented that stuff suffers in hell for eternity, the foul German bastard."

Tulloch had never seen his laconic sergeant so emotional.

"And now the Huns are back at their old tricks, murdering prisoners." Drysdale shook his head. "We must win this war, sir. We're fighting unadulterated evil."

Tulloch nodded. "We'll win, Sergeant. I'm not sure how, but we'll win. The first stage is to get our men back to Blighty and tell everybody what we've witnessed."

"Sir!" Drysdale whispered. "Look!"

The SS battalion roared past in a long column of trucks. Tulloch glimpsed Giorano in his staff car, talking to a uniformed man, and then the car was gone, with its flags fluttering from the bonnet and the SS soldiers staring stonily over the French countryside.

"Bastards," Hogg said and spat on the ground.

"Move on," Tulloch ordered. He did not have to warn them to be careful.

Hardie saw the bodies first. "Over there, sir," he gestured with his chin as his eyes roved across the landscape, searching for threats. "Three British soldiers."

Two were privates, and the third a corporal. All were wounded and then murdered, shot through the head.

"As you said, Sergeant," Tulloch said. "We're fighting evil."

"Hogg and Hardie, check these men for ammunition!" Drysdale ordered and accepted the fifty brass cartridges, which he distributed to the men. "Not much but better than nothing," he said.

"Move on," Tulloch ordered curtly.

Twice the Lothians melted into cover at the side of the road as a column of Allied prisoners shuffled past, with jubilant German soldiers guarding them.

"I hate these bastards," Hogg said, fingering his bayonet.

"I hate seeing our lads like that," Inglis agreed.

"Our turn will come, lads," Tulloch assured them. "Our job is to get back to Britain. After that, we can rejoin the regiment and get ready for the second leg."

"Maybe we're beat, sir," Cummings said. "Maybe we didn't get anybody off at Dunkirk, and we've thrown in the towel."

"Not a chance," Hogg told him.

They passed the remains of a Bristol Blenheim, with bullet holes riddling the roundel and the pilot's remains still inside.

Tulloch stopped them. "That aircraft fires .303 ammunition in its forward gun and dorsal turret," he said. "Break them open. We need bullets."

The men looked at him, unsure how to proceed.

"You heard the officer!" Drysdale snarled and led the way, tearing at the smashed turret and port wing to see what he could salvage.

The aircraft supplied twenty rounds for each man, and a shell-damaged farmhouse gave them stale bread, cheese, a fragment of pork, plus fresh water from an outside well.

"We want to get well clear of the environs of Dunkirk by daylight," Tulloch said, forcing the Lothians to march.

Refreshed by the food but depressed by the sights and sounds of the British defeat, they moved on. They avoided a group of drunken French soldiers waiting for the Germans to capture them, glowered at a company of exultant German soldiers and stared at a park of German panzers.

"How many of these bastards are there?" Aitken asked.

"Too bloody many," Innes replied.

"Push on," Tulloch ordered. "We're not here to sightsee."

By two in the morning, they had skirted Dunkirk and moved south, keeping close to the coast. Tulloch could hear the hush of surf, tantalising them with the prospect of freedom. A seagull swooped overhead, screaming.

"Look for boats," Tulloch ordered. "Any sort of boat."

"It will have to be large to hold forty of us," Drysdale said.

"Two small boats will do," Tulloch said. "Or three."

"Can you sail a boat, sir?" Drysdale asked.

"We'll learn," Tulloch told him. "We'll paddle with our hands if we must. Find out if any of the men have experience at sea."

"Sir!" Drysdale returned a few moments later. "Drummond used to fish from Musselburgh, sir, and some of the men have crossed the Forth on the Fife ferry."

Tulloch grunted. "Hardly hearts of oak and jolly tars, then. We'll have to do our best." He led them closer to the shore, so they could hear the welcome hammer of the surf on the sand and smell the clean tang of salt water.

*It's strange to think we're only about thirty miles from the south coast of Britain. The sea is like a defensive ditch, a moat holding back the enemy hordes, but now it's a barrier keeping us trapped on the European mainland.*

Tulloch heard the murmur of voices and touched Drysdale's shoulder.

The sergeant nodded and passed the message on from man to man. The Lothians halted, crouching on the soft sand, holding their rifles ready and with dry mouths and thumping hearts. Innes cradled the Bren, licked his lips, and stretched out, hoping for a target.

"Stay," Tulloch ordered, dropping to a crawl. He edged towards the source of the sound, hoping to find a group of fishermen around a reasonably sized boat or at least a few smaller vessels. The sand was cool under his hands, with the thump of the waves hampering his hearing.

The surf exploded in surges of silver-white, with moonlight gleaming from the surface of the sea, revealing a long, low boat drawn up on the beach.

Tulloch watched for a moment as half a dozen men moved

slowly inland, carrying rifles. He could not distinguish the colour of their uniforms, but there was no mistaking their purposeful walk.

*German sailors! Can we overpower them and take their boat? It'll be a squeeze, but we might all fit in, and better drown at sea than end up a prisoner of the Nazis.*

"Sergeant!" Tulloch whispered when he returned. "Half a dozen armed German sailors and a boat. If we take the Germans, we can grab the boat."

Drysdale nodded, showing his teeth in a gesture that could have been a smile or a grimace. "I'll tell the lads."

"No shooting!" Tulloch said. "We don't want to alert any German soldiers."

Drysdale nodded again. "I'll pass the message on, sir."

Tulloch felt very exposed, lying on the open beach with a breeze blowing hard sand over him and a scimitar moon throwing fitful shadows. The German seamen moved very slowly, two yards apart, as they patrolled the shore, prodding their rifles into patches of seaweed and peering over dunes.

*They're looking for British soldiers,* Tulloch thought; *well, the hunters are about to become the hunted. The Lothians are here.*

He crept forward, slithering over the shifting sands with his rifle in his right hand and his men spread out behind him. The sailors moved in a vee, dark uniforms against a dark sky and the hush of the surf as a backdrop. Judging his time, Tulloch shouted, "Now!" and stood up, ready to smash his rifle butt onto his target's head. Although the sailor lifted his rifle to defend himself, Tulloch knew his blow would brush aside the weapon.

"Wait, sir!" Drysdale yelled. "These are ours!"

"What?" Tulloch halted in mid-swing, altering the angle of his blow so it struck the sailor on the shoulder rather than the head.

"What the devil?" The sailor staggered and fell, staring up at Tulloch. "You're English!"

"No," Tulloch corrected, helping the man to his feet. "We're

Scottish; I'm Lieutenant Douglas Tulloch of the Lothian Rifles."

"Good God! You could have killed us!" The seaman was an officer with a determined chin on a young face. "I'm Lieutenant George Furness, HMS *Oystercatcher*."

The Lothians lowered their weapons, with the gleam of moonlight on naked bayonets a reminder of what might have been a disaster.

"We're looking for a lift home," Tulloch nodded to the boat as Furness dusted himself down. "Is that HMS *Oystercatcher*? Did you cross the Channel in that?"

"No." Furness shook his head, looking at the ragged soldiers who surrounded his men. "How many of you are there?"

"Forty-one, including me," Tulloch said.

"We'll need three trips," Furness decided immediately. "Maybe four. Are there any Germans nearby?"

"Thousands," Tulloch told him. "The whole German army, guns, horses, tanks and God-knows-what-else is just up the road."

"We won't waste time, then," Furness said. "Bring your men to the boat. *Oystercatcher* is a couple of miles offshore."

"I can't see her," Tulloch peered out to sea.

"You're not meant to," Furness told him. He glanced at the Lothians. "We'll take a dozen of your men, maybe fourteen at a pinch."

The Lothians hurried to the shore, with Tulloch and Eight Section acting as rearguard, now wishing a cloud could obscure the slender moon.

"Come on, Jocks," Furness said. He bundled fourteen of the Lothians into the small boat and pushed off, rowing for an unseen craft offshore. The men left on the beach heard the slight splashing of the oars as they watched the boat disappear into the night.

"I hope they remember to come back for us," Cummings said.

"They'll be back," Innes told him.

"Come on, lads; defensive screen here!" Tulloch ordered, spreading the remainder of his men in a semi-circle with their backs to the sea. They waited in tense silence, hoping not to see any enemy for what seemed like hours as the tide crept slowly closer and the night dragged on.

Seabirds called overhead, with one landing to inspect these intruders on his beach. An onshore breeze cooled the men as clouds eased over the sky, alternatively blocking and revealing the moon.

"Sir," Drysdale said. "The boat's returning."

Tulloch looked over his shoulder as he heard a quiet splash and saw the boat creeping closer, with the oars rising and falling like the legs of some giant aquatic centipede.

"Lieutenant Tulloch!" Furness whispered as the seamen held the boat steady in the surf. "Bring on the next contingent!"

"Sergeant Drysdale, take on another thirteen men," Tulloch ordered. "Cram them in and join them."

Drysdale pushed men onto the boat and stepped on himself as the seamen pushed off. The wind had risen with the tide, kicking spindrift and spume from the waves and raising a thin curtain of sand. Tulloch watched the boat struggle to sea, with waves breaking from the prow, now visible from the shore. He glanced at his remaining twelve men, noting that some were from Eight Section and reflected they were a long way from Waziristan. Another wave broke from the prow, white against the sea, and he realised HMS *Oystercatcher* was now visible as a vague grey shape on the horizon.

*If the Germans see the ship, they'll guess something's happening and come to investigate.*

The short summer night was easing to a close with a band of grey light already visible to the east. Tulloch curbed his impatience, knowing the navy was doing its best.

"Keep alert, boys," he warned. "This is the crucial time. When the boat returns, we're off home."

"Sir," Hardie whispered. "Something's moving up the beach."

# Chapter Twenty-Six

*Vengeance is in my heart, death in my hand.*
**Shakespeare: Titus Andronicus**

"Y ou've got eyes like a bird of prey, Hardie."
Tulloch lifted his binoculars. "A German patrol," he said. He heard them talking now, moving with the confident gait of men who were winning the war. **"SS, I think,"** Tulloch glanced over his shoulder, hoping to see the boat returning, but a thin offshore mist had risen, concealing everything beyond two hundred yards.

"Permission to fire, sir?" Hardie asked, squinting along the barrel of his rifle.

The Germans were in plain sight now, a dozen SS men walking easily between the dunes and the level plain of the beach, with the officer a few yards in front.

"That's the bastards that murdered the Norfolks," Hogg said, easing forward his safety catch.

"Sir?" Hardie asked again, and Tulloch sensed the restlessness of his men. To be so near rescue and have a German patrol stumble upon them was the cruellest of luck.

"There's that civilian!" Hardie said.

295

Francesco Giorano walked immediately behind the SS officer, looking as comfortable on this windy French beach as he had in Waziristan. Tulloch struggled between his desire to destroy this group of murderers and the realisation that to do so would hazard his men.

"Permission to fire, sir?" Hogg had first pressure on the trigger.

"Not yet," Tulloch snarled. "They might pass us by." He glanced over his shoulder again, where the sea broke in unending surf, and the mist was thicker than ever. A seagull cried, the call lonely, melancholic, yet familiar, a reminder of the friendly beaches of East Lothian and Fife.

When the tall German officer shouted an order, two SS soldiers hurried toward the Lothians with rifles at the high port. Tulloch cursed, glanced over his shoulder to see if the boat was back and aimed at the leading German.

"Fire," he said and loosed the first shot.

The Lothians fired at once, downing the two most forward Germans and wounding the tall officer, who crumpled with a loud yell.

"Got you, you murdering bastard," Hogg said, working the bolt of his rifle.

"He's still alive, Hoggie," Aitken said.

"I shot him in the guts," Hogg replied, firing again. "I want the bastard to suffer!"

The remaining men of the patrol hesitated, with some firing into the mist and others falling back to their parent body.

"They can't see where we are," Tulloch said. "Keep firing!" He peered into the mist, looking for Giorano, who had disappeared.

As the German fire ceased and the SS began withdrawing, Hogg yelled, "Gin ye Daur, lads! Come on, Lothians! Show them your cap badge!" He ran forward, bayonet fixed, and stopped at the writhing SS officer.

Hogg stared at the man for a second, poised his bayonet and thrust downward. "Hope you die slowly, Adolf."

Other Lothians had joined Hogg, with Tulloch on the flank, searching for Giorano. He saw a burly sergeant rallying the SS, aimed, and fired. When the sergeant crumpled without a sound, the others, seeing an unknown number of British soldiers appearing through the mist, decided that discretion overtook valour and withdrew.

"Aye, run, you windy bastards!" Hogg said.

"Don't follow them," Tulloch said, firing a final shot at the rapidly departing Germans. "Get back to the beach." He looked again for Giorano, frustrated that he had again failed to kill the Italian agent.

The Lothians withdrew towards the sea, most satisfied with their minor victory. Nobody tried to help the SS officer, who writhed and moaned as his life ebbed away.

"They'll send a larger force now," Tulloch said. "Dig in at the high-water mark, boys and get ready." He checked his watch and swore when he remembered it was broken. He felt as if he had been waiting for hours since the boat left, although it could not have been more than forty-five minutes.

"Where's the boat, sir?" Aitken asked. "Have they forgotten about us?"

"It will come," Tulloch said. Raising his binoculars, he stared out to sea, where *Oystercatcher* was plainly visible. *The Navy had better watch for German dive bombers.*

The first mortar bomb exploded on the beach a moment later. Fortunately, the soft sand absorbed most of the impact, so only a small fountain of damp sand rose. The Lothians stayed put, digging further into the sand and praying that the boat arrived before the Germans put in a major attack.

More mortars rained down, with the sand absorbing the majority but a few exploding in fire and fury, and then Tulloch saw a larger force of Germans advancing from inland. Black-uniformed SS were in front, with at least a couple of platoons of field-grey infantry backing them.

"Here they come, boys!" Tulloch opened the firing with a

snapshot at the SS, with Innes's Bren hammering a few seconds later. The bullets kicked up dry sand, helping conceal the attackers.

With the mist having cleared, the Germans could see how few men opposed them and opened into extended order. They advanced in a rush, depending on their numbers to overwhelm the Lothians' resistance.

"Rapid fire," Tulloch ordered, firing as fast as he could. For a moment, he was back in the hall of his childhood home, staring at the picture of the Thin Red Line with Colin Campbell commanding the 93rd Highlanders. Now he was the officer in command of a small force facing a charging enemy. *Nobody is here to record us for posterity.*

The SS advanced in short rushes, weaving and dropping as the Lothians tried to hold them back.

"Here comes the boat," Aitken shouted.

Tulloch glanced over his shoulder. The boat was two hundred yards distant, and he knew the beach shelved gently out to sea. "Wade out to them!" he ordered. "Come on!" He fired at the approaching Germans and ushered his men into the sea, with an early morning sun sparkling from the waves and bullets kicking up small columns of water. A man stiffened and fell to trail greasy blood in the water. Aitken yelled, spun, and dropped his rifle with a sinister stain on his right shoulder.

"Don't bunch," Tulloch shouted, swearing as a mortar bomb landed nearby, raising a twenty-foot-high column of water and sand. He saw the boat approaching with Lieutenant Furness in the stern and men hauling steadily at the oars.

Another mortar bomb landed in the water, raising a fountain of water. The Lothians pushed forward as the sailors lifted their oars to glide into shallow water.

"Come on, Pongos! Hurry up!" A grinning petty officer encouraged.

All aboard the *Skylark*! Sixpence for a trip around the bay, a shilling to cross the Channel!

The Lothians splashed forward, with the sailors unceremoniously hauling them over the gunwales and into the boat. Tulloch and Hardie fired toward the advancing Germand to keep them occupied.

"That civilian's on the beach, sir," Hardie said, working the bolt of his rifle.

Between the disturbed water and the blowing sand, Tulloch had not noticed Giorano arriving at the back of the SS. He stood on a slight eminence studying the skirmish through binoculars.

Tulloch raised his rifle, put Giorano in the vee of the backsight and fired. Giorano did not even flinch.

"Missed!" Tulloch said.

"You're last on board, sir," a long-jawed petty officer said, ducking as German bullets sprayed alongside. "In you come!"

"Not yet!" Tulloch said, nearly waist-deep in water. "I want another shot at that man!"

"Get in, Lieutenant!" Furness snapped the order. "We're a sitting duck here!" As if to emphasise his statement, a mortar shell exploded alongside, showering the men with a mixture of salt water and wet sand.

Tulloch took a last, hurried shot and pulled himself over the bulwark. He had a momentary fear that the Germans could shoot him when bending over the gunwale, and then he was inside the boat; the seamen were plying the oars, and the Lothians were firing their rifles. What seemed like a company of German infantry advanced across the beach, most firing at the small boat.

"Pull like buggery, boys," Furness ordered as shots splashed in the sea beside them or raised splinters from the gunwales. The seamen responded, grunting with effort as they dragged the oars through the water.

The German infantry strode into the shallows, firing, but with every stroke of the oars, the boat was further away from the shore and into choppy seas that bobbed their target up and down. More used to firing on ranges, the German soldiers could not correct their aim to correspond with the bucking vessel, and few shots were close. The Lothians' marksmanship was equally poor, although they may have unsettled the Germans.

Tulloch fired three more shots at Giorano, missing each time.

"Lieutenant Tulloch," Furness said quietly with his face troubled. "We don't make war on civilians."

"That's no civilian," Tulloch replied. "That's an Italian spy. He caused trouble for us on the Northwest Frontier, and he's instrumental in murdering British prisoners of war."

Furness nodded. "I see. My apologies, Lieutenant."

Hardie had been listening. "Would you like me to try, sir?"

"If you think you could do any better, Hardie," Tulloch said.

"I'll do my best, sir," Hardie said. Standing up in the rocking boat, he worked the bolt of his rifle and took a deep breath. Tulloch watched as he stood, balancing easily and sighting along the barrel.

"One, two, three," Hardie said, squeezing the trigger. He waited a second before speaking. "That's him, sir."

Tulloch lifted his binoculars. Giorano lay on the ground with an SS officer kneeling beside him. The Italian spy's head was at an impossible angle, and Russell and Pearson were avenged. "You got him, Hardie."

"Yes, sir," Hardie said, lowering his rifle and sitting on a bench.

"Who taught you how to shoot, Hardie?"

"The King's African Rifles, sir," Hardie replied.

"You must tell me sometime," Tulloch said as Innes pointed out to sea.

"There's HMS *Oystercatcher,* sir!"

Tulloch had never seen anything as beautiful as the Royal Navy sloop as it eased closer to the shore. The White Ensign hung above the four-inch guns that pointed shoreward and then fired with jets of flame and smoke, joined by the rattle of two-pound pom-poms and Oerlikons. The entire beach seemed to disappear under the weight of shells, with a cloud of sand and smoke rising skyward.

"That'll teach the SS not to mess with the Royal Navy," Hogg shouted. "Go on, Navy!"

Within a few moments, the boat was alongside *Oystercatcher*, with nettings draped along the hull to facilitate the Lothians' boarding.

"Get these men on board," a slender officer bellowed. "We can't hang around here much longer with the Luftwaffe on the prowl!"

Tulloch scrambled up the netting and rolled on board just as the sloop fired her guns again and then moved off in a sudden burst of speed. Seamen scurried to their posts all around.

"Up you come, mate," a rough-spoken seaman lifted Tulloch to his feet. "Oh, you're an officer. Sorry, sir."

"Thank you," Tulloch realised he still clung to his rifle. He automatically checked his men. "Where can I send my wounded?"

"They're already on their way to the sickbay," Lieutenant Furness told him. "It's all in hand." He eyed Tulloch curiously. "Italian spies, Lieutenant?"

"Yes," Tulloch said. "The Lothians can fight the SS, half the German Army and Italian spies all together."

Furness smiled. "Yet you needed the Navy to rescue you."

"Touché, Lieutenant. Thank God for the Royal Navy. To whom do I report?"

"Commander Warner," Furness said. "This way."

Standing on the bridge, Tulloch was surprised at how calm everybody was as *Oystercatcher* raced northwards towards the English coast.

Commander Warner was about thirty-five, with a strong featured face. "Glad to have you on board, Lieutenant. We were scouring the beaches for any stragglers after Dunkirk." He gave a slight smile. "We didn't expect to pick up forty men in one fell swoop."

"I'm glad you did, sir," Tulloch said. "Did you hear what happened to the rest of my regiment, sir?"

"No, Lieutenant. The evacuation was a bit hectic."

"I can imagine," Tulloch agreed. He thought of hundreds of thousands of British and French soldiers, many wounded, some demoralised, tramping into a single port for evacuation. At the same time, the Luftwaffe bombarded them, and the rearguard held off the German army. "How many men got off, sir? I think we were hoping for about twenty thousand."

Warner smiled. "A lot more than twenty thousand, Lieutenant. I don't know the exact figure but something north of three hundred thousand, including God knows how many French." He stared curiously at Tulloch. "What was it like ashore, Lieutenant?"

Tulloch considered his reply. "A bit hectic, sir," he used the commander's words.

Both men looked up when a seaman shouted a warning. "Aircraft approaching, sir," and added a bearing.

Commander Warner nodded calmly and gave an order to the helmsman, who threw *Oystercatcher* into a zig-zag course. The anti-aircraft gunners waited, scanning the skies as the tiny dots rapidly enlarged into a line of eight Stuka dive bombers.

"Permission to lend a hand, sir?" Tulloch asked. "My men have rifles and a Bren gun." *I think we have some Bren ammunition left.*

The captain nodded with a small smile. "Granted, Lieutenant, just don't get in the way and don't let anybody fall overboard. We won't be able to pick you up."

The Lothians lined the rails, aiming upward. Tulloch knew the possibility of a rifle or even a Bren hitting an aircraft, let alone bringing one down, was minimal, but fighting back was good for morale, and seeing so many men firing at them might unsettle the pilots a little.

"Here they come, boys!"

The Stukas came in a stick, diving nearly vertically with that terrible scream that Tulloch had come to dread. The sloop's anti-aircraft guns were hammering, the pom-poms covering the sky with the dark smoke of multiple explosions and the 20-millimetre Oerlikons pushing up a barrage of lead. The Lothians contributed as best they could.

"Ignore the noise!" Tulloch shouted. "Noise doesn't hurt!" He saw that each aircraft carried a single bomb, with the leading Stuka so close he could see the pilot inside his cockpit, wearing heavy goggles. Then the plane released its bomb, completed its dive, and zoomed upward, with another quickly taking its place.

HMS *Oystercatcher* shifted course as the first bomb exploded alongside, throwing up a fountain of water that cascaded onto the deck, soaking many of the Lothians. Men continued to fire, regardless, as the sloop twisted this way and that, bouncing over the water.

The second aircraft released its bomb harmlessly, and Tulloch thought he saw sparks coming from its undercarriage as the Oerlikon caught it when it rose.

*That's a bloody nose for you, Hitler,* he said to himself.

"Get them as they turn away!" Drysdale shouted. "That's when they're closest and slowest!"

"Aye, if we're still alive!" Lightfoot replied.

"Well, Lightfoot, if you're dead, you'll have nothing to worry about, will you!"

Tulloch saw a thin trail of smoke from underneath the second Stuka and concentrated on the remaining attackers. The sloop was unharmed as the captain steered for the previous bomb blast, dodging, weaving, and firing back.

Innes lowered his Bren. "Out of ammo," he said dejectedly.

"Me too," Hogg said. "But if the bastards come any closer, I'll run my bayonet through them."

Tulloch fired at the next Stuka, saw the pilot release his bomb from a higher altitude and then pull away with the remaining German aircraft following.

"We've scared them off!" Lightfoot said.

"Not us," a petty officer said calmly and pointed northwest. "Them."

A new row of dark specks had appeared in the sky above the smear of the British coast.

"That's a squadron of RAF fighters," the petty officer said as the anti-aircraft guns fell silent. "They'll see off the Nazis."

Tulloch nodded and shouted, "Cease Fire!" in case any of his men fired at the wrong side. They watched as the RAF fighters chased the Stukas away, with only the white trails in the sky a reminder of the recent action and the single, smoking German aircraft limping behind his fellows. One of the British fighters concentrated on the wounded Stuka, firing short bursts until the German aircraft crashed into the sea.

"And that's done for you, Adolf," Hogg said.

---

RAMSGATE WAS BUSY WHEN THEY ARRIVED, WITH AN ARRAY OF battered warships beside a host of civilian vessels of different sizes, many bearing battle scars. A row of ambulances parked beside the harbour, with men piling sandbags beside anti-aircraft guns and harassed naval and army officers organising defences.

"Here you are, Tulloch," Commander Warner said as he eased *Oystercatcher* into a vacant berth. "Home again."

"Thank you, Captain," Tulloch said. He led his tired Lothians off the sloop, counting his men and wondering that so many managed to get home safely after all the travail. A thin rain descended, and men and women beside the dock looked up in mild interest as the Lothians filed down.

"Form up!" Tulloch barked and inspected his men. Battered, bleeding, exhausted, and filthy, they formed two ranks. He stood in front of them as they stood at attention, each man holding his rifle, each man still a soldier. "Well done, lads!" He saw an officious, moustached Military Police captain striding towards him and knew the army was about to enfold his company in its arms.

"Who are you, and where have you come from?" the redcap barked.

"B Company, Lothian Rifles," Tulloch said. "And we've come from Belgium via France. Did the other Lothians make it?"

The redcap looked over the Lothians, noted the steel behind the weariness and nodded, with humanity showing behind the officiousness. "Some, Lieutenant. I'll get your men to a transit camp, and then you can rejoin your regiment. There is tea and food over there; grab some first, and I'll get back to you."

"Thank you, sir," Tulloch replied.

*The evacuation from Dunkirk has changed something. This redcap is nearly human, and the atmosphere has altered. A year ago, people despised soldiers and treated them with contempt; now, the civilians are rallying around as if we were all part of the same crusade.*

"Over here, lads," a civilian beckoned them to a covered stand where three women worked behind two urns of tea and a pile of sandwiches. "Tea and sandwiches, boys."

The Lothians crowded around, rifles on shoulders, joking and laughing as if they were on holiday rather than survivors of a major defeat. Tulloch saw Lightfoot turn away, wiping tears from his eyes as reaction set in, and a motherly woman emerged from behind the stand and wrapped an arm around him.

"Thank you," Tulloch mouthed to the woman.

"Don't you worry now, ducks," she spoke with a broad Kent accent. "You're safe now. My boy is at sea with the Navy, so I know what it's like." She led Lightfoot away, still with her arm around his shoulder.

Tulloch waited at the end of the queue, not wishing to push forward.

"Lieutenant Tulloch," a younger woman poured a mug of tea from the urn, added milk and a generous teaspoon of sugar, stirred, and handed it over. "I'm glad you made it back."

"Miss Clark," Tulloch looked at her in surprise. "I didn't expect to see you here."

"We must all do our bit," Amanda said. "I know you don't

take sugar in your tea, but you need it after that," she nodded in the general direction of France.

Tulloch realised she was correct and drank half the tea in a single draught. "That was welcome," he said.

"When I heard the Lothians had it rough, I wondered about you," Amanda leaned on the counter as the motherly woman watched with a knowing smile. "The rest of your battalion came ashore a few days ago."

"We got cut off," Tulloch did not go into details. Images of the SS murdering the Norfolks men and of Giorano and the SS officer came into his mind. He remembered Brown dying and the shell killing Kelly, Mackay asking for a Bren to take some of them with him and the long, desperate columns of refugees.

"You seem to specialise in getting cut off," Amanda said, only half joking.

"Not by choice," Tulloch replied."I heard it was rough over there," Amanda repeated.

"Aye. A bit." Tulloch said. He watched his men joking with the women, who chaffed back, knowing they were hiding their pain and relief. "I can still see everything. I wish I couldn't see it anymore, but I can."

Amanda listened with deep compassion in her eyes. "The Lothians are based only a few miles away," she took his mug and refilled it, passing over a bully beef sandwich. "You don't have far to travel."

"I hoped we'd return to Edinburgh to refit," Tulloch bit into the sandwich, wondering when he had last eaten.

Amanda shook her head. "We don't know the Germans' intentions," she said. "At present, they're busy with the French, but that won't last."

"The French might hold them," Tulloch said, more in hope than expectation.

Amanda shook her head again. "No, they won't. They'll look for an armistice or even surrender. The Italians will join Hitler, and then they'll both concentrate on us."

The motherly woman glanced over. "Take a break, Amanda," she said kindly. "It's quiet now, and we can cope. Take your man away for a few moments."

"He's not my man," Amanda denied.

The motherly woman smiled. "Whatever he is, he needs you." She nodded to the dock. "Go on, the pair of you. Your men are all right here, Lieutenant."

Tulloch did not argue. Amanda was a familiar female face, whatever their history. He did not object as she left the booth and walked beside him to the harbourside, where ships and boats continued to enter and exit.

"I'm glad you're safe," Amanda said after a few moments. "I thought about you a few times, and when you were not with the others of your regiment, I was," she considered her words carefully. "Unhappy."

Tulloch did not reply as they walked beside the harbour, keeping clear of the busy seamen and soldiers. Both looked up as a flight of aircraft passed overhead, heading out into the Channel.

"You don't like me, do you?" Amanda asked.

"That was a dirty trick you played on me in Simla," Tulloch blurted.

"We had a bad start," Amanda said quietly. "I was not happy to probe you with questions back in India, but it was my duty. I am sure your duty compelled you to do things you didn't want to do."

The memory returned.

*"Tulloch!" Russell screamed. "Don't let them take me alive!"*

*"God forgive me," Tulloch prayed, aimed his rifle at Russell's head and fired. He felt the weapon's vicious kick and fired again, seeing Russell's skull explode. "God forgive me,"*

"Yes, I have," Tulloch agreed soberly, suddenly understanding. He inched closer to Amanda. "More than once." He thought of the wounded men he had left behind men who had trusted him as their officer.

"God," Amanda said. "These days in India seem so long ago and a different, much simpler life."

When Tulloch closed his eyes, he could hear the scream of the diving Stukas and see the death of his men. "It was a different life," he agreed. "The world has changed since then."

Amanda shifted slightly closer. "Would you like to start again? You and me, I mean. If you trust me." She added, "Douglas," as if the name was an afterthought, although he knew it was the most significant word in her speech.

"You were doing your duty," Tulloch reminded her. "There is nothing wrong with that, Amanda."

Tulloch watched as a small Royal Naval launch entered the harbour with the White Ensign limp above a bullet-scarred hull. He noted the carefully wrapped corpse on the deck and the dribble of blood down her port side.

"You didn't answer my question, Lieutenant," Amanda urged.

"No, I didn't," Tulloch agreed.

"Well?"

Tulloch nodded and turned around to look at her. Tiny new lines around her mouth, nose and eyes only highlighted the strength of her face while she held her chin proudly. "I know nothing about you," he said.

"That's easily solved," Amanda said with a faint smile. "All you have to do is ask, and I'll tell you. I've made it my business to find out all I can about you."

"That wouldn't take long," Tulloch replied.

"Do you want to know about me?"

"I'll find out in time," Tulloch told her. He glanced over his shoulder where his company clustered around the stalls. "We'd better get back to our respective duties."

"I suppose so," Amanda said. "Try and stay alive, Douglas."

"You too," Tulloch said. "I'd like to find out about you." He gripped her hand and squeezed. "Yes, Amanda, I think we should start again."

# Chapter Twenty-Seven

*"O woman! In our hours of ease,*
*Uncertain, coy, and hard to please,*
*And variable as the shade*
*By the light quivering aspen made;*
*When pain and anguish wring the brow,*
*A ministering angel thou!"*
**Walter Scott: *Marmion***

The Lothian Rifles had settled into a large camp five miles from Dover, with the lush Kent countryside spreading all around. Tulloch's B Company marched from Folkestone and halted outside the new barbed wire fence, where a sentry eyed them warily.

"Heads up, men, march to attention!" Tulloch said. The sound of the Border pipes cheered them as they passed the first row of tents.

Colonel Pringle greeted Tulloch with a slow smile as he gripped his pipe between his teeth and extended his right hand.

"I heard you were back, Tulloch. What kept you?"

"A little fellow named Hitler," Tulloch said. "Him and a few thousand German soldiers."

"You brought back the rearguard," Pringle said. "We thought you'd gone in the bag."

Tulloch shook his head. "We managed to avoid that," he said. "I have some things to report, sir, and my men need to be fed and watered. They need a good night's sleep and to be re-equipped."

"The duty officer will take care of them," Pringle said. "Sit down and tell me what you have to report."

Tulloch told the colonel about the SS murders and Francesco Giorano.

"Write a report, Tulloch," Pringle sounded strained. "It seems that the Germans are going to fight a different sort of war, bombing civilians, strafing refugees and murdering prisoners of war." He pushed tobacco into his pipe. "I've heard all sorts of stories coming out of Germany," he said, "and discounted most of them as exaggerations. Maybe they were true." He lifted the silver lighter from his desk and set the flame to the bowl of his pipe. He looked up from under grizzled eyebrows. "If even half the stories are true, Tulloch, we must win this war. It's not about national prestige or guarding the empire or any of that. It's not even about losing territory. This war is a struggle between good and evil, as simple as that."

Tulloch agreed. "My sergeant says the same, sir. From what I've seen of the Germans so far, sir, we'd better not let them invade. They seem a very unpleasant bunch."

"Write your report, Tulloch, then get some rest. We don't know what the future holds."

"Yes, sir." Tulloch saluted and left the office.

Major Hume was in the makeshift Officers' Mess, cradling a glass of whisky and talking with the chaplain. Both looked up when Tulloch walked in.

"In your opinion, Tulloch, what went wrong over there?" Muir asked.

Tulloch sighed. "Everything," he said. "Everything that could go wrong, did go wrong from weak allies to poor equipment. We paid the price for two decades of neglect and cost-cutting. Or rather, the soldiers and airmen paid the price for poor decision-making by the politicians."

Muir nodded. "I can't argue with your assessment, Tulloch. As always, the men at the sharp end pay the price. We lost far too many good men, army, navy, and air force, in that debacle in France and that other disaster in Norway."

"We must alter and improve the army from top to bottom," Tulloch said. "Our men are as doggedly brave as they ever were, and our officers as cheerful and bold, but we need more to defeat the professionalism and efficiency of the Germans."

Muir nodded. "Yes." He sipped at his whisky. "I hope the Germans and Italians give us time for that. Oh, Mussolini will join in now, and he has a powerful fleet and air force. Mark my words, Tulloch, we'll be fighting the Italians in Africa within a few weeks."

Tulloch closed his eyes, aware he was accepted in the Mess and could speak freely.

"We need to be as ruthless as they are," Tulloch said. "We carry too many inefficient officers. Oh, they are jolly good chaps, no doubt, with all the right connections and social graces, yet if they can't function under high pressure, they're no good in war."

Hume looked at Tulloch across the rim of his glass. "You've given this some thought."

"I have," Tulloch agreed. "We need to create well-led fighting units trained for modern warfare and not throw our men into battle in penny packets. We need to use our tanks, artillery, and aircraft properly, with good communications so everybody, from the highest ranked general to the newest private, knows why he is there and what he is doing."

Hume listened, nodding, as he finished his whisky. "Yes, indeed."

"As Wellington said after the initial stages of the French Revolutionary War, we've learned how not to do it," Tulloch said. "Now we have to teach ourselves how to win."

They heard aircraft engines and strolled outside. A flight of seven Hurricanes passed overhead, one trailing smoke and stuttering from a damaged engine.

"That's the battle for France finished now. The French have packed it in. Have we lost the war?" Hume raised his eyebrows as he looked at Tulloch.

"Aye, we've lost France," Tulloch agreed. He heard somebody begin to sing.

"I love a lassie, a bonnie Kentish lassie,

She's as fair as the roses in the glen."

Tulloch thought of Brown, Kelly, Tait and all the other good men already killed but the singer was a fair-haired corporal with half a chest full of medals.

"We've lost the first battle of France," he said, "But we've only just begun the fucking war."

And then he thought of Amanda, and the world did not seem so dark.

# About the Author

Born in Edinburgh, Scotland and educated at the University of Dundee, Malcolm Archibald has written in a variety of genres, from academic history to folklore, historical novels to fantasy. He won the Dundee International Book Prize with *Whales for the Wizard* in 2005 and the Society of Army Historical Research prize for Historical Military Fiction with *Blood Oath* in 2021.

Happily married for over 42 years, Malcolm has three grown children and lives outside Dundee in Scotland.

To learn more about Malcolm Archibald and discover more Next Chapter authors, visit our website at www.nextchapter.pub.

# Notes

## Chapter 5

1. On the Grim : service on the North West Frontier, the border between British India and Afghanistan.
2. Chota Peg – a single tot of whisky.
3. Chota-Sahib: an inexperienced officer.
4. Pukka Sahib: a proper officer

## Chapter 6

1. Quaich: A shallow drinking cup with two handles, traditional to Scotland.

## Chapter 7

1. Duffy: a fight

## Chapter 8

1. Kafilah: caravan

## Chapter 9

1. Jock: generic term for a Scottish soldier.
2. Kotal: a mountain pass

## Chapter 13

1. The fishing fleet: every year, a host of unattached women flocked to Simla and other hill stations in British India, hoping to snare a husband from the single British officers or government officials. Those who failed to find a man were known as "returned empties."

*Notes*

# Chapter 15

1. Chibberow: 'Be quiet!"

# Chapter 19

1. This incident happened to the forward cavalry unit of the 3rd Division.

# Chapter 20

1. The Lady Victoria Colliery, Newtongrange, was a major colliery in Midlothian. Now it is the site of a museum.
2. Gonga: mad

# Chapter 22

1. A British patrol did destroy the staff car of Lt-Col Kinzel and captured these documents. On the 4th May 1945, Kinzel surrendered the German Northern Armed Forces to then Field-Marshal Montgomery at Luneburg Heath.
2. After the Battle of Mons in 1914, rumours spread that British soldiers had seen angels in the sky, helping them repel the German attacks. Other accounts mentioned ghostly archers. However, the stories seem to have been started by a newspaper writer who composed a fiction.

# Chapter 24

1. Burra Sahib: Important man.
2. The SS were guilty of war crimes during the British retreat to Dunkirk. One of the most notorious was the action of No. 3 Company of the 1st Battalion, 2nd SS Totenkopf Rifle Regiment. Hauptsturmfuhrer Fritz Knoechlein led them as they murdered ninety-seven captured men of the Royal Norfolk Regiment at
   Le Paradis. A unit of the Royal Scots was saved from murder by a German staff officer. On the 28th of May 1940, the Leibstandarte SS Adolf Hitler murdered more than eighty captured Warwickshire and Yeomanry soldiers in a barn.